"I can help you find those stolen VX mines," Bay said. "But you have to take me with you into the Big Bend."

"I work alone," Owen replied. "Besides, you wouldn't be able to keep up with me."

"Of course I would. I'm incredibly fit." She felt her stomach flutter as his eyes raked her from legs to belly to breasts . . . and lingered there appreciatively.

His heavy-lidded gaze lifted to her mouth, and she nervously slid her tongue across her lips. She felt a quiver of anticipation as his eyes locked on hers, hot and needy.

"You can't come with me," he said at last. "You'd be a . . . dangerous distraction."

JOAN JOHNSTON

THE TEXAN

ISLAND BOOKS

ISLAND BOOKS

Published by
Bantam Dell Publishing Group
a division of
Random House, Inc.
1540 Broadway
New York, New York 10036

ISBN: 0-440-23471-9

Manufactured in the United States of America
Published simultaneously in Canada
March 2001

10 9 8 7 6 5 4 3 2 1

OPM

*This book is
dedicated to my mother,
the most amazing
woman I know.*

Acknowledgments

Serendipity played a big part in the research for this book. I had just decided to set *The Texan* in the Big Bend and realized my hero would have to know enough about tracking to find someone in the desert, when I opened my copy of *Cowboys & Indians* magazine and found an article about Robert Haynes, a former Border Patrolman and Texas Deputy Marshal who'd started a business called Lone Star Tracking and was willing to give classes on how to track *in the Big Bend.*

I became Robert's first class—of one. Robert's sister Cathey Carter provided a cabin for me at Spring Creek, her ranch south of Marathon, Texas, and I spent the weekend as one of the family, learning a little of the skill it takes to find someone who's running in the desert. It's harder than you'd think. "It's *compression,* not *depression.*" Robert, you are the greatest! And thank you, Cathey, for your warm Texas hospitality.

I'm also indebted to Mike Hall, Doctor of Veterinary Medicine, who provided the expertise to deliver a foal in trouble. For technical advice and information I'm grateful to the Texas National Guard Public Affairs Office at Camp Mabry and Texas Ranger Headquarters, both located in Austin.

No writer works in a vacuum. I thank my writing friends for being there to provide support when I needed it.

Chapter 1

OWEN BLACKTHORNE STEPPED INTO THE AR-
madillo Bar and found trouble waiting for
him. "Damn that Creed kid," he muttered.

Luke Creed was arguing with the bartender, who was
refusing to serve him. The kid should have known better,
since he was three years shy of the legal drinking age in
Texas. The teenager wore baggy jeans and an oversized
black T-shirt that did nothing to hide the Texas-sized chip
on his narrow shoulders. His brown hair was cut in short,
youthful spikes, but his desperate brown eyes were ages
older, angry and bitter and disillusioned.

The Creed kid had been in and out of trouble con-
stantly over the past eighteen months since his father had
been murdered. He blamed the Blackthornes—one and
all—for his father's death. Since there was nothing the
kid could do to hurt the powerful family that was the
source of his grief, he took out his frustration on the rest
of the world.

Owen stepped up to the bar, letting Luke get a good look
at the silver badge on his shirt that announced the arrival of a
Texas Ranger.

The kid quickly made it clear he wasn't impressed by
the badge—or the man wearing it. He turned on Owen

and snarled, "Everywhere I go you Blackthornes turn up like a bad smell."

Owen ordered a beer from the bartender, at the same time eyeing the boy in the mirror behind the bar, which was lined with twinkling Christmas tree lights year round. In a low voice he said, "Take it easy, kid."

Luke puffed up like a banty rooster and said, "Go to hell." He turned to the bartender, his hands pressed flat on the bar. "I'm thirsty. How about that drink?"

Before the bartender could respond, Owen laid a dollar on the bar and said, "I'm buying. He'll have a Coke."

"Forget it," Luke said. "I'm not thirsty anymore."

"Then maybe you should leave," Owen suggested.

"You and what army are gonna make me?" the kid shot back.

Owen felt his adrenaline begin to pump. He hadn't come in here looking for a fight, and the last thing he wanted to do was arrest Luke Creed. He knew what it was like to rage against circumstances over which you had no control. He knew what it was like to hurt inside because someone you cared for was gone forever.

Maybe the kid was entitled to hate Blackthornes. It was Owen's mother who'd caused the death of Luke's father. Because there'd been no proof of what she'd done that would hold up in court, Eve Blackthorne had ended up in a sanitarium instead of jail. Hell. No one said life was fair.

The bartender set an icy bottle of Pearl, dripping with condensation, in front of Owen. Before he could pick it up, the Creed kid bumped it hard with his elbow. It toppled and fell, shattering on the sawdusted cement floor.

Owen swore as he jumped back to avoid the shards of broken glass and the yeasty splatter of foaming beer.

The kid sneered at him in the mirror and said, "Oops."

The bar got so quiet Owen could hear every word of the whispery Western ballad Wynonna was singing on the jukebox. He knew the patrons were hoping for a showdown. Owen was determined not to give them one.

He shoved the broken glass aside with his boot and stepped up to the bar. "Another beer," he said.

Luke turned his back to the bar, leaned his elbows on the laminated surface, and set one booted foot on the brass footrail, daring Owen to do something in retaliation. Anything to give him an excuse to strike out.

Owen figured the situation was about as bad as it could get. Then it got worse.

He saw the kid's eyes go wide, then narrow, and followed their focus to the door, where his brother Clay was standing in the entrance to the bar.

He and Clay were identical twins, both tall and broad-shouldered and lean-hipped. But Owen spent his life outdoors, so his skin was tanned, making his gray eyes look almost silver, and he had his share of crow's-feet from squinting past the glare of the searing Texas sun. Owen mostly wore Wrangler jeans, a yoked white Western shirt with a bolo tie, and cowboy boots.

His brother Clay, who'd been elected the youngest ever attorney general of the state of Texas two years ago at the age of thirty, had on a button-down oxford-cloth shirt with a rep striped tie, expensive wool-blend suit trousers, and cordovan shoes. As a concession to their meeting in the bar, Clay had pulled his tie down, and the top button of his blue shirt was undone to reveal a thatch of dark chest hair.

"Hey," Clay said as he stepped up to the bar beside Owen. "What's going on?"

The jukebox had begun playing Billy Ray Cyrus's

one-hit wonder, "Achey Breaky Heart." As they always did on Friday nights in the Armadillo Bar, the drunken crowd sang along at the top of their voices.

Over the noise, Luke Creed shouted an angry response to Clay's question. "I'll tell you what's going on. Your brother's being an asshole!"

"That's enough, soldier," Clay admonished.

"That National Guard bullshit won't wash in here," Luke said, his eyes glittering with malice. "We're not on weekend maneuvers now, *Major* Blackthorne. I don't have to obey you."

"A little respect for your elders wouldn't be out of line," Clay said sardonically.

"You're not my company commander unless we're both in uniform," the kid retorted. "Otherwise, you're just another asshole. In your case, a *thieving* asshole."

"Watch yourself, kid," Owen said in a measured voice.

But Luke was on a rant and reason wasn't working on him. "I know you stole those missing VX mines," he shouted in Clay's face. "If it's the last thing I do, I'm gonna find a way to prove it. One of you Blackthornes is finally gonna get what's coming to you."

"You're talking like a fool," Clay said, his voice even softer, which told Owen just how angry he was.

"I'm no fool," the kid snapped. "I know what I know."

"Exactly what is it you know about those nerve gas mines?" Owen asked Luke. Every law enforcement agency in Texas, and a bunch of federal agencies as well, had spent the past week searching for three crates of missing VX nerve gas mines. The mines had been dis-covered in mislabeled crates during recent maneuvers by a unit of the Bitter Creek National Guard and had been on their way to a disposal and storage facility in Pine Bluff, Arkansas, when they were hijacked.

"I know your brother met with someone at the armory two days before the mines were stolen," the kid said to Owen. "I heard the two of them talking about the schedule for when the mines were gonna be shipped to Arkansas. They shut up quick enough when they saw me watching them."

The kid focused his gaze on Clay and said, "But I heard what you said. I know you took those mines. I'll figure out why you took them and where you put them and then you'll end up in jail, where all you Blackthorne bastards belong!"

"Don't make accusations you can't back up," Clay said in a deadly voice.

"Who's gonna stop me?" the kid demanded.

Owen could see the kid was itching to take a swing and was on the verge of stepping forward to block him, when the door to the bar swung open, and the kid's sister stepped inside.

Owen watched as Bayleigh Creed did a quick visual search of the dining booths on the other side *of* the bar, where she obviously expected her brother to be. When she didn't locate him there, her gaze found its way back to the bar, where Luke was posed in a pugnacious stance. Owen saw the alarm in her eyes before she headed in their direction.

Owen had just enough time to admire the look of her in butter-soft jeans that cupped her butt and emphasized her flat belly and slender legs, before Luke threw a punch. The kid's fist hit Clay square on the nose and sent him staggering backward, as bright red blood spilled onto his starched blue shirt and his silk Armani tie.

Owen grabbed Luke by the scruff of his neck and the seat of his pants, and to the strains of "Achey Breaky Heart," frog-marched the kid past his sister, yanked open the door, and threw him out into the street.

"Go home and cool off," he said.

The kid's sister shoved her way past him and hurried to her brother's side. The asphalt parking lot was full of potholes, and the kid must have tripped on one, because he'd fallen forward onto his hands and knees.

"Luke, are you all right?" she cried.

The boy shoved his sister away as he rose to his feet. "Leave me alone."

Owen wondered if Bayleigh Creed was smart enough to know that her brother was more upset that she'd witnessed what had happened than he was about landing on the ground. From what Owen could see in the glow of blue neon light that spelled out "Armadillo Bar" in cursive across the whitewashed adobe wall, the kid was fine, and his job was done. He turned to head back inside the darkened bar.

He hadn't gone two steps before the boy shouted, "Hey, you!" and shoved him in the back.

Owen heard the kid's sister gasp as he turned to face the battling mosquito that refused to go away. He didn't want to swat it flat. It took all his self-control to keep his balled fists at his sides. He spread his legs in a wider stance, to give him leverage if it came to a fight.

"What is it you want, kid?"

"I want you Blackthorne bastards to pay for what you did to my dad."

There was nothing Owen could say to that. "You'd better take your brother home," he said to the kid's sister. "And tuck him into bed."

"Why, you—"

The kid charged, and Owen hit him once in the stomach, doubling him over.

Bayleigh Creed whirled on him like an avenging fury, her thick auburn hair swinging across her shoulders as she turned, her blue eyes blazing. She got into his space pretty quick, and he fought the urge to back up as she poked him in the chest with a pointed finger and said, "Why don't you pick on someone your own size?"

He saw the sprinkle of childish freckles across her nose and almost laughed. He managed to cough instead. *His own size?* He looked pointedly down at her, then looked her up and down. Slowly. Thoroughly. Until he saw the dark flush rising on her cheeks.

She barely reached his shoulder. Both of his hands would have fit around her waist. She curved in all the right places, even if there wasn't as much up top as he normally liked. Although, honestly, more than a handful was wasted.

"The kid came here looking for trouble," Owen said at last. "He found it." Even as he spoke, Owen realized explanations were futile.

He was a Blackthorne; she was a Creed. Their families had been feuding for generations. It didn't matter what he said. She was going to side with family.

"You shouldn't have provoked him," she said, her chest heaving in a way that drew his attention. "He's had a hard time dealing with Dad's death."

"I'll say," Owen muttered.

She glared at him, and he noticed her eyes weren't blue anymore, they were kind of violet. He wondered if they turned dark like that every time she got mad.

"He's just a kid," she said. "If you Blackthornes would leave him alone—"

"I can fight my own battles," her brother said as he straightened. He glowered at Owen. "I'll find enough proof this time to make sure that another one of you Blackthornes doesn't get away with murder."

Owen's eyes narrowed. "Are you accusing Clay of having something to do with the death of that Texas Ranger in the Big Bend?"

"It's all part of the same thing, isn't it?" Luke said. "That hijacked army truck was left just outside the borders of the Big Bend. Then that Texas Ranger goes into the Big Bend hunting for those mines. Supposedly, he's the best tracker in Texas, and he always finds what he's looking for.

"Suddenly, *pow*! He gets shot between the eyes. I figure whoever stole those mines killed that Ranger to keep him from talking. And your brother stole those mines."

"That's ridiculous," Owen said.

The kid smirked. "I'm going to make sure that brother of yours ends up on death row. See if I don't!"

"Luke," the kid's sister said. "Maybe you shouldn't be making accusations—"

"Stop treating me like I'm some stupid kid," the boy interrupted. "I know what I'm talking about."

"Why don't you come home with me and—"

"And what?" the kid snarled. "Swallow my medicine like a good boy? I'm gonna choke to death if I have to swallow any more—" The kid made a growling sound in his throat.

But Owen had no trouble filling in the missing word. *Pride.* It all came down to that, he realized. The Creeds had nearly lost Three Oaks when Jesse Creed died, and the family had been forced to come up with millions of dollars to pay estate taxes on the ranch. Even now, the

Creeds fought every day to make ends meet. To add insult to injury, the rich and powerful Blackthornes were responsible for this latest trial for the proud but struggling Creeds.

"Go home, kid, and sleep off whatever it is you've got in your system. You're delusional," Owen said.

"The hell I am!" the kid flared.

A few cowhands had collected around them, patrons of the bar who'd arrived but couldn't get through the front door because of the altercation between Owen and Luke.

"Get going or get arrested," Owen said flatly.

"I'm going," Luke said, his throat working and his eyes glazed with angry tears. "But tell your brother he isn't going to get away with it. I won't stop till I can prove he's guilty."

He watched Bayleigh Creed's wide, frightened eyes as her brother jumped onto his Harley, kicked it to life, and roared down Main Street so recklessly he nearly ended up a smear on the pavement.

"Luke," she cried. "Stop!"

But it was too late. The kid was gone.

He noticed she was trembling. "Maybe you'd better come inside and sit down," he said.

"You can go straight to hell." She turned and marched past him. She'd taken about three steps when she stopped, pivoted, and marched right back past him in the opposite direction, her back ramrod straight. A moment later she reached her pickup, yanked the battered door open, and stepped inside.

She was a spitfire, all right. His eyes crinkled at the corners and his mouth cocked up on one side in an almost-grin as he remembered her challenge. *Why don't you pick on someone your own size?* "I don't think you'd qualify, Mizz

Creed," he murmured, as he stared at the disappearing tail-lights on her truck. He shook his head and laughed.

"What's so funny?" Clay asked.

Owen turned to find his twin at his side. "How's your nose?"

"It hurts," Clay said. "At least the bleeding's stopped. Did you figure out what that kid's problem is?"

"He's a little loco, I guess," Owen said. "He thinks you're behind the theft of those VX mines."

"That's crazy, all right," Clay agreed with a disbelieving shake of his head. "Still want to have a beer?"

Owen sighed as he remembered why he'd come to the bar in the first place. To seek solace from his brother for the death of his friend Texas Ranger Hank Richardson—the man who'd been shot between the eyes by whoever had stolen those VX mines. "Yeah," Owen said. "A beer sounds like a good idea."

Owen felt Clay's comforting arm around his shoulder as they headed back inside. They collected a couple of beers at the bar and grabbed a booth that had just emptied, where they could have a little more privacy.

They didn't say anything for a while, just listened to the nasal performance of a favorite Clint Black tune on the jukebox.

When the song ended, Clay took a long swig of beer, set his bottle down on one of the silver dollars that was laminated into the tabletop, and said, "I can't make it to Hank's funeral tomorrow, Owe."

Owen felt his throat tighten with emotion. He kept his eyes lowered, so Clay wouldn't see how devastated he was by his brother's news. He wasn't sure he could handle the funeral on his own. He wanted his brother beside him in case he needed a strong shoulder to lean on.

"I don't think I'll be missed," Clay said. "Every police officer in Texas is liable to show up here in Bitter Creek tomorrow to pay their respects to Hank."

None of them is my brother, Owen thought. *I can't turn to one of them, if I start to fall apart.* "Isn't there any way you can rearrange your plans?"

" 'Fraid not. I've got some business in Midland tomorrow with Paul Ridgeway."

Owen took a sip of beer while he contemplated Clay's revelation. Paul Ridgeway was the FBI's special-agent-in-charge of coordinating all the law enforcement agencies investigating the theft of the VX mines. He had also *almost* been Clay's father-in-law.

Clay had been engaged to Paul's only child Cindy until she'd been murdered a year ago, two weeks before their wedding. Paul had tracked down his daughter's murderer, who'd turned out to be a vagrant, and shot him when he resisted arrest. But he'd had a difficult time dealing with his daughter's death, and Clay had spent a lot of time with him over the past year, keeping him company on hunting trips and attending football games. Offering comfort.

The same comfort Owen needed now. The same comfort Owen had offered his brother at Cindy's funeral. He'd been there when Clay fell to pieces the morning Cindy was buried. He'd hoped to have Clay's support when he buried his best friend tomorrow.

Then he remembered Luke Creed's accusations. Owen knew Clay hadn't stolen the mines. That was absurd. But maybe Clay knew something about their theft. After all, it was soldiers in Clay's National Guard unit, a heavy mechanized engineer battalion that specialized in laying mines during combat, who'd discovered the mislabeled crates of nerve gas mines.

"Does your business with Paul have anything to do with those missing VX mines?" Owen asked pointedly.

"My business with Paul is absolutely personal," Clay said with a grin that acknowledged the contradiction in terms.

"Which means you're not going to tell me."

"Nope."

"You're a secretive sonofabitch," Owen said.

"Yep. At least to the secretive part."

Owen dutifully laughed. "I wish you could be there," he said.

"I'm sorry, Owe. I can't."

Owen concentrated on tearing the label off his beer. His nose stung, and his throat ached. The grief he felt was terrible. But he wasn't going to cry. He wasn't.

It had been so long since he'd cried, he wasn't sure he could. And he had an awful, frightening feeling that if he let even one drop fall, he might not be able to stop the humiliating flow of tears. It had happened once before.

When he was nine, he'd gone hunting with his father and shot his first white-tailed buck. He hadn't killed the deer, and it was thrashing in the underbrush and shrieking in agony—something he hadn't known a deer could do.

His father had refused to kill the buck for him, saying it was up to him to end the animal's suffering. Tears had spurted from his eyes as he held the knife to the deer's throat, unable to cause the pain that would end its pain forever. He'd seen the disappointment in his father's eyes.

Worse was yet to come. His father had agreed to kill the buck for him the moment he stopped crying. Owen had tried to stanch his tears, but every time the deer shrieked, his throat clenched and more tears fell. Until at last he'd found himself on his knees with the knife in his hand slitting the deer's throat himself to end its torment.

Once the deer was dead, his tears had stopped abruptly. Nothing that had happened to him since—no joy or pain or sorrow—had wrung a tear from him. But he'd never lost someone so close to him before, and Hank Richardson's death was turning out to be a lot harder to handle than he'd expected.

Owen was glad his beer was gone, because it was impossible to swallow past the knot of anguish in his throat. It felt as though a steel band were tightening around his chest. Hank would have given him one of those fierce, rough hugs that men share when emotions are running high, and no one's about to admit they're hurting so bad inside they can't breathe.

But Hank wasn't here. And it did hurt to breathe.

He felt Clay's hand tighten around his forearm. "It'll be okay, Owe. Not right away. It takes a while. I know."

Owen swallowed painfully. He felt his eyes watering and bit his lip hard to keep the tears at bay.

"How's Julia holding up?" Clay asked.

He raised tortured eyes to meet his brother's gaze and said in a raspy voice, "How do you think?" It was easier to handle the pain if he turned it into anger. Easier to rage than to cry. "She's eight months pregnant, for God's sake! I told Hank he should let someone else go into the Big Bend after those stolen munitions, especially with Julia so close to her time, but he wouldn't hear of it."

"Texas Rangers are notorious for that sort of glorious sacrifice," Clay said quietly. "I mean, heading off into the wilderness alone to hunt down the bad guys. It's too bad Hank got ambushed. Is there any evidence from the scene you can use to help you find his killer?"

"We found a note in Hank's handwriting in the lining of

his hat that said, 'Find the perfect lady, and you'll find the thief.' "

Clay frowned. "Does anyone know what that means?"

"Not a clue," Owen said. "But I intend to find out."

"On your own?"

"Rangers work alone," Owen said. "It's the nature of the beast."

"Under the circumstances, I'd think you'd want some backup," Clay said.

"Are you suggesting I should bring along a posse?"

Clay smiled. "The thought had crossed my mind. What makes you think you'll have any better luck finding those stolen munitions than Hank had?"

"Hank must have gotten close, or they wouldn't have killed him. I'll start where we found his body and work the trail from there."

"Will you have any trouble getting assigned to the case? I mean, the Big Bend is a long way from your normal hunting grounds," Clay said.

"I've already arranged it with my boss, and he worked it out with the FBI."

Clay took another swallow of beer. "Will you be okay tomorrow?"

"Yeah," Owen said, his throat swelling with emotion again. "I just wish I could go to sleep and wake up and discover this is all a bad dream."

But it wasn't a dream. Hank was dead.

Owen was afraid he would break down like some sniveling kid, if he didn't get away. He stood abruptly.

"Owen?"

In his brother's eyes he saw all the pain he was suffering reflected back at him. He felt like howling but gritted his teeth and kept the sound inside. "I have to go."

Clay stood, and the twins exchanged words without speaking, a gift they'd shared from the womb.

Take care of yourself, Owe.

I will, Clay. You know I have to find the man who killed Hank. I owe him that.

I wish I could be there for you tomorrow. Are you sure you'll be all right?

"I'll be fine," Owen said aloud. "I'll be even better when I find the man who killed Hank. He's going to pay for what he did. If it's the last thing I ever do."

Chapter 2

A SINGLE BULB ILLUMINATED THE SWOLLEN belly of the mare, lying on her side in a deep bed of straw. The mare made a soft, grunting sound as her belly rippled, but the sharp contraction did nothing to move the foal along the birth canal. Too tired even to lift her head, the suffering beast stared with expressive, defeated eyes at the woman kneeling beside her.

Bayleigh Creed had spent long hours studying at the veterinary college at Texas A&M and had been a licensed vet for more than a year, handling just this sort of emergency. The foal was turned so the hooves, instead of the nose, were presenting first. It was the equivalent of a human breech birth. Not an impossible situation, but a difficult one, that sometimes turned out badly.

"I know I should have called you sooner," Summer Blackthorne said, as she sank to her knees beside the priceless championship cutting horse. "I thought I could handle it myself. I was sure I could handle it myself," she said, an edge of defiance in her voice. "But I couldn't get the foal turned." The young woman lifted frightened eyes to meet Bay's gaze. "Can you save her? Ruby is . . . She's like family."

"How long has Ruby been in trouble?" Bay asked, as she rolled up her sleeves and moved to the mare's hindquarters.

"From the start," Summer admitted in a low voice.

Bay clamped her jaw tight to keep from giving the young woman a piece of her mind. She'd gotten her fill of troublesome Blackthornes last night at the Armadillo Bar. Here was another one making her life difficult—Owen and Clay's little sister—who just might be worse than all the rest put together.

Summer Blackthorne had a reputation for running wild. She'd dropped out of a dozen colleges. Well, maybe only a half dozen. But everyone in Bitter Creek, Texas, knew she was the apple of her father's eye—and spoiled rotten.

But not totally uncaring of the harm she might have caused by her reckless behavior, Bay conceded, as she glanced at Summer's anguished hazel eyes and ragged appearance. Blond curls had come loose from a thick ponytail, and her expensive, tailored white Western shirt had obviously been used like a throwaway rag to wipe her hands. But then, money for new clothes was easy to come by for the wealthy Blackthornes.

At least the girl had called Bay. Finally.

"I had no idea how quickly Ruby would tire," Summer said, as she caressed the mare's neck with a trembling hand.

"Let's hope you didn't wait too long."

Bay had been shocked to receive the frantic call from Summer, since Blackthornes and Creeds never crossed paths if they could help it. But it wasn't always possible to avoid each other. Especially when the Creed ranch was lodged, like a chicken bone in the throat, in the very center of the vast Bitter Creek ranching empire.

Three Oaks, the ranch where Bay had been born, was a small island in a sea of Blackthorne grass. It measured a mere five miles east and west and twenty miles north and south, but that hundred square miles of land had been bitterly fought over by Blackthornes and Creeds since the Civil War. And neither of them seemed willing to give up or give in.

The quarrel had once again become deadly eighteen months ago, when Summer's mother had arranged the murder of Bay's father. Actually, she'd been trying to kill Bay's mother—whom she suspected her husband of secretly loving. But the man who'd been hired to do the shooting had missed and ended up killing Bay's father, instead.

As far as the local sheriff was concerned, her father's death had been a hunting accident—a hunter's bullet tragically gone astray. The Creeds had learned the truth when Summer's eldest brother Trace told Bay's elder sister Callie—after he'd married her—that his mother had admitted to her family that she'd arranged the whole thing.

Bay fought down the surge of helpless rage she felt every time she remembered how Eve Blackthorne had escaped punishment for her crime. After what had happened last night, she wouldn't have come near Bitter Creek, except she'd known it was the mare that would end up suffering if she stayed away.

"Why didn't you call your regular vet?" Bay wondered aloud, as she began manipulating the foal to see if she could turn it, or whether she was going to have to help it be born feet first.

"I didn't tell him Ruby was foaling before he took off for Houston. I thought I could handle it myself."

It was stubborn pride, Bay decided, that had kept the girl from calling for help. Bay recognized the flaw because the Creeds had more than their own share of it.

"Bitter Creek is a big ranch," Bay said. "Why didn't you call one of your hired hands or your father or—"

"My father's the last person I'd tell I can't handle the situation," she retorted. "And in case you haven't noticed, it's Saturday night. The hands are all in town spending their wages. Everyone else is tied up at that wake my brother Owen is holding up at the Castle for Hank Richardson, that Ranger who was killed in the line of duty. It's really sad, because Hank's wife is eight months pregnant, and now the baby's going to grow up without a father."

Bay gritted her teeth to keep from reminding the girl that because of Eve Blackthorne, *she* no longer had a father. It was typical of the Blackthornes to ignore what it was awkward to remember. And in a country without a king, only a family as domineering and dynastic as the Blackthornes would have the nerve to call their home "the Castle."

On the other hand, Bitter Creek was an eight-hundred-square-mile cattle ranch with enough oil underground to please an Arab sheik. The house itself was huge, thirty thousand–odd square feet filled with Tiffany and Chippendale and a heritage that went back a hundred and fifty years. Bitter Creek certainly possessed all the elements of a fiefdom, and the Blackthornes were bona fide Texas royalty.

"An unbelievable number of cops showed up for the funeral," Summer said, interrupting Bay's thoughts. "Surely you noticed all those police cars in town today."

Bay had noticed. And wondered. But she hadn't

stopped to find out, because she'd been on her way to an emergency at the Franklin ranch. A mule named Hobo, a family pet, had eaten a plastic bag that had gotten stuck in its throat. It had been a near thing, but Hobo was fine, and the Franklins had promised to dispose of their plastic more carefully.

She'd had another call after that, to the Henderson ranch, and another later in the afternoon from the Stephensons. The call from Summer had come just as she stepped out of the shower at Three Oaks. She'd pulled her wet, shoulder-length hair back from her face with a couple of butterfly clips and brushed her hands through her bangs to get them out of her eyes. She'd stared at the heap of dirty clothes on the bathroom floor for a full thirty seconds, then decided she couldn't bear to put them on again.

So she'd donned a clean pair of jeans and a newly pressed Western shirt, yanked on her boots, and driven hard and fast to Bitter Creek. And found a young girl—alone in the barn with her beloved mare—in desperate trouble.

Bay cocked her head at the strains of plaintive fiddle music carried on the evening breeze from the wake at the Castle. Clearly, death was being mourned there. But damn it, new life was trying hard—and failing—to find a foothold here. Surely the girl could have found someone to help!

"I can't believe you couldn't find one person who'd be willing to leave that wake to help out a poor dumb beast," Bay said, unable to keep the edge from her voice.

"Of course my brother Owen would have come, if I'd asked him!" Summer shot back. "I couldn't—I didn't—ask for help. If you had any idea— If you only knew how hard it is for me to convince my father— Oh, never mind that now! Please. Help Ruby."

The mare whinnied and tried to raise her head.

"Keep your voice down," Bay said quietly. "You're upsetting your horse."

"What can I do to help? Give me something to do," Summer pleaded.

"Talk to your horse. Encourage her."

Bay could see from the look on Summer's face that the girl didn't think it was enough. But Bay knew that to please Summer, the mare would try harder to live through the ordeal to come. Unlike people, animals loved honestly, unjudgmentally, and without reservation. It was one of the reasons she'd become a vet.

"Easy, Ruby," Summer crooned to the animal, as she smoothed a hand down the mare's sweat-slick neck. "Easy, sweetheart. It won't be long now. The doctor will help. Everything will be fine soon."

Bay hoped Summer was right. One of the foal's forelegs had somehow gotten bent at the knee. That would mean disaster, if she couldn't get it straightened out. She had the bent leg in her grasp, but had to wait for a contraction to pass before she could begin to untangle it.

At that moment, the cell phone attached to her belt began to play "The Yellow Rose of Texas." Bay smiled every time she heard the song. Yellow roses were her favorite flower, and her older brother Sam had arranged to have the tune programmed on the cell phone he'd given her for her twenty-fifth birthday.

Normally, Bay would have let the caller leave a message. But Luke hadn't come home last night. Throughout the day, she and her mother and her brother Sam had been waiting for some word from—or about—Luke. But there had been nothing. After his scuffle with the Blackthornes, her brother had gone tearing off on his Harley-Davidson.

And simply disappeared.

Bay had begun to suspect the worst, and she wasn't sure her mother could handle another tragedy so soon on the heels of her father's death. She'd made Sam promise to call her immediately if he heard anything.

This might be that call.

"Would you answer my cell phone?" Bay said to Summer. "Just unsnap the cover and remove it."

"Can't that wait?"

"No, it can't," Bay said, keeping her voice calm in deference to the mare. "Hit the call button and find out who it is."

Bay made herself stay focused on the mare's labor, while she listened to Summer's responses to the caller.

"She's right here," Summer said. And then, "This is Summer Blackthorne."

Summer held the phone away from her ear. "It's your brother Luke. Swearing a blue streak. Wants to know how the hell I got hold of your cell phone."

Bay couldn't take the risk of releasing the foal's foreleg. The mare was losing strength fast, and she might not get another hold as good as the one she had. "Put the phone to my ear."

"Wouldn't it be better—"

"Do as I ask!" Bay could hear her brother still ranting at Summer. "Luke!" she interrupted. "Shut up and tell me where you are. The Big Bend? That's five hundred miles from here! What in the world are you doing in country that far west of the Pecos? Of course I'll tell Mom you're all right, but what are you—"

The mare's belly rippled, and Bay urgently bent for-

ward, away from the phone, to make one last desperate
tug on the foal's foreleg before the contraction began.
The knee unbent as the contraction hit, and Bay felt the
foal move along the birth canal. "Thank you, God," she
muttered.

It was then Bay realized she'd missed whatever Luke
had been trying to tell her. "Put the phone back to my
ear," she snapped at Summer.

The mare whinnied anxiously, and Bay forced herself
to speak calmly despite her agitation. "Luke? Are you
there? I missed what you just said. What does Clay
Blackthorne—?" Bay cut herself off as she realized who
was perched on bended knee beside her, then continued
without mentioning names.

"So he met with some men in Midland and now
you're following them and— That sounds awfully far-
fetched. Luke, I don't think you should—" Bay saw the
curiosity on Summer's face. She turned her back on the
girl and whispered, "If you're so sure he's involved, why
not go to the military police or the FBI or the Texas
Rangers or whoever hunts down—"

Bay closed her eyes and bit her lip as she listened to
her brother's urgent voice. "Luke, please don't try to handle this yourself. You might—"

The mare grunted and began to expel the foal. Bay
saw the umbilical cord slide down and realized that it
would be crushed between the foal and the edge of the
birth canal, cutting off the flow of oxygen. She had to get
the foal out quickly, or it would suffocate.

"Damn, damn, damn," she muttered.

"What's wrong?" Summer asked anxiously.

Bay leaned away from the phone and frantically
searched in her medical bag for the OB chain she'd

brought with her. She wrapped it around the foal's hocks, ready to pull as the mare pushed.

"Hold the damned phone where I can hear it!" she snarled.

"I'm doing the best I can," Summer snarled back.

"Luke? Repeat what you said. I didn't hear it all."

The mare shuddered as another contraction tore at her belly. Bay leaned toward the struggling animal, groaning with frustration as she once again lost the sound of her brother's voice.

Bay raged against the fates that had put her here, helping the enemy, when her own flesh and blood might be in mortal danger. She was torn violently between the demands of her heart and her head. But Luke was beyond her immediate help. The foal could be saved.

"Come on," she urged the mare. "Push, damn you!"

Bay grasped the chain that was looped on the foal's hocks, wrapped it around her wrist and forearm, and leaned back, pulling with all her strength, as the mare labored to expel her burden.

The foal didn't move.

"Help me!" she yelled to Summer. "Hurry!"

The girl dropped the cell phone, grabbed the end of the chain and, grunting with effort, pulled along with Bay.

Moments later, the tiny animal slid out onto the straw and lay motionless, covered in the birth sac.

"He isn't breathing!" Summer cried. "Do something!"

Bay tore at the sac, wiping the colt's mouth and nose clear with a cloth. Then she hauled its hindquarters into the air, much as a human baby might be held by its feet to free its breathing passages of liquid. But the foal remained lifeless.

"Oh, God. I killed him. I killed Ruby's foal."

Bay took one look at Summer's stricken face and realized the girl had already given up. But Bay had been raised in a family that didn't know the meaning of the word *quit*. She willed the foal to *live*. And then called on all the medical skills she possessed to make it happen.

She performed chest compressions, CPR intended to start the tiny heart. But the foal lay still.

"Daddy will never trust me now," Summer moaned. "Oh, Ruby, I'm so sorry. So sorry."

Bay ignored the girl's sobs. She was too busy inserting an endotracheal tube down the foal's nose. She reached out to turn on the attached oxygen cylinder and realized with horror that it was empty! She'd used the last of the oxygen earlier in the day to save the Franklins' mule.

It took Bay only a second to realize that the little air she could blow through the tube from her own lungs was better than no air at all. She yanked the cylinder free of the tubing and blew into it, counting *three, four, five, six,* then counted the compressions as she performed them, *three, four, five, six,* before she once again sent her own, life-giving breath into the tiny chest.

She felt the heartbeat a half second before the foal made a tiny snuffling sound. She quickly slid the tube out as the foal coughed and began to breathe on its own.

"That's it, little one. Come on. Breathe. Breathe," she urged.

The foal's nostrils quivered as it took a shaky breath.

"He's breathing!" Summer said with a tearful laugh, as she scooted closer to the foal. "Oh, thank you, God. And thank you, Doctor."

Bay shared a delighted grin with Summer Blackthorne as she rubbed the colt vigorously with a soft towel. Ruby raised her head and whickered a hello to her son.

The relieved smile on Bay's face faded as she remembered the last words her brother had spoken to her. "Where's the cell phone?" she asked, quickly wiping her hands on the towel.

"I dropped it in the straw," Summer admitted.

Bay sieved her fingers through the prickly straw until she found it. She put the phone to her ear, but the call had been disconnected. "Damn it all to hell! Luke, you crazy fool!"

"Is your brother in trouble?" Summer asked.

"Why should you care?" Bay said bitterly. "You Blackthornes don't give a damn about us Creeds."

Summer didn't deny it.

Bay was distracted again by the need to ensure that the afterbirth was delivered. Once she was certain the mare was in no more danger she said, "Make sure Ruby gets on her feet and that the colt nurses within the next half hour."

Bay picked up the cell phone again and hit the button for "call return," but a Mexican voice answered the phone. "Is my brother there? He's a boy—a man—about six feet tall, slim, with brown spiky hair."

Manny, the twelve-year-old boy who'd answered, said, "Guess your *hermano*'s gone. 'Cause there's no one here but me."

"Where, exactly, are you?" Bay asked.

"This is the pay phone at the Rio Grande Village," the boy replied, "and I got to make a call." And he hung up.

Bay stared at the dead phone in disbelief. What had happened to Luke? Had he been accosted by the two men he was following? Or had he simply run out of change for the pay phone and left to continue his pursuit?

She made a growling sound as she shoved her cell phone back into its case, then crossed to the sink at one end of the birthing stall, turned on the water full blast, and began washing herself clean.

Now what was she supposed to do? Her brother had sounded as crazy and out of control on the phone as he'd sounded last night at the Armadillo Bar. Maybe he *had* taken something that made him delusional. Or maybe he'd finally gotten his fill of the Blackthornes and was fighting back the only way he knew how.

"What if Ruby can't get up?" Summer asked fearfully.

"Then you figure out a way to get her up! And if you can't you have only yourself to blame." Bay was angry at Summer for putting her in this situation, angry at her brother for charging into trouble without thinking, angry at Summer's father Blackjack, for loving Bay's mother Ren, causing the the machinations of Blackjack's jealous wife that had resulted in her father's death.

Bay shook the water off her hands, then struggled to calm herself as she unrolled the sleeves of her plaid Western shirt and snapped the cuffs.

She took one last look at the dejected girl and debated whether to give her any comfort. She could explain to Summer that the mare was merely exhausted and should recover shortly. But she remembered her murdered father, and thought of Luke's dire situation, and kept her peace. Maybe a little worry would make the girl more cautious next time.

In the end, she relented and said, "Ruby's going to be fine. But you have my number. Call me if you need me."

Without another word, Bay collected her medical bag and left the barn. She felt agitated. Frustrated. And yes, she admitted, frightened. What had Luke gotten himself into? How much danger was he really in? And what could she possibly do about it from five hundred miles away?

Bitter Creek was situated on the eastern side of the bottommost tip of Texas—south of San Antonio, east of Houston, and north of Brownsville. The Big Bend National Park was located on the opposite side of the state, where the line of the Texas border dipped into Mexico, following the "big bend" in the Rio Grande.

The Big Bend National Park was about the most desolate, perilous place you could be in West Texas. Even in these modern times, people still got lost there and died of thirst. The desert landscape was rife with poisonous snakes and sharp-thorned cacti. Cell phones didn't always work in the rugged mountains and deep canyons, which explained why she hadn't been able to reach Luke when she'd dialed his number earlier in the day, and why her brother had finally called her from the pay phone at the Rio Grande Village.

Luke had said he planned to stay in the Big Bend until he either found the missing VX mines—or had enough evidence to put Clay Blackthorne in jail. Who should she call for help? The Park Rangers? The FBI? The Texas Rangers?

There was a Texas Ranger only a quarter mile away at the Castle—Clay Blackthorne's twin brother Owen. She ought to drive right up to the Castle and confront Owen Blackthorne at his wake and demand that he arrest his brother and rescue hers.

She shuddered at the thought of confronting him after what had happened last night. Owen hadn't believed her brother last night when he'd made accusations against Clay. Why should he believe Luke twenty-four hours later?

Bay had ample evidence that when push came to shove, the Blackthornes took care of their own. Owen's mother had never been made to pay for her part in Jesse Creed's death. Instead of being tried in court, she'd been committed to some fancy, five-star sanitarium. No wonder Luke was so certain Clay would escape justice. No wonder he was so desperate to find proof of Clay's wrongdoing.

Bay brushed at some straw clinging to her still-damp auburn hair. Damn it, the law was the law. And she wasn't about to leave her baby brother hanging in the wind.

She jumped into her pickup and gunned the engine, eating up the quarter mile between the stable and the house. When she got to the front door of the Castle, she slammed on the brakes, burning rubber, then swerved into a tiny space, narrowly missing two black Cadillac limousines—front and back—that must have brought dignitaries to the funeral.

Bay shut off the ignition, not waiting for the sputtering truck engine to die before she shoved open the door and got out. She'd just lost a father. She couldn't afford to lose a brother, too. She charged up the front steps, determined to confront Owen Blackthorne and—

Bay had no idea what she was going to say. She gravitated toward the sound of deep male voices and turned left from the high-ceilinged central hallway into a room fogged by pungent cigars and choking cigarette smoke.

The old-fashioned parlor was full of big men, but Bay easily found Owen in the crowd. He wasn't the tallest man or even the one with the broadest shoulders. But in a roomful of close-cropped heads, his wavy black hair crept a good two inches over his collar. And while every other Texas Ranger there wore a dark tie and still had his sleeves buttoned at the cuff, Owen's yoked shirt was open at the throat, exposing dark curls, and his rolled-up sleeves revealed strong, sinewy forearms.

Bay felt dozens of curious—and even a few lustful—male eyes on her. She kept her shoulders back, her chin up, and her eyes focused on Owen Blackthorne as she crossed the width of the parlor to where he sat on an aged, saddle-brown leather sofa. His sharp cheekbones and bronzed skin gave him the look of some long-ago savage.

Last night, he'd proved just how uncivilized he could be. Bay had lain awake for hours after she'd gotten home, thinking about their encounter. He'd stared at her like she was some helpless lamb, and he was a starving wolf. She'd made herself stand still for his scrutiny and had felt his eyes devouring her legs, her belly, her breasts . . .

She'd experienced the same perusal from any number of men before Owen Blackthorne had come along—and been totally unmoved by it. Bay felt the same unwelcome reaction looking at Owen Blackthorne now that she'd felt last night. A fluttering in her stomach. An erratic heartbeat. And a hot flush of awareness that made the too-warm room in which she now found herself seem suffocating.

It was disturbing to find herself vulnerable to such a barbaric man. He was the enemy, a callous, coldhearted Blackthorne. His mother had arranged the murder of her father. His brother now threatened hers. And Owen himself had been responsible for the high school football injury to her brother Sam that had left him paralyzed, imprisoned for life in a wheelchair.

Owen's attention was focused on the very pregnant woman dressed in black, who was sitting beside him. Bay realized she must be Hank Richardson's widow.

Mrs. Richardson held a lace-edged white handkerchief

against her nose, and her cheeks were streaked with tears. Her tragic appearance only made her look more ethereally beautiful. Bay watched as the widow suddenly grabbed Owen's hand and placed it on her burgeoning belly. It seemed the baby had kicked, and she wanted him to feel it moving inside her.

When Bay saw the look of wonder Owen exchanged with the woman, an excruciating shard of envy knifed through her. She would never share that particular joy with a man.

The painful knot in her throat caught her unawares.

There was no way she'd be able to speak if Owen glanced up and noticed her now. She stumbled backward over the Texas Ranger behind her, nodded an apology, then turned and shoved her way through the mass of uniformed police officers, not stopping until she reached the cool, clean air outside.

She took several deep breaths to calm herself. When she looked around, she realized she'd fled out the back door instead of the front. The covered porch was dark, except where the glow of light from the kitchen knifed through the open screen door.

Her hands bunched into fists, and she made a growling sound in her throat at her ridiculous behavior. It had been foolish to run away, but Bay knew she couldn't go back inside. When the screen door opened, she made a startled sound.

"Oh. Sorry. Thought I'd catch a smoke," a young waiter said.

In the young man, Bay saw the messenger she needed. "I could use some help," she said.

"Certainly, ma'am," the waiter said, standing erect at the urgency in her voice.

"Do you know who Owen Blackthorne is?"

"Yes, ma'am."

"Find him and tell him there's an emergency at the barn. A mare is in trouble, and he's needed there."

"Yes, ma'am!"

As the waiter turned and hurried back inside, Bay wondered if she'd worded her message strongly enough. Maybe she should have said *A mare is in desperate trouble.*

Summer had said her brother Owen would have come, if he'd known Ruby was in trouble. Well, Bay would just see if the girl was right.

She slipped into the shadows and waited, like a she-wolf, for her quarry.

Chapter 3

BAY CAUGHT HER BREATH WHEN OWEN BLACK-
thorne stepped into the cool night air. He was
close enough to touch. His shaggy black hair
looked rumpled, as though he'd shoved both hands through
it in agitation. When he started to move off the porch, Bay
reached out and grasped his sleeve.

A second later she was slammed back against the wall,
a powerful male hand at her throat choking her. She
could feel the heat of him, the solid maleness of him.
And panicked. She clawed at Owen's flesh with her nails
and drove her knee upward toward his genitals. He thrust
her upraised knee aside, and the full weight of his over-
six-foot frame shoved hard against her from shoulders to
thighs.

Bay froze, staring up at him in mute horror. Her body
trembled in shock. She tried to speak, but there was no
air to be had beneath the crushing pressure of his grip on
her throat.

"What the hell ... ?" He released her throat and
grabbed her arms to yank her into the narrow stream of
light from the kitchen doorway.

She gasped a breath of air, coughed, then gasped another, pressing a shaky hand to her injured throat. She

wrenched to free herself, but he let her go without a struggle and took a wary step back. She rubbed her arms where he'd held her, wishing she'd approached him more directly.

"What are you doing out here, Mizz Creed?" His voice was clipped but controlled. The violence she'd felt in his touch was still there in his eyes, which glittered with hostility.

"It's *Dr.* Creed," she rasped, glaring back at him.

He lifted a black brow. "Well, *Dr.* Creed."

She opened her mouth to say *I need your help.* But the words wouldn't come. There was nothing wrong with her voice. She just hated the thought of asking a Blackthorne for anything.

"I haven't got all night," he said. "There's an emergency at the barn—"

"Ruby's foal has already been delivered safely," she said. "I made up that story because I wanted to speak privately with you."

"You delivered Ruby's foal?"

She saw the confusion on his face. "Your sister tried to manage by herself and ran into trouble. Since your vet was out of town, she called me."

Owen grimaced, but to his credit, didn't berate his sister in front of her. Neither did he thank Bay for saving the foal. "You've got me here now," he said. "What is it you want?" His hands fisted on his hips in a way that made her think he was itching to wrap them back around her throat.

She lifted her chin and met his gaze. Big mistake. His gray eyes had turned into shards of ice. His body was wired tight, like frayed barbed wire ready to snap and tear flesh.

Her stomach clenched with unaccustomed fear, which she told herself was unreasonable. She'd simply surprised him, and he'd reacted to the threat like the lawman he was. He couldn't know how frightening it was for her to be imprisoned against the wall by his large, muscular frame. She swallowed past the soreness in her throat and said, "My brother's in trouble."

"Which one?"

"My younger brother Luke."

His eyes narrowed, and his hands left his hips and crossed over his broad chest. "I knew I should have arrested him last night. What's he done now?"

"Luke hasn't done anything," Bay retorted. "But he seems convinced your brother Clay has."

Owen snorted with disbelief. "What's your brother accusing Clay of doing now?"

"The same thing he accused him of last night."

His lips curved in amusement. "What is it you expect me to do? Arrest my brother?"

Bay put ice in her voice to take the smile off his face. "I believe my brother is in danger, and that your brother is the one threatening him."

"I'd be more inclined to think the opposite," Owen said. "Your brother's the one who attacked mine last night."

Bay was starting to feel some of Luke's frustration. She was tempted to turn and walk away. But what if her delay in seeking help cost Luke his life?

When Bay didn't speak, Owen shook his head in disgust and turned back toward the house.

"Wait!" Bay reached out to stop him but jerked her hand back, remembering how he'd reacted the last time she'd touched him without warning.

Her raspy call was enough to turn Owen around, but he was obviously irritated at her jumpiness. "Look, lady, I've got better things to do than stand here—"

He was interrupted when the screen door creaked open, and an older man wearing a Texas Ranger badge and a salt-and-pepper mustache stuck his head out the door. "So this is where you went."

The Ranger gave the two of them a speculative look, then joined them on the porch, waiting to be introduced.

Owen finally said, "This is Dr. Bayleigh Creed, one of the two local vets. Dr. Creed, this is my boss, Ranger Captain Tex Mabry."

Bay managed a smile. "Good evening."

"Am I interrupting something? I hope?" the captain said, returning her smile. He glanced from Bay to Owen and back again, recognizing the tension between them but uncertain of its source.

"You're not interrupting a damned thing," Owen said. "What is it?"

The captain eyed Bay as though he expected her to leave, but when she merely smiled back at him, he turned to Owen and said, "I got a call from the FBI office in Midland. The Park Rangers found a motorcycle abandoned on a dirt road in the Big Bend near where Hank was shot. Apparently it belongs to one of the guardsmen in Bravo Company who discovered those three crates of mislabeled VX mines. We may have a suspect at last."

"You got a name?"

"Check with Paul Ridgeway. He'll have it." Mabry tipped his hat up with a finger and said, "You be careful out there, Owe. I don't want to lose another man to these bastards." He turned to Bay and said, " 'Scuse my language, ma'am. But the men who hijacked those VX mines are mean sonsofbitches."

Bay had paled as she listened to Captain Mabry. It had to be Luke's motorcycle they'd found. Which meant her brother was now on foot in the Big Bend. Even worse, in the flicker of an eye, he'd gone from being a man chasing down suspects, to a man accused of stealing the VX mines himself!

She remembered how Luke had come home two weeks ago excited by his discovery—along with a half dozen other soldiers—of some mislabeled crates of VX nerve gas mines. She'd given him a hard hug, realizing how close her family might have come to losing him. In college, she'd done a paper on chemical warfare, so she knew how deadly VX nerve gas was.

A single VX nerve gas mine exploding in Dallas or Houston or San Antonio would be devastating. Every living thing within a range of eight miles would die a grisly death within minutes. It was appalling to think someone had stolen *three crates* of them.

But it hadn't been her brother.

A chill went down her spine as she considered the danger Luke was in. Not only did he have to watch out for the two men he was chasing, but now Owen Blackthorne was heading into the Big Bend to hunt him down. Dear God. She had to find Luke and get him out of there.

"Are you all right, Dr. Creed?" the captain asked.

Bay felt Owen's hand at her elbow and barely resisted tearing herself free. "I'm fine," she said, forcing herself to smile. "Just a little tired. It's been a long day."

Owen eyed her keenly and said, "Isn't Luke a private in Bravo Company?"

"Your brother Clay is his company commander," Bay replied, meeting Owen's incisive stare with one of her own.

Stalemate.

"Your brother rides a motorcycle," Owen said.

"So do a lot of Texans."

"I wonder how many of them also serve in Bravo Company," Owen said.

Bay searched her mind for someone in Luke's National Guard unit who also rode a motorcycle and blurted, "Bad Billy Coburn rides a Harley."

" 'Bad' Billy Coburn?" Captain Mabry interjected. "Sounds promising."

"He's a troublemaker, all right," Owen confirmed.

"We've already interviewed all the men in Bravo Company once, but you might want to talk to this 'Bad Billy' character again before you head into the Big Bend tomorrow," the captain said.

"Or maybe I should start with the doctor's brother," Owen said, staring into her eyes.

Bay resisted the urge to look down and the even greater urge to fill the silence with a declaration of Luke's innocence. She felt invaded by Owen's stare, which sought out her secrets. But she'd learned from her father never to back down. So she stood her ground and met Owen's probing inspection with one of her own.

She thought she saw Owen's lips curve in a grudging smile before he finally turned to his boss and said, "I'll check them both out in the morning."

"I'll make sure Ridgeway e-mails you everything he has before you leave tomorrow," the captain said. "Good night, Dr. Creed," he said, tipping his hat to her.

Once the screen door had closed behind him, Owen

turned to Bay and said, "Where's your brother, Dr. Creed?"

"Where's yours?" Bay shot back.

Owen scowled at her, but she refused to be intimidated. It wouldn't take much effort for him to discover that Luke had called her from the Big Bend—his sister had been there when the call came in. But Bay wasn't going to volunteer any information that might help the Texas Ranger find Luke.

When Owen's eyes narrowed, Bay knew he was remembering why she'd called him outside in the first place.

My brother's in trouble.

Bay resisted the urge to blurt out her fears. She would never convince Owen Blackthorne that Luke was an innocent bystander. And she didn't want her brother caught in the crossfire when the Texas Ranger caught up with the real hijackers.

But how could she possibly find Luke on her own? The Big Bend National Park sprawled over an area larger than Rhode Island, with hundreds of miles of paved and unpaved roads and remote, primitive trails. Most of the Big Bend was desert, made green by plants that needed little water—acacia, candelilla, ocotillo, and cactus. Beyond the desert rose the imposing Chisos Mountains, covered with pine and juniper.

"Whoever stole those mines has already killed once," Owen said. "If your brother's involved—"

"He isn't," Bay said too quickly.

"When you brought me outside, you said your brother was in trouble," Owen persisted. "What kind of trouble?"

Bay thought fast. "He didn't come home last night.

My mother's worried. I thought you might be able to help us locate him."

"What part does my brother supposedly play in his disappearance?"

Bay arched an indignant brow. "Your brother was fighting with mine last night. I thought he might know what's become of Luke."

"Do you think your brother might be involved in this hijacking?"

"Of course not!" But if she found it impossible to believe her own brother was involved, it was even more absurd to imagine Owen's brother having anything to do with the theft of the VX mines.

Why would Clay Blackthorne, the attorney general of the state of Texas, son of one of the wealthiest men in the country, want to steal a bunch of nerve gas mines? It was far easier to believe that Luke Creed, son of a widowed mother who could barely make ends meet, had stolen the mines to sell them for cold, hard cash.

Luke's wild allegations would more likely be seen as an attempt to make trouble for his company commander, a man with whom Luke had recently brawled, and against whom Luke—indeed, his whole family—bore a grudge.

Was her brother in way over his head? Should she tell Owen Blackthorne what she knew? But how could she trust a Blackthorne to give her brother a fair hearing?

She stuck her hands under her armpits to prevent Owen from seeing how they were shaking.

"If you know anything," he said. "If you can give us any help finding—"

"The truth is, I can help you find those mines." Bay couldn't believe the enormous lie that had just come out of her mouth. She took a deep breath and added, "But you have to take me with you to the Big Bend."

"I work alone."

"Then we're finished here," Bay said, turning to leave.

Owen caught her before she'd taken two steps. "You're not going anywhere until you tell me what you know."

"I'll tell you everything when we get to the Big Bend."

"I can't take you with me, Dr. Creed. It's too dangerous. If you help me out, I'll make sure your brother gets a chance to tell his story in court."

Bay gave an unladylike snort. "I don't believe you."

She was surprised at the anger that flared in his eyes before he said, "I'm not in the habit of lying."

"I've never met an honest Blackthorne," she said. "And I sure as hell don't trust you."

"I ought to arrest you for obstruction," he muttered.

"Go ahead!" she challenged. "Then I can tell them how you manhandled me." She glanced toward his tight grasp on her arm, then put her fingertips to her aching throat, and said, "I'm sure I'll have the bruises to prove it."

He looked down in surprise to where his fingers were clamped on her forearm, as though he'd had no notion of how tightly he was holding her, and abruptly let her go.

She rubbed her arm and said, "When do we leave?"

"You wouldn't be able to keep up with me."

"Of course I would," she replied. "I'm incredibly fit."

She felt her stomach flutter as his eyes raked her from legs to belly to breasts . . . and lingered there appreciatively. His heavy-lidded gaze lifted to her mouth, and she nervously slid her tongue across her lips. She felt a quiver of anticipation as his eyes locked on hers, hot and needy.

"You can't come with me," he said at last. "You'd be a . . . dangerous distraction."

She heard herself swallow. "Then I'll go by myself."

"The lawmen posted at the park entrance will have orders to keep you out."

"Then I'll go around the entrance," she said stubbornly. "There are other ways to get into the park."

"It's not safe—"

"You *owe* me," she said, cutting him off.

"How do you figure that?"

"Your mother put my father six feet underground. Your brother Trace stole my sister Callie's heart and spirited her away to live with him on some cattle station in Australia. And you put my brother Sam in a wheelchair for the rest of his life."

Owen's jaw tightened, and his face paled. "It was an accident. We were playing football."

"Maybe it was," she conceded. "But your mother certainly caused my father's death. And Trace was ruthless in his pursuit of Callie. I'd say the debt is all on your side, and it's time to pay up. I'm coming with you to make sure my brother gets home alive and well. You owe my family that."

"The Big Bend is too hazardous a place to go with some civilian traipsing along behind me," he said.

"I'm willing to take my chances."

"I'm not."

Bay played her ace. "Luke called me on my cell phone while I was delivering Ruby's foal."

Owen hissed in a breath of air.

"Ask Summer," Bay said. "She'll confirm that I'm

telling the truth. I know where to look for my brother. I can save you a great deal of time and effort. But only if you take me with you. You can pick me up at Three Oaks tomorrow morning, right after you talk to Bad Billy Coburn. I'll be waiting for you."

Bay turned and marched away. She didn't look back. But she could feel his eyes on her, assessing her, devouring her. And her stomach responded with that appallingly delicious flutter.

THE FOREMAN'S HOUSE WHERE SAM LIVED WAS DARK, AND Bay presumed her brother must be at the Homestead, a half mile farther down the road, which blazed with light on the lower floor. She parked in back of the house and could see through the screen door that her mother and elder brother were sitting at the large trestle table in the kitchen.

As she stepped inside she asked, "Have you heard from Luke?"

Her mother had risen to pour Bay a cup of coffee from the electric pot on the counter and set it in front of her as she joined them at the table. Bay put several spoonfuls of sugar in her coffee and added enough cream to make Sam laugh.

"I'll never get used to the way you drink coffee," he said.

"There's still plenty of caffeine in it, which is the only reason I swallow the foul-tasting stuff." Bay sipped at the steaming coffee, swallowed before her tongue could burn, and said, "I think Luke might be in serious trouble."

"That irresponsible whelp," Sam muttered. "When is he going to grow up?"

Bay met Sam's eyes and lifted an admonishing brow. It had taken him eleven years to start pulling his own weight. Bay was still getting used to the changes in her brother over the past year. When Sam had woken up in the hospital after his accident on the football field, a cripple for life at eighteen, he'd railed against his fate. For the next eleven years, he'd been a surly, miserable creature, drunk as often as not.

Her father should have brought Sam to heel sooner, but since it was Owen Blackthorne who'd crippled him, Sam had been allowed to nurse his grievance against the world in general, and the Blackthornes in particular. It was only after their father had been killed and their mother wounded in the same hunting accident—which had been arranged by Eve Blackthorne with the help of her husband's *segundo* Russell Handy—that Sam's behavior had changed drastically.

Sam freely admitted it was a Blackthorne who'd been responsible for the turnaround. Owen's elder brother Trace had wanted Bay's elder sister Callie for his wife, but Callie had argued that she couldn't be spared from Three Oaks. So Trace had set about to make it possible for her to leave the ranch.

He'd threatened Sam into sobering up, then arranged for a special van that Sam could drive by himself, and finally remodeled the foreman's house so Sam could live there on his own.

When Bay had come home after her final semester at Texas A&M, she'd found a totally different person from the Sam she'd always known. The scraggly beard was gone, and his shoulder-length chestnut-brown hair had been trimmed up over his ears. He was wearing a newly ironed Western shirt and crisp jeans and boots with a spit shine. Most importantly, his brown eyes had been clear and bright, without the red lines that spoke of a night's dissipation, and his voice had possessed a pleasant Texas drawl without the slur that had so often marked his speech when he was drunk.

Over the past year, he'd taken a greater interest in their Santa Gertrudis cow/calf business, and there was growing hope that this year they might recognize a profit that had been noticeably absent in years past.

Bay hated giving thanks to a Blackthorne for anything. But Trace was clearly responsible for initiating the changes in Sam.

Sam had the grace to look sheepish, but said, "Where is Luke? What kind of trouble is he in now?"

Bay kept her eyes focused on her cup as she said, "While I was delivering a foal at Bitter Creek he called me . . . from the Big Bend."

"What the hell was he doing there?" Sam demanded.

"Sam." That was all it took for her mother to silence her brother. "Go on, Bay."

"Luke's motorcycle has been found abandoned near where that Texas Ranger was shot."

"Oh, man. What a mess," Sam muttered.

"Luke had nothing to do with the theft of those VX mines," Bay said certainly.

"That crazy idiot. I wouldn't put anything past him," Sam said.

"You can't think he's involved!" Bay protested.

Sam rubbed his forehead. "No. I guess not." He looked at Bay and said, "But he's been gone a lot lately. Last night's not the first time he hasn't slept in his own bed. He messes it up so it looks like he slept in it, so you and Mom won't worry about him."

Bay saw the tightening around her mother's eyes and mouth that revealed she wasn't as calm inside as she appeared on the outside.

Her mother had worked in the house during the years of her marriage, so the harsh Texas sun hadn't gotten to her complexion. She didn't wear makeup, but she didn't need it. Her figure was trim, almost girlish. The fine lines around her wide-set hazel eyes were the only sign that she'd endured fifty-one years of ranch life.

"What did Luke say when he called you?" her mother asked.

"I didn't hear it all," Bay admitted. "But I know he's convinced Clay Blackthorne is involved in the theft of those VX mines."

Her mother hissed in a breath of air.

"Even I find that hard to believe," Sam admitted.

"I went up to the Castle to see Owen Blackthorne—"

"Why the hell would you—"

"If you let me finish a sentence, I'll tell you," Bay snapped at her brother. "I thought he might be able to help."

"Like he helped me into this chair?"

Bay heard the bitterness in her brother's voice. He was never going to forgive Owen Blackthorne. He didn't think his injury had been an accident.

"I'm going with him when he heads into the Big Bend tomorrow morning," Bay said.

"The hell you are!" Sam said.

"Someone has to go," she said, eyeing her brother and then letting her gaze drop to his paralyzed legs. It wasn't playing fair, but right now she was more interested in winning her point.

"I could use a drink right now," Sam said.

Without a word, her mother crossed and poured Sam a cup of coffee and set it down in front of him.

"How did you convince Owen to let you go along?" her mother asked.

"He hasn't exactly agreed to take me yet," Bay admitted. "But I'm sure he'll come around. I told him I know where to find Luke."

"Do you know where he is?" her mother asked.

"I wish I did! About the time Luke called, I got busy delivering the foal, and by the time I got back to the phone, the call had been disconnected. I hoped Luke might have phoned here."

"He didn't," her mother said. "Where was he when he called you?"

"The pay phone at the Rio Grande Village."

"Sam, get the number of the store from information," her mother instructed. "It's doubtful Luke's still there, but maybe someone can tell us if he bought supplies and which direction he headed."

It only took a moment to get the number and for Sam to dial it. The phone rang only once before it was answered. Sam said, "Who's this?" and quickly hung up the phone. His eyes were bleak when he met Bay's gaze.

"Who was it?" Bay asked.

"FBI," Sam said. "Do you think they'll be able to figure out who called?"

"I wouldn't think so," Bay said, and then changed her mind. "Yeah. They can probably get hold of the phone records."

"Do you think Luke'll call again?" Sam asked.

"How can he?" Bay said. "His cell phone probably doesn't work in that rugged terrain, because he didn't use it to call me. And I doubt he'll try to use the phone at the Village if it's being watched by the FBI."

"Do you think he'll know it's the FBI?" Sam asked.

Bay pursed her lips. "They weren't too subtle on the phone with you, were they?"

"So what do we do now?" Sam asked.

"I'm going to the Big Bend tomorrow with Owen Blackthorne. We'll find Luke, and I'll make sure he gets home safely."

Bay saw the struggle her mother was having between wanting Bay to stay safe at home and knowing that Bay might be Luke's only chance to return home alive.

Sam pounded his useless legs. "God, I hate being tied to this chair. I'd go there myself if I could."

"Blackjack is coming here tomorrow to check on some of the two-year-old cutting horses we're training for him," her mother said. "Maybe he knows someone who can help us locate Luke."

Bay exchanged glances with Sam. After their father's death, the patriarch of the Blackthorne family had hired their mother to train cutting horses for him, which gave him an excuse to come around and check things out. "Do you really think Jackson Blackthorne would be willing to help us, Mom?"

"Despite what your father believed, the Blackthornes aren't all ogres."

Bay felt her heart skip a beat. Enmity for the Blackthornes had been a part of her life from the cradle. She'd never heard a good word spoken about them around this table. Her mother's pronouncement was blasphemy in this household—or would have been if her father had still been alive.

Bay searched her mother's eyes, uncertain what it was she sought. Had her mother made peace with Jackson

Blackthorne? Could the generations-old feud simply be called off?

Even if her mother was willing to forgive and forget, Sam was not. "The Blackthornes are all sonsofbitches, every blackhearted one of them," he said vehemently. "And Blackjack has the blackest heart of all."

Her mother didn't argue. She merely rose and said to Sam, "Keep your cell phone handy, in case Luke finds a way to call you," and left the room. They heard her tread on the stair to her bedroom.

"What's gotten into her?" Sam said irritably, once she was gone. "When did the Blackthornes become our friends?"

"I don't like them any better than you do," Bay said. "But that doesn't mean they don't have their uses. I suspect Blackjack has friends in high places who can find out things we wouldn't be able to learn on our own."

"I suppose Mom'll bat her eyelashes at him, and he'll tell her whatever she wants to know."

Bay was irritated by the suggestion that her mother would actively flirt with Jackson Blackthorne. "The fact she's willing to ask for information doesn't mean there's some kind of romance budding between them."

Sam's lips twisted cynically. "When was the last time you saw them together?"

Bay felt her shoulders tense. "What are you saying?"

"I'm saying that if Eve Blackthorne wasn't in the picture the two of them might very well end up together. And I'm not so sure it won't happen anyway."

Bay shoved herself out of her chair so abruptly, it scraped loudly against the hardwood floor. "Mom would never get involved with a married man. She'd have to be crazy to do something like that."

"Crazy in love," Sam said so softly Bay wasn't sure she'd heard him right.

"I'm going to bed," she said.

"You'll need plenty of rest if you're going to be trudging around the Big Bend. That's a treacherous place, Bay. Watch your step."

Bay stopped at the kitchen doorway and turned back to her brother. "Sam."

"What?"

"Mom . . ." She bit her lip, wondering if there was anything either of them could do to save their mother from the kind of hurt that would come her way if she fell in love with a married man. "Nothing," she said at last.

"I'll find a way to stop him from hurting her," Sam said. "No matter what I have to do."

Sam's threat sounded deadly. Bay didn't know what to say. But she couldn't make herself warn him off. So she simply said, "Good night, Sam."

"Watch yourself around Owen Blackthorne," he said.

"What?"

"I saw how he looked at you when he showed up at Dad's funeral."

Bay scoffed. "The man has absolutely no interest in me."

"Just be careful. Whatever else you might say about those Blackthorne men, they're charming bastards. He just might steal your heart when you aren't looking."

"Don't worry, Sam," she said. "I don't have a heart to lose."

Chapter 4

AS HE MADE THE TWENTY-FIVE-MILE DRIVE to Bad Billy Coburn's ranch from the Castle the next day, Owen considered Bayleigh Creed's ultimatum. He still chafed at the reminders of how his family had victimized hers. Hell, he hadn't started the feud between their families. And his brother Trace had fallen in love with her sister Callie. How could you blame him for that?

Owen had done the best he could to make sure his mother paid for the murder of Bay's father. In a fit of anger, his mother had admitted her involvement to her family. But Russell Handy, the man she'd conspired with—who was both her lover and his father's *segundo*—had taken all the blame on himself, confessing his guilt to the police and refusing to name any other responsible party. Handy had been convicted of murder and was serving a life sentence in Huntsville. Nevertheless, Owen had arranged to have his mother committed to a sanitarium.

Owen had paid a higher price for his efforts than anyone knew. It hadn't been easy pointing a finger at his own mother. And as she was led away by two burly male nurses dressed all in white, she'd let him see just how much she despised him for it.

The rough hit he'd put on Bay's brother Sam on the football field that had left him paralyzed had been an *accident*. Oh, he'd been mad, all right. But he hadn't been mad at Sam. Sam had just gotten in the way . . . and gotten hurt.

He'd kept a rigid control on his temper ever since. But his reflexes had been honed by his years in law enforcement, where any hesitation might cost him his life. Which was why he'd ended up with a stranglehold on the good doctor when she'd surprised him on the back porch.

Owen just wished he hadn't ended up body to body with her. There'd been no way to control his physical response to her soft, feminine curves; that had been instinctive and instantaneous. She wasn't very tall, but she was all legs, and she'd fit him in exactly the right places. Something he would rather not have known, considering he was a Blackthorne and she was a Creed. It figured that since he never wanted to see her again, circumstance was throwing her in his way.

He'd learned from Paul Ridgeway that Bay's brother Luke had been positively identified as the owner of the motorcycle abandoned in the Big Bend. Owen couldn't afford to pass up the chance that Bay could lead him right to Hank's killer.

On the other hand, having her along was going to be a pain in the ass. He ran a finger across the three tender welts on his throat, where she'd scratched him. She reminded him of one of those small, prickly animals that put up dangerous spikes if you got too close.

His brow furrowed as he remembered the look in her eyes when he'd pinned her against the wall. It wasn't just surprise and fear he'd seen in her eyes. More like panic and terror. He wondered if she'd been attacked sometime in the past.

Her reactions certainly hadn't been those of a helpless female. Somewhere along the line, Bayleigh Creed had taken a self-defense course. His lips twisted ruefully, as he thought of how close she'd come to doing serious damage to the family jewels. Luckily, his reflexes had been faster than hers.

He was sorry he'd frightened her, but she should have known better than to come at him like that in the dark. Hell. He was probably going to have to apologize to her. He hated apologizing even more than he hated losing his temper.

And he dreaded the thought of staring into those violet-blue eyes of hers while he did it. A man could lose himself in those deep blue wells. Actually, when he'd waylaid her last night, they'd merely been dark and shadowy, wary and wounded.

Owen swore under his breath. Hank had recently argued that Owen needed to take a break from the job. That he was walking a ledge, ready to go over. Maybe his friend had been right. Was it reasonable to expect someone dangerous to accost him on his own back porch?

But after the grueling day he'd spent burying his best friend—and controlling his emotions while he did it—he'd been wired pretty tight. His quick reflexes, which had kept him alive in more than one dangerous situation, had simply gone into overdrive. But he didn't need a break from the job. And he didn't want one. He loved his work.

It was all he had.

Owen veered away from that thought, refocusing on the problem at hand. Bayleigh Creed. At least he'd stayed cool enough not to seriously hurt her. But she was going to have a helluva sore throat for a couple of days. Which might keep her quiet if they had to spend time on the trail together.

Had he decided, then? Was he going to take Bay with him?

No. No way. No how. That woman was not going with him into the wilderness.

As Owen pulled up to the dilapidated Coburn homestead, he saw Bad Billy slouched in a rickety chair on the covered back porch. His long legs extended over the broken porch rail, his booted feet crossed at the ankle. A day's growth of dark beard masked his cheeks and chin, and he wore a battered Stetson that was crushed so far down over his shaggy black hair that it left his eyes in shadow.

Western courtesy should have had the younger man rising to greet him. As Owen cut the engine on his pickup, Bad Billy Coburn merely caught the cigarette that hung from the corner of his mouth with two fingers, flicked the ash to the sun-seared porch with a third, and set it back between his lips.

Owen had taken only two steps from his pickup when Billy said, "That's far enough."

His voice begged for an excuse to fight, and Owen had to resist the urge to give it to him. "I imagine you've been keeping up with the news about the hijacking," he said.

"Don't have a TV. Don't read the paper."

Owen stuck his hands in his back pockets to keep them from bunching into fists. He'd dealt with plenty of wise-ass punks. But there was an air of menace about Bad Billy Coburn. Everybody knew Billy had been beaten regularly by his father the first fourteen years of his life. As small as the town of Bitter Creek was, the kid's bruises had gotten noticed.

But there wasn't much anyone could do about it when

Billy insisted he'd gotten the marks from being clumsy or from the rough ranch work he did. The signs of brutality had ended abruptly when Billy reached the eighth grade. It was easy to figure out why. Billy had suddenly sprouted and grown taller than his father, eventually topping him by a good half foot.

As a teenager, and into his early twenties, Bad Billy Coburn had earned his name, becoming a dangerous sonofabitch to cross. He was suspended so often, it was a wonder he'd graduated from high school. Owen had heard that Billy scored amazingly high on the college boards—which meant he was plenty smart. But he didn't have the grades to get into an affordable state university, and his family didn't have the money for a private one.

Over the next few years, Bad Billy Coburn had drunk too much, fought on a whim, and looked for trouble wherever he rode.

The drinking had stopped two years ago, when Owen's brother Trace had fired Billy from his job as a Bitter Creek cowhand for getting into a drunken brawl that involved their younger sister Summer. Because Billy was such a good man with a rope, he'd managed to get other ranch work. But the kid didn't get along well with others, so the jobs never lasted very long.

Owen figured Billy had the intelligence to plan the theft of the VX mines, and he might finally have gotten sick and tired of living hand-to-mouth and decided to do something illegal about it. So the question was, had Bad Billy Coburn crossed the line from troublemaker to terrorist?

Owen surveyed the lanky cowboy coiled in front of him, malevolence lurking in his dark eyes. "Got any ideas who might have stolen those mines, Billy?"

"Sure don't."

"Make a guess," Owen said.

"You can bet someone in Bravo Company was involved. No one outside the few of us who discovered those mines even knew they existed. But we all knew they'd have to ship them somewhere to be destroyed."

Owen's hands came out of his pockets and hung at his sides, not far from the Colt .45 he carried in a holster at his hip. "You were one of the guardsmen who found the mines?"

Billy nodded curtly.

"How many others were involved?"

"Maybe a half dozen enlisted men. And your brother Clay. He's our CO."

"Was Luke Creed one of those men?"

"Yep."

"Was Luke particular friends with any of the half dozen guardsmen you mentioned?"

Billy shrugged. "I wouldn't know about that."

"Were you friends with any of them?"

The young man's gaze was shuttered, defiant. "I don't need any friends."

Owen felt a stab of pity at that bald statement of the isolation in which Bad Billy Coburn lived his life. It must have shown on his face, because Billy's features tightened.

"Give me some help here, Billy," he said.

"I wouldn't piss on you if you were on fire," Billy retorted.

Resentment for all the years he'd stood alone against the world simmered in Bad Billy Coburn's dark, sullen eyes.

"Look, kid—"

Billy lurched from his chair, and it clattered backward onto the porch. He took one step into the harsh sunshine, his eyes narrowing, his mouth flattening into a hard line, a muscle jerking in his cheek. He dropped his cigarette and crushed it with his boot.

Suddenly, Billy was no longer the skinny, beleaguered kid who'd been six years behind Owen in school. His shoulders were as broad as Owen's, and he was not more than a hairsbreadth shorter than Owen's six-foot-four-inch height.

"Get the hell out of here," Billy said coldly.

Owen didn't think Billy was involved in the theft of the mines. But somebody ought to keep an eye on him, just in case. He'd report his suspicions to Paul Ridgeway, and let the FBI handle it. Owen had turned to leave, when he heard a voice that stopped him in his tracks.

"What's going on out here? I heard—"

Owen pivoted and felt the hairs rise on his neck as he watched his sister shove her way past the broken screen door, tucking the tails of her Western shirt into her skintight jeans as she came. She jerked to a stop when she noticed him.

"What the hell are you doing here, Summer?"

"That's none of your business, Owen."

Owen shot a look at Billy Coburn that would have flattened him, if it had been a blow. The lanky cowboy took a step closer to Summer, and Owen was astonished to see his sister back herself up until her shoulder was wedged against Billy's broad chest, so they provided a solid front of defiance. He waited for Billy to put his arm around Summer, cementing the picture of a happy couple, but it didn't happen.

"Would you mind explaining what you're doing here

at this hour of the morning?" Owen asked his sister. Billy's father had died driving drunk about a year ago, but Owen realized he hadn't seen or heard Mrs. Coburn or Billy's teenage sister Emma since he'd arrived. Then he remembered it was Sunday. They were probably both at church. Which was why Summer was here now, so she could be alone with Billy. He frowned, as he remembered how she'd been tucking in the tails of her shirt.

Summer opened her mouth, then shut it again, before she finally spoke. "I'm here visiting my friend."

"Billy Coburn doesn't have any friends," Owen said. "He told me so himself."

"I told you I didn't *need* any friends," the dangerous young man corrected. "Your sister is just what she said. A *friend*."

A frown of confusion creased Owen's brow. "What could you and Bad Billy Coburn possibly have in common?" he asked his sister.

"His name is Billy," Summer replied heatedly. "Plain Billy."

They'd had this argument before. Owen nodded curtly, conceding the point. "Answer the question."

"You're not my father, Owen."

"Does Dad know you hang out here?"

She made a face. "What I do in my free time is none of Daddy's business, either."

Owen noticed that Billy edged protectively closer to her, although his hands remained at his sides. If they had been intimate, Owen felt sure Billy would have touched her. So they must be "just friends." But Owen couldn't imagine why Billy was keeping a respectful distance. He was reputed to be as wild in his dealings with women as he was in the rest of his life.

God knew, Summer had a mind of her own. He'd be wasting his time telling her to stay away from Bad Billy Coburn, that he was a good-for-nothing, hell-seeking wastrel, who'd never amount to anything. But he could make his position clear to Billy. He met the other man's taunting gaze and said, "If you lay a hand on my sister, I'll make sure you live to regret it."

Summer shook her head in disgust. "You're wasting your threats, Owen. I told you, Billy and I are *friends*."

"I don't think much of your choice of friends, little sister."

Billy's eyes narrowed at the insult, and the same muscle flexed in his cheek. He took a half step forward, but Summer laid her hand gently on his forearm.

Billy stopped. But he vibrated with rage.

"I think you should leave now, Owen," she said.

Owen resisted the urge to grab his sister out of Bad Billy's clutches and haul her away with him. But the days were long gone when she'd been a toddler learning to walk, and he'd been her big brother, holding her hand, making sure no harm came to her. At twenty-one she was an adult, able to make her own decisions, no matter how ill-considered he thought they were. He made himself back off.

"Shall I tell Dad you'll be home for Sunday brunch?" he asked.

"Dad won't be there himself. He's gone to Three Oaks to see Mrs. Creed."

Owen felt acid rise in his throat. Eighteen months ago, when his father had heard from his mother's own lips that she'd been unfaithful to him with his *segundo* Russell Handy, Blackjack had vowed to divorce her. His mother had said she'd make him sorry if he tried. She was doing her best—from the sanitarium where she'd been caged—to prevent the dissolution of their thirty-three-year marriage.

Owen hadn't expected his father to start courting the Widow Creed before the divorce was final. To be honest, even though Blackjack had said he wanted out of the marriage, Owen hadn't really believed his father would go through with a divorce. Texas divorce laws didn't necessarily divide things fifty-fifty. They allowed the judge to give either spouse as much of the marital property as the judge deemed fair. With the right lawyers, his mother could skin his father alive.

Which left Owen with only one conclusion: the old man must really want that Creed woman.

"Daddy took his championship cutter Smart Little Doc over to Three Oaks this morning, to stand stud to Mrs. Creed's mare Sugar Pep," Summer explained.

Owen felt a surge of relief but managed not to sigh. "You mean he's there on business."

"Why else would he go to Three Oaks?"

Owen was grateful for his sister's naïveté—or willing blindness—whichever it was. Although, even a blind man could have sensed the yearning between his father and Lauren Creed whenever they got anywhere near one another, even before Jesse Creed's death. It had been a major source of friction between the Blackthornes and the Creeds over the past thirty-odd years, keeping the feud between their two families alive.

Owen wondered if his father was really at Three Oaks this morning to see Lauren Creed on business, or whether his business with her was entirely personal.

He focused his gaze on Billy and said, "If you think of anything that might help us find the man—or men—who took those VX mines, call me."

Billy merely touched his hat brim, his dark eyes burning with resentment.

As Owen reached the door to his pickup, Summer called after him, "You won't tell Daddy I was here, will you?"

He glanced back at her over his shoulder and saw how she was the one clinging to Billy, rather than the other way around. "You wouldn't ask that, if you thought that being here was a good idea," he said. Before she could protest further, he added, "I'll keep my mouth shut." He gave Billy a warning look and said, "Just be careful."

Owen stepped into the pickup, turned the key, and gunned the engine, throwing up a cloud of dust as he left the Coburn ranch behind him, heading for Three Oaks. Maybe Bay had heard from her brother. Maybe she'd changed her mind about telling him what she knew.

And maybe you can see for yourself whether your father is making a fool of himself over the Widow Creed.

BAY HAD SPENT A SLEEPLESS NIGHT AND HAD WOKEN UP tired and irritable. Not a good combination for someone who had to start the day by confronting a ferocious beast with the coldest gray eyes this side of the Arctic. She'd been absolutely certain Owen Blackthorne would show up on her doorstep this morning. So when she heard the knock at the kitchen door on her way downstairs, followed by a gruff male sound of greeting to her mother, the slam of the screen door, and the mention of Luke's name, she gave a mighty sigh of salute and marched into the arena.

And discovered Jackson Blackthorne kissing her mother.

Not just a peck on the cheek. Not just a brush of the lips. His large, workworn hands were splayed on her mother's jean-clad rear end, and she was arched into his body, her breasts pressed flat against his broad chest. Their eyes were closed and their mouths were meshed and the way their jaws were moving it was clear his tongue must be halfway down her throat.

Bay's outcry was totally involuntary. She fervently wished she'd simply backed out of the kitchen. Because what they did next was more revealing—and terrifying to witness—than the kiss itself.

While they both jerked when they heard her, they didn't spring apart like guilty teenagers. His hands slid to her mother's shoulders reluctantly, and her hands, which Bay only then realized had been thrust into Blackjack's thick black hair, slid down to his shoulders, and they slowly separated until they were looking into each other's eyes.

Bay couldn't see her mother's expression, but Blackjack's gaze was tender . . . loving . . . and regretful.

Of course it was, Bay thought bitterly. Their secret was out. Bay was normally gone making rounds to see her animal patients long before her mother was up, and Sam lived in the foreman's house. Her mother must not have realized Bay was still home. Otherwise, she might have been more discreet in greeting her lover.

But now Bay knew. And there was no putting this snarling cat back into the bag.

Bay felt a sharp, visceral pain when her mother turned within the circle of Blackjack's arms and remained close to him, rather than moving away. She didn't dare acknowledge the torment she saw in her mother's eyes.

"Daddy's barely cold in his grave," she said in a raspy voice. She put her hand to her throat. It hurt to talk, but it was the ache inside, rather than the bruises outside, that was causing the problem.

Her mother's voice was surprisingly calm. "Your father's been dead for more than a year. I've been worried about Luke, and Jackson's been a great comfort to me."

"When did you start sleeping with him?" Bay demanded, snapping her chin in Blackjack's direction.

The blood left her mother's face in a rush, and if Blackjack hadn't been holding her, she might have fallen. "Bay—"

"Your mother and I never came near one another before your father's death," Blackjack said.

"So you say!"

Bay watched as he exchanged a poignant glance with her mother, before he added, "I love your mother. I plan to marry her."

"You're already married!" Bay wrapped her arms around her midriff to keep her jangled insides from flying apart. "What about your wife?"

"I'm getting a divorce," Blackjack said in a voice Bay found annoyingly calm.

"When?"

Blackjack's eyes turned bleak, and he exchanged another glance with her mother. "Soon."

"That's not good enough. When? A year? Two years? Ten years? Never?"

"Stop that, Bay!" her mother commanded.

The authoritative tone halted Bay's tirade long enough for her mother to say, "We love each other. We want to be together. And when we can marry, we will."

"But he's a Blackthorne!" Bay protested, as though her mother had decided to take a venomous snake to her bosom. And this was the biggest, baddest snake of them all, a rattler with fangs that could bite deep and leave poison to fester.

"It's about time this feud ended," her mother said.

"Does Sam know?" Bay demanded.

Her mother shook her head.

"What about Luke?"

Her mother winced. "He . . ."

"He caught you. Like I did," Bay said.

"He saw us kissing in the barn a couple of weeks ago," her mother admitted.

"Is that why Luke was fighting with Clay on Friday night?" she asked, focusing her anger where it belonged, on Jackson Blackthorne. "Has Clay been persecuting Luke because of this . . . thing . . . between you and my mother?"

"My sons know I plan to divorce their mother," Blackjack said.

"But do they know you're having a sordid affair with mine?"

"Bay!" her mother said. "That's enough."

The screen door screeched open, then slammed closed. Bay leaned around her mother to see who'd arrived, praying it was Luke, hoping it wasn't Sam. And gasping when it turned out to be Owen Blackthorne.

"I couldn't help overhearing." Owen's voice was hard, his powerful body restless. He had the haunted, hunted look of a wolf caught in a steel-jawed trap.

Blackjack had taken a step back from the kitchen door, but kept Bay's mother in the circle of his arms. The two of them turned to face their children.

Bay had never thought she would side with a Blackthorne on anything. But she was in perfect agreement with Owen that their parents had no business being together. Bay saw how her mother clung to Blackjack's strong, encircling arm, her bastion of safety in the coming storm. There was a recognizable current that ran be-

tween them, something so blatantly sexual that it made
Bay uncomfortable.

She glanced at Owen to see if he had picked up the
same signals. His gray eyes told her nothing. They were
so very cold. So very remote. So detached from what was
happening.

Maybe that was how he stayed in control. She could
see his body quivering. His hands had balled into fists so
tight his knuckles were white.

"How long has this been going on?" Owen asked
through tight jaws.

"Like I told Bay, Ren and I never went near one another until after Jesse was dead," Blackjack replied with
that same annoying, unruffled calm he'd exhibited since
Bay had discovered him kissing her mother. As though
he could not be judged. As though he could do no wrong.

Owen's features revealed so little, Bay had no idea
what was going on inside his head. When he spoke to his
father at last, she was horrified by what he said.

"Maybe Mom isn't guilty of killing Jesse Creed after
all. Maybe you're the one who arranged his murder."

"You know better than that!" Blackjack said, his calm
shattered at last.

"Do I?" Owen challenged. "Mom wanted Mrs. Creed
dead. Somehow, it was Jesse who got killed."

Bay's heart was pounding a hundred miles a minute.
Was Owen making this up because he was angry with his
father? Or was there some truth to it? She'd assumed that
Eve Blackthorne would never have been put in a sanitarium unless her husband and sons had positive proof that
she'd been responsible for arranging Jesse Creed's murder. Owen seemed to be suggesting there was room for
doubt.

"Mom told us she asked Russell Handy for help getting rid of Mrs. Creed. It's just as likely you asked Handy for help getting rid of Jesse. Especially after that last confrontation between the two of you at the Rafter S auction, where you threatened to kill him. Maybe Handy was really working for you instead of Mom."

"That's ridiculous," Blackjack said flatly.

"We all figured the shooter was aiming at Mrs. Creed and missed—hitting Jesse by mistake," Owen continued. "What if he hit exactly who he'd been told to aim at? What if Jesse was meant to die all along?"

"That's enough," Blackjack said, his voice ragged with fury.

Owen wasn't done. "Handy never said anything one way or the other about who ordered him to arrange Jesse's murder. *Because you told him to keep his mouth shut.*"

"You know damn well why I did that!" Blackjack said. "Your mother would have spent the rest of her life in prison. Is that what you wanted?"

"I remember being relieved when you said you'd make sure Handy never spoke to anyone about what he'd done. At the time, I believed you wanted to protect Mom from prosecution. I have to wonder, seeing you here with Jesse's wife, whether that was a self-serving lie."

Bay's heart was beating so fast it hurt. Complicated as Owen's reasoning was, it made perfect sense. She saw from the look on her mother's face that she didn't want to believe that the man she loved had arranged to have her husband murdered. It was equally clear, from the way her body had tensed within Blackjack's embrace, that she couldn't discount it entirely. And certainly, the argument between father and son was painful for her. She put her hands on the arm that surrounded her and pushed it away.

"This is all nonsense, Ren," Blackjack said as he released her. Bay saw the anxiety in his eyes, the concern that Owen's accusations might have found fertile ground.

"I'm sorry you've been hurt by seeing us together," her mother said to Owen. "I love your father."

Bay felt her heart skip a beat as her mother glanced at Blackjack with anguished eyes.

"I . . . I never meant to hurt anyone," her mother said hurriedly, as she brushed past Owen and pushed her way out the screen door.

The three of them stood frozen as the door slammed behind her.

Blackjack swore a string of epithets, before he bolted for the door.

Owen stepped in his way. "Leave her alone, Dad."

"You crossed the line this time, Owen. You and your goddamned suppositions! I love that woman, and by God, I am going to marry her. Now get the hell out of my way!"

Bay saw Owen's indecision before he stepped aside and let his father charge past him.

"Goddamn it all to hell!" Owen muttered. He looked up and their gazes met and she saw the naked pain in his eyes. Immediately, his lids lowered, and she felt shut out.

He yanked his Stetson down until his eyes were shadowed and said, "Have you heard from your brother?"

"No."

"Are you going to tell me where he is?"

"No."

"I'm not taking you with me. And that's final."

Bay was desperate. She had to think of something that would force his hand. "Please—"

"No," he said, his voice colder and harder than she'd ever heard it.

"Then I'll go on my own!" she said fiercely. "And whatever happens to me will be on your head. If I get lost and die of thirst—"

"Damn you Creeds!" He jerked off his Stetson and swatted it against his thigh, then crushed it back down on his head. "Are you ready to go?" he said through gritted teeth.

"Yes."

"Then get your stuff, and let's get the hell out of here."

Chapter 5

"HOW ARE WE GETTING TO THE BIG BEND?" Bay asked as the kitchen screen door slammed behind her.

"We're flying," Owen replied.

"I figured that. Flying from where? San Antonio or Houston?"

"Flying from right here. We're taking the jet."

Bay stopped at the door to Owen's pickup. "*The* jet? You mean the four-million-dollar Cessna CJ1 Callie flew in when Trace took her to Houston? The one with the Circle B brand painted on the tail?"

He smiled. "That's the one."

"Don't tell me you're the pilot."

"All right. I won't."

Which meant, of course, that he was. "I don't trust you on the ground. Why should I trust you in the air?"

"We need to get where we're going in a hurry," Owen said as he opened the door to the pickup for her. "There's a jet sitting on the landing strip at Bitter Creek, and I'm a qualified pilot. You've talked your way into coming, but I'd be just as happy to leave you behind."

"You're not getting rid of me that easily," she said.

He grimaced, took her backpack from her, and swung

it into the back of his pickup, then gestured her into the front seat of the black extended-cab Silverado. She was inside the luxurious pickup before she realized she'd let him take her backpack and open her door. Well, she'd soon cure him of thinking she was some fragile female. She could take care of herself.

"I don't know what you're so worried about," he said. "You're a pilot yourself so—"

"I only fly a helicopter during roundups."

He lifted a dark brow. "That's a helluv— That's a lot more difficult and dangerous than fixed-wing flying."

For some reason it irritated Bay that he'd edited the profanity from his speech. She didn't want his deference. She wanted them on equal footing. So she added the profanity that he'd edited. "I'm not going to argue with you. I'd just feel a helluva lot better if we had a qualified pilot."

"I am a qualified pilot," he said as he started the pickup and headed toward the bump gate that led from Creed to Blackthorne property.

"You know what I mean."

"You mean, you'd rather not trust your life to one of those dastardly Blackthornes."

He surprised a laugh out of her. "You must admit your father's a hard-hearted man."

"I'm not my father," he said curtly.

"You're cut from the same mold," she countered. "You crippled my brother."

In the blink of an eye he'd hit the brakes, grabbed her arms, and pulled her up nose to nose with him. "That's the last time I want to hear those words out of your mouth. Is that understood?"

She scowled at him and said, "Let go of me."

He shook her once and demanded, "Answer me! Is that understood?"

She knew better than to taunt an enraged animal. But she couldn't help herself. "You are what you are." She stared at the vicious grip he had on her arms. "A man with a nasty temper that gets out of hand. You hurt my brother. And now you're hurting me."

He let her go instantly and turned back to face the road, his hands gripping the steering wheel so hard she thought he might break it in two. Through tight jaws he said, "This isn't going to work. I'll arrange for someone to take you home when we get to the landing strip."

"Oh, no you don't," she said, folding her arms across her chest. "One little temper tantrum isn't going to scare me away."

"I can't guarantee it won't happen again."

"I work every day with cantankerous beasts who growl and bite, when I'm only trying to help. I think I can handle you."

"I'd like to see you handle me," he said, eyeing her up and down.

She ignored the double entendre, but she was pretty sure he wasn't sizing her up as an adversary on the tae kwan do mat. She put a hand to her stomach, which was doing a strange flip-flop. "Don't think I couldn't take you down," she said seriously. "I've trained in the martial arts."

He smirked. "That I've got to see." He started the truck again. "But not right now."

Owen did a thorough flight check of the Cessna before he pronounced it ready to fly. He took Bay's backpack from her again and put it in the forward baggage com-

partment. When he opened the door to the passenger
compartment, two foldout steps appeared.

"Pretty nifty," Bay said as she entered the cabin,
which had a recessed floor that allowed her to stand upright. She looked at the four facing seats, two on each
side, and said, "I'd rather fly up front with you."

"Suit yourself," he said, stooping as he headed for the
front of the airplane.

"It has nothing to do with wanting your company," she
assured him. "I just want to make sure you can fly this
thing."

"What help could you be if I can't?" he asked.

"I did a paper in college on airplane hydraulic systems," she said, surveying the cockpit.

"You're kidding, right?"

She buckled herself in. "I had to take a lot of science
classes to become a vet, so I tried to do papers on things
that interested me."

Bay noted the Citation CJ1 was equipped with the
best, most modern com/nav/ident avionics gear. The soft
camel leather seats and burled wood trim were evidence
of the luxury in which the Blackthornes indulged.

Her family had once owned a secondhand helicopter
they used for roundups, but they hadn't been able to keep
up the payments, so the bank had taken it back. Now they
rented a helicopter when they needed one.

"You wrote a paper on hydraulic systems?" Owen repeated dubiously, as he checked generators, flaps, thrust
attenuators, and speed brakes.

"What did you write about in college?" she asked.

"As little as possible," he replied.

"What did you study? I mean, what was your major?"

"Clay and I both studied government. Clay went on to Harvard Law. I went into law enforcement."

She rolled her eyes. "I can imagine what your father said when you did that."

"I don't think he noticed," Owen said, as he set aside his clipboard.

Bay shot Owen a sideways look as he powered up the jet's FJ44-1A engine and confidently pushed the control yoke forward for takeoff. She wondered if he realized how much he'd revealed in that simple statement.

Bay knew something about being shunted aside by a parent, but she'd never resented the attention her father had paid to her injured brother. Sam had needed a lot of help when he first came home from the hospital.

Later, when Sam had learned how to lift himself in and out of bed and how to manage his own care, her father had still given her brother the bulk of his free time. Bay had finally concluded that her brother and her father spent so much time together because they could feed on each other's hatred of the Blackthornes.

She shuddered to think how Sam would react when he realized their mother was having an intimate relationship with Blackjack. With any luck, her mother would come to her senses and call the whole thing off before Sam got wind of it.

Bay waited until they were safely in the air to speak again. "Why didn't you become a lawyer like your brother?"

"I hated the thought of spending the rest of my life in an office. I like the wide open spaces."

"I can appreciate that," Bay said. "I feel the same way."

"And I wanted to be a Texas Ranger, like a lot of Blackthornes before me."

"Creeds have been Texas Rangers, too," Bay said. "Jarrett Creed, who married my great-great—however many greats—grandmother, Cricket Stewart, was a Ranger. In fact, they met when he recovered some horses that were stolen from her father."

"I've heard that story," Owen said with a laugh. "Is it true Cricket had three pet wolves?"

"Rogue, Rascal, and Ruffian," Bay confirmed. "She raised them from pups. I keep forgetting our families are related—were related—in the beginning. I'd give a lot to know the truth about how and why Cricket Creed ended up marrying that English Blackthorne fellow. Her son Jake believed Blackthorne forced his mother into marriage because he wanted her land."

Bay glanced at Owen. "It wouldn't surprise me if it were true."

"It's not," Owen said. "My brother Trace showed me a diary Cricket wrote that proves they fell in love. Trace loaned the diary to your sister Callie. Didn't she share it with you?"

"I guess she didn't have time before your brother rushed her off to Australia," Bay said, unable to keep the resentment from her voice.

"Sounds like you don't believe your sister and my brother fell in love, either," Owen said.

"Trace swept Callie off her feet, all right. It helped that she needed the money he could provide to pay my father's estate taxes, after your mother had him murdered."

There it was again. The most recent wrong the Blackthornes had done the Creeds, staring them both in the face. The reason her brother Luke had gone after his brother Clay. To prove, once and for all, that the mighty Blackthornes weren't as righteous and law-abiding as they wanted everyone to think.

Bay missed her father so much sometimes her chest physically ached. She felt cheated because he'd never had a chance to see her become a successful vet, especially when he was the one who'd made her believe she could be a good one. Deep down, she knew her father had been thinking of all the money he'd save on vet bills, but she didn't think he would have pushed her, if she hadn't loved it as she had.

She angled herself toward Owen and asked, "Do you really believe that *both* your parents might have conspired—independently—with Russell Handy to kill my father?"

She saw Owen's throat working and noticed he avoided her gaze as he answered, "It's possible. Handy was my father's right-hand man. If Dad ordered him to squeeze the life out of someone, he'd have done it."

"Then Blackjack's getting away with murder, too," Bay said.

Owen frowned. "I suppose that's one way of looking at it. But there's no more proof my father committed the crime than there is against my mother."

"Somebody should have pressed Russell Handy for the truth." She watched Owen shift uncomfortably in his seat. "You did!" she realized suddenly. "You went and talked to him! What did he say?"

"He wouldn't admit anything. Except that he loved my mother. And respected and admired my father."

Bay realized they were descending. The CJ1 had made the five-hundred-mile trip across South Texas in a little more than an hour. Owen set the jet down smoothly on the short landing strip in the tiny West Texas town of Alpine, which was only an hour's drive from the entrance to the Big Bend National Park.

"If you find you can't keep up with me, I want you to say so right away," Owen said.

"I won't be turning back," Bay said.

"The sooner you quit, the less backtracking I'll have to do to get you headed back home," he said flatly.

"Don't you worry about me. I'll keep up."

"We'll be picking up some safety equipment in Alpine."

She gave him a questioning look. "Rappelling equipment, you mean? Climbing stuff?"

"Nerve gas stuff," he said bluntly. "Rubber safety suits and atropine-oxime autoinjectors."

Bay felt her body go cold. "You're kidding, right?"

"I'm not only hunting down the man who killed my best friend. I'm looking for those missing VX mines. If I find them, there's a chance that in the confusion one of them might go off. So yes, we'll be picking up gas masks and rubber suits, along with an antidote for VX gas. But honestly, if I thought we'd be needing them, you wouldn't be coming along with me."

"I did a college paper on chemical warfare," she said.

Owen eyed her sideways. "What did you learn?"

"A single drop of VX nerve gas on your skin is enough to kill you."

"I think they told me that when they offered me the rubber suit."

"What else did they tell you?"

"If I even suspect I'm exposed, I need to inject myself with the antidote immediately."

"Did they tell you VX gas can hang around in the air for days on end?" She pursed her lips thoughtfully. "Although, heat can make it evaporate more quickly."

"Thank God we're headed for the desert," Owen said.

Bay frowned at his flippancy. "Organophosphate poisoning is gruesome. It attacks the nervous system and reacts with neurotransmitters—"

"You're losing me," he said. "Too many big words."

"I can use small ones," she said. "When you're exposed, you get a headache and your eyes hurt and your chest gets tight. Then you get bronchospasms—"

"Lost me again," he interrupted.

"You start wheezing," she corrected. "And drooling and hallucinating and vomiting. Are those words small enough for you?"

"I'm getting an ugly picture of what this stuff does to you."

"There's more."

"How long was this paper?"

She ignored him and said, "You start to sweat. Probably because you realize it's all over. You begin defecating and urinating, your arms and legs twitching, unable to breathe. Think of it. Just one tiny drop. And you die a swift, agonizing death."

"Guess we can forget the rubber suits."

"You'd be smarter to bring along a gallon of Clorox."

"Clorox?"

"The brand doesn't matter. Just some household bleach. It works to neutralize the gas and decontaminate surfaces. Assuming we're still alive."

"Remind me to stop by the Safeway in Alpine," Owen said.

Bay stared soberly at Owen. "Until you forced me into that ridiculous recitation, I never really considered what we might be walking into."

"Does that mean you've changed your mind about coming?"

She shook her head. "I have to believe that whoever stole those mines knows how dangerous it would be to detonate one of them."

"Or that they won't want to waste one in such an unpopulated place," Owen said.

Bay felt a chill of alarm run down her spine when she saw the three men hovering near the entrance to the small terminal building in Alpine. Despite the searing June heat, they were wearing dark suits, white shirts, and wide ties knotted tightly at their throats. Since the FBI special-agent-in-charge of investigating the theft of the VX mines was headquartered in Midland, only a four-hour drive away, Bay wondered if one of the men might be Paul Ridgeway. Owen must have been in contact with him to make all those arrangements.

Her suspicions were confirmed when Owen smiled, held out his hand to the man in the middle, and said, "Hi, Paul."

"Owen. Good to see you." Ridgeway was the shortest of the three men and wore wire-rimmed glasses that made him look businesslike rather than trendy. He was nearly bald, and what hair he had left had been cut severely short.

There was no mistaking the fact that Paul Ridgeway was in charge. He reminded Bay of a bulldog, with his powerful neck, square flat face, and short legs. Seeing the way he stood braced on both feet, she wouldn't have been surprised if he turned out to be as fiercely tenacious as one of those small, tough animals.

The other two agents were long, lean, and sharp featured. Definitely Dobermans.

"It was nice of you to meet us, Paul," Owen said. "But we really don't have time for more than hello and goodbye."

Bay felt Owen's hand in the small of her back, urging her inside to pick up their camping gear, which a baggage worker was bringing inside. She barely managed not to jump at the frisson of feeling it caused. She didn't need any further encouragement. The sooner they got shed of this threatening pack of lawmen, the happier she would be.

"You're going to be delayed long enough to give us a chance to talk with Miss Creed," Ridgeway said as he joined Owen.

The other two men flanked Bay, one walking beside her, the other slightly behind, like watchdogs. All that was missing were the bared teeth and the growl.

Bay did her best to keep the panic she felt off her face. What if they kept her here? What if they sent Owen into the Big Bend alone?

She glanced at Owen to see whether he was going to leave her at the mercy of this pack of wild dogs. When she saw the twitch of irritation in Owen's jaw, she nearly sighed aloud with relief.

"The airport has put a room at our disposal," Ridgeway said. "This shouldn't take long. Then you can both be on your way."

"What is it you think Dr. Creed knows?" Owen asked.

"We'll find that out when we speak to her," Ridgeway replied.

The four men were two steps beyond Bay when they

realized she had stopped. When they turned to face her she asked, "Am I under arrest?"

"Why, no, Dr. Creed," Ridgeway said.

"Then I feel neither the inclination nor the necessity to speak with you. Excuse me, please." She saw her backpack sitting on a baggage cart and walked past them to retrieve it.

When the four men caught up to her, Ridgeway's jaw was jutting. "Surely you realize the seriousness of the accusations against your brother."

"Of course I do. There's nothing I can tell you."

The agent lifted a skeptical brow. "Then what is it you're doing here?"

"Protecting my family's interests."

"Would you mind explaining that?"

"Not at all," Bay said as she grabbed her backpack, slid her arms through the straps, and slung the forty pounds easily onto her back. "I'm going along to make sure nothing happens to my brother if—when—he's found, so he'll have a chance to explain himself to you."

"So you think he's hiding in the Big Bend?"

Bay realized the clever trap Ridgeway had set. She'd stupidly fallen right into it. "My brother isn't *hiding*, Mr. Ridgeway. He's *missing*, maybe even *lost*." She shrugged as nonchalantly as she could with forty pounds on her back. "I don't know how Luke's motorcycle ended up where it was found. Maybe he left it there. Maybe someone moved it there. I have no way of knowing that."

Bay took a deep breath. "But I'm certain my brother had nothing to do with the theft of those VX mines, and I'm going along to make sure he gets a chance to prove it."

"You're risking your life—and a lot of other lives—by not telling us what you know," Ridgeway said.

"I've told you everything I know." Bay turned to Owen and said, "I'm ready when you are."

"You heard the lady," Owen said to Ridgeway, as he slung his own backpack over one shoulder.

"With a little more time—" Ridgeway protested.

"The longer we stand here talking to you, the colder the trail is getting," Owen pointed out. "Have you made all the arrangements I requested?"

"There's a pickup waiting out front with a horse trailer attached. The safety equipment is in the pickup, and you've got the best two mounts I could find on short notice."

"Then we're out of here," Owen said.

Bay saw the anger flicker in Ridgeway's dark eyes, as he considered his alternatives. She waited with bated breath to see whether he would take the steps necessary to keep her at the airport.

Ridgeway put a hand on Owen's shoulder and said, "You be careful out there. I wouldn't want to have to face Clay and tell him that anything happened to you on my watch."

"I'll be fine," Owen said.

Ridgeway's glance slid to Bay as he said to Owen, "Watch your back."

Bay sympathized more than ever with her brother. She hated the way it felt to be suspected of wrongdoing when she was completely innocent. She turned her back on Ridgeway and headed for the door. A moment later, Owen joined her.

"You seemed pretty sure of yourself back there," he said, as he threw his backpack into the bed of the pickup, which was filled with the promised equipment.

"Why wouldn't I be?" Bay had stopped to admire the two chestnut quarter horses in the Sooner trailer, one with a white blaze and the other with four white socks. As she lifted her own backpack over the side of the black, heavy-duty Dodge pickup, Owen took it out of her hands and set it beside the one-man tent and sleeping bag the FBI had provided for him.

"I could have done that," she said.

"Sure you could. But my daddy taught me a gentleman always helps a lady."

Bay was so startled at what he'd said, and the chagrined way he'd said it, that she laughed. "Oh, my God. Chauvinism is alive and well—"

"We call it chivalry, or Southern courtesy, ma'am," he said. She realized he was heading around the truck to open the door for her.

She stepped in front of him and said, "It's going to be a long trip if you refuse to let me pull my weight. I can get my own door, Mr. Blackthorne."

For a minute, she thought he was going to make an issue of it. Then he touched the brim of his hat, shot her a rakish grin that turned her insides to mush, and said, "Whatever you say, Mizz Creed."

She was so flustered, she took a half step backward, slid into the seat when he opened the door for her after all, and said, "My friends call me Bay."

Bay flushed as she realized what she'd said. As he came around the hood and got in, she said, "That is—I mean—You know what I mean!"

He belted himself into the driver's seat and started the engine, before he turned to her and said, "My friends call me Owe. You can call me Owen."

She stared at him in disbelief. "Oh. You. *Blackthorne,* you."

He laughed and put the truck in gear.

OWEN WAS BECOMING MORE AND MORE CERTAIN THAT HE was on a wild-goose chase. Bay had remained vague about exactly where her brother was in the Big Bend, and no matter how many questions he asked, he couldn't pin her down to an exact location.

"Where are you taking us?" she asked.

"Luke's motorcycle was found in the Basin at the foot of the Chisos Mountains," he said, as they continued south on U.S. 385 from Marathon, "which is also where Hank's body was found. We'll start looking for him there. Unless you have a better suggestion."

"Did you ever think that maybe they took Hank as far as possible from where they're really hiding those mines and then shot him? That they might have put Hank's body and my brother's motorcycle where they did simply to lead you astray?"

"Of course it's a possibility. Why do you bring it up? Do you have information that suggests we should start looking somewhere else?"

She made a face and asked, "How far is it from the Basin to the Rio Grande Village?"

"Once you're inside the park, you head one direction to reach the Basin and the opposite direction to get to the Village. They're about thirty-five miles apart. Why do you ask?"

"Just wondering."

He watched as Bay chewed worriedly on her glistening lower lip and found himself wondering how much she really knew . . . and how her mouth would taste. He focused his eyes back on the narrow two-lane road when he realized she'd caught him staring. Not that he would have run into anything. There wasn't much but cactus, creosote, and roadrunners for the next forty desolate miles.

"I want to check for any tracks your brother might have left near his motorcycle before it rains, and they're gone," Owen said.

"Wouldn't it have been better to bring along a couple of bloodhounds, if you're planning to track him down like an animal?"

"Don't need dogs," Owen said.

"You're that good?"

Owen shrugged. "I usually find what I'm looking for."

Both Park Rangers and FBI agents guarded Panther Junction, the entrance to the Big Bend. They'd been expecting Owen, and once he provided identification, they waved him through. Fortunately, the Big Bend National Park was so remote that it had fewer visitors in a *year* than someplace like Yosemite in California had in a single *week,* so it was easy to keep an eye on who was coming and going.

The powers that be had decided it would cause more problems if they closed the park—and had to explain why to the newspapers and the public—than if they left it open and guarded the main roads in and out.

The danger of creating panic in metropolitan Texas cities—with its consequent human and economic repercussions—seemed greater than the remote risk that some tourist would run into the hijackers, who were well hidden. In fact, despite constant satellite surveillance and aerial radar heat imaging, no sign of them had been found.

Once they were inside the park Bay asked, "Isn't there a store at the Rio Grande Village?"

"What is it you need?"

"Chocolate."

"It's a hundred degrees in the shade," he said. "Chocolate is going to melt."

"Well, actually, it isn't chocolate I need. It's something else. I didn't want to embarrass you."

"What?"

"Tampax."

He eyed her sideways. "Why didn't you bring some from home? Or pick some up at the Safeway?"

She flushed. "I didn't think of it. Not that it's any of your business, but my periods aren't regular."

He made a disgusted sound. "This is exactly why I didn't want to bring you along."

When the fork in the road came, Owen made the turn east toward the Rio Grande Village.

As they headed south, the vegetation changed, and the grass disappeared, replaced by tall stalks of ocotillo and spiny masses of lechuguilla. Mexico's high Sierra del Carmen Mountains rose majestically ahead of them in the distance, and as the sun headed downward, the cliffs took on the rosy hue for which they were named.

"I want to drive back to the Basin before dark," Owen said. "That's where I have the best chance of picking up a trail." He turned to her and asked, "Do you really have any idea where your brother is? Or did you just say that so I'd bring you along?"

She eyed him sideways. "When I'm sure there's no possibility you can leave me behind, I'll tell you what I know."

There wasn't much to the Village, just a campground and picnic sites, the store, laundry and shower facilities, a service station, and trailer facilities. Bay jumped out of the truck when they arrived and ran inside.

Owen checked out the campground. He figured Luke might have come here for supplies, and since there were so few tourists, a stranger on a Harley would have gotten noticed. But no one in the campgrounds remembered seeing anyone on a motorcycle.

Owen kept remembering how crazy Luke had been acting at the Armadillo Bar. How desperate he was to find a way to send Clay to jail. No. *To death row.*

Was it possible the kid had stolen the mines so he could pin the theft on Clay? Implausible, but possible. Could Luke Creed have shot Hank? Between his training as a weekend warrior and growing up on a ranch in Texas, it was a sure bet he knew how to use a gun to kill. But was he clever enough to have outwitted Hank? Probably not. Unless Hank had let himself get distracted by thoughts of his wife and unborn baby.

Owen's stomach churned. He didn't want to think about what would happen if the kid pulled a gun on him—and he had to shoot him down in front of his sister. Damn! He wished he'd left Bayleigh Creed at home.

Owen saw a couple of Mexican kids hanging around outside the Village store and figured it might be worth his while to question them. Before he could approach them, Bay came out of the store carrying a handful of candy bars and headed straight for them.

She laid a Snickers on the palm of the tallest boy. When she added a Baby Ruth, the kid began talking a mile a minute. The instant he saw Owen coming he ran, along with his pals.

Owen's instincts told him to go after the kid, but Bay stepped in front of him and smiled. That warm, appealing smile hit him like a fist somewhere in his solar plexus and left him speechless, with his mouth bone dry and his body hard as a rock.

By the time he'd recovered his senses, the kid was long gone. "What did the kid tell you?" he asked irritably.

"What makes you think he told me anything?" Bay said as she crossed past him.

"Why'd you give him the candy bars?" Owen persisted.

She shot him an anxious look from beneath a Stetson she'd pulled low on her forehead—as much to keep down the sprinkling of freckles that dotted her nose and cheeks, he guessed, as to protect her eyes from the sun. "He saw my brother use the phone here," she admitted.

"Why did you let him get away?" Owen demanded. "Maybe he knew—"

"He saw Luke late last night," she said, meeting his gaze. "And he wasn't anywhere near the Basin."

"Where was he?"

Bay shook her head. "I'm not telling you anything until I'm sure—"

"Right. I hear you." Owen realized from the stubborn thrust of her chin that she wasn't going to give in. He had a better chance of following a fresh trail than an old one. It made more sense to start here than in the Basin. "Let's ride while there's still daylight."

Owen unloaded the horses, and they each saddled up, distributing everything they had to take along between the bedroll behind the saddle and the saddlebags.

Two hours later, when Bay stopped on the rocky trail and pulled out a map for the sixth time, Owen finally lost his patience. "Where is it we're supposed to be headed?"

"The Dead Horse Mountains," she replied calmly.

"The Dead Horse Mountains are a big place. Where, exactly?"

"I'm not quite sure."

Owen pulled his horse to a stop. "We've been riding for two hours, and you're not sure where we're going?"

"Oh, I'm sure we're headed in the right direction," she said. "I'm just not sure which of these trails to take."

She held the map out to him and pointed to a junction where the Strawhouse and Telephone Canyon Trails intersected. "My brother is somewhere in here." She paused and added in an almost inaudible voice, "I think."

Owen bit back an oath. He'd been raised not to swear around ladies, but as she'd pointed out, it was going to be a long trip if he had to mind his manners when the *goddamned* woman was going to be so provoking. "I knew this was going to be a total waste of time. I should have—"

"That Mexican boy I spoke with—his name is Manny—said that while Luke was talking on the pay phone at the village, some men dressed in 'army clothes' grabbed him—" Her voice caught, and her eyes welled with tears. "Grabbed him and pushed him into a pickup."

"Aw, damn," Owen said.

"Manny said he saw those same men at the trailhead for the Strawhouse Trail later on last night," she said in a choked voice. "Doesn't it stand to reason my brother must be in here somewhere?"

"What makes you think he isn't lying dead in the Basin, where the Park Rangers found his motorcycle?" Owen said.

He watched her eyes darken from sky blue to lavender, as she fought back tears. "Manny said his family's traveled those trails for generations."

"Smuggling, most likely," Owen interjected.

"Anyway," Bay continued, glaring him into silence, "he admitted he went back after dark to see if the men were still there—whether they'd left anything behind in their pickup, which they'd parked at the trailhead, that he might use—"

"You mean steal," Owen interrupted.

"What's important," Bay said with asperity, "is that he saw my brother—alive."

He watched her struggle to control the wobble in her chin before she spoke again. "I think the men who took my brother parked his Harley in the Basin to lead everyone in the opposite direction from where they're actually holding him."

"Why would they keep him alive, when they killed Hank?" Owen demanded.

Bay met his gaze with dark violet eyes and said, "You're forgetting what my brother did in the National Guard. He knows how to arm and detonate those VX mines."

Chapter 6

LAUREN CREED HAD MADE THE TRIP FROM the kitchen door of Three Oaks to the stable so many times over the past eighteen months, she could have found her way in the dark. So it didn't matter that she was blinded by tears. There was work to be done. A stallion and a mare to be put together in a way that would allow them to mate without one sexually excited animal injuring the other.

Blackjack's championship stallion Smart Little Doc pranced in an adjoining corral to her own quarter horse mare Sugar Pep. Ren could see the bay mare was restless, trotting back and forth along the fence, her tail up in response to Smart Little Doc's urgent neighs and high-spirited crowhops.

As Ren reached the corral, she swiped surreptitiously at her tears before she turned to the cowhand she'd left to watch over the two animals. "What do you think, Slim? Is it about time to put them together?"

"Sugar Pep is ready, Boss. That big old boy still seems a mite excitable, though."

Ren watched the championship cutting horse lower his head and kick up his heels, showing off for the mare. Then he reared and pawed the air, his neigh challenging any and all comers to a battle for dominance. "I'll take it from here, Slim," she said, dismissing the cowboy.

Slim handed over the lariat he'd kept ready, in case either of the horses needed to be lassoed and subdued. "Here you go, Boss."

Ren still felt odd whenever one of the hands addressed her as "Boss." For all her married life, her husband had run Three Oaks without any help from her. It wasn't that she hadn't offered to share the load. But Jesse had said the most important job in the world was taking care of their family. And that responsibility was hers.

Unfortunately, there hadn't been enough housework in the world to keep her mind off the mistake she'd made, the consequences of which she'd lived with every day. Ren had loved Jesse Creed when she'd married him, pregnant with his child. But she'd been desperately *in love* with Jackson Blackthorne.

Ren had met Blackjack quite by accident, on a hot July day when she was barely seventeen. She hadn't been able to persuade Jesse to sneak away from riding the fenceline with his daddy and go swimming with her, so she'd gone alone. She'd ridden off to one of the deep, quiet spots along Bitter Creek that was shaded by a broad, leafy cottonwood.

Ren hadn't brought along a swimsuit, so she'd stripped down to her plain white bra and bikini panties and waded in. The deep pond of water that had formed at a bend in the creek had been icy cold and wonderful, and she'd put her head back and closed her eyes and floated in the dappled shade. When she'd heard galloping hoofbeats, she'd smiled, thinking Jesse had decided to join her.

Ren could feel his heated gaze on her and wondered why he didn't say anything, then realized that in all likelihood he could see her dark nipples through her wet cotton bra. A quiver ran through her, as she felt his gaze caressing her. "Come on in," she invited in a husky voice, her eyes still closed. "The water's fine."

She smiled as she heard the snaps pop on his Western shirt, the rattle of his belt being unbuckled, and the sound of him hopping one-footed as he pulled his boots off, before she finally heard the brush of denim sliding down his legs.

She waited for the splash, but realized when she felt the gentle ripple of waves that he hadn't whooped and done a cannonball as she'd expected. He'd come into the water silently. She imagined him with water covering him to his waist, and her lips curved into a Madonna-like smile, as she waited for him to come and kiss her. That, too, was a tradition, one she felt sure he'd observe. But he was taking too long.

"Kiss me," she murmured, floating in the water with her eyes closed, as though suspended on clouds in the sky.

One of his arms slid under her shoulders to support her, and she felt his warm breath on her cheek as he leaned over her. His lips barely teased her own before he withdrew.

Oh, she wanted more. So much more. And she told him so. "More, please."

His mouth returned to hers, unbearably soft, incredibly gentle. Jesse had never been so tender, and she felt a place inside her open and flower with love. She lay quiescent, her eyes too heavy-lidded with pleasure to open, and only his arm to support her as she floated languorously in the water. "Oh, that was lovely. Again."

His mouth returned, hungrier, and his tongue probed the

seam of her lips. She opened to let him in and realized that he tasted . . . different . . . but in a good way. His tongue slid to the frenulum behind her upper lip and teased, something he'd never done before, and she gasped at the pleasure of it. He retreated, and his lips caressed the edges of her mouth and then her cheeks and eyelids with tiny, reverent kisses. She felt exalted. Worshiped.

"Oh," she said with a moan. "Oh."

It felt so wonderful. Why hadn't they ever done this before? She started to open her eyes, and his large, callused hand gently covered them.

"Easy," he said in a rough, gruff voice. "Easy."

She relaxed against his arm in the water, willing to trust him. "I want to hold you," she said. "I want you to hold me."

He seemed to hesitate, then whispered, "Keep your eyes closed."

She smiled at the silliness of such a request, but was more than willing to play along with his game. "All right," she whispered back.

She was surprised at his strength when he lifted her out of the water, surprised at the hardness of his biceps under her hands, as she slid them up his arms and around his neck. The hair at his nape was soft and thick and luxurious. Her mouth searched for his and found it, warm and waiting.

She groaned with satisfaction as his tongue probed deeply into her mouth. She felt him release the catch on her bra and pull it up out of his way, so he could reach her breasts. She let her head fall back and felt the dappled sunlight on her eyelids as he suckled first one breast and then the other. She moaned as the breeze hit her damp nipples and turned them into tight buds.

"Oh, God," he said in a low, guttural voice. "You're so beautiful."

She couldn't help smiling. She would have opened her eyes, but he put one large hand over them once more and murmured, "Don't. This is a dream. Let's play it out."

Oh, yes. It felt like a dream. A wonderful dream.

She let him remove her bra and heard it hit the water with a small splash. She felt a raw curl of feeling deep inside, as her breasts brushed against the rough, wiry hair on his chest. She hadn't remembered Jesse having so much hair on his chest, but she was feeling too much pleasure to question something so inconsequential.

She pulled his head down so she could kiss him more easily, put her tongue into his mouth. Oh, the sounds he made! Carnal, lustful sounds. She felt desirable and desired.

He pulled her roughly up along his body so she felt his naked erection against her belly. She was startled at first at the thought of him naked, but then she realized she was glad. She reached down to touch him, but he caught her wrist in an iron grip and put her hand back around his neck.

"Not yet," he rasped.

He caught her buttocks in his hands and pulled her hard against him, so she could feel the heat of him pulsing against her.

"I want to feel you inside me," she begged. "Please."

A groan rumbled deep in his throat, a desperate, animal sound of need. She felt him rip her bikini panties in two and growled low and fierce in her throat as she realized he was going to give her what she craved. Her mouth latched onto his neck, biting hard as he lifted her and thrust inside, deeply, to the hilt.

She felt full. Unbelievably full. But her body was too far gone to question the anomaly her mind had recognized. She bucked against his body, the water thrashing around them. He held her buttocks tight against him, releasing her only to thrust again. She clenched her inner muscles, as she felt him release his seed, milking him dry.

Her head fell on his shoulder, and she linked her fingers behind his neck to keep her arms from sliding down. She felt his chest heaving against her own as he held her tightly against him, their bodies still connected to one another.

"Oh, God," she heard him say.

And realized it wasn't Jesse's voice she heard.

"Oh, God," she whispered, as she slowly lifted her head . . . and opened her eyes.

His eyes weren't dark like Jesse's. They were stone cold gray. It wasn't Jesse Creed she'd just made love with. It was Jackson Blackthorne.

"Put me down." She was amazed at how calm her voice sounded. Amazed at how bereft she felt, as their bodies disentangled. Amazed that she had no bones in her legs. And only belatedly felt the shame that flushed her cheeks and caused her to hide her naked breasts with her hands.

She stiffened when he tried to help her stay upright in the shallow water and said, "Don't touch me."

"Will you let me explain?"

She was too wounded to listen. "How could you? You knew I thought you were someone else."

"Why didn't you stop me?"

She knew what he was asking. Why hadn't she recognized the differences between one man and another?

Why hadn't she known it wasn't Jesse who'd been making love to her?

Maybe she had. Most certainly she had.

Ren frowned, confused by her own actions. There had been so many differences. She'd noticed them all. Why hadn't she opened her eyes? *Because then the dream would have ended.* Why hadn't she stopped him? *Because it had felt so right.*

"Why didn't you stop?" she countered.

"Because I wanted you," he said boldly. "I saw you floating there, so beautiful . . . so desirable . . . so utterly irresistible."

Ren wasn't immune to flattery. Especially when she'd received so little of it from Jesse. Jesse didn't seem to think she needed to hear those sorts of things. But she did. Every woman did.

"Is there a chance I've gotten you pregnant?" he asked.

Ren gasped, as she remembered why she'd been so anxious to have Jesse meet her at the pond. The news she had to tell him. That she was pregnant with his child. She looked at Blackjack with stricken eyes.

"If I've gotten you pregnant—"

"No," she interrupted. "There's no chance of that."

She didn't know why she hadn't told him she was already pregnant. That she would most certainly be a married woman as soon as she and Jesse could arrange the wedding.

"Can I see you again?" he asked.

"No."

"Why not?"

The Blackthorne arrogance she'd heard so much about was evident in his demanding voice. Ren discovered she didn't mind it so much, when what he wanted was her. She'd wanted her dream lover to seduce her. She'd loved every moment she'd spent in his arms. But that was all there could ever be between them.

He leaned across the distance that separated them and touched her lips with his.

And she was lost. She stepped into his embrace and felt his arms tighten around her.

"I have to have you again," he said, as he lifted her up and carried her out of the water and onto the bank.

They'd spent the rest of the afternoon together, loving and talking and then loving again. She hadn't questioned the insanity of what she was doing. She'd only known that it felt right, no matter how wrong it was. He was another part of herself. They belonged together.

She wished she'd known then what she knew now. That her conscience would force her to give up Blackjack and marry Jesse, whose child she carried. And that even when she realized, within a year of marrying Jesse, that she'd made the wrong choice, it would be too late. Because Jackson Blackthorne had already married Eve DeWitt and had a child of his own on the way.

But that was then. And this was now. New decisions had to be made, new choices that would affect the rest of her life. She focused her gaze on the stallion and mare in the adjoining corrals.

"Penny for your thoughts?"

Ren jerked as Blackjack touched her shoulder. "Just remembering—" She cut herself off, but not before a light flared in his eyes.

"It's been a long time, Ren. Too many years. I want you. I always have, and I always will."

Oh, he was a wily-tongued devil. How did he know

just the right thing to say? She walked away from him and slid open the gate between the two corrals, watching as the stallion, head up and tail flowing, danced into the corral with the mare.

Ren felt Blackjack join her as they watched the two animals circle one another, felt his big body tense as he watched the violent, bestial coupling.

The mating of stallion and mare was never civilized. To someone unschooled, it might even seem brutal, a fierce, powerful animal claiming its mate. But sex was necessary for the survival of the species. And while people might want to mask the ferocity of the act, animals never did.

The stallion's teeth bared and clamped on the mare's throat as he mantled her, his front hooves finding surface on her gleaming coat, their manes flying in the wind as he plunged into her. Their bodies glistened with sweat and their eyes rolled wildly, as he demanded she take his seed.

Ren grasped Blackjack's forearm, her fingernails biting hard into his flesh, as the stallion neighed in triumph. She was shivering, shuddering, when the animals finally uncoupled. She didn't resist when Blackjack pulled her into his arms, and she burrowed her face against his powerful chest and slid her arms around his waist and held on tight.

"I didn't kill Jesse, Ren," Blackjack said. "You have to believe me."

She had only his word for it. Even his own son suspected him. He'd threatened to kill Jesse only three weeks before her husband had died. Ren remembered his exact words: *I should have killed you a long time ago, Jesse.* What if he'd done it? She'd seen enough examples of Jackson Blackthorne's willingness to make hard choices when he was after something he wanted.

The bank he controlled refusing loans to struggling ranchers. Flooding the market with beef and lowering the price, causing more disaster, and gobbling up small ranches when they went belly-up.

She wondered if he'd been so ruthless when she'd met him thirty-five years ago, or if he'd only become that way as he'd fought against adversity over the years to survive and succeed. Would Jackson Blackthorne have become a different—more compassionate—man if she'd relented and married him?

Over the years, the Bitter Creek Cattle Company had become a gigantic ranching empire, until the only property within a hundred miles that Blackjack didn't own was Three Oaks. Had he murdered Jesse to get it? Or was she what Blackjack had wanted? Was he guilty, as his son had accused him of being? Or as innocent as he professed?

"Oh, God," she whispered. "I have to believe you. I can't give you up. Not now that we've found each other at last."

"You don't have to," he replied. "I'm yours, Ren. Always and forever."

She forced herself to step back and look at the man she loved. Had always loved.

He'd aged well. At fifty-five, there were crow's-feet at the corners of his eyes and harsh lines drawn on either side of his mouth. His jawline was still straight and firm, probably from the arrogant thrust of it all these years, she mused.

He was only an inch or two taller than Jesse, but his shoulders were broader, more powerful. His waist was still trim, and he was as lean of hip as he'd ever been. He looked weathered, like a piece of wood that had met wind and sun and only been polished to a brighter sheen. She still wanted him. Lusted after his body, as only teenagers were supposed to do.

It was foolish for her to be feeling all the hopes and dreams of youth. She was fifty-one. Her periods were irregular. She had gray hair at her temples and in other places she wished she did not. If she were a brood mare, she'd already have been put out to pasture. And yet, inside, she still craved the feel of his body on hers, still wanted to join with him, still yearned for the savage need, coupled with tenderness, that he'd shown her that long-ago day.

But she wasn't a teenager. She was a mature woman, who'd lived a long life and learned lessons from it.

Ren felt a place inside her shrivel up, as though it had been touched by fire and burned to ash. She imagined years of lying in bed at night untouched. It didn't bear thinking about. But what other choice did she have? Blackjack wasn't free to love her. He had a wife.

"I think it would be best if we kept our distance from one another until your divorce is final," she said.

"That could take years!" Blackjack protested. "Every day is precious. And life is too damned short!"

Ren hadn't forgotten the heart attack that had nearly killed Blackjack two years before. "Are you all right?" she asked, laying her hand on his heart.

"My heart will be fine. So long as you don't break it."

"I don't want to hurt you, but I can't bear sneaking around like this. I won't openly commit adultery with you. That isn't fair to my children. Or to yours."

She could see the struggle on his face to find a reason

she would accept to continue the clandestine meetings that had begun only a month before. So far, she'd managed not to have sex with him. But she didn't think she could resist much longer. Quite simply, she didn't want to resist.

"This is crazy, Ren. I won't give you up."

"Then hurry up with that divorce," she said with a smile meant to ease the pain she could see in his eyes.

"Eve wants too much," he said. "She wants it all," he amended.

"Is Bitter Creek so important to you?" She knew the answer to her question before he gave it.

"I wouldn't know who to be without the ranch," he said. "And I can't pay Eve what she wants without selling it."

He leaned over and touched his lips to hers with so much gentleness that she couldn't help but feel his desperation.

"I've got a hunting cabin where we could meet," he urged. "It hasn't been used since Trace left for Australia. No one would know. Please, Ren. I'm fifty-five," he reminded her with a self-deprecating grin. "Who knows how much longer I'll be a virile man."

She laughed, as she knew he'd intended. She wanted to give in. She wanted to be with him. But she wanted more than just sex. She wanted to spend the rest of her life with him.

She laid her palm on his cheek and said, "I want more, Jackson. I want to share the joy of living day to day with you. I want the right to sleep beside you at night. And I want to grow old with you, the two of us sitting in rocking chairs on the back porch, when our bones are too brittle for sex."

She saw the bleak look in his eyes and almost gave in. But there was too much at stake. "You'll have to choose," she said. "Between her and me."

But what it really came down to was a choice between Bitter Creek and Ren. She could see the struggle on Blackjack's face. He knew exactly what she was asking. *Is a piece of land—all right, eight hundred thousand acres of land—more important to you than I am?*

"You're the one who married Jesse, when I begged you not to," he said angrily.

It was hitting below the belt. Fighting dirty. She should have known he would. He was fighting for his life. She wrapped her arms around herself and said, "You know why I did that. I was carrying his child. It wasn't his fault that I did what I did with you that day at the creek."

"I love you, Ren."

She swallowed hard. "I know."

"But that isn't enough for you, is it?" he said in a harsh voice.

"No," she said softly. "It's not."

"You can send Smart Little Doc home when he's done here," he said.

And then he was gone.

Ren gripped the top rail of the corral with both hands to keep from running after him. She was doing the right thing. She had to keep believing that. Especially over the long, lonely nights to come.

BILLY HAD FELT SICK TO HIS STOMACH AS HE WATCHED Owen Blackthorne drive away. He had immediately turned to Summer and said, "You should be going."

"He won't say a word to my father," she said. "Owen isn't like that."

"You should be going anyway. My mother will be home soon with Emma."

He watched as Summer wrinkled her nose like a child smelling burnt toast. "What have I ever done to make your mother dislike me so much?"

"You're rich," Billy replied.

"That's not fair."

Billy snorted. "Who said life was fair?" He slid his arm across her shoulder like a brother might. He yearned to make the touch a caress, but he didn't dare.

He had nothing to offer her as a prospective husband. He'd never been to jail, but he'd come close too many times to count. And he had a steady job, though it was the worst kind of menial ranch work. Yet he did it, to keep his mother and sister fed and to make what few repairs he could on the ranch with the limited funds he had left.

In the year since his father had died, he'd been a model citizen. But it was way too late for anyone in Bitter Creek to see him in another light. He was "Bad" Billy Coburn. Always had been and always would be.

Which was why he had to get out of here. Anywhere else would be better. He hated his home. Hated the memories he had of growing up here. He would have left a long time ago to seek his fortune, but he hadn't been willing to abandon his sister while she still needed him. Once Emma graduated from high school in the spring and could get herself a job, he'd be gone. One year. He had one more year to wait.

If he was ever going to have a chance to make something of himself—to make himself worthy of becoming Summer's husband—he had to go. But he was afraid, with good reason, that Summer wouldn't be here waiting for him when he got back. Her father was intent on selling her to the highest bidder, and Billy lived in fear that one of these days Blackjack might offer her a suitor she took a hankering to. And then she would be lost to him forever.

But he couldn't ask her to wait. She had no idea his feelings for her went as deep as the ocean. She thought they were just good friends.

"You have to go," he repeated.

She slid her arm around his waist and laid her head on his shoulder. He forced himself to relax, so she wouldn't feel the sexual tension caused by her closeness. He couldn't help breathing in the smell of her shampoo, something flowery and feminine. He let himself kiss the top of her head, because that was the sort of thing a friend might do.

She wrapped her other arm around him and turned to put them body to body. He edged his hips away, so she wouldn't discover his reaction to her touch was a great deal more than friendly.

She sighed and said, "I wish you didn't have to go away next year. I don't know how I'm going to survive once you're gone."

They'd talked often about their plans for the future. It was her dream to run the Bitter Creek Cattle Company one day. That had become a lot more likely when her eldest brother Trace inherited a huge cattle station from a distant relative and moved lock, stock, and barrel to Australia. Neither Owen nor Clay had any interest in running the ranch. Which left her as her father's only choice.

Yet he still didn't seem all that anxious to choose her.

Billy's dreams were all about becoming a rich and powerful man, so he could prove how wrong everyone had always been about him all his life—and so he would be worthy of the woman he loved.

"You're the only one who seems to care that my daddy's willing to trade me in marriage for more land," she said.

"All you have to do is say no," Billy said in a voice that was more harsh than he'd intended.

"It sounds easy when you say it like that. I love my daddy. I feel like I've been a disappointment to him, getting thrown out of so many colleges. Of course he should have known better than to send me away. Everything I want in life is right here in Bitter Creek."

"You might be sorry one of these days that you didn't get an education." Billy would have given anything for the opportunities she'd thrown away.

She shook her head. "Education doesn't have to come from a book. Daddy could teach me how to run Bitter Creek, if he wanted to. But he doesn't think I can do the job. Then I go and do something stupid, like what I did last night, and prove him right."

Billy felt her shudder in his arms.

"I almost killed Ruby and her foal," she said in a tremulous voice. "Thank God for Dr. Creed."

"You've told me you won't make that mistake again," Billy said. "So you learned something from the experience."

She looked up at him, her hazel eyes misted with

tears. Billy felt his soul connect with hers, as he lost himself in those deep golden orbs.

Summer's brother Owen would have known instantly what drew Summer Blackthorne and Bad Billy Coburn to one another, if he'd ever seen in Summer's eyes what Billy was seeing now. Billy recognized the look, because he'd seen it so often in his own mirror. A need for acceptance. A desire to please someone you feared you could never please. And a feeling there must be something wrong with you, something that, if you only knew what it was, you would fix, because then you could get the acceptance you craved.

"I just want Daddy to see how capable I am," she said, staring up at him. "I want him to teach me how to run Bitter Creek someday." She nuzzled her face against his shoulder. "He only sees a brood mare he can mate with some expensive stud and get him a *grandson* to follow in his bootsteps."

Billy pulled her snug against his body, forgetting his arousal in the urgent need to give her comfort.

He felt her stiffen, sought the reason, and realized she must have felt his erection. She shoved him away with the flat of her palms and stared up at him, her eyes wide with surprise. Or maybe shock was a better word.

Billy knew instantly what he'd lost. The wariness in her gaze spoke for itself. She'd always trusted him implicitly. Like a brother. But it was a lover's body she'd felt. He could see she was astonished that he'd become aroused by touching her.

He let his hands drop to his sides. He didn't think excuses would work, but he was willing to give them a try. His mouth curled up on one side in a cock-eyed grin.

"Sorry about that. The feel of a female body does that to a man, whether he wants it to happen or not."

"It shouldn't happen between us," she said with certainty. "We're *friends*."

He shrugged. "You're female. I'm male. Sometimes it happens."

"Not to *us*," she insisted. She stared into his face suspiciously. "Or has it?"

"It might have happened once or twice. No big deal."

She stared at the visible bulge in his jeans, then glanced up at him, her face flushed and said, "It looks pretty big to me."

Billy couldn't help grinning. "Summer, you can't be this naïve. This is how a man reacts when he's around an attractive woman."

"You find me attractive?"

He saw the startled interest in her eyes and realized he'd opened another can of worms. He didn't want her judging him as a prospective suitor. There was no way he could match up to the men her father presented to her on a silver platter.

"Any man would find a pretty girl like you attractive," he said, backpeddling as fast as he could. He flipped one of her golden curls back from her shoulder and said, "Curls this bouncy, and eyes like topaz jewels, and a nose this nosy." He tapped her playfully on the nose. "What man wouldn't react like I did?"

"A *friend* wouldn't."

"I'm a man, Summer, not a eunuch," he said, unable to keep the irritation from his voice. "I've never once touched you as a lover, never kissed you like one. Think about it, and you'll realize I'm right."

He saw her mind working. He was disturbed by what she said next.

"Do you have a lover?"

He touched the blush on her cheek with the backs of his knuckles. Her skin felt as hot as it looked. It was also amazingly soft. "You never did know when to keep your mouth shut."

"Do you have a lover?" she asked again, her heart in her eyes.

"If I did, it wouldn't change what we have between us," he said. Had she really imagined that he'd been celibate all the years they'd been friends? Maybe she hadn't wanted to see him as a man, or more likely, she simply hadn't wanted to imagine him with other women.

"I guess that means you do." She was looking at him with her head cocked like a little bird.

"Are you seeing me with another woman?" he teased.

"I'm wondering what it would be like to be kissed by you."

"Let's not go there," he said. "I don't want to mess up our friendship."

"It wouldn't," she said, grinning suddenly. "I'd like to know how it feels. I mean, as an experiment."

"Put the wrong chemicals together, and they explode."

She frowned. "Are you saying you don't think I'd like it? Or that I would?"

"It doesn't matter, because I'm not going to kiss you."

She looked up at him shyly, from beneath lowered lashes, and gave him a cajoling smile. "Just one teeny, weeny little kiss?"

He laughed at her antics. Inside his stomach, about a million butterflies had taken flight. "Don't play games with me, Summer." He said it with a smile, but it was a warning.

One she ignored.

She crooked her finger and wiggled it, gesturing him toward her. "Come here, and give me a little kiss."

She was doing something sultry with her eyes, something she'd never done before. She'd turned on some kind of feminine heat, because he was burning up just looking at her. "Stop this," he said in a guttural voice.

She canted her hip and put her hand on it, drawing his attention in that direction, then slid her tongue along the seam of her lips to wet them. "I'm ready, bad boy. What are you waiting for?"

His heart was beating a hundred miles a minute. He was hot and hard and ready. And if he touched her, he was going to ruin everything.

"I'm not going to kiss you, Summer."

He saw the disappointment flash in her eyes. Saw the determination replace it.

"All right. I'll kiss you."

He could have stopped her. He was the one with the powerful arms and the broad chest and the long, strong legs.

But he wanted that kiss.

"Fine," he said. "Don't expect fireworks. I'm only doing this because we're friends." And if she believed that, he had some desert brushland he could sell her.

Suddenly, she seemed uncertain, and he felt a pang of loss. Silly to feel it so deeply, when kissing Summer had been the last thing he'd allowed himself to dream about. Although, to be honest, he hadn't always been able to control his dreams. She'd been there, all right. Hot and wet and willing.

He made himself smile at her. "Don't worry, kid. It was a bad idea. To be honest, I value our friendship too much—"

She threw herself into his arms, clutching him around the neck, so he had to catch her or get bowled over. "Whoa, there," he said, laughing and hugging her with her feet dangling in the air. "It doesn't matter that you've changed your mind about wanting that kiss. I'm just glad to be your friend."

She leaned back in his embrace, searching his eyes, looking for something. Before he could do or say anything to stop her, she pressed her lips softly against his.

His whole body went rigid.

"Billy," she murmured against his lips. "Please. Kiss me back."

"Summer, I don't—"

She pressed her lips against his again, damp and pliant and inviting.

He softened his mouth against hers, felt the plumpness of her upper lip, felt the open, inviting seam, and let his tongue slide along the length of it.

"Oh." She broke the kiss and stared at him with dazed eyes. Eyes that sought reason where there was none.

He wanted to rage at her for ruining everything. They could never be friends now. Not now that he'd tasted her, not now that she'd felt his want and his need. He lowered his head to take her mouth, to take what he'd always wanted.

"Stop that this instant, you jezebel! How dare you stand there in broad daylight on the porch of my house fornicating with my son!"

Billy felt Summer jerk free of his arms and drop to the porch. They turned to find his sister gawking and his mother red-faced and furious.

"There's no reason to be calling names," he said to his mother.

"I knew this would happen. I knew it!" she raged. "You swore to me there was nothing going on, Billy. I should have known better. God never intended men and women to be friends, he meant for them to lie down with one another. But I won't have you lying with that Blackthorne bitch. Not ever. Do you hear me? Never!"

"That's enough, Mother," Billy said, leaping to the ground past the two broken back steps. "Nothing happened here but a simple kiss."

"I want her off my property. Now. I don't ever want to see her here again."

Billy saw that Summer was frozen on the porch, staring at his mother, her face fiery red. He realized the only way she could leave was to walk past his mother, who would likely hurl more hurtful words at her. He put himself between his mother and Summer and said, "You'd better leave, Summer."

Billy desperately hoped his mother would hold her tongue until Summer was gone, but as Summer passed them, his mother said, "Tell that mother of yours, when you get home, that she'd better keep an eye on you. Because I'm not having this, do you hear? I'm not having fornication between her blood and mine."

"Her mother's in a sanitarium," Billy said, hoping to distract his mother long enough for Summer to make her escape.

His mother turned her head sharply and stared at Summer. "You mean you don't know?" She laughed raucously. "Your mama's home, girl. They let her out."

Summer stopped, mouth agape, eyes wide with shock. "You've seen my mother? Here in Bitter Creek?"

"That mother of yours had the nerve to show up in church this morning. As if she could be forgiven her sins.

There's no redemption for the likes of her. It's the devil who'll claim her soul. And it can't be soon enough for me!"

Billy locked eyes with Summer. She looked lost. Frightened. She desperately needed a friend to hold her, to share her joy at the return of her mother and her fear of what this might mean to her father.

But he couldn't be her friend anymore. Things had changed unalterably between them. They had played a dangerous game. And they had both lost.

Chapter 7

"WHY IS THIS CALLED THE TELEPHONE CANYON Trail?" Bay asked.

"Because the army ran a phone line down the canyon during World War I."

"Why would they want to do that?" Bay asked.

"I have no idea. Don't you ever shut up?"

"I don't see why I can't ask questions."

"I need to keep my eyes on the damned trail," Owen said.

Bay figured he'd decided it was okay to swear in front of her—at least for the duration of this journey. "Anyone can look and talk at the same time," she muttered.

She was so worried and frightened, she couldn't stop talking. The farther they traveled into the wilderness, the more precarious her brother's situation seemed—and the less certain she was that she could get out of here on her own if she found her brother and then decided they needed to escape from Owen.

She'd visited the Basin before, which was mostly green with foliage. But she'd never realized how godawful this part of the Big Bend was. No trees, no water, just rock and sand and plants that had adapted to life in the desert by growing deadly spines to keep from being eaten. The canyon walls showed layers of history, proof they'd been here for a million years or more. Bay felt small and insignificant. And frightened.

But she wasn't about to admit she was scared and get a lecture about how she should have stayed at home in the first place.

"It's really hot, isn't it?" she said.

He shot her a baleful glare.

"That was a rhetorical question. It didn't require an answer. You could easily have kept your eyes on the trail instead of making a face at me," she said testily.

Owen rolled his eyes. "Lord save me from the logic of women."

"Women can be every bit as rational as men."

"Don't make me laugh," Owen said. "In a crunch—"

"I don't know what kind of women you've been meeting, but I guarantee you I'm the picture of calm in an emergency."

"I'll have to see that to believe it."

"I suppose you've never panicked in a crisis," Bay said.

"Nope."

She ground her teeth. "I'll have to see that to believe it."

"My job doesn't allow for mistakes in a crisis," he said.

"Neither does mine."

He eyed her assessingly. "I suppose that's true. Why would you choose a life-and-death job like being a vet?"

"I focus on the life part of the job," she said. "And do my best to limit the deaths."

"Me, too," he said.

She searched the ground ahead of her and said, "I don't see anything. Are you sure my brother came this way?"

"If you'll recall, you're the one who told me this was the way to go."

"You're the one who knows how to track people down," Bay shot back.

Owen had explained that it was possible to follow a trail from footprint to footprint by using a stick to measure a man's stride and then laying the stick down on the ground in every direction until you found the next sign of passage.

He'd also explained that while you could certainly follow the trail that way, you'd be moving so slowly that you'd never catch up to the man you were chasing. The trick was to look for sign as far ahead along the trail as you could find it, move up to that point, and then look ahead again.

Bay hadn't been able to discern anything that looked remotely like a trail left by her brother and the two men who'd abducted him. "Have you seen any sign at all?" she asked Owen.

"They're traveling single file. I saw an army boot print when we crossed the top of the ridge, about a mile back."

"You did?" Bay said excitedly. "Why didn't you say something?"

"It was only a boot print."

"Can you tell if it's one of the guys who kidnapped Luke? How many folks do you suppose are hiking around out here in army boots?"

"Lots of hikers wear army boots."

"If you noticed one boot print, how come you haven't been able to find more?" Bay asked. "I mean, since you're such a mighty hunter."

"Because they've brushed them out."

Bay stared at him a moment. "That means you've

been following their trail by watching for what—brush strokes on the ground?"

"Something like that," Owen said. "I haven't seen anything since we crossed the sandy bottom of that arroyo. They might have taken another path, or a switchback I didn't notice. We might have to backtrack to pick up their trail."

Bay grimaced. She didn't relish repeating the trip they'd just made. She was hot and sweaty and tired. Telephone Canyon Trail was nearly twenty miles long, and the first three miles had been steeply uphill and difficult to follow. Her knees ached from bracing herself in the stirrups as they'd traveled a half mile back downhill to the Ernst Basin. It had been slow going through a sandy arroyo, and then uphill again a mile and a half to the top of a ridge, the highest point on the trail. The view had been awesome, but another reminder of just how easy it would be to get lost in this vast place. Then it had been more stress on her knees, as they headed back downhill to the bottom of Telephone Canyon.

And that was only six and a half miles of riding. They still hadn't reached the rock cairn that marked the junction with Strawhouse Trail, which was more than two miles farther on.

Owen had stopped his horse and was surveying the terrain ahead of them.

"What do you see?" she asked.

"Not a damned thing. My guess is that we'll find more tracks in the morning."

"In the morning? You mean we're stopping?"

"There's no sense moving when we don't know which direction to go."

"That kid I bribed with candy said he saw those men head into this canyon with my brother. Doesn't it stand to reason they'd be in here somewhere? Why can't we keep moving?"

"This trail disappears, crosses other trails, reappears, and runs through a maze of thick, thorny brush. We're going to get lost if we can't see exactly where we're going, and we're running out of daylight."

"Don't you have some military gadget that lets you see in the dark?"

He lifted a brow. "You've been watching too many movies."

She made a face. If he only knew. She saw every movie that came out. She *loved* the movies. Which is why she knew all about modern military gadgets. Infrared imaging wasn't new, however. It had been around for aeons. "I know there's gear you can use. Surely you brought something along."

He sighed. "I have night-vision goggles, but I didn't bring anything to help my horse see in the dark."

"If you can see, why can't you guide your horse?"

"I don't want him bucking me off when he gets stabbed in the leg by some cactus and thinks he's been bit by a snake."

"What about when the moon rises?" Bay asked. "Couldn't we move on then?"

"There's only a quarter moon. It won't give us enough light to see faint brushmarks."

Bay felt a terrible foreboding that if she didn't find Luke today, she might never see him again. "Can't we at least keep searching now, while there's still light to see?"

"We're stopping while there's still enough light to find ourselves a flat place to camp, here in the bottom of the canyon."

Bay looked at the narrow trail and the sharp-thorned

lechuguilla and ocotillo that lined either side of it. "I think it's already too late for that."

"If I remember correctly from my trips here with Clay when we were teenagers, there's a wide, flat space around the next bend. It's got rock on three sides, so it's a better spot to fight off an ambush."

Bay's heart began to pound in her chest, spiked by adrenaline. "You think we might get ambushed?"

"Better safe than sorry," Owen said.

Bay reached for her canteen and took a long drink of water to calm her scattered nerves. "Why aren't you drinking?" she asked irritably.

"If you didn't talk so much, you wouldn't get so thirsty."

Bay pressed her lips flat. Well, if that was the way he was going to act, she'd keep her mouth shut and see how he liked the silence.

Obviously, he liked it fine. It was eerily silent. Only the crunch of their horses' hooves in the sandy soil, the jangle of a bit, and the creak of saddle leather could be heard. There wasn't a bird cry from what little blue sky she could see above her, nor the rustle of wind in any of the desert plants along the trail. Nothing from the outside world seemed to penetrate the depths of Telephone Canyon.

Bay searched for the compression—rather than *depression*—of sandy soil that Owen had taught her was evidence of a footprint, but she didn't have the skill he'd developed over years of hunting down criminals. Everything looked compressed to her.

She was quiet for ten minutes. Which was a long time, really. She wanted to ask another question, but she didn't want him snapping at her again. Too anxious to sit still, she stood in the stirrups to stretch her legs, then moved her bottom back and forth in the saddle until she found a comfortable spot to settle.

She dallied her reins loosely around the saddle horn and reached up to unbutton the top two buttons of her blouse, then leaned over and shook the cotton cloth back and forth to cool herself. Her Stetson came off next. She settled it on the saddle horn while she lifted the hair off her neck with both hands, so what little breeze there was could reach the sweat on her nape.

"What the hell kind of strip show are you putting on?"

Bay nearly fell out of the saddle at Owen's angry outburst. She jerked upright, knocking her hat off the horn and onto the ground. Her horse saw the shadow when it fell, figured it for a dangerous, horse-eating jackrabbit, and shied violently toward Owen's mount.

His horse took exception to being bumped and kicked out with both hooves, striking Bay's horse in the rump, which made him buck. Bay grabbed for the reins, but they fell loose from the horn, and she was helpless to restrain her mount when he began to run helter-skelter down the canyon, sunfishing and crowhopping.

Bay was thrown up onto her mount's neck, where she held on for dear life. She heard Owen galloping behind her and knew it was only a matter of time before he caught up to her. But a narrow passage was coming up, and there wasn't room for both her and her horse. She was going to be scraped off. Unless she jumped first.

From her precarious perch, Bay stared down at the rocky soil racing past her nose and thought of all the movies she'd seen where cowboys leaped from their horses and got up and walked away. Surely it couldn't be that difficult.

In a moment, when they reached that narrow passage, the choice was going to be taken from her. Bay closed her eyes and launched herself as far as she could from her horse's flashing hooves.

And landed like a sack of wet cement.

She skidded for maybe two feet along the rocky bed of the canyon. On her face. And her right hip. And her left hand.

When she stopped, she lay there stunned for a moment, then gave a shaky laugh. "Oh, that was not at all like it is in the movies."

Owen reached her a moment later and dropped on one knee beside her. "You little fool! Are you all right? Are you hurt?"

Being called a fool hurt a lot. The rest of her was in serious pain. She lifted a trembling hand toward her scraped cheek.

"Don't touch it," Owen said, catching her wrist.

"It hurts." Bay realized she was crying now, and her whole body was shivering. "I think I'm in shock."

"No wonder. That was quite a fall."

He ran his hands over her, checking for injuries in a way that did nothing to ease the strain on her racing pulse. Bay wanted to tell him she was fine, that nothing was broken, but her heart was in her throat.

"Why on earth didn't you just hang on?" he demanded. "I'd nearly caught up to you!"

"I didn't think my horse and I would both fit through that passage," she croaked. "Cowboys are always leaping from their horses in the movies, and they never get hurt."

"You forgot to roll."

"Oh. I knew I did something wrong."

Owen had already slid his hands under her knees and

behind her shoulders before she realized he intended to pick her up. "I can walk," she protested.

"Sure you can. I'm just giving you a little helping hand. Guess we're going to be camping here tonight."

Bay looked around and realized the ground where she'd landed was as lopsided as the first birthday cake she'd ever baked. But she was willing to sleep on an angle, if it meant she didn't have to get back in a saddle right away.

"If you put me down," she said. "I'll help you set up camp."

He set her down in the shade of the canyon wall and went down on bended knee beside her. "Let me take a closer look at you." He took her chin in his hand and gently tipped her face up so he could look into her eyes.

"You have really beautiful eyes," she murmured, staring back at him. "Did you know they change color? Sometimes they're silver and sometimes they're pewter and sometimes they're dark, like storm clouds."

His lips quirked. "Yours turn violet when you get mad . . . or excited."

She flushed and lowered her eyes.

"Your pupils look okay to me," he said gruffly.

"I didn't hit my head. I fell on my face."

"I see that," he said, catching her hand before she could touch her right cheek. "You've got some stones and sand in those scratches. They'll need to be cleaned out. Where else are you hurt?"

She held out her left hand and realized as she did so that her sleeve was torn away all the way to her elbow. "Oh, God. I didn't even realize I'd skinned my arm. My hand is what hurts." She held out her hand to him. It looked raw. She tried to imagine what her cheek must look like.

She reached down and touched her hip. Her jeans were ripped, but they'd held up better than her cotton shirt. "I hurt my hip, too."

"Let me see."

She made a face at him and yelped when her cheek protested even that slight movement. "You don't need to see my hip. It's fine."

"If the skin's broken, it'll need cleaning, too," he said, unbuckling her belt.

"Stop that."

"Think of me as your doctor," he said, as he unsnapped and then unzipped her jeans.

"My doctor doesn't usually undress me," she snapped. "And my patients already come undressed."

He laughed. "Lift your hips," he said. "Up!" he ordered, when she hesitated.

She put her good hand on his shoulder to brace herself and lifted her hips as he pulled her torn jeans down. To her surprise, her bikini underwear was shredded, and the skin underneath was bloody. "Uh-oh."

She was still staring at the injury on her hip when she felt him pulling off her boots. She started to protest, saw the warning look in his eyes, and shut her mouth. He pulled her jeans off, leaving her legs bare above her white boot socks. "Was that really necessary?"

"You're decent," he said, straightening the tails of her Western shirt over her shredded bikini underwear. "I can put your boots back on if you like."

Bay shook her head and laughed. "Just get the first-aid kit, and let me take care of myself."

He grimaced. "If I'm not mistaken, you packed the first-aid kit in your saddlebags."

Bay winced. "You're right." She stared down the canyon

as far as she could see. There was no sign of her horse. "How long do you think it'll take him to stop running?"

"He won't have gone far. But I need to set up camp before it gets dark. And I'm not hunting for your horse in the dark, for the same reason I'm not hunting for your brother in the dark."

"Where am I supposed to sleep? My bedroll and tent are with my horse."

"You should have thought of that before you started that little striptease of yours."

"You're the one who shouted and scared me half to death. I was only trying to cool off."

"And heating me up in the process!"

"I can't help it if you have a vivid imagination."

"It didn't take much imagination to see your breasts," he shot back. "You opened your blouse right up and bent over and flapped your shirt like you were waving a red flag at a bull!"

"I was getting some air!"

"You slid your butt around that saddle like you were sitting right on my lap."

"That's ridiculous!"

"Then you lifted your arms to hold your hair up and those perfect little breasts of yours—"

"That's enough," she interrupted. "You're crazy if you think—"

"You mean you weren't inviting me to kiss my way around those wispy curls at your nape?"

"I most certainly was not!"

"Could've fooled me."

She searched for the worst insult she could think of to sling at him. "You—You—Bullying Blackthorne!"

"Damned contentious Creed!"

She glared at him, and he glared back.

"I've got a tent to set up and a camp to make," he said through clenched teeth. "You sit there, and don't get into any more trouble."

"I can help," she said, starting to get up. She cried out as she felt a sharp pain in her injured hip.

"I said stay put! As soon as I get the camp set up, I'll clean you up. Bandages will have to wait till I can find your horse tomorrow."

Her chin jutted. "I can take care of myself."

He ignored her and set to work putting together their campsite. He set up the one-man tent in nothing flat and unrolled his sleeping bag inside. She didn't say a word when he handed her a flashlight, picked her up, and moved her inside the tent. It was getting dark, and she knew the scorpions and centipedes would be coming out to hunt.

Owen unsaddled his horse, rubbed him down, watered him, and hobbled him with a ration of grain in a feedbag, then joined her in the tent with a handful of cloths and his canteen.

"With any luck, your horse will come back this way looking for food and water," he said. "Otherwise, he's going to get damned thirsty. There's no *tinaja* in this canyon where he can get a drink."

"Is it possible he can find his way out the other side?"

"Possible. Most likely, once it gets dark, he'll stay put where he is until morning."

Owen wet down a handkerchief with water from his canteen that had warmed in the sun. There wasn't much room inside for the two of them. Bay edged backward and crossed her legs Indian style.

"You need to lie down, so I can lay this across your injured cheek."

"I can lean my head back."

"Lie down."

"I don't like being ordered around," she said.

"Please lie down," he amended.

"That's better," she muttered, as she uncrossed her legs and scooted forward so she could lie down. "Ouch," she said, as he laid the damp cloth on her face.

"Sorry. If we don't get all that sand out of there, you're liable to get an infection. Let that soak a minute." He wet another handkerchief and said, "Give me your hand."

She opened her mouth, but before she could speak he said, "Please give me your hand."

She held out her hand, and he laid the second handkerchief across her palm. "That stings."

"Good."

"Beast."

"Brat." Without asking permission, he lifted the tail of her shirt and gently pulled down what was left of her panties, exposing her bare hip. "I don't like hurting you," he said, as he laid a dampened strip of cotton he'd torn from one of his T-shirts on her wounded flesh. "But this has to be done."

She hissed in a breath as the wet cloth hit her abraded flesh. "Oh, God."

Before she could focus on that pain, he was lifting the cloth off her cheek.

"I need to wet this down again."

He repeated the process over the next half hour, laying cloths on her wounds to soak them clean, then replacing them with more cloths. The warm cloths seemed to ease the pain, as well as remove the sand and grit.

"I think that about does it," Owen said at last.

"Thank you," Bay said.

"How do you feel?" he asked.

No one had ever made her feel more special, more pampered, more cherished. But all she said was, "Better." Her stomach growled, and she laughed. "Now I'm hungry."

"Supper's coming up," he said with a smile of truce.

"Could you get my jeans and boots for me?"

"No sense you getting dressed. You can eat in the tent."

"Are you planning to share this tent with me tonight?" Bay asked.

"Hadn't figured on sleeping out here on the ground."

"You will unless I get my jeans and boots."

"Yes, ma'am," he said with a wry grin.

Bay shook out her boots before bringing them inside the tent, to make sure no snakes or scorpions had taken up residence. It was hard to get her jeans on because her knee was also skinned, and it hurt to bend her hip.

"Need any help?" Owen asked.

"I ought to make you put them on, since you took them off," she grumbled.

Before she knew it, Owen was on his knees in front of her and had her jeans in his hands. He held them so she could put her legs inside, then slid them up until they reached her hips.

"Lift," he said.

She braced her good hand on his shoulder and lifted her hips, as he pulled her jeans up around her waist. He started to reach for her zipper, but she put her hand over his. "I can get that."

They were nose to nose with one another, and she realized he really did have the most beautiful eyes she'd ever seen. She laid her hand on his bristly cheek, marveling at how much dark beard had grown in the space of a day. She wanted to thank him for taking such good care of her. But not with words. No sense giving him the chance to hurl them back at her. She leaned forward the inch that separated them and pressed her lips lightly to his.

"What was that for?"

"To thank you for taking care of me."

He pressed his lips lightly against hers.

"What was that for?" she asked.

"You're welcome."

Her stomach growled. Bay was willing to ignore it. She had something much more interesting than dinner to contemplate. Who would have thought a man as hard as Owen Blackthorne would have lips so utterly soft. Or be so gentle. Or caring.

"You can pack tomorrow, to make up for all the work I'm doing tonight," he said, as he backed away.

Or so obnoxious, she added mentally. "I'll be glad to do my share right now."

He grinned at her. "Like I said, you're a distraction."

Owen offered her a selection of *MREs,* better known to the military as a *Meal, Ready-to-Eat,* and Bay chose the chicken noodle soup. Owen warmed it using a sizzle sack. He added a saltwater pouch to the bag of chemicals, put in the packaged *MRE,* and twenty minutes later they had hot chow—without the need for a fire.

Bay sat cross-legged on the ground to eat and worried about all the scorpions and centipedes that might need to cross her path to get from one side of the canyon to the other. "The desert seems a lot more alive after dark," she said to Owen, trying her best to hide her unease.

"Yeah. It's amazing how many animals there are out here that you never see till the sun goes down."

That did absolutely nothing to calm Bay's nerves. "Like what?" she asked.

"Like—"

Bay heard a flutter of wings, and then something grabbed at her hair. She opened her mouth to scream at the same time she swatted desperately at her hair.

Owen clamped his hand over her mouth before any sound escaped. "Easy, easy," he said, as she struggled violently against his hold. "It was only a bat."

Bay cringed at the thought of a *bat* in her *hair*!

"Think you can keep from screaming if I let go of your mouth?"

She nodded vigorously.

He let her go, and she shuddered.

"Oh, God," she said. "A *bat* was in my *hair!*" She ruffled her hair as though she were trying to free it of feathers.

"Bats are a good thing. They eat a lot of insects," Owen said.

"Ick," Bay said, and shuddered again.

Owen slid his arms around her. She pressed close to him, as she tried to still her trembling body. "I feel silly," she admitted.

He rubbed his hands up and down her back and said, "My sister isn't afraid of much, but she hates bats, too."

Bay ducked her head and said, "It's just that they look like . . . flying rats."

She heard Owen chuckle. The husky sound, and the moist warmth of his breath against her temple, made her feel safe. She put her arms around him, which brought her soft breasts into contact with his rock-hard chest.

His arms tightened around her.

Suddenly Bay didn't feel the least bit safe. In fact, the

emotions she was experiencing felt downright dangerous. "Owen?"

She felt his hesitation before he let go of her and sat back so he could look into her eyes. "Are you okay now?"

She nodded. "I'm fine." She was a great liar when she needed to be.

"I think maybe it's time for bed," he said.

"It's so early," Bay protested. "I don't think I'll be able to sleep." Oh, she was tired, all right. But still scared of what might go bump in the night. Exhausted, but aching all over. She was sure there was no comfortable way she could lie down to sleep.

"We'll be getting up at first light," he reminded her. "You'd better grab what shut-eye you can."

It took a bit of maneuvering to get them both inside the tent. It was amazingly cold in the desert once the sun went down, since there was no foliage to hold the heat. They ended up spooned together inside the sleeping bag, with Bay's uninjured cheek lying on her hand.

Bay tried not to notice the warmth of Owen's body. Tried not to notice the muscles in his chest and thighs as they pressed against her. Or how much she liked the musky smell of him.

"This is cozy," Owen murmured.

"This is all your fault," Bay replied peevishly. If not for him, she'd be safe in her own sleeping bag. Alone. Instead of lying here *loving* how it felt to be snuggled up next to a *Blackthorne.*

"I've got no complaints," Owen said.

"My father would roll over in his grave if he could see me with you like this." She felt Owen tense and knew she was ruining the budding closeness between them. But she couldn't seem to stop herself. "My brother was in that wheel-chair at the breakfast table every morning to remind him that a Blackthorne had turned his eldest son into a cripple. And there were no consequences for what you'd done."

"No consequences," he muttered. "That's a laugh."

Bay turned her head to look at Owen over her shoulder, because there was no way to turn her entire body in the tiny space. "Were you ever punished? I never heard about it, if you were."

"I got kicked off the football team my senior year."

Bay snorted. "That's no punishment."

"It meant I wasn't scouted for college football. Which meant my football career ended before it ever started."

Bay was startled by his revelation. "You wanted to play football professionally?"

"I was big enough and fast enough and strong enough."

"A Blackthorne playing football for a living? I can't imagine it."

"Neither could my father," Owen said. "Or my brother Clay. But it was my dream. It ended when your brother got hurt."

"It's hard for me to feel sorry for you," Bay said. "You walked away from your mistake. My brother will never walk again."

"If I could change what happened that day, I would," Owen said. "I can't. I tried apologizing to your father, but he wouldn't listen to me."

"Have you tried apologizing to Sam?"

She felt Owen move restlessly behind her. At last he said, "I've thought about it a lot of times. Once or twice I tried to see him, but he avoided me. Maybe I'll try again. If you think it would help."

"Apology or no, Sam will never accept the idea of your dad and my mom getting together," Bay said. "It's pretty hard for me to accept it myself, and I've seen them kissing. Everything's been crazy since my dad was murdered."

"Do you think that might have something to do with why your brother stole those mines?"

Bay stiffened. "I'm positive Luke didn't take those mines. As positive as you seem to be that your brother didn't do it. I'm sorry about what happened to your friend."

"Being sorry isn't going to help your brother if he was in any way responsible for getting Hank killed."

"My brother came to the Big Bend for the same reason you and I did. To find the real culprits."

"Why didn't he just go to the authorities?" Owen asked.

Bay took a deep breath and said, "Because he knew the authorities would want proof when he accused your brother of stealing those mines."

"Your brother's crazy."

Bay lifted Owen's arm off her hip and shoved it back onto his own. "I guess we'll see about that."

There was no room to shift without bumping against hard male flesh. No room to turn without encountering the smell of a man who'd spent a day in the sun—a scent she found strangely alluring. No room to escape the brush of his soft hair against her temple.

"You're more restless than two bobcats in a potato sack," he growled at last. "Come here."

He cinched a strong arm around her waist and hauled her back against him. Snug enough to feel what a profound male response all her moving around had produced. She should have felt frightened. Instead, she felt secure, protected by Owen Blackthorne's embrace.

"Now go to sleep," he snarled.

Bay would have said that was impossible, but she closed her eyes and started counting roadrunners and soon felt herself drifting off.

She didn't know what woke her. Had no idea how long she'd been asleep. But she suddenly realized Owen wasn't in the tent with her. And despite the fact they were supposed to be totally alone, she could hear him talking to someone.

Chapter 8

BAY CREPT OUT OF THE TENT AND CRAWLED cautiously toward Owen, until she could see him in the shadowy grayness between dawn and daylight. "So you did bring secret spy stuff!" she crowed.

Owen swore, as he swiveled on his knee to confront her. "What woke you up?"

"I heard you talking to someone. Who's on the other end of that satellite line?"

"FBI Special-Agent-in-Charge Paul Ridgeway. I have to contact him at five A.M. every morning to let him know exactly where we are." He held up a global positioning device.

"Even if we haven't found anything?"

"It was two days before the Rangers realized Hank was in trouble," Owen said. "Even with satellite photos, it took them another day to find his body. This way, if anything happens to us, the cavalry knows where to come running."

"Why didn't you tell me you had all this stuff?" Bay asked.

"It was none of your business," he said bluntly.

Bay made a disgusted sound in her throat.

"Sounds like you're in fine voice this morning," he said wryly. "How are you feeling?"

Bay surveyed the scabs on her hand and arm and tried a nonchalant smile that ended when she realized that the scraped skin on her cheek wouldn't tolerate the strain. "Everything's still a little sore, but I'll be fine."

"I want to see if we can find your horse before we have breakfast."

"Sounds like a good idea."

They both went to work, folding up the sleeping bag and tent as though they'd been working together all their lives. Bay managed her ablutions while Owen repacked the satellite phone and the global positioning device. When she rejoined him, he said, "You'd better have a drink of water before we start."

She took the two-quart canteen, stared into it, then swished it around. "This is nearly empty. Is this all the water we have?"

"I've got another full canteen."

"Thank goodness." She hadn't yet quenched her thirst, when she felt Owen taking the canteen away from her.

"Better save some of that till we catch up to your horse."

"You said he'd be easy to find this morning."

"Maybe he will. Maybe he won't."

Owen stepped into the saddle and reached a hand down as he took his foot out of the stirrup, so Bay could mount behind him. Once she was settled, he said, "Hang on. And don't be wiggling around. We can't afford any more accidents."

Bay glowered at him. She clamped her hands on either side of his waist at his beltline, but his Colt .45 was holstered on one side, which kept her from getting a comfortable hold. She put her right hand above the gun, but that meant it was practically under his armpit. Then she moved it below the gun, but that put her hand low on his hip, close to his crotch.

"Sonofabitch." He grabbed her hands and pulled them around his midriff. "Now hang on."

Bay kept her breasts rigidly distanced from Owen's back, but her nipples puckered anyway. It was that damned washboard of male abdominal muscle under her hands. The man could do commercials for those workout machines they advertised on TV.

The horseflies were a surprise. Where had they come from? She let go with one hand and swatted at one that seemed determined to bite her on the nose. And knocked Owen's hat askew.

"That does it. Off."

"It wasn't my fault," Bay said. "I was getting bitten."

"Off." He grabbed her arm and levered her out from behind him and onto the ground.

"You're not going to make me walk!" she protested.

He stepped out of the saddle. "We're both going to walk, since the terrain here is mostly uphill, and give my horse a breather."

Bay pursed her lips. She couldn't very well insist that he let her ride, if he was going to walk, too. She wished she could change into her hiking boots, but they were tucked in her saddlebags, which were with her horse. He seemed perfectly happy in his lizard cowboy boots, but she knew they couldn't be comfortable, since they weren't meant for walking.

She followed him up the trail, a safe distance behind his horse. "I've been looking, but I haven't seen signs of any tracks being brushed away. Have you?"

"Your horse destroyed whatever signs there were

when he came through here," Owen said. "Maybe we'll find some again after we find him."

They traveled the two-plus miles to the cairn of stones marking the junction of the Strawhouse and Telephone Canyon Trails. From the hoofprints in the loose sand, it was plain even to Bay (and she was no tracker) that her horse had taken the turnoff to Strawhouse Trail, rather than continuing along the Telephone Canyon Trail. "What do we do now?" she asked.

"We need the water and medical supplies your horse is carrying. We'll have to go after him."

"What if the men who have my brother went the other way?" Bay asked.

"They did go the other way," Owen said, as he pointed out the faint compression marking the definable sole of an army boot a good dozen feet ahead of them on the Telephone Canyon Trail.

"Why don't I go after my horse, while you stay on the trail of the men who kidnapped my brother?"

He lifted a brow. "You mean you're going to trust me not to shoot your brother on sight?"

"Don't even joke about something like that."

"You don't know how tempted I am to be rid of you," Owen said. "But I think we'd better stay together."

"I'll be glad to take the less full canteen of water. I won't need as much as you and—"

"I said we'll stay together."

Bay realized she didn't really want to be out here alone. "Fine."

"Mount up," he said.

She stared at him. "Shouldn't you mount up first?"

"I think it's safer if I ride behind you."

Bay didn't argue with him. Time was passing, and the

longer it took to find her horse, the longer it was going to take to find her brother. She mounted quickly, then extended her hand and took her foot from the stirrup.

Owen grabbed the saddle horn with his left hand and threw himself onto his horse behind her in a feat of such grace and strength that she only barely managed to stifle an admiring "Oooh."

He surrounded her with his arms and took the reins from her, then clucked to set his horse in motion.

Bay realized as they entered a narrow creekbed choked with vegetation that there wasn't much "trail" to the Strawhouse Trail. "Is the whole trail this bad?"

"No. It gets worse."

They hadn't gone very far before Owen reined to a stop. "The foliage in this wash is too dense to ride through. Which means we're going to have to walk above it, along the side of the trail, and lead the horse."

Bay took one look at the lechuguilla, sotol, and cat-claw cactus that rimmed both sides of the wash and groaned. "Good Lord. Why didn't my horse stop here? This must have been impossible to travel through in the dark."

Owen shook his head. "Beats me. Maybe he went a little loco."

Bay was grateful for her cowboy boots when they began walking through the spiny cactus. "This stuff is dangerous."

"Yep."

Bay slipped, and Owen leaped to catch her before she could fall. "Thanks," she said.

"Uh-oh."

His voice was so quiet, Bay didn't realize at first that in rescuing her, he'd slid into a lechuguilla. Several of the needle-sharp three-inch spines had pierced Owen's boot and were embedded in his calf.

"Stand still," she said. "Let me help."

She slid a pocket knife from her boot, where she'd sewn a leather holder for it, and used the knife to cut the spines away from the bush. One by one, she pulled each of the spines out of his flesh, then out of his leather boot, and finally through his denim jeans. "Did I get them all?" she asked at last.

He moved his leg and said, "Whatever's left is more a nuisance than anything else. We'd better get moving. The sun is getting hot."

Long before they reached a faint trail on the west side of the wash that marked the end of the heavy vegetation, Bay noticed Owen was limping. "Are you okay?"

"Hurts like hell."

She glanced at the leg of his jeans above his boot. "You're bleeding."

"Probably a good thing. Get rid of all the dirt."

Bay chewed on her lower lip. "Doesn't it seem a little strange to you that we haven't found my horse yet?"

"Yeah, it does," Owen admitted.

"What do you think happened to him?"

"We know he came this way," Owen said, pointing to the recent hoof marks in the sand. All of a sudden, Owen's horse jerked against the reins and began to whinny. "Whoa, boy. Easy, boy."

Bay searched ahead to see what might have frightened him. "Oh, no."

"What is it?"

"My horse. He's down. It looks like he's been hurt."

Bay hurried toward the spot where she could see bits of the chestnut's body through the vegetation, anxious to do what she could to help the animal, which was lying in the center of the sandy wash. As she approached, a half dozen turkey buzzards that had been dining on the concealed carcass were frightened into flight around her, their black wings filling the canyon from wall to wall.

Bay screamed in fear and backpeddled as fast as she could. Owen caught her, and she turned and pressed her face against his chest. His arms surrounded her and held her tight.

"It's all right," he said. "You're okay. I have you."

She clutched at him, her body trembling violently. She felt his hands smoothing her hair, heard him saying quiet words, but couldn't make sense of them. As she calmed, she realized there was something odd about the scene she'd witnessed.

Suddenly, she leaned back and looked up at Owen. "There was no saddle. No saddlebags." She pulled herself free, and holding her hand over her mouth and nose to stifle the smell of the decaying horse, crossed back to look at it. "Where are the saddle and saddlebags? What could have happened to them? Did he buck them off?"

Owen walked around the dead animal, examining the carcass and the ground around it. "He sure as hell didn't buck off the bridle. And that's gone, too." His mouth formed a grim line. "Somebody else found your horse last night," he said. "And left us a message."

Bay gasped as she looked where Owen was pointing. Her horse had been shot—right between the eyes. "That's horrible!"

"These are not nice men."

Bay's gaze slid uneasily back and forth along the trail, as she searched for some sign of the depraved soul who'd killed an innocent animal to make his deadly point. "Why didn't we hear the shot?" she asked.

"Most likely muffled by these canyon walls."

"You said they took the other trail," Bay said accusingly.

"That footprint might have been put there to fool us into going in the wrong direction. Or maybe they split up." Owen pointed to the compression of an army boot that showed beneath the horse's tail. "At least one of them was here."

"What do we do now?" Bay asked. "Go back? Or keep going?"

"If I were alone, I'd keep going. I think the smart move is to make sure you're safe and then come back here on my own."

"We can't be far behind the men who took my brother. We can catch up to them, if we keep going." Bay knew she was a liability now, but any delay might endanger Luke's chances for survival. If the two men they were hunting would shoot a poor defenseless animal, she didn't want to think what they might do, or might already have done, to her brother.

Owen shielded his eyes and peered up at the scorching sun. "We need to get out of the sun during the heat of the day."

Bay waited with bated breath, as Owen looked back in the direction they'd come, then forward along the Strawhouse Trail.

"Hell," he muttered. "I don't like either of my choices."

"Please, Owen."

He met her gaze and frowned. "Let's go," he said brusquely. "There are some limestone caves up ahead."

Bay sighed in relief when he continued down the trail they'd been following. As they headed south, the wash widened into the Ernst Valley. They no longer had to dodge cactus, but now her calves ached from walking in loose sand. "How much farther?"

"Another couple of miles."

Bay wasn't going to beg Owen to stop. If he could keep walking—limping—on that injured leg of his, she could manage on her aching hip.

At least they didn't have to worry about being ambushed. She could see for miles in every direction. "There must have been one whopper of a fire here," she said as she surveyed the charred vegetation that lay ahead of them as far as the eye could see.

"Yep. 'Bout ten years ago. Started by lightning in the spring. Burned for four days, then petered out on its own."

"What was there to burn?" Bay asked, looking at the desert landscape.

"Sotol. Yucca. Brush. Grass."

"Why hasn't it grown back?"

He shrugged. "Not enough water, I guess."

Which reminded Bay they were walking in the desert with less than three quarts of water between them, when they ought to be drinking a gallon of water a day—each. "Where's the closest water?" she asked.

"The Rio Grande. But I'm not sure you'd want to drink that."

"How far away is the river?"

"Eleven or twelve miles."

"We can walk that in what—maybe four hours?" Bay said, relieved.

"If we were traveling on a flat surface, maybe. There's a place farther on where the trail is blocked by boulders. We're going to have to do some climbing before we get where we're going."

Bay stared at Owen's horse. "How is your horse supposed to get over country like that?"

"He won't."

"So you're saying that eventually we're going to end up carrying our supplies on our backs?"

"I'm saying we're going to end up carrying our supplies on our backs *in the dark.*"

"Oh, shit," Bay said.

OWEN DIDN'T KNOW WHAT WAS WRONG WITH HIM. SOMEthing had gone haywire inside, and he couldn't look at Bayleigh Creed without having sexual fantasies that were mostly visions of the two of them naked, with him buried deep inside her. Anybody looking at the waif in blue jeans and a ripped shirt, with one cheek scabbed over and a handkerchief bandaging her hand, would think he'd gone loco. Maybe he had.

There was nothing remotely sensual about her appearance. Except he couldn't look into those violet-blue eyes of hers without getting a fluttery feeling in his stomach. The memory of her nipples stabbing him in the back made his groin draw up tight. And watching her fanny move in those butter-soft jeans as she walked along the trail in front of him had made him hard as a rock. It was not a comfortable way to travel.

Owen swore, low and soft.

Sunlight gleamed off her auburn ponytail, as she glanced at him over her shoulder. The auburn curls at her temple had been tickling his nose when he'd woken up in the tent with her. He imagined what all that silky auburn hair would look like draped across his body. And felt about a hundred butterflies take flight in his gut.

"Keep moving," he said curtly.

The guttural sound that came from her throat made him think of hot, sweaty sex.

Owen didn't want to contemplate the difficulties of getting involved with the daughter of a man his mother—or maybe his father—had arranged to have murdered. That alone should have been enough to discourage his interest. He couldn't understand how she was having this effect on him now, when their situation was so fraught with danger. But maybe that was exactly why he was reacting the way he was. Danger heightened sexual tension. Yeah, that must be what it was.

Owen knew the significance of the message that had been left for them back in that dry wash, even if Bay didn't. They were being warned off, given a chance to get the hell out of Dodge. He knew he should have backtracked, especially since they'd lost half their water, along with the rubber suits and gas masks that would have protected them if they ran into any VX nerve gas.

Fortunately, he'd put the atropine-oxime autoinjectors into his shirt pocket to keep them handy, figuring that if they needed them, they'd need them in a hurry.

Unfortunately, the hijackers weren't going to need anything as deadly as VX nerve gas to kill them. Or even a couple of bullets. If he and Bay didn't keep moving, if one of them got injured, or if anything delayed them from getting to the end of this trail—like a standoff with the hijackers who'd taken this same route—they would die of thirst.

They'd been walking through a broad valley, and he began searching the limestone walls above them for one of the caves that had been inhabited by some prehistoric people—in a day when there must have been water here.

He spotted one of the lower caves and pointed it out to Bay. "We'll stop here and wait out the heat of the day."

He watched her stare down the valley ahead of them, knew she was calculating whether they could make it without stopping, and saw the small shake of her head as she turned back to join him.

"How much farther will we have to walk when it's dark?"

"A couple of hours."

Bay stared up at the opening in the limestone that was easily eight or ten feet above the ground. "How do we get up there without a ladder?"

"We'll use a trick my brother Clay and I worked out," Owen said.

"What's that?"

"I'll hold the horse near the opening, and you stand on the saddle. That'll give you enough height to grasp the edge of the cave with your hands and pull yourself inside."

"Women don't have the same upper body strength as men," she pointed out. "I did a paper on it."

He grinned. "I'll give you a shove from the bottom."

In the end, she turned out to be strong enough to make it on her own. He handed up the saddlebags, then loosened the cinch and hobbled the horse below the cave, before he joined her. The cave wasn't large, but they were out of the sun.

"Snakes can't climb, can they?" Bay asked as she cautiously walked farther inside.

"No snakes," he said. "Maybe a few spiders. Scorpions could be a problem," he said as he retrieved the nearly empty canteen.

He saw her shiver as she said, "I sure hope I don't accidentally sit down on a scorpion. At least you can see a snake coming."

Owen watched her use her boot to scrape away a few cobwebs and debris along one wall.

"I get the feeling we should have brought a whole posse of Texas Rangers along with us," she said, as she sank down in the space she'd cleared.

Owen smiled wryly as he remembered Clay had made the same suggestion.

"I can't believe we could be in such terrible trouble from such a small accident," Bay said.

"The Big Bend is notoriously unforgiving," Owen replied. "People have died of thirst out here even when they stayed with their car and their car was on a road. This place is just too damned big and too damned remote."

"Which is why those hijackers picked the Big Bend to hide out in, I suppose," Bay said with a sigh. "And why my brother must have felt he had to keep an eye on them, rather than calling for help. It's easy to see how someone might disappear in this place and never be found."

"Right now, we need to worry about getting ourselves out of here alive."

"Don't worry about me," she said. "I'm doing fine."

Maybe now she was, Owen thought. But the heat was dehydrating her, and since she was a great deal smaller than he was, she was going to find herself in trouble long before he did. He handed her the canteen. "Take two swallows. No more."

When she was done, he took one swallow himself. He intended to conserve what water they had until he was sure they were going to make it out of here without anything else going wrong. He threw the rolled-up sleeping bag to her. "Get some sleep. It's the best way to pass the time."

He saw how carefully she moved in deference to her sore hip as she unrolled the bag, unzipped it, and laid it flat. "You might as well join me." she said.

"I'm going to keep watch for a while."

She stopped and tipped her head sideways. "Watch for what?"

"The bad guys," he said with a wry smile.

She frowned. "We're supposed to be chasing them, not the other way around."

"Yeah. But we might be getting a little too close for comfort."

Her eyes widened. "Do you think they've been watching us?"

He shrugged. "Maybe. Don't worry about it right now. Get some sleep."

She lay down with her hands cupping her head, making her breasts jut. He forced himself to look away, but it was too late. His blood was pumping, and his jeans no longer fit comfortably. He limped to the opening of the cave and stared out.

"You seem to know this trail pretty well," Bay said.

"Yeah. Clay and I came here every summer to spend time by ourselves." He thought of the accusation her brother had made—that his brother was involved in the hijacking of the VX mines.

Owen had refused to even consider the possibility, because he couldn't conceive of a reason *why* Clay would be involved. But he hadn't spent much time with his brother over the past ten years since they'd graduated from college. Clay had gone one way, and Owen had gone another.

And there was that coincidental visit by his brother to Paul Ridgeway in Midland, where Clay had been seen by Luke with two men who'd traveled on to the Big Bend—and then abducted Luke.

Owen knew Clay was ambitious. His brother believed political power was the road to important social change. The Texas Rangers, along with the FBI, had been investigating the possibility that the mines had been stolen by a Texas-based white supremacist group, the Rattlesnakes, who'd bought stolen guns in the past and met secretly, fomenting civil rebellion against the government. Had Clay decided that change came too slowly within the boundaries of the law and decided to step outside it with help from a couple of friends from Midland?

Owen tried to imagine himself doing such a thing and couldn't. Clay was his twin. They used the same toothpaste, ate the same favorite foods. His brother was the other half of himself. Innately, they were the same person. There was simply no way Clay could be involved.

When Owen looked back into the cave, he saw Bay had turned on her side, with her good hand beneath her good cheek. Her eyes were closed, and she was breathing deeply and evenly. She looked so helpless, when she was anything but. She was prickly and persistent, and she'd turned his world upside down.

Somehow, he managed to keep his distance from her for the rest of the afternoon. When the sun was low in the sky, he retreated back into the cave and tapped her on the shoulder. "Wake up, sleepyhead."

She bounced upright, and her head caught him on the chin, knocking his teeth together and catching his lip between them.

"Ouch!" he yelped.

"I'm sorry. I get called so often in the middle of the night for emergencies that I'm used to popping out of bed."

He massaged his chin and worked his jaw and dabbed at his split lip. "I'll remember that."

She leaned toward him and moved his hand out of the way. "You're bleeding."

She unwound the handkerchief from her hand and used it to dab at his lip. She moved the cloth away and used a finger to plump his lip where his teeth had left a tiny cut. "Speaking as a physician, I'd say you'll recover."

"Not if you keep that up for long," he murmured, looking into her eyes.

She seemed startled, then looked back at him. Their eyes caught and held. "We really shouldn't do this," she murmured.

"I know," he said, as he lowered his mouth to hers. "Be gentle with me. I'm wounded."

Her lips were incredibly soft, a little damp, and giving. He pushed his mouth against hers, his heart thrumming as he felt her cautious response. He wanted to taste her and captured her nape to hold her steady as he slid his tongue along the seam of her lips. She opened wide.

A moment later he was inside, his tongue lapping at the honeyed taste of her. She was equally ravenous, he discovered. Her hands didn't seem to know where to go, and he felt them moving across his chest and finally clasping him around the neck. He wrapped his hand around her ponytail and angled her head back so he could thrust his tongue deep into her mouth.

And he was lost.

They were a tangle of arms and legs as he lowered her

to the sleeping bag, both grabbing at buttons and snaps and belts and boots. Trying to get naked, anxious to put flesh next to flesh. Anxious to touch. To caress.

"Hurry, hurry," she said breathlessly. "I can't wait."

He was afraid he wouldn't last long enough to get inside her. She was fire in his arms, and he was on a very short fuse. "Don't wait on me," he said, as he plunged himself deep inside her.

Lord, have mercy. She was so hot and tight and wet. She wrapped her legs around him, and he could feel her nails piercing his back as she cried out and surged upward, driving him in to the hilt. His mouth found hers, and his tongue mimicked the hard thrust of his body. He was out of control, his body forcing hers against the hard ground, the blood pounding in his ears, his lungs shrieking for air.

He couldn't take it all in fast enough. The smell of her heated flesh, the taste of her mouth, the touch of her silken hair. He thirsted, and she was life-giving water. He needed her, had to have her, could not survive another moment without the completion she promised.

"Can't . . . wait," he gasped.

"No need . . . to wait," she gasped back, as her body began to convulse around him.

He threw his head back in a grimace of excruciating pleasure as he spilled his seed within her.

He pulled her close as he collapsed beside her, his chest heaving in concert with hers, their bodies slick with sweat, as they sucked enough air to stay alive.

He felt her easing away and said, "Don't. We have to talk."

She looked up at him with the knowledge of what they had done in her eyes. She looked terrified. And unhappy.

"We can figure out a way to make this work," he said.

She shook her head. "No, we can't."

"Our families—"

"This has nothing to do with your family or mine. There are . . . personal reasons . . . why I'm not going to get involved with you."

He sat up abruptly. "Are you telling me you've got a boyfriend—or a husband—out there somewhere?"

"Nothing like that," she said, turning her face away. "I've just decided that . . . I'm never getting married."

He thrust a hand through his hair, shoving it back from his face. "I see." But he didn't really. He grabbed his underwear and dragged them on, then pulled on his jeans. "I wasn't proposing marriage. I was only suggesting—"

"Sex?"

He grinned. "You must admit, what just happened was pretty incredible." He paused with his shirt half on. "I wouldn't mind repeating the experience."

From the speed with which she began dressing, she didn't share his feelings. "I'm not proud of what I just did," she said. "I haven't forgotten who you are, or who your family is. Ordinarily, I have a lot of self-control. I can't explain what just happened. I can't imagine what Sam would think if he ever found out I had sex with the man who crippled him."

"I—" Owen cut himself off. There was no way he could excuse himself. Nothing he could say that would undo the past. He tucked his shirt in, zipped up his jeans, and buckled his belt. "Our families don't have to get involved in this."

"How can we keep them out?" she asked bleakly.

"I thought we managed fine."

She shook her head. "I wanted to know what it would

feel like to make love to you. I had a lapse in judgment and indulged my curiosity." She shoved her feet into her boots. "That's all that happened."

"The hell it was."

He yanked her onto her feet and had his mouth open over hers in two seconds flat. He shoved her legs apart, unzipped her jeans and thrust two fingers deep inside her. She moaned and bucked and shook her head in denial, but it was too late.

He already knew she was wet and ready.

Owen looked into her eyes and said, "That sweet little mouth of yours can tell tales all day long. But your body doesn't lie. You want me every bit as much as I want you."

He let his thumb caress her, and she writhed in his arms.

"Don't," she said. "I don't want this."

She stared at him with heavy-lidded eyes, violet eyes still dazed with passion.

"Oh, you want it all right. Every bit as much as I want it." He abruptly released her, stepped back, and said, "Let me know when you decide to let us both have it."

She sank back onto the sleeping bag, wrapped her arms around her legs and rested her chin on her upraised knees. "I don't think I could stand to get hurt again, Owen."

"Again?"

"I had a . . . bad experience."

He opened his mouth to deny that he'd ever harm a hair on her head, but she cut him off.

"There are things you don't know about me. Things I have no intention of telling you. Reasons why I won't have a casual affair—"

A loud voice from outside the cave interrupted her. "Hey, you two in there. Throw out your weapons and come out with your hands up."

Owen shoved Bay flat and used his body as a shield to cover hers. He met her startled gaze and said, "I guess we found the bad guys."

Chapter 9

BAY WAS TERRIFIED. SHE'D KNOWN THE HIjackers were dangerous, but frankly, she'd been more worried about dying of thirst. It seemed she was going to be spared that fate—and get shot instead.

"You've got ten seconds to throw out your guns before I start shooting."

Bay realized the hijacker's bullets wouldn't have to hit them. They could easily ricochet off the rock walls of the cave and kill them.

"Stay down!" Owen ordered brusquely.

"No problem." Her legs felt like they were made of Jell-O.

She watched as Owen crawled to the saddlebags at the back of the cave and pulled out the SIG P226 pistol the Texas Rangers had issued to him. Staying low, he made his way to the front of the cave, then stood with his back to the wall and said, "I'm throwing out my weapon."

When the SIG hit the ground, the hijacker said, "Don't tell me that's all you've got. I know better."

"I had a rifle in a scabbard on another horse—"

"I've got that," the hijacker said.

Which answered for certain the question of what had happened to her horse, Bay thought.

"I know you've got another handgun," the hijacker said. "You cops always carry two."

Owen swore under his breath, then retrieved his Colt .45 automatic from its holster. "Here it comes."

Bay lifted her head enough to see he'd thrown it far beyond the hijacker. When the man's head turned to see where it landed, Owen launched himself from the ten-foot-high cave opening like a panther.

Bay scrambled to the cave entrance in time to see Owen come crashing down on top of the hijacker. His weight forced the man's face into the ground, and the hijacker's gun went flying. The hijacker twisted and slugged at Owen, who reeled backward and then took a jab of his own.

The two men were evenly matched, and both were desperately trying to reach the hijacker's machine gun. Bay realized she could help, if only she could get to the ground.

She sat at the edge of the cave with her feet dangling, trying to decide if she could drop ten feet without breaking an ankle. Probably not. She quickly turned onto her hands and knees and slid over the ledge so her body hung down, and she only had half the distance to fall. She reminded herself to *roll,* and let go.

She hit the ground harder than she'd expected, but bent her knees as she fell and rolled right onto her feet. The hijacker had his fingers on his weapon when Bay snatched it out of his reach and pointed it between his eyes.

"Hold it right there," she said.

Owen hit the distracted hijacker on the chin and knocked him out. Then he stood and took the nine-millimeter Uzi from her trembling hands.

"Thanks, Red," he said, as he smoothed her auburn hair away from her face and pulled her into a one-armed embrace. "You did good."

"So did you." She peered around his shoulder at the hijacker and exclaimed, "That's one of the Dobermans!"

"What?"

"He's one of the FBI agents who met us at the airport in Alpine with Paul Ridgeway. He reminded me of a Doberman pinscher," she explained.

"Yes, he is," Owen said, turning with her to stare at the unconscious man. "And yes, he does."

"What's he doing here?" Bay asked. "I mean, is he one of the hijackers? I think he must be. He knew what happened to my horse. How is that possible?"

"Whoa," Owen said. "Slow down. First things first." He handed the Uzi back to her and said, "Be careful. When you pull the trigger, this shoots lots and lots of real bullets."

He crossed to the downed man, pulled the army web belt from his camouflage pants, turned him over on his stomach, and lashed his hands behind him.

Bay looked around, but there was no one to be seen in any direction. "Where do you suppose he came from?"

"He didn't walk far today. His combat boots still have a spit shine."

Bay looked down at the boots, the bottoms of which matched the footprints they'd been following. "How did he get here? There aren't any roads nearby where he could have driven in, are there?"

"Helicopter," Owen said.

"Really? Why didn't we hear it?"

Owen shrugged. "Maybe it was one of those black helicopters, the quiet ones, or maybe the sound got baffled by the terrain. There's plenty of room in this valley to land a bird. It's the only thing that makes sense."

"Then my brother must be somewhere nearby."

"Stands to reason."

If he's still alive. And he won't be for long, if he's one of the hijackers. Bay heard the words, even if Owen didn't speak them.

The agent was rousing, and Owen jerked him onto his feet. "Where's your camp?" he demanded.

The Doberman just growled.

Owen crossed to Bay and held out his hand for the Uzi. He took it and turned back to the agent. "I don't need you. I can follow your tracks back to wherever you came from. It's up to you whether you live or die."

"You're not going to shoot me," the Doberman snarled.

Owen frowned. "No, you're right. That would make too much noise. Bay, give me your knife."

Bay already had the jackknife out of her boot before she realized what Owen wanted it for. She hesitated, but his hand remained outstretched, so she opened the knife and laid it on his palm.

She cried out in alarm when Owen pressed the edge of the razor-sharp blade against the agent's throat. A stream of blood quickly stained the man's army-green T-shirt. As a vet, Bay had made enough incisions that the sight of blood shouldn't have bothered her. But she felt nauseated at the thought of watching a man get his throat cut.

"Your choice," Owen said, his gray eyes hard as flint. "I'd as soon kill you as not."

"I'll show you where it is," the agent croaked.

Owen wiped the bloodied knife on the agent's sleeve, folded it against his own thigh, and handed it back to Bay.

She was panting with fear and forced herself to take several deep breaths to keep from hyperventilating. She'd been shocked by Owen's unexpected savagery, appalled by his ruthless infliction of pain. Gone was the tender, passionate lover. In his place was a man who could kill, a dangerous predator.

And her brother might very well become his prey.

Suddenly, Bay wasn't nearly so anxious to get to the hijackers' camp. She'd come along on this journey in the first place because she'd feared Owen might make himself judge and jury and take revenge for his friend's death without giving her brother a chance to defend himself. She'd naïvely believed that her mere presence would be sufficient to curb his violence. Obviously, that wasn't the case.

She realized the agent was still bleeding. "Do you have another handkerchief with you?" she asked Owen in a quavery voice.

He pulled one from his jeans pocket and handed it to her.

With hands that shook, she tied it around the wound in the agent's neck. "You might want to get a tetanus shot, if you haven't had one lately," she told the wounded man.

"That's enough tender loving care, Red," Owen said.

He stepped between her and the FBI agent and reached into the man's back pocket. "James Brophy," he read aloud, as he held open a folder containing a badge and an ID. "Who are you working for, James?"

"The FBI," the agent replied with a smirk.

"And who else?" Owen demanded as he snapped the agent's FBI identification shut.

The agent's lips flattened into a thin, recalcitrant line.

"Where's your partner?" Owen asked.

He spat at Owen's feet.

"He's not going to tell us anything," Owen said in disgust.

"What have you done with my brother?" Bay asked anyway. "Where is he?"

James Brophy remained mute.

"We'd better get moving," Owen said. "We want to find that camp before somebody misses their dog and comes looking for him."

It only took a matter of minutes to collect all the guns, repack the saddlebags, and tighten the cinch on the saddle. Owen gave his horse a drink, took a sip of water for himself, and offered one to Bay.

His frugal use of their water supply told Bay that Owen didn't think they were out of the woods—or rather, the desert—yet. She hadn't really thought about what they would do when they found the hijackers.

"Shouldn't we contact the FBI now, and let them go find the bad guys?" she asked.

"The satellite link only works in the morning," Owen said. "We might as well find the exact location of their camp. That way I can send map coordinates and tell the cavalry where to land their helicopters."

Bay realized they were going to have to wait for the cavalry—FBI, ATF, National Guard, Texas Rangers, Park Rangers, she'd welcome any or all of them—to show up. Even if they flew in like bats-out-of-hell, there was going to be a window of time when she and Owen would have to survive on their wits.

Of course, the Uzi would be a big help.

Owen used the agent's own bandanna, which had been tied around his head, to gag him. "I'll be watching the trail, so don't get any bright ideas about leading us in the wrong direction. Get moving."

Bay watched the ground ahead of them as the agent left the marked Strawhouse Trail and edged past a ten-foot-high lip of stone and made his way through a seemingly impenetrable wall of limestone.

"There's an opening in the rock," Bay marveled.

"Looks that way," Owen said.

The crack in the limestone was maybe five feet wide, tall enough for a man, and about twenty feet long. The bright sunlight that lit the entrance to the passageway was just dimming when it was replaced by bright sunlight marking the exit.

Bay noticed Owen had a hand on the agent's shoulder and a gun pointed at his back, to keep him from bolting as they reached the end of the tunnel. She touched Owen's arm to get his attention. When he glanced back at her, Brophy tried to make a run for it.

Owen instantly swung his Colt .45 in an arc that caught the hijacker on the temple and leveled him.

"You didn't have to hit him!"

"Quiet," he warned. "We must be close."

Bay dropped on one knee beside Brophy and checked his pulse. "He's still alive."

The agent groaned as Bay probed at the knot growing where the barrel of Owen's Colt had struck him. "He's going to have a doozy of a headache."

Owen moved the groggy man close to the limestone wall and covered him with limbs from a creosote bush growing near the tunnel exit, then took the gag from his mouth and used the kerchief to tie his ankles together. He handed Bay his SIG and said, "Do you know how to use this?"

"I'm not shooting anyone."

He made a disgusted sound in his throat. "Don't be a fool. If it comes to a choice between you and—"

"I don't think I can do it," she said. "I don't think I could ever kill a human being."

She flushed as he searched her face. She wondered what he hoped to find. She'd hunted game with her father and brothers. She'd used a rifle to destroy animals that were too ill to be saved. But she was in territory she'd never traveled now, a dark place where she would never willingly have chosen to go.

He held out the gun and said, "Take it."

"I won't—"

"Take the damned gun, Red. You can choose later whether you're willing to kill someone or die yourself."

Bay took the pistol and stuck it gingerly in the front of her jeans. She could feel the cold metal through her cotton underwear.

"Now, you wait here—"

"No! I'm going with you."

He shook his head. "It's too dangerous, Red. Wait here. I'm just going to take a look at their camp and—"

"I don't trust you," she blurted.

He flinched as though she'd struck him. "This is my job, Red. It's what I do, and I'm good at it. Nobody's going to get killed that doesn't deserve it."

Her chin lifted. "There's no telling who you might think deserves to get shot. I'm going with you."

"Damn it, Red. No."

"You can't stop me. So you might as well tell me what I can do to help."

"Stay the hell out of my way!" His eyes were as dark as she'd ever seen them. "I want you behind me at all times," he said brusquely. "Do what I say when I say it. No argument. Understood?"

She nodded, because her heart was in her throat, and she couldn't speak.

Owen hobbled his horse, but he didn't loosen the cinch. "We might need to get out of here in a hurry," he explained.

He stopped at the end of the tunnel and searched the terrain in front of them. The hijackers' camp was nowhere to be seen. "It's got to be there. Maybe beyond that wall," he said, pointing to a curve in the limestone. "Stay close, and be ready to hit the ground."

There was nothing beyond the limestone wall but a large, open valley. Swiftly and quietly, Owen followed what seemed to Bay a nonexistent trail, as though it were written in neon arrows. They reached another limestone crevice, narrower than the first and barely tall enough for a man to stand upright.

"I don't like this," he said. "It's a natural place to set booby traps or an ambush."

Bay kept her hands balled up, so Owen wouldn't see how much they were shaking. "Why don't we wait for the cavalry to arrive?"

"That agent's going to be missed long before tomorrow morning."

"So what? It doesn't follow that they have to find us," Bay argued. "Couldn't we hide somewhere?"

She watched Owen consider her suggestion and saw the moment he rejected it.

"I'd rather check things out first. If he did come in on a helicopter, it's possible there's only one other man, or maybe two, at the camp. If that's the case, I might be able to manage the situation myself."

"What if there's a dozen men or two dozen?" Bay asked.

He shot her a crooked grin. "Then we find a shady spot and hide out till morning."

Bay realized that while she was shaking in her boots, Owen was enjoying himself. The prospect of danger didn't seem to frighten him, as it did her. He relished it, maybe even invited it. She only hoped his confidence didn't override his caution.

"What kind of booby trap should I be looking for?" Bay asked. "Not a VX mine, right? One of those mines has a range of—what?—eight miles? They'd be in danger of poisoning themselves, too."

"Not in an enclosed space like this," Owen said, his hands brushing the limestone walls on either side of him. "All they'd need to do is block off either end of this narrow passage, which they could do with a small explosive charge that's triggered the same time as the mine."

"I wish you hadn't told me that," Bay said. "We don't have any protective gear with us."

"I have the atropine-oxime autoinjectors right here," Owen said as he patted his shirt pocket.

"You do? Thank goodness for small favors. Although, I don't know how much good it'll do us to survive the nerve gas, if this passage is sealed at both ends like a tomb."

Owen laughed. "I'll bet you love to tell scary stories by the campfire at night."

"I like to know my options. I like to plan ahead."

"You always seem to plan for the worst possible outcome," he pointed out.

"In my house, there was always more bad news than good."

It was a reminder of the differences between them that had brought them to this place. She had lived hand-to-mouth, sometimes not certain where the next meal was coming from. He had led a privileged life, where every meal was served on china plates and eaten with silver.

"What's that?" Bay asked, cocking her head.

Owen stopped and listened. "Chopper."

"They're getting away!" Bay said, as she ran past him, anxious to discover whether her brother was being flown away in the helicopter.

"Stop! Don't move!"

Bay stopped, but not before she'd tripped a fragile wire that was stretched across the passage. "Oh, God." She turned back to Owen and saw from his grim expression that she'd done something awful. "I'm sorry."

"Don't move," he repeated.

She waited for an explosion, but it didn't come. "Why didn't something explode?"

"You might only have tripped a sensor somewhere that would let them know we're here. Or the charge might be delayed."

"Delayed? Then shouldn't we be trying to get out of here?"

"I want to look around your feet before you make another move," he said. "Stand still."

Bay had no idea what Owen was hunting for and didn't like the "Aaah" sound he made. "What did you find?"

"A timer."

Bay felt her heart begin to gallop. "How much time is on it?"

"Twenty-nine seconds."

OWEN WISHED HE KNEW WHAT SUBSTANCE WAS ABOUT TO explode. Was it plain old TNT? A claymore? Or a VX nerve gas mine? He had less than thirty seconds to decide whether to give each of them a shot of the atropine-oxime antidote. He didn't want to waste it now, if he was going to need it later.

It made more sense to run.

He grabbed Bay's hand, and they dashed pell-mell for the sunlight they could see ahead of them. Owen was doing his best to keep an eye on the ground in front of them, but he missed seeing the second tripwire until he was right on top of it.

"Jump!" he ordered, as he yanked Bay's arm to lift her over it.

The toe of her boot snagged the wire, and the limestone walls behind them exploded. The force of the blast threw them free of the cave, as crumbling limestone sealed the opening.

Owen wrapped his arms around Bay while they were still in the air and used his body to protect hers as they hit the ground. He landed in lechuguilla, and the thorny spines pierced his back like knives.

But they were both alive.

Owen hugged Bay tight. "Are you all right?"

"I think so. I . . . Owen, is it possible VX nerve gas exploded in there?"

He lifted her chin and searched her eyes. "What's wrong?"

"I feel . . . odd. There's something . . . I feel sick and . . ."

Owen tensed. "Red? Are you all right?" In a matter of seconds, her eyes had become red-rimmed. Her nose had started to run. She was wheezing.

"Jesus Christ." It was definitely a prayer. Owen fumbled in his shirt pocket for the two atropine-oxime autoinjectors.

And found only one.

He tried to catch his breath and realized his chest felt constricted. His symptoms seemed to be a few moments behind hers. Already, she was lying prone, and her muscles had begun to spasm. The VX nerve gas was at work.

She was dying.

Owen looked at the injector in his hand and realized he had to save her. Even if it meant he was going to die.

He tore her shirt open, placed the autoinjector next to her heart, and pulled the trigger. It wasn't nearly as dramatic as the foot-long needle Nicolas Cage had used in *The Rock* to keep his body from turning to mush.

But it worked. Bay immediately started breathing more easily.

Owen staggered upright and began a 360-degree search for the other injector. If he could find it, he might yet save himself. He didn't understand why he didn't have more symptoms, why he hadn't succumbed as quickly as she had. Maybe she'd been exposed to more of the gas. And she was a lot smaller than he was.

But all it took was a drop.

Owen fell to his hands and knees, then collapsed facedown. And realized he couldn't get up again.

THE ANTIDOTE WORKED SO QUICKLY THAT BAY'S SYMPTOMS were gone within a minute of getting the injection. She remembered immediately what had happened. It felt like every inch of her body had been pummeled in a boxing ring. It even hurt to breathe. But she had survived.

She rolled over and lifted her head to search for Owen. She saw him lying facedown not far away and crawled over to him, which seemed infinitely wiser than trying to get onto her feet. She breathed a sigh of relief when she saw the pulse beating at his throat.

She nudged his shoulder and said, "Owen, are you okay?"

Then she realized he was wheezing.

"Owen," she cried. "What's wrong? Why isn't the antidote working on you?"

"Lost . . . injector . . . find . . ."

"Hang on. I'll find it!"

She shoved herself onto her feet and stumbled toward the area where they'd first fallen coming out of the cave. The sun was nearly down, and the shadows created by the desert plant life made it hard to see anything on the rocky ground. She moved in outward circles, praying that she'd find the injector before it was too late.

She nearly fell as something rolled under her boot. She saw the injector, grabbed it, and ran as best she could back to Owen. At the last second, she realized she needed him on his back in order to put the shot in his heart. She fell to her knees and used all the shoulder muscle she had to heave him over.

He was drooling, and his body was twitching. How long had it been since the explosion? One minute? Two? Three? Was she too late?

"Owen, I'm here. I found the injector. Hold on."

She yanked open his shirt, put the injector against his heart and pulled the trigger. She held her breath waiting to see if it would work, ticking off the seconds.

Ten. Twenty. Thirty.

The twitching stopped.

Forty. Fifty. Sixty.

Owen opened his eyes.

Bay smiled at him. "Those are the loveliest red-rimmed eyes I've ever seen."

Owen managed a wobbly grin. "Ditto."

"I can hardly believe we survived a dose of VX nerve gas," she said.

"Thanks to you."

"And you." She laid her hand on his heart and said, "I owe you my life. If I hadn't been able to find that other injector—"

"You did. So we're even." He pushed himself into a sitting position and said, "Keep your hands off your clothes. There may be VX residue on them. If we get it on our skin now, it's lights out, that's all she wrote, say good-bye, Shirley."

"How long does the antidote work before you can get reinfected by nerve gas on your clothing?" Bay asked.

"I didn't think to ask," Owen replied.

"Then wouldn't it make sense to take off our clothes now?"

"It would if we had anything to replace them with," Owen said. "But I don't see how we're going to walk out of here barefoot."

"We won't walk out of here at all if we get exposed to VX gas particles on our clothing after that antidote wears off," Bay pointed out.

Owen grimaced. "Strip down to your underwear. Leave on your socks and put your boots back on after you get your jeans off."

When Bay was done she looked down at herself,

dressed in a plain white bra, torn bikini underwear, and cowboy boots. "I feel like I'm dressed for the midnight show at the Crazy Horse Saloon," she muttered.

Her mouth went dry when she looked at Owen, who was left wearing cowboy boots and black Calvin Kleins. The knit cotton underwear hugged him lovingly from waist to thighs. He was a female's fantasy come to life.

They stared at each other, enjoying what they saw. And realizing just how close they'd come to losing their lives.

"You look good, Red," he said.

"Good and thirsty," she said, as she realized how dry her mouth was.

"I guess no one heard that explosion, since we're still here all alone," Owen said, as he looked around the clearing in which they found themselves. "I lost the Uzi when we got blown out of that cave. Do you still have my SIG?"

She picked it up off the pile of clothing she'd turned inside out and handed it to him. "It was mostly protected by my clothes. Do you think it's safe to carry?"

"Let's put it this way. I'll feel a lot safer with it than without it."

"I see your point," Bay said.

"We're going to need food and water," Owen said. "We better see if we can find the hijackers' camp. It's got to be somewhere close."

"I don't usually go calling dressed like this," Bay said.

Owen grinned. "Me, neither. We can worry about that when we actually find the camp."

Bay pointed to a spot beyond Owen's shoulder. "I think we've found it."

Owen turned to look at a distant light that had appeared in the growing darkness. "I think you may be right, Red." He leaned a hand on her shoulder to brace himself as he rose to his feet. He tottered like a baby for a step or two, then seemed to find his balance.

"Your turn," he said, extending a hand to her.

When she was on her feet, it seemed like the most natural thing in the world to step into his supporting arms, which encircled her as she clung to him.

She pressed her cheek against his heart and said, "This is ridiculous. We can hardly stand up. How are we going to make it to that light? And why do I have the feeling that if we do get there, we'll be jumping out of the frying pan and into the fire?"

"We don't have much choice. We need water. That camp is our only hope of getting it."

They staggered toward the light together, sometimes one and sometimes the other bearing the weight of both.

"How long does it take for the effects of this VX stuff to wear off?" Owen asked.

"I think maybe two weeks."

"I was hoping maybe two hours."

Bay managed a smile. "That would be lovely, but it's not very likely."

"I don't think either of us could have gotten much of a dose of gas," he said. "I didn't start getting symptoms until you were already down. And I don't think my symptoms were nearly as bad as yours."

"I feel as weak as a baby, and I have a headache."

"We haven't had much water over the past few hours, and it's been damned hot. Could be just dehydration."

But dehydration could kill them, too. Bay hoped the light in the distance really was the hijackers' camp, and that they would be able to remain undiscovered and still get hold of some water.

It took them half an hour to walk a distance they might have covered in five minutes if they'd been well. Owen insisted that they stop beyond the glow of the light, which turned out to be a single Coleman lantern set on a folding metal table outside a four-man tent. The entire area was covered with camouflage netting, but beneath that was a layer of something thin and silvery, like tinfoil.

"That's why heat-imaging radar never picked them up," Owen muttered. "They've got some kind of reflective ceiling over the camp, and the camouflage netting above it keeps them from showing up on satellite photographs. Whoever stole those mines knows what he's doing."

"Well, Brophy's an FBI agent. I imagine the FBI knows all about that sort of thing," Bay said.

"Yeah. But if these guys are so good at hiding themselves, how did Hank find them?"

"We found them," Bay pointed out.

Owen shook his head. "They found us. If that FBI agent hadn't shown up when he did, we'd have stayed on the trail and would probably be halfway back to the Rio Grande Village by now. Instead, we took that little detour, and God knows where we are now. No, there's something here I'm missing. I wish I could think, but my head's pounding."

Bay didn't suggest the obvious. That the reason Hank had been shot was because he'd recognized one of the hijackers. Maybe one of the FBI agents. Or perhaps Owen's brother Clay.

They lay prone in the dark, staring at the camp, but Bay saw no signs of life.

"Where are they?" she whispered.

He put a fingertip to her lips, mouthed the word "Quiet," then pointed toward the tent.

Bay's eyes went wide as her brother stepped out of the tent. With Clay Blackthorne right behind him.

Chapter 10

BILLY COBURN KNEW MORE ABOUT THE MISSing VX mines than he'd told the Texas Ranger who'd come asking questions. But he hadn't been about to accuse his company commander, Major Clay Blackthorne, of wrongdoing, to his brother's face. Especially when Clay's brother was a Texas Ranger. Billy knew how the system worked. Clay was a rich man's son. Billy was a nobody, down on his luck. Somehow, they'd turn everything around, so he ended up in jail.

He couldn't help wondering what was going to happen when that Ranger managed to track down the thieves and discovered his brother was one of them. The incident Billy had witnessed sure had looked damned suspicious.

During maneuvers two weeks ago, he and Luke Creed had been sent by the first sergeant to pick up another crate of claymore mines. They'd come around a corner and caught Clay Blackthorne talking to a short guy in civilian clothes who looked like a wrestler—all neck, with a face that seemed flattened by one too many landings on the mat. He and Luke had only heard the end of Major Blackthorne's sentence—"intercept them on the way to Arkansas"—before the major saw them and clammed up.

It hadn't meant much at the time, but when the VX mines had been hijacked two days later, Billy had thought back to what he'd seen and heard.

Major Blackthorne hadn't been merely surprised at being discovered, he'd been distressed. The fact the other man was a civilian, and had no business near the camp, seemed significant. The words themselves were damning.

Luke had apparently nosed around and managed to find out enough to get himself in deep shit. Billy had minded his own business, but it looked like he was going to be dragged willy-nilly into the line of fire anyway.

If Luke Creed had disappeared, there was every chance he'd been caught snooping by the bad guys. It wasn't going to take long for Clay Blackthorne to make the connection between Luke and Billy. And if the hijackers had shot a Texas Ranger, it wasn't going to bother them even a little bit to put a bullet into someone with as few friends and as little influence as Bad Billy Coburn.

Which was another good reason why he should keep Summer Blackthorne at a distance. Not that Billy thought her own brother would hurt her, but if the bad guys did come after him, she might get caught in the crossfire. Billy planned to tell her today that they shouldn't see each other for a while—at least until the situation with the VX mines was resolved.

His mother's hysterics had nothing to do with his decision. She'd always been uncomfortable around Summer. Billy figured she just didn't want her only son getting hurt by some spoiled little rich girl, who was only slumming, and would break his heart if he ever fell in love with her.

If his mother only knew. It was way too late to protect him from that kind of pain. He'd been in love with Summer Blackthorne from the first moment he'd laid eyes on her, when she was sixteen and he was twenty. He'd been working for her father, mucking stalls in the barn, when she'd shown up to saddle her horse for a ride.

Summer Blackthorne had been the most beautiful girl Billy had ever seen. She was also far above the touch of a humble cowboy. As the boss's daughter, she'd expected his homage. And been intrigued when she didn't get it.

He'd known from the start that he didn't have a chance with her, which was why he'd ignored her. Now that he knew her better, Billy realized that he'd done the one thing that was sure to get her attention.

His aloofness had kept her from ever realizing how he really felt about her. And her repeated attempts to break through his indifference had finally resulted in the friendship that had grown between them over the years. She'd confessed that she liked being with him because she could relax and be herself.

She'd told him a great many things he knew she never would have told a man she loved. Because they revealed how vulnerable she was. How very alone she felt in a houseful of servants. How her brothers stifled her, because they wanted to keep her safe. How little she understood her mother, who kept her at far more than arm's distance. How much she loved her father, who couldn't imagine the dreams she had that reached far beyond becoming a wife and mother.

Billy wished he hadn't ruined everything by kissing her. Or, he thought wryly and more truthfully, by letting her kiss him. It wasn't going to be easy to convince Summer to forego her visits for a while. Somehow he had to do it.

He'd decided to meet her away from the house, at a shady spot near a stock pond on his property, where they wouldn't be seen by his mother. He'd ridden there on horseback, taking advantage of the opportunity to repair some downed barbed wire fence along the way. Summer drove to meet him in her brand-new, cherry-red Silverado.

She was already waiting for him when he arrived, wearing a tailored Western shirt, designer jeans that hugged every curve, and hand-tooled Western boots with her family's Circle B brand on them, made especially for her by a bootmaker in Dallas. The clothes on her back would have fed his family for half a year. She had no concept of what it meant to be poor, and he could never explain it to her.

Not that he'd ever tried. He'd known all along that he would only have her in his life for a little while. Until she fell in love—or her father found a man for her to marry. He'd planned to take off for parts unknown to seek his fortune long before he had to watch her walk down the aisle with some other man.

She was sitting on the hood of her Silverado, leaning back with her palms flat on the shiny red finish, knees crossed, booted toe bouncing, waiting for him to come to her.

"Hey," she said with a smile that made his chest ache. "I thought you'd never get here."

"Had to fix some fence," he explained.

"I would've been glad to help."

"It's done now." He dismounted and tied his horse to

one of the cottonwoods that shaded the pond, then crossed to her. She reached out her arms, and without even thinking, he grabbed her by the waist to help her down.

He hadn't intended to slide her along his body. It just happened. Every nerve ending came alive when the softness of her hips and breasts collided with the hardness of his own.

"We're not going to do this," he said in a harsh voice.

"Billy," she whispered. "Please."

She looked up at him. And he looked down at her. And groaned in submission.

His head swooped down, and he plundered her mouth. He told himself it didn't matter, because this wasn't going anywhere. One kiss. He'd take one last, desperate, soul-filling kiss. Then he'd tell her she had to stay away from him.

For her sake. Because it was dangerous to hang around him, when he was a man without a future.

And for his sake. Because she was only going to rip his heart out and leave him to suffer without one the rest of his life.

One touch. That was all he wanted. He made a grating sound of satisfaction at the feel of her breast filling his hand, the weight and softness of it, the nipple budding beneath his fingertips. He caught her moan of surprise and delight in his ravaging mouth.

His body ached with wanting her. Needing her. He already felt the fear of losing her.

He yanked open her shirt, popping the buttons, which pinged against the front fender. He dragged the cloth halfway down her arms, unhooked the front clasp of her bra and shoved it aside—and admired the feast before him.

"You're so beautiful," he breathed. "So perfect."

He saw the hot flush rising on her chest, skating its way up her throat, and sought her eyes with his own. He stroked her hot cheeks tenderly with his knuckles, then brushed her long blond curls behind her shoulders, leaving her breasts bare.

"Nobody's ever seen me like this," she admitted shyly. "I'm glad you're the first, Billy."

He hadn't imagined she was untouched. She'd attended a dozen different universities—and gotten thrown out of every one. She'd told him how she ran with a wild, wealthy crowd. How she'd dated so many rich, shallow boys. He hadn't asked for details. He hadn't wanted to know.

"I'm glad, too," he said, his throat suddenly thick with emotion. It was a wonderful gift. One he'd treasure all his life. He was wearing an undershirt with the arms torn out and cut to leave his midriff bare, and he yanked it off over his head, then pulled her close, flesh to flesh. "God, Summer," he whispered in her ear. "I can't believe . . ."

"I know . . ." she whispered back. "I never thought . . ."

He felt her mouth against his throat, felt her hot breath beneath his ear. Felt himself getting harder, when he'd thought he was as hard as he could get.

He found her mouth and kissed her reverently. That didn't last any longer than it took for her tongue to find its way into his mouth. He sucked hard on it and heard her guttural groan.

He wanted her like he'd never wanted a woman in his life. His heart was beating so hard his chest hurt. His body throbbed. His brain had shut down, because all the blood had left his head and journeyed to other regions. He grabbed her buttocks in both hands and spread his legs wide and pulled her into the cradle of his thighs, rubbing against her, with only a scrap of cotton and a layer of denim between them.

"Oh," she moaned. "Yes."

"Oh," he moaned. "No."

He clutched her tight against him, holding her there so she couldn't move, even though he could feel her wriggling against him. "We have to stop, Summer."

"Why? It feels so good, Billy. It feels so right."

Her eyes were heavy-lidded, her pupils dilated, her lips swollen and pouty from his kisses. He tasted her lips and told himself it was for the last time. "This isn't a good idea."

"Why not?"

She rubbed her breasts against the swirls of dark hair on his chest, and he felt her nipples tighten into buds. His hands left her rear end and circled her back, holding her tightly in his embrace to stop the exquisite torture. Unrestrained, her hips thrust against him again.

He laughed. "Stop it, Summer. You're killing me."

She rubbed herself against him and said, "You don't feel dead."

But he was dying to have her, when he knew it wasn't something a friend would do. "You should be saving yourself for that special man in your life," he said, putting her away from him.

She grabbed the sides of her shirt to cover her breasts, then crossed her arms for good measure. "I hate it when other people think they know what's best for me. I have a mind and a will of my own, Billy. If I want to do this with you, I will."

He grabbed her by the arms and looked deep into her eyes. "Are you willing to marry me, Summer? To live in my house and work this ranch with me?"

Startled, she gaped at him. "Are you proposing?"

"I'm asking if you really want to be with me, Summer. Enough to give up your life at Bitter Creek and become a part of mine."

"I don't get my trust fund until I'm twenty-five."

He shook her. "What does that have to do with anything? Do you want to marry me or not?"

"How do I know? Until a few days ago, I never thought of you as anything but my friend."

"A moment ago you were ready to give me your virginity."

She flushed. "Why are you doing this, Billy? I wanted to give you . . . this gift."

"And then what?" He didn't want that kind of memory. The kind a man never got over. The kind that would keep him from loving any other woman. He let go of her arms and took a step back. "Make up your mind. Do we do this? Or go back to being just friends."

"Can we still be 'just friends'?" she asked, her brow furrowed. She tried buttoning her shirt, realized half the buttons were missing and gave up. "How am I supposed to forget your kisses? What it feels like to have you touch me?"

"We remember those things. We just don't repeat them," he said.

"For how long?"

"This isn't a game, Summer. I'm not a toy you can

play with when the mood strikes and put back in the box."

He didn't see the slap coming. But he knew he deserved it. Maybe it was better if she left angry. So long as she left. He wasn't sure how long he could resist the urge to drag her back into his arms.

She made a whimpering sound in her throat and met his gaze with golden eyes welling with tears. "I'm sorry. I've never hit anyone in my life. I feel awful."

She needed a friend to hold her. She needed a friend to commiserate with her. She needed a friend to love her.

Billy knew she was depending on him to be that friend. He pulled her into his arms and held her, commanding his unruly body to forget any ideas it had about doing anything more than comforting the woman in his arms.

"I don't want to lose your friendship," he said.

"I don't want to lose yours," Summer replied, her arms wrapped tightly around his waist.

Her shirt had come open, and her breasts were warm against his chest. He reached between them and pulled her shirt closed. Then he hugged her again, let her go, and stepped back. "We can make this work," he said.

"Yeah. Right." She lifted her shirttail to dab at the tears in her eyes. "I like you so much, Billy."

"I know," he said with a lopsided grin. "I like you, too." That was the problem.

She stuck out her hand, and he saw it was trembling. "Friends?"

He took her hand, shook it once, and let it go. "Friends."

BLACKJACK HAD BEEN STUNNED WHEN HE ARRIVED HOME after spending Sunday afternoon with Lauren Creed, to discover his wife sitting behind his desk with a drink in her hand.

"Surprised?" she asked, as she swiveled the chair to face him.

"How the hell did you get out?" he demanded.

"The wheels of justice are slow, but they do eventually turn."

"I was supposed to be notified when you were being released."

She pointed to the blinking red light on his answering machine. "I believe they did call. You weren't in."

"How did you manage to get them to let you go?"

"I finally found a doctor and a lawyer and a judge you didn't control," she said with irritating calm. "And, after all, I'm not really crazy. It was a simple matter to convince the doctor that I was as sane as he was. Even simpler for the lawyer to seek a court order from the judge for my release. And here I am, a free woman."

"You had a man murdered."

"So you say. But really, Jackson, there just isn't any *proof.* Why, you had as much reason to want Jesse Creed dead as I did. More, if you consider your behavior with the lovely widow while I've been locked away in that hellhole."

Blackjack gritted his teeth. "Keep Ren out of this."

"I wish I could," Eve said. "I'm afraid she's in it up to her lovely eyeballs. You've been a very naughty boy, Jackson."

"I told you eighteen months ago that I wanted out."

"Since we're still married, your behavior is called adultery. I would hate for this to get messy, but—"

His hands tightened on the back of the horn-and-rawhide chair in front of the desk until they were white at the knuckles. "Don't threaten me, Eve."

"Stay away from her, Jackson. Or you won't like what I'll do."

"Don't threaten her. Or me. Or you won't like what *I'll* do," he said furiously.

"Actually, I was thinking it might hurt you more if I take Bitter Creek away from you," Eve said. "I can do it. Especially since you've provided such lovely ammunition for me to use in court. I have pictures of the two of you together."

Blackjack felt his heart beating hard in his chest. "You hired someone to follow me?" he said through tight jaws, incensed at the thought of someone intruding on his and Ren's privacy.

"How else was I going to keep track of you, when I was locked away behind bars?"

"Don't push me, Eve."

"Then stay away from that woman."

He choked back a strangled oath.

"You don't look well, Jackson. Have you been taking your heart medication while I've been gone?"

"I was fine till you walked in the door."

"Don't let me keep you, if you've got business," she said.

"You're sitting at my desk," he pointed out.

She stood. "It's all yours. I've accomplished all the business I had to do here today."

It took him a full fifteen minutes to get his pulse back to normal after she'd left the room.

They avoided each other as much as possible in the days that followed. But Eve's threat against Ren was difficult to ignore. Blackjack felt like he had a boot on his neck holding his face in the mud, and he was going to strangle if he couldn't find a way to escape.

He missed Ren. When he was with her, she filled a place inside him that had been empty for far too long. But he had no one but himself to blame for the situation he was in.

All those years ago, when he'd found out Ren was pregnant so soon after her marriage to Jesse Creed, he'd wondered if the child might be his. He'd confronted her, but she'd told him that she'd already been pregnant when they met at the pond. He'd begged her to leave Jesse and marry him, but she hadn't trusted him to love another man's child. Especially when he was a Blackthorne, and that other man's child was a Creed.

His father hadn't forced him to marry Eve, just pointed out the advantage of owning the fifty thousand acres of DeWitt grassland she would bring to the marriage. Since he'd believed Ren was lost to him forever, he hadn't seen a reason in the world not to have the land.

And he'd gotten himself a beautiful, educated, talented wife in the bargain, who'd borne him three fine sons, Trace and Owen and Clay, and a beloved daughter, Summer. Eve was the perfect hostess. A critically acclaimed artist. A good businesswoman.

And she'd never refused him in bed. Sex was the one thing they never fought about. Eve had been a passionate and creative and desirable sexual partner. His body had always been satiated. But his soul had never been satisfied.

It wasn't her fault he was in love with another woman.

He might have lived the rest of his life in the kind of marriage a lot of people had—a convenient economic alliance of partners, who were also parents, and had a good time in the sack—if he hadn't nearly died two years ago of a heart attack.

Having his mortality shoved in his face had made him think about what he wanted to do with the rest of his life. He'd decided while he was still in the hospital that he didn't want to spend whatever years he had left in an alliance with a wife he'd never loved. He'd been thinking of divorce long before he'd learned his wife had been having an affair with his *segundo* Russell Handy. That discovery had merely propelled him into speaking the word "divorce" for the first time.

Blackjack didn't know why Eve was so insistent on staying married to him. He was going to have to find out exactly what price she wanted to set him free—short of giving her the ranch. Thirty-three years of being his wife didn't make up for the hundred and fifty years that Bitter Creek had belonged to Blackthornes. She could have all the money she wanted. So long as she didn't insist he sell the ranch to get it.

He was sitting at his desk, debating whether to call Ren, when the phone rang. He picked it up, hoping she'd called him, but it was Paul Ridgeway.

He didn't have good news.

Blackjack hung up the phone and put a hand to his heart, which was beating erratically. He hadn't thought Paul's news would hit him so hard. He felt breathless. His first thought was to call Ren, because the news concerned her, too. But he realized he owed his wife the courtesy of telling her first.

He knew exactly where to find her.

As she had for so many years of their marriage, Eve had disappeared into her studio at the end of the hall on the second floor to paint. She took pictures of interesting subjects, then corrected the flaws she found in the photographs, transforming the blemished world into perfect beauty on canvas. She was a nationally renowned Western artist, but Blackjack figured she kept herself busy painting so she wouldn't have to face the emptiness of their marriage.

He knocked on the door to her studio and waited, knowing she rarely answered the door when she was working. And she didn't. This couldn't wait, so he opened the door and walked in.

The sun through the skylight was blinding in the white-on-white room, and he waited a moment for his eyes to adjust. He could smell oil paint and turpentine before he actually saw the oily rags and tubes of oil paint that were scattered on the counters that lined the walls. The chaos in the room was at odds with the rest of the house, which the hired help kept as close as possible to the perfection found in his wife's paintings.

He stopped to screw the lid on a can of pungent turpentine before he crossed to her side and said, "I have bad news, Eve."

She didn't miss a brushstroke. She was so totally focused on what she was doing, he wondered if she even knew he was there. Her safari-style smock was bedaubed with vivid colors, and she was holding a palette of greens, which he realized were intended for the mesquite tree she was painting.

When he put a hand on her shoulder, she jerked, then stared at him in irritation. "I'm working, Jackson."

"Stop that for a minute and listen to me," he said. "I

have something important to tell you. It has to do with Owen."

"I'm listening."

"I just got a call from Paul Ridgeway with the FBI in Midland. The same day you got home, Owen went into the Big Bend to track down the man who killed his friend Hank Richardson. He took Bayleigh Creed with him. The FBI decided they wanted the two of them out of there, so they sent Park Rangers to Owen's last known location. All they found was a dead horse."

Eve made a face. "I suppose now you'll run to Three Oaks to comfort the girl's mother."

"I came here because I thought you might need some-one with you when you heard the news," he said through gritted teeth.

"Well, I don't," she said bluntly.

"Then you won't mind if I go to Three Oaks and see Ren," he said, heading for the door.

"Jackson."

He stopped and turned back to her. "What is it, Eve?"

"Do they know for sure whether Owen is dead?"

"They haven't given up hope of finding him. But it doesn't look good."

"Did you call Clay?" she asked.

"No. I'll take care of it."

"I'll do it," she said, dropping her palette and brush on a nearby butcher block table with a clatter. She pulled the safari jacket off, and he was surprised to see she wore a plain, round-necked white T-shirt tucked into unbelted Levi's. He hadn't seen her in jeans since the last time they'd gone riding together. He couldn't remember how many years ago that had been.

She looked surprisingly young. And natural. And

touchable. He found himself staring when he realized she
wasn't wearing a bra. She took a step toward him, and it
dawned on him she was also barefoot.

He'd been celibate for eighteen months, and if they'd
been a happily married couple, they would be holding
each other right now. They might even have sought relief
from their mutual fear for their son through vigorous,
tension-relieving sex.

"It's been a long time for me," Eve said.

"And for me." He hadn't had sex with Ren, but only
because she'd exercised enough restraint for the both of
them.

"I can wait to call Clay."

It was the closest he knew Eve would come to an invi-
tation to bed her.

There was no question he found her physically desirable. And she was his wife, their union sanctioned by
God and the government. Sex had always been good between them. She knew all the ways to touch him, to turn
him on, to make him want her. His body certainly craved
the release hers promised.

But he found himself strangely unable to acquiesce,
because it would have felt like he was cheating . . . on the
woman he loved.

By making the choice to stay faithful to Ren, Blackjack
realized he was turning his back on any hope of a reconcilia-
tion with his wife. He felt a sharp pang of loss, a deep-seated
grief for the final death of the dream of marital happiness that
must have been lurking inside him all these years.

His nose stung, and he swallowed noisily past the sudden lump in his throat. "I'm . . . sorry."

He saw the tears well in her eyes, watched her brush
angrily at them.

"This isn't over," she said. "Not by a long shot!"

"Eve . . . I . . ."

"Out. Get out! Get out!" She was shrieking like a harpy, her hands curling into claws, as she grabbed for something to hurl at him.

Blackjack turned his back on his wife and walked out the door, closing it firmly behind him.

Chapter 11

 BAY'S FIRST INSTINCT WAS TO CRY OUT TO her brother. Owen saved her from that folly by clamping his hand over her open mouth and pulling them both to the ground.

"Whoa there, Red," he whispered. "Let's find out exactly who we're dealing with before we let them know we're out here."

She dragged his hand away and hissed, "Admit it! Your brother's one of the bad guys. Look at Luke's face. He's been tortured!"

"I'll admit it looks bad," Owen said. "But—"

"Don't try to make excuses. The fact you're not standing up waving a big hello to your brother tells me you don't think he's so innocent."

Bay was shivering with cold. They were hidden by the dark and a few creosote bushes, but they couldn't stay where they were indefinitely, considering they didn't have even a layer of clothing to keep them warm.

"Come here," Owen said, wrapping an arm around her waist and sitting her between his legs with her back against his chest. "We can share our body heat."

"If I weren't freezing I wouldn't come within a mile of you," she muttered.

"Then I'll have to be thankful for the cold."

His big body was amazingly warm—and male—and when she shivered again, it wasn't because of the cool night air.

He rubbed his hands up and down her arms. "Hypothermia and dehydration. Lethal combination."

"We're not going to sit here all night, are we?" she asked. "Can't we sneak into their camp and—"

"Might be more tripwires," Owen said.

Bay scoffed. "They're not going to explode any VX mines around here."

"They might have conventional mines set up to protect their perimeter. This looks like a military-type operation."

"Why is your brother doing this?" Bay asked.

"I don't know," Owen said. "I'm going to ask him first chance I get."

Owen was rising, and Bay grabbed his arm to hold him in place. "What are you going to do?"

"Find a way to talk with my brother alone."

"Aren't you afraid—"

"Clay isn't going to hurt me."

"Are you absolutely sure about that?"

Bay heard the slight hesitation before he said, "Yeah, I'm sure."

"What am I supposed to do while you're gone?"

"Stay put," he said. "I don't want you setting off any explosives that'll get us both killed."

"Let me go with you."

"I don't want you getting hurt, Red."

There was something about the sound of his voice that gave her pause. "Don't tell me you care."

He ruffled her hair as though she were five instead of

twenty-five. "All right, I won't. Just stay put." He picked up the SIG from where he'd laid it on the ground and checked to make sure a round was chambered.

"How long will you be gone?"

"As long as it takes," he said.

"How do I know you won't hightail it with your brother and leave me and my brother here to die?"

He gave her a quick, hard kiss. "I guess you'll have to trust me." A moment later he was gone, and she was alone.

Bay drew her knees up to her chest and wrapped her arms around them as much to comfort herself as to stay warm.

Trust me.

Was it possible that in a matter of days she'd forgotten everything she'd learned at her father's knee and was willing to trust one of the black-hearted Blackthornes? How could she not trust Owen, when he'd saved her life at the risk of his own? Of course that might merely have been the act of a lawman doing his duty. Or the natural instinct that compelled a man to save a woman or child. The fact he'd rescued her didn't necessarily mean that he cared for her. Or that she ought to trust him with her heart.

But her pulse was still racing from that quick, hard kiss. And she liked the warm feeling she got inside whenever he used the affectionate nickname he'd given her. She'd never let anyone get close enough to assume that such familiarity would be welcome.

Was it welcome?

Bay wasn't sure she wanted Owen to care for her. She certainly wasn't about to allow herself to care for him. Because then she'd have to tell him the truth about herself. She'd have to dredge up all that pain and lay it open for him, and she really didn't want to do that. In the past, she'd simply enjoyed the sexual relationship most men were willing to engage in without asking for more than the pleasure to be found in it by two consenting adults.

It was the situation that was causing the problem. They'd been thrown together, then forced to rely on each other, when normally, she was perfectly capable of taking care of herself. She liked being in control of her life. She liked making her own decisions without thinking about the consequences to another person. She'd known that she would have to spend her life alone, and she'd prepared herself for it.

Owen was making her rethink her choice. He was making her want more. And she didn't like it one bit.

She could avoid a lot of heartache by nipping this whole relationship thing in the bud. Sex was fine. Sex was great, in fact. More than that was not.

Bay heard a noise in the dark and stayed perfectly still, like a fawn in the forest, or a lion cub on the savannah, knowing that if she couldn't be seen, she would be safe.

Then she remembered night-vision goggles and realized she might not be as invisible as she thought. If that was the case, there was no escape. And to run might cause her to trip one of the mines Owen seemed to think might be laid around the camp.

A voice from the dark said, "It's me."

"Oh, thank goodness," Bay said, launching herself into Owen's arms as he appeared beside her.

"If this is the welcome I get, maybe I should go away more often."

Bay could see his white-toothed grin in the moonlight

and pulled away, embarrassed at how she'd turned to the enemy for comfort. "What are you doing back here so soon? What did you find?"

"The camp is empty."

"It can't be! We just saw your brother and mine—"

"This place seems to be a little valley completely surrounded by limestone cliffs. Clay and Luke must have gone out through another crack in the wall. I couldn't find it in the dark. And I wasn't about to go stumbling around, considering what happened the last time we headed into one of those crevices."

"Where is everybody?" she asked. "Do you think they'll be coming back—" Bay stopped herself in midspeech when she heard the distinctive whine of a helicopter rotor starting up.

"Damn!" Owen said. "I completely forgot about that chopper we heard earlier. It must be outside the cliffs."

"Your brother's leaving! And he's taking my brother with him!"

In her anxiety over Luke's fate, Bay forgot all about the possibility of booby traps and ran toward the camp. Hobbled was more like it, but she still moved faster than Owen. She reached the camp before he caught up to her. "We have to catch them," she said, struggling against his hold.

"Red, it's too late," he said, pointing toward the sky.

As Bay stared upward, she saw a helicopter rising above the cliffs. In the eerie light from the instrument panel, her brother and Owen's brother were visible in the cockpit.

Her arms wobbled above her as she waved at them and shouted hoarsely, "We're here! We're here! Come back!"

"Don't waste your energy," Owen said. "They can't see you or hear you."

She turned on him, letting him feel the full brunt of her frustration. "You left me sitting there on my hands doing nothing while you let your brother get away! Now we're stuck out here freezing to death and dying of thirst and—"

"There's plenty of food and water here," Owen said, gesturing toward a stack of metal containers.

"What happens when that runs out? Who knows how long it'll be before we're strong enough to walk out of here? What's going to happen when they come back? We'll be sitting ducks. And if they don't come back, we might never get out of here!"

"Oh, I think we can count on them coming back."

"What makes you so sure of that?"

Owen pointed to a stack of crates by the limestone wall. "They left the VX mines. And a lot more munitions besides."

Bay stared at the huge mound of crates. "What's in all those boxes?"

"From what I can tell, they're all different kinds of mines. The VX mines that were stolen seem to be a small—but admittedly lethal—part of a much larger operation."

Bay stared with rounded eyes at the three wooden crates Owen had indicated as the ones containing the VX mines. "Are they safe?"

"They've been sitting in those crates for a lot of years. I don't know any reason why they'd spring a leak now. Unless all this moving around has worn through some rusty spot on one of them."

"Don't even think it," Bay said, shuddering.

. . .

OWEN HADN'T LET ON TO BAY, BUT HE'D BEEN BOTH ASTON-
ished and troubled to find Clay at the hijackers' camp.
Since there was no one else here, he'd been forced to
conclude that either the FBI agent they'd encountered or
Clay himself had worked over Luke Creed. What he
couldn't for the life of him figure out was how his brother
had gotten involved in this mess.

It wasn't until he'd seen the stockpile of mines that
Owen realized that he—and Hank—had stumbled onto
an operation much larger than either of them had suspected. If all of those mines had been stolen in Texas, the
Rangers would have heard something about it by now.
Which meant they'd come from other depots in other
states around the country. And that meant the bad guys
were very well connected.

So what the hell had Hank's note meant? Who was the
perfect lady? And how was finding her the key to finding
the thief or thieves? Owen didn't see anything here to explain Hank's clue. Why the hell hadn't he written a little
more, given him a little more help?

He knew it was entirely likely the federal government—either the FBI or ATF or the Justice Department
or the military or all of them combined—had decided to
conduct its own investigation of the munitions thefts
without informing the Texas authorities.

It made sense that the government wouldn't want the
American public to find out that someone was stealing
mines from depots around the country. Terrorism was becoming a real fear for Americans, and judging from the
quantity of mines Owen could see under the camouflage
netting, someone had a real urge to see things explode.

Since the FBI was coordinating the investigation here in Texas, maybe Paul Ridgeway had asked Clay to get involved. Since Cindy's death, the two of them had become as close as father and son. Or maybe, since Clay was the state attorney general, the FBI had figured he had the "need to know" about the full extent of the problem, and he'd come here hoping to rescue Owen—and found Bay's brother instead.

Owen had known Clay was hiding something when they'd spoken at the Armadillo Bar. He just wished he'd pressed his brother for more information when he'd had the chance. It had simply never occurred to him that Clay had anything to do with the hijacked VX mines. He clung to the belief his brother was working on the right side of the law. In which case, it was reasonable to believe Clay had just rescued Luke.

Owen opened his mouth to tell Bay the conclusion he'd reached and shut it again. She wasn't going to believe him until she saw her brother safe and sound. And that wasn't going to happen until they got out of here.

Then he remembered the FBI agent who'd accosted them at the cave. James Brophy had been standing right beside Paul Ridgeway at the Alpine airport, which explained how he knew they were headed into the wilderness. But who did the man work for? Some American militia group? Some Arab terrorists? Some South American rebels? Who was running this show? Why were there so few people guarding the mines? Where was everybody?

And when would they be back?

Owen wished the hijackers had swiped a few M-16s. He had nothing but Bay's jackknife and his SIG to defend them—unless he set up his own perimeter of mines.

Which was definitely an idea worth considering.

BAY SPENT THE NEXT HOUR GOING THROUGH THE CAMP
with Owen, figuring out exactly what supplies they had.
They found bottled water and stopped to quench their
thirst.

"Go ahead and drink your fill," Owen said. "We need
to rehydrate our bodies."

While Bay was drinking, she kept rummaging. "Look
what I found!" she said excitedly. "Tide detergent."

"You're excited because we can do our laundry?"

She pointed to the front of the box. "Tide whitens and
brightens with *bleach*. We can use it to neutralize any remaining VX gas residue." She read the side of the box
and grimaced. "Damn. There's no chlorine bleach in this
stuff."

"At least we'll have clean clothes."

"Sure, if we can find some clothes that haven't been
doused with VX nerve gas," she grumbled. She rum-
maged some more and gave a cry of delight as she held
up a small plastic bottle of Clorox. "Thank goodness.
Now all we have to do is wash ourselves to be rid of
whatever VX residue is left."

Owen threw her an army-green T-shirt and a pair of
camouflage pants. "Here's something to put on once
you're VX-free."

They both stopped what they were doing and washed
themselves down in Clorox. Even diluted, the smell was
overpowering.

"Whew. This is one perfume I won't be trying again,"
Bay muttered. When she'd rinsed off with clear water,
she pulled the army-green T-shirt over her head and knotted the excess material at her waist, then toed off her

boots and pulled on the camouflage pants. They were too big in the waist, but the hips fit. She rolled them up about six inches, then pulled her boots back on.

"The latest in *Survivor* fashion," she said with a grin.

The military clothes made Owen look like a soldier. Strong. Fit. Capable of killing.

He started to pull down the shirt and stopped. "Ah. I think I need some help."

"What's the problem?" The shirt looked like it would fit just fine. She saw Owen wincing and asked, "Are you hurt?"

"I landed in some lechuguilla when we came flying out of that tunnel." He turned his back to her, and in the light of the Coleman lantern she could see a half dozen puncture wounds in his back and shoulder.

"Are the spines still in there?"

"Yeah. I think maybe some of them are."

"Come over here, closer to the light, and take off that shirt."

He pulled the shirt up over his head, then crossed to her and turned his back to the light, so Bay could examine him. She didn't like what she found. At least four of the wounds had razor-sharp spines broken off in them.

"Why didn't you say something sooner? This must have hurt like hell."

He shrugged. "There wasn't anything we could do in the dark. Didn't seem worth mentioning."

"You'll be sorry if you end up with an infection," she scolded. "I need to get these spikes out. Did you find a first-aid kit around here anywhere?"

"There's one in the tent," Owen said. "I'll get it."

"Let's both go. It'll be easier for me to work if you're lying down on one of those cots." She took the Coleman lantern with her and followed him into the four-man tent. It was high enough inside for her to stand easily, but Owen had to keep his head bowed. He retrieved the first-aid kit from a foot locker and handed it to her.

"Lie down," she said, as she set the lantern on an empty crate that was apparently being used as a bedside table. She rooted around in the first-aid kit and held up a couple of autoinjectors. "Bet I can guess what these are for."

"Let's keep them handy," Owen said, taking them from her and setting them on the crate between the two cots.

"I was looking for tweezers," Bay said. "You'd think they'd have a pair, considering all the cactus around here. Ah. There they are. Now, a little alcohol, and I'll be in business."

Owen's shoulders were so broad they extended to the sides of the canvas army cot, but his hips were narrow enough to leave space for her to sit beside him.

"This might hurt," she said, as she dabbed the first of the wounds with cotton she'd soaked in alcohol.

"It sure as hell does," Owen growled, as he reared up. "I thought you were supposed to be gentle."

"Don't be a baby," she said. "I have to swab these clean, or you're going to get an infection."

"I don't like doctors," he said flatly.

"Neither do I," she said. "They're always poking and prodding and giving you bad news."

He turned his head to look at her. "You sound like you're speaking from experience."

She didn't answer him. The conversation had been so innocent, she hadn't realized she was stepping into deep water. "You want some rawhide or something to bite on? This might hurt."

"Very funny," he said. "I think I can keep from screaming."

"Here goes," she said.

Bay knew she was hurting him. The spines were more than two inches long and stuck deep into his flesh. She was most concerned about getting the entire spine out without breaking off part of it inside. To her surprise, after Owen's first rumblings, he didn't make another sound. When she was finished, she dabbed each of the wounds again with alcohol and gently covered them with Band-Aids she'd found in the first-aid kit.

"I'm done," she said at last. "I did the best I could to get all the spines out without doing minor surgery."

"I can vouch for the fact you were thorough, Doctor." He rolled over, and she saw that sweat had beaded on his forehead and upper lip. "If there's anything left in there, it'll work itself out in time."

Bay untied the knot in her shirt and used the cotton cloth to dab his face dry. "I'm sorry I hurt you."

He caught her wrist and pulled her toward him. "You can kiss me and make it better."

She leaned over and gave him a peck on the lips. "There. Happy?"

"You sure are stingy with those kisses, Red."

"What's for supper?" she asked, rising and heading for the zippered doorway to the tent. She heard the cot creak as he rose and followed after her.

"You can pick your own poison," Owen said, as he crossed to one of several cardboard boxes stacked next to the table, reached inside, and held up a dozen *MREs*, each one a hardy *Meal, Ready-to-Eat.*

Bay inspected each package, reading the labels aloud. "Creamed Ground Beef. Yuck. Spaghetti with Meat Sauce. Maybe. Meat Loaf. Nope. Lentil Stew. No, no, no. Pork Chow Mein. Promising. Oh, here's the one I want. Boneless Pork Ribs in Barbecue Sauce. Mmmm. Sounds delicious."

"You got it," Owen said as he set up one of the military chemical heaters—a version of the sizzle sack made for use with *MREs*—on the table.

"The fact military munitions have been stolen, and the presence of these *MREs*, suggest it's someone in the military who's responsible for the thefts," Bay said. "Like your brother, the commanding officer of Bravo Company, 186th Combat Engineer Battalion."

"Clay is also the state attorney general," Owen said. "He could be working for the government investigating the thefts."

"Are you suggesting your brother was here to *rescue* my brother?"

"Maybe. This can't be a very large operation," Owen said as he poured water in the chemical heater and set Bay's *MRE* inside. "Look around you. There's only one tent. It's a four-man tent, but there are only two cots—one for your brother and one for the FBI agent we left in the tunnel. Or maybe there are normally two guys here, and they left your brother tied up somewhere at night. Which means my brother might have found his way here, and when he found the camp abandoned, took off with your brother."

Bay wanted to believe that scenario. If it was true, it meant her brother was safe and on his way home. "Why didn't Clay take the VX mines with him?"

Owen made a face. "Probably too dangerous. Or

maybe he figured he'd have time to tell the authorities where to find them before the thieves could move them somewhere else. Those crates are too big for one man to carry. And look around you. There's no communications equipment here. Surely that Doberman had some way of contacting the outside world. Clay must have taken the communications satellite or whatever with him, leaving this guy cut off—"

"You keep painting your brother as the good guy."

"That's because I know my brother."

"If he's really working for the government on this, why didn't he say something before he let you come charging into the Big Bend?"

"Maybe he thought he had the situation under control."

"If he is the thief, he'd hardly be likely to confess it to you," Bay said pointedly.

"It's entirely possible he got a lead about where the munitions were and followed it on his own," Owen argued.

"Or maybe he figured that even if you caught him, you wouldn't prosecute him, since you let your mother get off scot-free after she had my father killed."

Owen swore under his breath. He busied himself setting up another chemical heater and dropped in the beef stew he'd chosen for himself. When he was done, he looked her right in the eye and said, "If I thought my brother was guilty, I'd arrest him just like any other criminal."

"Easy to say when he's not here," Bay retorted.

Owen cocked a brow. "He's the state attorney general. He won't be too hard to find."

Bay had to concede that was true. She also had to ad-

mit that she was having as much trouble as Owen obviously was coming up with a motive for Clay Blackthorne
to be involved in the hijacking of a few crates of nerve
gas mines, especially when there were mines here from
all over the country.

They ate their meals sitting on benches across from
one another at the table. Bay was too tired to make idle
conversation, and they spent most of the meal in silence.

"You didn't eat much," Owen said, when she set down
her fork. "Not as appetizing as it sounded?"

"I wasn't hungry."

"You need to keep up your strength. We may have to
walk out of here."

"Won't someone come looking for us when you don't
report in?"

"Probably," Owen said. "But what are they going to
find? Your horse is dead, so it won't give off a heat signa-
ture, and by the time the turkey vultures are done, there
won't be much to pick up on a satellite photograph—assuming the view isn't obstructed by the canyon walls."

"What about your horse?" Bay asked.

"I'm guessing that once Mr. James Brophy was fully
conscious he worked his hands and feet free and is, at
this very moment, on his way home on my horse."

"Won't he come here?"

Owen dropped his spoon in his bowl. "He was awake
enough when we left him to hear the explosion when the
tunnel caved in. If he takes a look, he'll figure the VX gas
turned us into mush, and we're buried under a ton of rock.
It's a good bet he has to go the long way around to get back
to this camp. Which means it might be a couple of days before someone else shows up here in a helicopter."

"If they think we're dead," Bay reasoned aloud, "and

my brother's been picked up, why would they bother coming back here at all?"

"The answer to that question depends on whether you think my brother rescued your brother or relocated him. If Clay rescued your brother, Brophy will think Luke got left here by himself. If Luke was left tied up in the tent, Brophy may assume he'll die of thirst, in which case, there won't be any reason to come back until they need the mines."

"If Clay's one of the bad guys," Bay continued, picking up where he'd left off, "they'll know there's no one here, because he took Luke with him, and they believe we're dead."

"We're wasting our time speculating," Owen said. "We need to get our strength back and get out of here."

"Which means, I suppose, that it's time for bed."

"At least we won't have to sleep on the ground," Owen said.

"Or together," Bay added.

"Now that I'm sorry about," Owen said, as he discarded the *MRE* packaging. He saved the boiled water from the chemical heaters, since it was likely to become precious.

"You said I squirm too much at night," Bay said, as she grabbed the Coleman lantern and headed into the tent.

He stepped in after her and murmured in her ear, "I can handle it, Red."

She stiffened. "I can't, Owen." She turned to face him, refusing to back up, refusing to move any closer. "I don't want to get any more involved with you than I already am."

"I've already figured out your secret, Red. The one you're using as an excuse to keep your distance."

Bay paled. "You couldn't possibly—"

"You were attacked. Raped, probably. You've done a good job of recovering. I'd guess you had a good counselor. And you took a self-defense class to make sure it didn't happen again. How am I doing?"

Bay swallowed over the knot in her throat. "Date rape, actually. I had a professor who took me under his wing and helped me get over the trauma. I fell head over heels in love with him. Of course, he never bothered to tell me he was married and had two kids. I got over *that* with some good counseling. And yes, I did take a self-defense class, so it won't happen again."

She'd told him almost everything. All but the most important thing. Which didn't matter, because she wasn't going to let herself care for him.

Owen pulled off his shirt, revealing a torso that could have been cast in bronze. "The girl I loved in college dumped me for the quarterback," he said. "They're married now and have two kids. I got over it with a six-pack of Lone Star. Then I took a women's studies class, so it wouldn't happen again."

Bay laughed. "You made that up to make me feel better."

He held up his hand, palm forward, and said, "I swear it's all true."

"Did you ever fall in love again?" Bay asked.

Owen shook his head as he crossed past her and settled on one of the cots. "Too busy doing my job. How 'bout you?"

"My job keeps me pretty busy, too." Bay wasn't sure whether she felt disappointed or relieved that their sleeping arrangements put them on opposite sides of the tent.

Owen pulled off his boots and slid into his sleeping bag. She did the same, pulling the bag up to her neck to stay warm.

She turned on her side and watched as Owen crossed his arms behind his head and stared aimlessly at the ceiling. "You can turn out the lamp now," she said.

Owen reached over and turned off the hissing Coleman lantern. It was dark in the tent, and Bay listened for the night sounds. And eventually heard an owl. And a locust. And Owen shifting restlessly on his cot.

She smiled and closed her eyes. She was almost asleep when Owen spoke again.

"There's something else that keeps me busy."

"What's that?"

"I have a camp for kids with disabilities."

Bay pushed herself up onto her elbow. "What? Where?"

"It's in the Hill Country near Fredericksburg. I started it with the trust fund my grandmother—my father's mother—left me. It's called Sam's Place. It was my way of trying to make up for what happened to your brother."

"Why didn't you ever say anything? Why didn't you tell Sam?"

"I funded it anonymously. I just . . . wanted you to know."

She shoved the sleeping bag out of her way, left the cot, and crossed to Owen in the dark. She sat beside him and caught his ears with her hands, so she'd know where his face was.

Then she kissed him. Gently. Lovingly. Thoroughly.

When he tried to kiss her back, she lifted her head. "No, Owen. That was just to say 'Thank you.' On behalf of the Creeds, your apology is accepted."

She left him and crossed back to her cot and slipped

into her sleeping bag. "Good night, Owe," she whispered.

"Good night, Red. Sleep tight. Don't let the bedbugs bite."

"You would have to mention bugs," she muttered.

Owen laughed.

Chapter 12

FIRST THING THE NEXT MORNING, OWEN MADE a foray into the crevice through which Clay and Luke had disappeared—and took one of the autoinjectors with him. Bay was waiting for him when he returned with an expression on her face that looked suspiciously like concern.

"Is it booby-trapped?" she asked.

"Nope."

Bay frowned. "Why not? It seems logical they'd want to guard against anyone getting in here."

"Maybe that other trap was set just for us," Owen suggested. "After all, the hijackers knew we were coming down the Strawhouse Trail. They'd already left a warning for us to go back—which we ignored."

"I don't like these people," Bay said. "They're mean."

"And determined to hurt a lot more people, judging from that stockpile of mines."

"I don't want to stay here," Bay said. "Isn't there any way we could get back to a road where someone could find us?"

Owen shook his head. "I'm familiar with the marked trails, but I don't know where we'd end up if we left through that crevice. If we start wandering around in the

Big Bend, we could end up good and lost. Besides, we need to give our bodies more time to recover from exposure to that VX gas."

"My headache is gone," Bay said. "And my stomach feels fine. How about you?"

"I'm good. Just not a hundred percent."

"We're going to die of boredom before those hijackers come back to kill us," Bay said. "I need to be doing something. Sitting around isn't my style."

"Must be that Creed work ethic," Owen said, as he headed back toward the center of the camp.

"It's easy to work when you won't have food on the table if you don't," Bay said as she fell into step beside him.

"Was it really that tough for you growing up?" Owen asked.

"I can't eat macaroni and cheese without gagging."

"You're kidding," Owen said, as he settled into one of the chairs at the table. "You raise some of the best Santa Gertrudis beef in the country at Three Oaks. Why eat macaroni and cheese?"

"We had to sell our beef to pay bills," Bay said as she sat down across from him.

"Surely you could have butchered a steer now and then."

Bay shook her head. "You can't imagine what it's like to be poor, because you've been rich all your life."

"Three Oaks is a huge operation. Are you telling me your profit margin is so small—"

"I'm telling you it's infinitesimal," Bay said. "And it got worse when my father was murdered. The government took fifty-five percent of my dad's estate for inheritance taxes before Mom got a penny. If your brother Trace hadn't agreed to pay the taxes, we might have lost the ranch. Since he did, we're back where we started—living hand-to-mouth and eating macaroni and cheese."

"Why are you still living at home?" Owen asked.

Bay shrugged. "It made more sense than getting a place of my own, since I was going to work in the neighborhood. I can help Mom with chores when I'm not on call. Where do you live?"

"When I'm not out hunting down bad guys, I stay in one of the managers' houses at Bitter Creek."

Bay shot him a cheeky grin. "So you haven't left home, either."

"I guess you could say that."

"Where would you live, if you could choose anywhere in the world to settle down?" Bay asked.

"I could never leave Texas," Owen said. "Because I'd have to give up being a Texas Ranger."

"You could be a policeman somewhere else," Bay said.

"It wouldn't be the same. Texas Rangers are—"

"Mythic," Bay interrupted. "Larger-than-life heroes swaggering around in hand-tooled boots and ten-gallon hats with six-shooters slung low on their hips."

Owen chuckled. "If the boot fits . . . I like working alone, hunting down criminals with only my wits and my reflexes to save me in a pinch."

"You're forgetting that great big gun you carry."

"That, too," he said with a smile. "I like knowing that what I do makes a difference."

"I can understand that," Bay said, lifting her hair off her sweaty neck to try to catch the breeze. "I feel that way whenever I save an animal that would die without my help."

Owen knew she was totally unconscious of the picture

she presented. With her arms up, her breasts were jutting against the soft cotton T-shirt, and he couldn't help remembering how nicely they'd fit into his palms.

"I need something to do," Bay complained.

"I can think of something to keep us busy, but I'm not sure you'll want to do it."

"Name it," she said.

Owen knew what he wanted to do. It started with slipping that T-shirt off over her head and ended with him inside her. Considering everything, he decided that wasn't such a good idea right now. "We can do an inventory of these boxes and see what's inside them," he said. "Maybe we can figure out where they all came from."

"Wonderful idea!" A moment later, Bay was headed for the stack of munitions boxes.

"You've sure got a lot of energy."

"I told you. I'm going crazy doing nothing." She turned when she reached the boxes and said, "What about something to write on? Have you seen a paper or pen?"

Owen shook his head. "Neither one. Which leads me to believe they don't hang around here much."

"They drop off the stolen goods and run, huh?"

"Yeah," Owen said thoughtfully. "Whoever stuck all these mines here doesn't live a long way off, not if they have to get here often. Since this is about the most remote place you can be in Texas, it figures that even if the mines were stolen from stockpiles all over the United States, the thief—or thieves—live in Texas."

"What makes you think the mines were stolen from a lot of different places?" Bay said. "Is there something on the boxes to tell you—"

"If this many mines had been stolen in Texas, the

Texas Rangers would've known about it. Which means they came from out of state. The army probably investigated on its own—if it noticed the thefts—but they might also have involved the FBI or the ATF."

"Hard to believe someone could steal this much truly dangerous stuff and not get caught."

"Part of the problem might be that the army—and whichever federal law enforcement agencies are helping them out—is keeping the whole thing under wraps, so they don't frighten the public."

"I see what you mean. I'd hate to worry about another Oklahoma City bombing happening in my hometown."

"While the local police have been kept in the dark, the government might very well have told the Texas state attorney general what was going on. Knowing Clay, when those VX mines got stolen right from under his nose, he threw himself into the thick of things."

"I hope you're right." Bay sighed. "How are we going to keep track of what's what without pen and paper?"

"You can carve notches in one of those crates with your knife," Owen said.

Bay grinned. "I have to say that appeals to my sense of adventure. It's like we're marooned on a desert island somewhere. Just the two of us. We could be here for years and years."

"I hope not," Owen said. "We've only got about a week's worth of food."

Bay stared at him. "That's not much at all. Are you sure that's all we have?"

"Did I mention there's less than two weeks' worth of water?"

"When did you figure all this out?" Bay asked irritably.

"What happened to your spirit of adventure? The two of us alone on a desert island?"

"My island has *water*," she said flatly.

"I don't think we're going to be alone here very long."

Bay looked transfixed. "Who is it you think will be coming here?"

"The bad guys, of course."

"We don't have anything to defend ourselves with. Just my knife and your pistol."

"Sure we do." Owen pointed to the stack of boxes. "We just have to figure out how to use them to our advantage."

Owen was far less sanguine about their chances of surviving than he'd led Bay to believe. But there was no sense scaring her. Better to let her play *Survivor* and hope for the best.

They spent the next five days doing an inventory of the weapons, deciding which mines to set and how to lay them so no innocent person would be hurt by accident. They spent the nights sitting near a wood fire they made using broken-up mine crates, telling stories and singing silly camp songs.

As the week wore on, instead of feeling better, Owen felt worse. He started to wonder if maybe he'd gotten a larger dose of VX gas than he'd thought. His back and his legs ached. He felt feverish and lost his appetite.

He hid his condition from Bay, hoping he would get better. On the morning of the sixth day, Owen couldn't rise from his cot.

When Bay returned from her morning trip to the bushes, smiled at him and said, "Rise and shine, lazybones," he opened his eyes and croaked, "Can't do it, Red. Too sick."

•   •   •

BAY WAS BENDING OVER OWEN A MOMENT LATER, A PALM on his forehead. "You're burning up with fever! How long have you been sick?"

"Few days," he muttered.

"How many days?" she insisted. "Where does it hurt?"

"My back. My legs. All over."

"Men!" she said in disgust. "You're such stupid creatures. Why couldn't you have told me you weren't feeling well? Why do you have to put on this macho act until you're so sick you can't move?"

"No sense worrying you," he said. "If it's the gas, there's nothing you can do to save me."

"If it was the gas making you sick, I'd be sick, too. More likely, we'd both be dead!" Bay dragged Owen's shirt off over his head and said, "Turn over."

Bay saw the problem immediately. Red streaks radiated from three of the four Band-Aids on his back. "These wounds are infected. What I need is penicillin. And we don't have any."

"See. Wouldn't have made any difference if I'd said something sooner."

"I might have been able to cut out whatever was causing the infection and cut out the infection along with it, if you'd told me sooner," Bay said angrily. "You said your legs hurt, too. Get those camouflage pants off, so I can take a look."

"This isn't the way I pictured getting naked for you," he said.

Bay was terrified when she realized he was too weak even to sit up and pull off his pants. She shoved his hands out of the way and unsnapped and unzipped his camouflage trousers and pulled them off.

As she'd suspected, two of the wounds in his calves where she'd pulled out lechuguilla spines had also become infected.

"You're a mess!" she said. "What am I going to do with you?"

"Bury me?" Owen quipped.

"If you weren't in such bad shape, I'd make you pay for that," Bay said. "I can use hot cloths to soften these wounds enough to drain them. But I don't think that's going to be enough."

"I don't suppose you did a paper on this?" Owen asked.

"Don't be ridicu—" Bay stopped herself and smiled. "I did! Oh, if I can just remember. It was a paper on herbal remedies. You wouldn't believe how many desert plants are antimicrobial."

"Give it to me in English," Owen said.

"You can crush the seeds and boil the bark and make an antiseptic that can be used directly on the wound. Or I can make a tea you can drink. There are poultices to help with the inflammation and to draw out poisons," she said excitedly. "If I can just remember which herbs are used for what."

"I'm sure if you put your mind to it—"

"What if I'm wrong?" Bay interrupted. "What if I give you a remedy that doesn't work? Or one that's meant to cure something that isn't wrong with you?"

"So what? A couple of wrong things won't matter as long as you give me at least some of the right thing. What can you remember?"

"Mesquite, because it's so common in South Texas. I think it has to be dried, or you have to use gum from the trunk, and I'm not sure I can get what I need soon enough to do you any good. But I think the pods can be boiled for tea."

"All right. One mesquite tea," Owen said, as though he were ordering from a menu in a restaurant. "What else?"

"Catclaw . . ." Bay hesitated. "Catclaw something."

"Cactus?" Owen suggested.

"Not cactus. I remember thinking at the time it must be a mistake, because it's a different word than cactus."

"Acacia," Owen said. "There's catclaw acacia."

"That's it!" Bay said. "That works like mesquite. But it doesn't have to be dried first."

"I've seen some of that around here. I can describe it for you."

"Good. I think sage has some medicinal value, too."

"You know what that looks like?"

"Yes, I do." Bay put her fingers to her temples. "Oh, I wish I could remember exactly what to do."

Owen laid his hand on her thigh. "Go out and hunt your herbs, Red. Or should I call you 'Medicine Woman'?"

Bay laughed through the tears that were blurring her vision. "Let's wait and see how you feel after you've been dosed with a few of my remedies."

She started to rise, but he tightened his hold to keep her in place. When she met his gaze he said, "Thanks for taking care of me, Red. I mean . . . considering everything."

She lifted a brow. "You mean, considering you're a Blackthorne, and I'm a Creed?"

"Yeah. That's what I mean."

"This doesn't change anything, Owen." The shorter, more affectionate name wouldn't come out. Last night things had gotten too familiar . . . too frightening. So she'd taken a step back. "We still live on opposite sides of the fence."

"We could both move."

She stared at him in confusion. "What?"

"I said I have to stay in Texas to be a Ranger. I didn't say I had to stay in Bitter Creek. I wouldn't mind moving to the Hill Country near Fredericksburg. How about you?"

She rose and said, "Maybe you ought to make sure you're going to live, before you start planning to pick up stakes and move halfway across the state."

"Bring on the tea," Owen said. "I'll swallow whatever you put in front of me."

Bay smiled. "Be careful what you wish for. Some of these remedies are liable to taste like what they are— bark and leaves."

Owen was cursing loudly long before she'd finished washing out his wounds with a mesquite concoction made from leaves, twigs, bark, and pods boiled in water.

"That hurts like the devil!" he complained.

"You shouldn't have hidden the fact you weren't feeling well. It would have been a lot simpler to treat you before you got so sick."

He nearly came off the cot when she applied a boiled poultice of flowering white sage to his back. "Too hot?" she asked sweetly.

"No," he said through gritted teeth.

"I need to go collect some catclaw acacia. Will you be all right?"

"I'm not going anywhere," Owen said.

It was surprisingly difficult for Bay to collect the leaves and seed pods she needed from the catclaw acacia, because the stems were covered with "catclaws," which looked like rose thorns and were twice as sharp. Bay had a few wounds of her own before she was done.

She crushed the green leaves and pods with a stone and threw them into a pot of boiling water to brew cat-claw acacia tea. When it was done, she brought a cup to Owen.

"Can you turn over by yourself?" She was surprised at the effort it took him to do so. She feared he was much sicker than he'd let on, and that he really needed a hospital and a people doctor. "I'll help you sit up," she said.

"I can do it."

In the end, he couldn't. Bay didn't lecture him, merely put a hand on an unwounded part of his back and helped push him into a sitting position.

When he tried to take the cup from her she said, "Let me help. I don't want to have to start over collecting this stuff. That catclaw acacia fights back."

He drank the tea, making faces as he did.

"How does it taste?" she asked.

"Like leaves and bark."

Bay smiled. "I told you so."

When he had drunk the whole cup, Bay helped him lie back down on his stomach. "I want to keep hot poultices on your back until I see some of the swelling and redness go away."

It was a sign of just how sick he was that he didn't argue.

By dawn the next morning, his calves were looking much better. But Bay conceded that no amount of hot poultices was going to force out the broken-off spikes that were the source of the infection in Owen's back. His skin was red and tender to the touch. Despite the teas she'd forced down his throat, his fever was raging. If she didn't act soon, Owen would end up with gangrene. Then it would be too late to do anything but watch him die.

She sighed heavily.

"What is it?" Owen asked as he turned his head in her direction.

She dabbed away the sweat on his forehead with a torn piece of an army-green T-shirt. "I didn't know you were awake."

"I just woke up," he said in a slurred voice. "What's wrong?"

"I need to cut out the spikes in your back."

He ran his tongue along dry lips and said, "I figured that was coming."

"Well?"

"I've been trying to imagine a scenario where we get rescued in the next day or so. I don't think that's going to happen. If you think it'll help, Red, maybe you better make like a doctor and operate."

"I don't have any anesthetic," she said. "You're going to feel it when I start cutting. I know there's some desert plant that would make you sleepy, but I've tried and tried, and I can't remember what it is."

"Don't worry, Red. I'll be fine," Owen said. "Maybe you ought to get me something to bite on, so I don't make you slice too deep by screaming at the wrong moment."

"You're not helping by making jokes," she snapped.

"I wasn't joking."

"Oh." Bay's hands were shaking by the time she'd cut a piece of sotol, a desert plant with long stems that could be turned into walking sticks, for Owen to bite down on.

"Why so nervous, Red?" Owen said. "You're qualified to do surgery, aren't you?"

"On animals," she said. "In an operating theater. With

surgical instruments and enough anesthesia to ensure the patient suffers no pain. I'm going to be using a jackknife to cut into you, for God's sake!"

"Think of the alternative. If you don't operate, I'm going to die a slow, lingering—and very smelly—death from gangrene."

"When you put it that way, I suppose I have no choice," she said acerbically.

"I trust you, Red."

"I don't want this responsibility, Owen."

"Too late to worry about that now. I'll try to stay still and keep down the noise."

"Feel free to moan and groan," she said. "At least that way I'll know I haven't killed you on the operating table."

When Owen didn't say anything she said, "That was a joke."

"Oh," he said. "Ha ha."

Bay tried to reassure him by smiling. "I'm a good surgeon, Owe. I'll get you through this okay."

"Thanks, Red."

He didn't speak after that, because he had his jaws clamped on the piece of wood to keep from screaming. Bay made a neat, precise incision, found the first offending spike and used the tweezers to pull it out. Bay knew she was hurting him, because when she cut, every muscle in his back tensed.

His face ran with sweat, and despite his gritted teeth, a groan issued from his throat.

"One down," she said.

He groaned loudly at that announcement.

"Don't be a baby," she said. "It's just a little surgery without anesthesia."

She knew she'd made him laugh, because the sound ended in a gasp when she made the next incision. There were three spikes in his back, and she had them all out in five minutes. They were the most grueling five minutes of her life.

"I have to sew up these incisions," she said. "I give you fair warning the stitches may be a little crooked. I never could sew a straight seam. Can't cook worth a damn, either—except for macaroni and cheese—and you know that makes me gag."

He was laughing again. She could feel it in his body, which was better than seeing his muscles stretched taut with pain while she'd been cutting. There had been no needle or thread in the first-aid kit, so she'd improvised.

Ironically, she ended up using a lechuguilla spine for a needle and peeled a yucca leaf into thread-sized lengths. She made quick work of the sutures. Ordinarily, she would have wanted them close together to minimize the scar. But she made the stitches as far apart as she dared, because she couldn't bear his pain.

"You're going to have some really sexy scars back here, Owe."

"Do girls go for that sort of thing?"

She was surprised to hear him speak and realized he'd spit out the piece of wood. It was marred with impressions of his teeth. "Scars like this are a sign you've survived in battle."

"Some battle," he said ruefully. "Me and a cactus going three rounds, and I nearly bit the dust."

Bay wanted to tell him the worst was over. Maybe it was. The offending spikes had been removed. She'd used more of the acacia concoction to rinse the three wounds before she'd sewed them up. Now she had to make sure

Owen rested and kept drinking the foul-tasting teas she brewed, so his body could heal.

"You'll make a good mother," Owen murmured. "You're tender and gentle and caring."

Bay felt her throat swell closed. He couldn't know how it hurt her to hear him say that. She knew she ought to tell him the final secret she'd been keeping from him, but he kept on talking, so she remained silent and listened.

"My mom never spent much time with us kids. We had servants to take care of us. But I never stopped wanting her to notice me. I remember once I fell and skinned my knee. I couldn't have been more than six or seven. I landed pretty hard, and it was nice and bloody. I figured if anything would get her attention, that would."

He stopped, and she heard him swallow hard.

"Anyway, she was up in her studio, painting. I knew I wasn't supposed to interrupt her, but I did it anyway. She took one look at me and yelled, 'Get out! I'm working!' "

"What did you do then?" Bay asked, her heart aching for the little boy he'd been.

"I got out. I never washed my knee, and it got infected. My dad was pretty pissed off when he noticed it. He took me to the doctor, and I ended up getting a shot of penicillin in my butt. I've got a scar there. On my knee, not my butt," he clarified with a laugh.

"I'm so sorry, Owe."

"I didn't tell you that to get your sympathy. I just wanted to explain a little about why we Blackthornes are the way we are."

"You're not at all like your mother," Bay said certainly. She pursed her lips. "I suppose that means you must take after your father."

Owen grinned. "That ogre? Are you sure?"

"At least he took you to the hospital. He must not be quite as heartless as I've always thought." She made a face and said, "I suppose he must have a few redeeming qualities to make my mother fall in love with him."

They looked into each other's eyes and smiled, and a comfortable silence fell between them.

Bay reached out and brushed aside the lock of hair that always fell onto Owen's forehead.

Owen brushed his knuckles against her cheek, where the scab had fallen off and left pink skin behind.

She reached up and twined her fingers in his. "You should go to sleep," she said.

"I'm not tired."

"Don't argue with the doctor," she said, putting her fingertips over his eyelids and urging them closed.

"How about a bedtime story?"

"What did you have in mind?" Bay said, as she sank down cross-legged on the floor of the tent beside him.

"There must be a good story about the Blackthornes and the Creeds. Something from a long time ago."

"When we all used to sit around the fireplace on winter nights, my father would tell this sad story about Jarrett Creed."

"You mean Cricket's husband before she married the first Blackthorne? Jarrett was killed in the Civil War, right?"

"Wrong. Cricket *thought* he was killed. He was wounded and got captured and sent to Andersonville. You know, that really cruel prison. His leg was torn up by a musket ball, and he had to go into the prison hospital."

"But a pretty nurse saved him, and he fell in love with her," Owen said.

"Whose story is this?" Bay said. "You're supposed to be falling asleep."

"My eyes are closed."

"Try shutting your mouth."

"Okay, Red. Tell your story."

"Cricket received a letter saying that Jarrett had died in the battle at Antietam. She had borne five children, four sons and a daughter. The daughter had died of pneumonia when she was a child. Three of Cricket's sons—and she thought her husband, as well—were killed in the war. Her one remaining son was reported missing and presumed dead.

"Cricket had lost everything that was important to her, so she left her home and went to live with her older sister Sloan, at her cattle ranch, Dolorosa. That's when this mysterious Blackthorne fellow showed up. Seems he made some kind of wager with Cricket, and he won, and they ended up getting married."

"They fell in love," Owen interjected.

Bay glared at him, and he shut his eyes. "Now, this is where the story gets good. See, Jarrett finally gets released from prison and comes home. And what does he find?"

"Nobody."

Bay growled.

"Sorry, that slipped out."

"He hears some carpetbagger named Blackthorne *and his wife* have taken up residence at Lion's Dare, the cotton plantation he'd owned before the war. Meanwhile, Jarrett has no idea where his wife is, and all his sons are reported missing or dead. So he heads for Dolorosa, where his sister-in-law Sloan is living. Sloan gives him the bad news: Cricket is married to another man. And she's expecting his child."

"I thought all her sons were grown men? How old was she, anyway?"

"Young enough to bear your great-great—however many greats—grandfather," Bay said with asperity. "Do you want to hear the end of this story, or not?"

"I'm listening."

"Anyway, Jarrett wants his wife back. Things are complicated, because she's pregnant with another man's child. To make matters worse, Jarrett is no longer a whole man."

"Right. He's missing a leg," Owen piped up.

"No, his leg is stiff, so he limps, but he's still got both limbs."

"Then what's wrong with him?" Owen asked.

"He's blind."

"Whoa," Owen said. "Why didn't I ever hear about any of this in my family history?"

"Because this is a story about *my* forebears," Bay said.

"What happened next?" Owen asked. "What did Jarrett do?"

"Nobody knows."

"What kind of ending is that for story?" Owen complained.

"The only one we have," Bay said. "All we know is that Jarrett disappeared and was never heard from again."

"I *hate* that ending! Couldn't your father have made up something more satisfying?"

"The truth is the truth."

"That's a tall tale if I ever heard one. Jarrett Creed died in the war. That's what Cricket wrote in her diary. I've seen it myself."

"He didn't die. He came back. Then he disappeared again."

Owen made a *hmmmph* sound in his throat. "That was a terrible story. I'm going to sleep."

"It's about damn time," Bay said with a sigh.

Chapter 13

IN THE DEEPEST PART OF HER SOUL, DORA Coburn knew she'd made the wrong choice twenty-five years ago. But who would have believed that one mistake could cause so much pain for so many people?

Dora was waiting in the shade of a live oak, in the parking lot of the First Baptist Church, for Eve Blackthorne to bid the talkative preacher farewell and return to her shiny black Cadillac. Dora's hands were shaking. Her knees felt like they were going to buckle at any moment. And her eyes kept filling with tears, which she swiped away with a balled-up Kleenex.

Dora had done a lot of soul-searching in church and had admitted that there was no way she could keep her son from seeing Summer Blackthorne. Billy was like a wild bronc with the bit in his teeth. He'd had a sniff of that little Blackthorne filly, and he would be back for more. Head bent, hands folded in fervent prayer, Dora had acknowledged that she had no choice except to appeal to Mrs. Blackthorne to marry off her daughter to some rancher who would take her far away from Bitter Creek.

Otherwise, both their children were going to commit the kind of sin for which there was no forgiveness.

Eve Blackthorne was coming. She looked incredibly beautiful, her blond hair cut short and styled in that windswept look Dora had seen on Meg Ryan in the *Star* magazine she'd picked up shopping for groceries in the H.E.B. Mrs. Blackthorne's countenance was serene, as though she didn't have a worry in the world—and never had. And her tailored, tiny-sized, off-white suit and snakeskin pointy-toed shoes must have cost at least a thousand dollars—each.

Dora stepped away from the base of the live oak and immediately squinted, putting a hand up to protect her eyes from the searing Texas sun. She took a step in Eve Blackthorne's direction and said, "Mrs. Blackthorne, we need to talk."

Dora saw the other woman looking her up and down and cringed inside. Over the past twenty-five years, hard work and unhappiness had etched Dora's face with too many wrinkles. She knew she looked fifty-five, when in fact she was only forty-four. She wore a fraying print jersey dress she'd bought at Kmart in a woman's size, to accommodate the extra pounds that had stuck to her waist and hips from too many cheap meals of tortillas and pinto beans and rice. She'd scraped her long, gray-streaked brown hair back from her face into a no-nonsense bun.

And she now wore black plastic-framed glasses that hid the entrancing brown eyes that Jackson Blackthorne had once said reminded him of rich, dark chocolate.

Whatever Eve Blackthorne thought of her now, once upon a time, Dora had been young and beautiful enough to catch Jackson Blackthorne's eye. She'd worked part-time after school at the Lone Star Cafe in town as a waitress, and Blackjack had come in for a cup of coffee after school board meetings or hospital board meetings or bank board meetings before heading home.

Dora hadn't meant to let things go so far. After all, Jackson Blackthorne was a married man. But she'd been flattered, because he'd been so rich and powerful. And she'd been moved to comfort him, because he'd seemed so sad and lonely.

She'd given him her virginity. And he'd gotten her pregnant.

Dora had gone straight to the Castle from the doctor's office to tell Blackjack the awful news and ask for his help. Her parents were sure to throw her out when they discovered how she'd sinned. And she didn't know what she'd do, if Blackjack refused to help her.

She hadn't been at all sure he would.

He'd never said he loved her. He'd told her bitterly, after the first and only time they'd ever made love, that he could never divorce his wife.

But she'd gone to his house anyway, because she needed enough money to survive until she could have the child and give it up for adoption. So she'd knocked on the back door of the Castle and asked the maid who answered, if she could speak to Blackjack.

Eve Blackthorne had shown up instead.

Dora had been terrified, knowing Blackjack would be furious if his wife ever found out about them. She'd started to run, but Mrs. Blackthorne had called her back. "What do you want?"

"I . . . uh . . . Is Jackson—I mean, Mr. Blackthorne here?" Dora had stuttered.

"Why do you want to see my husband?"

Dora had flushed to the roots of her hair. "I'm . . . uh . . ." She couldn't get it out.

"I can guess why you're here," Eve had said, standing in the doorway holding the screen door open.

Dora didn't see how Mrs. Blackthorne could have guessed her secret. She'd only found out an hour before that she was pregnant.

"I need to talk to Jacks—I mean Mr. Blackthorne," Dora said, deciding to bluff it out.

"I ask myself, what problem could a very beautiful— and very young—girl have that would cause her to seek out my husband?" Mrs. Blackthorne said. "Only one an- swer comes to mind."

Dora swallowed hard. "What is that?"

"Jackson's been distracted lately. I thought it was work. Now I see it was you." Her nose pinched tight, like she'd whiffed something putrid. "I presume you've got- ten yourself pregnant."

"I had some help!" Dora shot back. Her face flamed as she realized what she'd admitted. "We only did it once." As if that made it better.

"Come inside," Mrs. Blackthorne said. "We need to talk."

"I'd rather see Jackson," Dora said, not liking the shrewd look in Mrs. Blackthorne's ice-blue eyes.

"Come inside, girl. I insist."

Dora balked.

"I know you need money. I'll make sure you get it."

Dora was surprised that a betrayed wife would be the one offering her money, but the ways of the rich were a mystery to her. Eve Blackthorne had apparently sus- pected her husband was cheating on her, which meant Blackjack must not have been sleeping with his wife. Or had done something else to convince her he was having an affair with another woman. Only, it hadn't been an af- fair. Just a one-night stand.

"Come on in. I won't bite," Mrs. Blackthorne said with a smile meant to allay her fears.

Dora shivered. Eve Blackthorne was like the snake in the Garden of Eden. Tempting where Dora knew better. She stepped inside and heard the screen door slam behind her, as she followed Mrs. Blackthorne through an amazingly large and modern kitchen and down a high-ceilinged central hallway to a room with a large oak desk.

The walls of the room were lined with more books than any human being could read in a lifetime. Mrs. Blackthorne closed the door behind them, then crossed and sat in the big swivel chair behind an enormous oak desk and gestured Dora into one of the two horn-and-rawhide chairs in front of her.

"I just need enough money to support myself until I can give the baby up for adoption," Dora said quickly.

"I'm surprised at you, Dora. You aren't being very clever about this. You could earn a great deal more by keeping the baby."

Dora gaped at her. "But . . ." She'd never even considered the possibility. "It would be a bastard."

"Not if you got married."

"I would never trick a man by doing that to him," Dora said scathingly.

"What if your husband knew when he married you that it was another man's child?"

"I don't understand why you're talking like this," Dora said. "I don't know anyone I'd consider marrying. And anyway, I'm too young to get married. I'm still in high school."

"What if I promised you a stipend every month to support the child, if you got married?"

"A stipend? What's that?"

"A monthly allotment, a monthly check to support the

child . . . for as long as the child remains a secret from my husband."

Dora couldn't understand why Mrs. Blackthorne wanted the child kept a secret from her husband. Dora could have told her that Blackjack wasn't going to divorce his wife and marry some girl he'd had sex with once. Maybe Eve Blackthorne was afraid that if Blackjack knew about the child, he'd want to adopt it himself. Dora could understand why a woman wouldn't want her husband's bastard living under her own roof. People would know. People would talk. It would be humiliating for her.

For the first time, Dora considered the idea of keeping the baby. She'd done her share of baby-sitting, and she liked babies. If she had enough money to support it, she wouldn't even mind having this one. But she didn't think there was much chance of her finding a husband. And she said so.

"I appreciate the offer, but I don't see where I'm going to find a husband who'd want to marry me."

"I'll take care of that," Mrs. Blackthorne said.

"How are you going to talk some man into marrying me that I've never even met?"

"The cowboy I have in mind won't just be getting a pregnant wife, he'll be getting a ranch in the bargain."

Dora's eyes goggled. "You can't buy a man like that!"

"Of course I can. You'd be amazed what money can buy."

Dora felt queasy, and she didn't think it was her pregnancy causing the problem. "I don't think I'd want to marry anyone who'd agree to a bargain like that."

"You can take the deal I'm offering you, or find some other way to survive. You won't be getting a penny from my husband. I'll see to that."

"I can't marry a stranger."

"You had sex with one."

Dora opened her mouth to say Jackson Blackthorne hadn't been a stranger and shut it again. The truth was, she hadn't known Blackjack that long before she'd had sex with him.

"Think of what I'm offering you," Mrs. Blackthorne said. She ticked off each item on her fingers. "First, you'll have a steady income, so long as the child remains a secret from my husband. Second, you'll have a home of your own—I'll see the ranch is put in both your names, so your husband can't divorce you and take it all."

Dora hadn't even *thought* of that!

"Third," Mrs. Blackthorne continued, "you'll have a father for your baby, so no one need ever know he's a bastard. Fourth, you'll be able to stay right here in Bitter Creek, instead of moving away to some big city and having to give your baby away to strangers to raise. And fifth, you'll be working for yourself on your own ranch, instead of working for someone else the rest of your life."

Dora felt overwhelmed. "I can't think. I don't know what to do."

Mrs. Blackthorne's offer sounded so reasonable. And it would settle a future that had been cloudy at best. The only problem was, Dora would have to spend her life married to some man she didn't love. Some man she hadn't even met.

On the other hand, on TV she'd seen how parents in foreign countries arranged marriages for their children to strangers. They learned to love one another. She supposed that if you worked hard enough, anything was possible.

She imagined a scene where she held her child, and her adoring husband had his arms securely around both of them. It was the sort of dream she'd never allowed herself to dream, when she'd first feared she might be pregnant. Maybe it was possible. Maybe it could happen.

"Who did you have in mind for me to marry?" she asked.

Dora saw from the cat-in-the-cream smile that spread on Mrs. Blackthorne's face that she knew she had won, that all she had to do was provide a proper groom and the marriage was inevitable.

"His name is Johnny Ray Coburn."

Dora hadn't known what a devil's bargain she was making that day. Hadn't realized how it would eat at Johnny Ray to know he was raising a rich man's son—and being paid to do it. Hadn't known what a mean drunk he would be. Hadn't known how envy and hate could eat at a man, until he beat an innocent child . . . and the wife he realized too late that he'd paid too high a price to marry. Hadn't known how shiftless and lazy a man could get, knowing a Blackthorne check was on its way each and every month to put food on his table.

Dora knew Eve Blackthorne would be as anxious as she was to end the relationship between Billy Coburn and Summer Blackthorne.

Because the two of them were related by blood.

Dora took the few steps necessary to bring her close enough to be heard by Mrs. Blackthorne without her voice carrying to those few people still searching out their cars in the church parking lot. "We have a problem," Dora began.

"What is it you want now?" Mrs. Blackthorne demanded.

Dora flushed at the insinuation that she'd come to beg for more money and quickly said, "I caught your daughter kissing my son."

"I see. What is it you expect me to do?"

Dora stared wide-eyed at Mrs. Blackthorne. "It must be obvious what I want. I want the two of them separated."

"Then send your son away."

Dora was aghast. "I can't do that. His income is all that's keeping the ranch afloat since Johnny Ray died in that accident."

"We had an agreement. I'm not paying more. That's blackmail."

Dora felt like she'd entered the Twilight Zone. "It's not money I'm after," she said through clenched teeth. "You must see the danger in my son and your daughter getting too close, being more than friends. We've got to separate them."

Eve grimaced. "Very well. I'll take care of it."

Dora breathed an inward sigh of relief. Disaster had been averted. She blamed herself for letting things go as far as they had. She should have nipped the friendship between her son and Eve Blackthorne's daughter in the bud. Well, it was taken care of now. And the dark, ugly secret she'd held clasped to her bosom for twenty-five years was still safe.

JACKSON BLACKTHORNE HADN'T DARKENED A CHURCH DOOR-way since he'd married his wife thirty-three years ago. He welcomed the respite from his wife's company that her Sunday morning absence provided. They hadn't stopped fighting since he'd come home from Three Oaks the previous

Sunday and found her sitting at his desk going through his papers.

He felt his body tense as he heard the front door open. He knew she'd come looking for him, because they hadn't finished their most recent argument before she'd left for church.

As Eve entered the room, she gently tugged off her gloves, one finger at a time, and set them on the wet bar.

"Would you like a drink?" she asked.

Blackjack could have used one, but he didn't want to be obliged to her even for that. "No, thanks. There's been no word about Owen or the Creed girl."

She poured herself a scotch and drank it like a man, neat, without ice. "Too bad. So sad."

"You're a damned cold bitch," Blackjack said.

"Are you just now noticing?" she said with an icy smile.

The sad truth was he'd blinded himself to her faults because that was easier than divorcing her.

"Owen put me in that sanitarium," she said. "I will never forgive him for that."

"He was doing his job."

She caressed the crystal glass with her thumb and peered down into it, as though debating whether to have another. Then she set the glass aside. "I won't miss him. But I'll be sure to grieve publicly, if that's what's bothering you."

Blackjack felt physically sick to his stomach. Once upon a time he'd admired her stoicism. Now he saw it for what it was. Self-denial. She was a woman with empty spaces that she refused to fill with the things she wanted—especially love. She hadn't been happy for a long time, and he didn't see how staying married to her was going to do either of them any good. But she didn't

want a divorce. And she knew all the right things to say
to make him think twice about demanding one.

"Well, I'll miss Owen if he's gone," Blackjack said.
"He was—is—a good man."

"We still have Clay," his wife said. "He's the twin
who's always showed the most promise, anyway."

"What makes you say things like that?" he asked, furious at her cruel dismissal of Owen.

She lifted a shoulder in a negligent shrug. "You can't
choose your children any more than they can choose their
parents. I never liked Owen much. He always lacked the
courage to face the realities of life."

"Don't talk about him as though he were already
dead," Blackjack snapped.

Eve pursed her lips. "He's been missing for a week in
the desert. What makes you think he's still alive?"

"He's a Texas Ranger, for God's sake. Only the best
get chosen for that honor. And he knows the Big Bend.
He'll find a way to get out and bring the girl with him."

"Would you like to make a bet on that?" Eve asked.

"I can't imagine why I ever married you," Blackjack
said. "What kind of mother are you?"

"I'm what you've made of me," she said, spreading
her arms wide. "A little crazy. A little vengeful. A little
sad. Thanks to you, I have no illusions left. I see things as
they really are. The world is not a nice place, Jackson.
People disappoint you. People live despicable lives. People die for foolish reasons. The way Owen and that Creed
girl will probably die."

Blackjack tensed as Eve crossed and stood behind him
to look over his shoulder at the papers in front of him.

He didn't hide the contract with Lauren Creed, in

which she agreed to train a half dozen cutting horses for him. He braced himself, expecting his wife to object to it, and was surprised when she brought up another woman entirely.

"I had an interesting conversation with Dora Coburn after church," she said.

Blackjack tensed and swiveled the chair around to face her. "Oh?" His one indiscretion in his marriage had occurred twenty-five years ago. But he'd never ceased to worry that his wife would discover it—and use it against him.

"It seems Dora caught Summer kissing her son Billy. She wanted me to do something about it. Can you imagine the gall of the woman? Suggesting *I* do something about it? I'm not responsible for the situation. I haven't been home for the past eighteen months. You're the one who's been looking after our daughter. How could you let her throw herself away on a piece of trash like that boy?"

"I've told her before to stay away from him," Blackjack muttered. "Summer said they're just friends."

"The boy's own mother caught them kissing. If you don't watch out, that care-for-nothing cowboy is going to pluck your darling ripe peach."

"I can handle Bad Billy Coburn."

Eve laughed. "Sure you can. If you handle him like you've handled our daughter, those two are going to make you a proud grandpa before you know it."

Blackjack came out of his chair so fast that Eve cried out in alarm and backed up against the wall. There was nothing he could do about Owen's situation, but he could, by God, still save Summer from herself. "I'll roast in hell before I let that saddle tramp ruin my daughter."

He turned to his wife, and she pressed herself tighter against the wall. He made an irritated sound in his throat. "I don't know what they did to you in that damned sanitarium, but you've been jumpy as a bullfrog ever since you got home."

"It was not a nice place, Jackson," she said as she edged past him and headed back toward the bar. "I will never forgive you, either, for your part in sending me there."

"You don't have to forgive me. Just give me a divorce." The words were out. And he had no desire to take them back. "I'll give you half of everything. I just need enough time to pay it out without selling the ranch."

He waited for her answer while she poured herself a second drink.

She turned with the glass in her hand, drank it in a single gulp, then said, "I don't want a divorce. Why would I make it easy for you to give me one?"

"You don't love me."

"Who says I don't?"

"More to the point, I don't love you."

"I've known that for a long time," she said. "But I'm not giving you up. You're mine."

"Like a beef on a spit," he said angrily.

"A very nice beef," she said, appraising him as she would a powerful bull on the hoof.

Her look left him physically stone cold. But it raised the hairs on the back of his neck, as though he were facing some dangerous predator. "You cheated on me, Eve. I'm not going to forget—or forgive you for—that."

"How dare you! When you—" She cut herself off and turned back to the bottle to pour herself a third drink.

He stared at her. What had she started to say? Could

she possibly know about Dora Coburn? It simply wasn't possible. He'd been faithful to his wife both before and after that single lapse. Except for those few weeks when he'd considered, and then actually consummated his affair with Dora Coburn, he'd come every night to his wife's bed to slake his fierce appetites. And she'd never refused him.

But that was before Jesse had died. That was before he'd known there was a chance he could have the woman he'd always loved.

"Why make us both miserable?" he said. "Let me go."

She drank the third scotch as neatly as the second and set it down, then turned to him and put her hands behind her on the bar, making her breasts press against the soft white suit. "No, Jackson. I still want you. It's been a very long eighteen months."

"I'm not interested."

He saw the rage flare in her eyes. Maybe if he'd seen distress or pain, he'd have found a way to soften the blow. But it was time she faced facts. "It's over, Eve. I'm getting out."

"Over my dead body."

He snorted. "Don't think it couldn't be arranged."

Her eyes narrowed. "Are you threatening me?"

"That isn't my style. If I were going to do it, you'd already be dead."

She laughed gaily. "Oh, I do love fighting with you, Jackson." She picked up her gloves and said, "Will you join me for brunch?"

Acid churned in his stomach. "I'm not hungry."

She was almost out the door, when she stopped and glanced back at him over her shoulder. "By the way, if you're looking for Summer, I believe she told me this morning that she was going to visit Bad Billy Coburn. I guess, since Dora brings Emma to church with her, that means your daughter and that hell-raising boy spent the morning together . . . alone."

"I get the picture," Blackjack said in a voice as gritty as sand. "I said I'll take care of it."

"I'll believe it when I see it."

It was the goad he needed, and he was sure she knew it. That didn't stop him from picking up the phone to call the bunkhouse and arranging to have a few handpicked cowboys meet him in back of the house. He surveyed the men he'd chosen, rough men, loners who'd drifted in and stayed, because they had nowhere else to go.

"I'm going to teach a man a lesson, and I'm going to use force to do it. You have a problem with that, you're welcome to stay behind."

One man tugged down his Stetson. Another blew out a breath of smoke. The third stared at the toe of his boot, which was digging into the dirt. The fourth stuck his thumbs in his pockets.

"All right," Blackjack said. "Let's go."

They piled into the extended-cab pickup with him, and he drove the twenty-five miles to Bad Billy Coburn's ranch. He saw his daughter's cherry-red Silverado parked in the shade of a live oak near the house. A quick search revealed his daughter and Bad Billy standing by the stable near two saddled horses. It wasn't clear to Blackjack whether they were just leaving or just returning from a ride.

He drove past the ramshackle house and pulled up in front of the weathered barn. "Tom, you take my daughter and put her in her truck and take her home."

"Yessir, Boss," the cowboy said.

"Hurt a hair on her head, and I'll cut out your heart and feed it to you on a platter," Blackjack warned.

"I hear you, Boss," Tom said.

Tom would have to bear whatever punishment his daughter dished out. Summer wouldn't strike out at him, once she realized he wasn't fighting back; she was too fair-minded for that. Once she was gone, Blackjack would be free to deal with Bad Billy Coburn.

Summer looked surprised—and delighted—to see him when he stepped out of his pickup. That delight turned to alarm when she saw the other four men get out of the truck.

"Tom is going to take you home," he announced to her.

She took a step backward and sideways, so she stood between him and Bad Billy Coburn. "What are you doing here, Daddy?"

"I have business with Bad Billy," he replied.

She opened her mouth to argue with him, but Billy put a hand on her shoulder and said, "This is between me and your father, Summer. Go on home."

She looked at him again, then at Billy. "You really have business with Daddy?" she asked suspiciously.

Billy nodded. "Now go on home. I'll see you later."

Blackjack felt his gut twist when he realized his daughter was going to do what Bad Billy Coburn asked without a bit of fuss.

With a defiant look at him, she turned and gave the tall, lean cowboy a kiss on the mouth. "All right, Billy. Just don't let him buffalo you. Daddy's more bark than bite."

One of the cowboys snickered, and Blackjack shot him a look that shut him up.

When Tom started after her, Summer turned to him and said, "I can get home on my own."

Tom touched the brim of his hat and said, "Gotta go with you, Missy. Boss's orders."

She rolled her eyes in disgust, then turned and marched toward her truck without stopping, Tom on her heels.

Blackjack waited until there was nothing but a trail of dust to show she'd been there, before he turned to one of the cowboys and said, "Get the rope." Then he focused his gaze on Bad Billy Coburn.

He hadn't realized how tall Johnny Ray's boy had grown. The kid was lanky, all muscle and sinew. His crow-black hair needed a cut and hung over his frayed collar beneath a dirty gray felt Stetson that was stained with sweat around the braided leather band. His deep-set eyes were dark, his mouth sullen, and his stance defiant. Not a character you'd want to meet on a dark night, Blackjack thought.

"I want you to stay away from my daughter," Blackjack said.

"I'll see Summer so long as she wants to see me," Billy replied.

"I thought you'd say that. I'm here to change your mind."

He watched Billy survey the three hard men arrayed against him. "Is this all the help you brought?" the kid said with a sneer.

Blackjack couldn't help admiring the kid's guts. But he had a point to make. He'd discussed what he wanted done during the drive. All it took was a nod for two of the cowhands, Hardy and Marcus, to reach for Billy's arms, while the third man, Leon, who'd returned with a lariat, tried to get a noose over Billy's head.

He had to hand it to the boy. He didn't go down easy. Billy broke Leon's nose and kicked Marcus in the balls, before the three men were able to wrestle him to the ground and get the rope cinched around his neck.

The kid had dished out plenty of hurt himself, and when Marcus raised his boot to repay Billy by stomping him in the groin, Blackjack caught him by the collar and yanked him away. "This is my fight, not yours."

Marcus shot him a surly look but stepped aside.

"Get him on his feet," Blackjack ordered.

When Billy stood before him again, his hat was gone and his shirt was torn. The boy's nose was crooked and spurting blood, probably Leon's vengeful handiwork. One eye was swollen, and the boy had a split lip. He was breathing hard, and he was mad as a peeled rattler, but he wasn't begging for mercy. He wasn't saying a damned thing.

"I'm gonna give you one more chance to save your hide," Blackjack said. "I want your word you'll stay away from my daughter."

Billy glared at him from his one good eye and said, "You can go to hell."

"Tie him to the corral," Blackjack said.

Billy struggled, but he was no match for the three hard men who hog-tied him to the corner post of the corral.

"Teach him I mean business, boys," Blackjack said.

In the truck he'd told them he wanted the kid roughed up, but he didn't want him in the hospital. But Blackjack hadn't figured on Billy getting his licks in first and enraging the three men he'd brought along.

When Blackjack heard Billy's ribs crack, he said, "That's enough."

Marcus raised his fist to punch Billy again, and Blackjack laid him flat with one blow. "I said that's enough."

He crossed to Billy, grabbed hold of his hair, and yanked his head back. "I don't want you near my daughter. You're not to take her calls or see her if she comes here. Otherwise, I'll be back to finish you off."

"Fuck you," Billy said.

Blackjack admired the boy's grit. But he couldn't afford to let that offense go unpunished. "Someday, you'll learn when to keep your mouth shut."

Blackjack nodded to Hardy, who hit Billy one last time, knocking him unconscious.

"Let's go, boys," he said, as he took one last look at Billy's bloodied face. "We're done here."

Chapter 14

DORA HAD BEEN WASHING LAUNDRY AND hanging it on the clothesline out back because the dryer was broken. She was coming out the kitchen door with another basket of wet clothes, when she realized Jackson Blackthorne's pickup was parked near the barn. It wasn't hard to recognize, with the Circle B brand painted in white across the black cab door. She wondered what he was doing here. And what business he could possibly have with Billy.

Dora frowned, as she watched Blackjack getting back into his pickup—along with three burly cowboys. As they drove away, she suddenly knew why they'd come. She shrieked Billy's name and took off at a run for the barn.

"No no no no no no," she cried. And then, "Please, God. Please, God. Please, God." And again, "No no no no no no."

Dora stopped in her tracks when she saw her firstborn child tied to the corner post of the corral, his face bloody and his body battered. She felt her insides clench and twist. It had always hurt inside whenever Billy had come to her with a cut or a scrape from playing. Or a bruise that Johnny Ray had put there with his fist.

"Billy," she whispered. "Oh, Billy."

She awkwardly dashed the rest of the way, clutching the stitch in her side, heaving for breath, because she hadn't run this far in twenty years. When she was standing before her son, Dora felt a chill of dread go through her.

He looked dead.

His own father killed him. Beat him to death because I complained to that Blackthorne bitch. I should have known better! I should have found some other way to keep the two of them apart. This is all my fault.

The words poured out of her, an apology for all the wrongs it was too late to repair. "I'm so sorry, Billy. So sorry. I should have left the first time Johnny Ray laid a hand on you. I should have stopped him from hitting you. But I was afraid. I was always so afraid. I'm so sorry, baby. I'm so sorry."

She was afraid to touch him, because she might hurt him. Her throat was swollen closed with grief. Because no one could ever hurt him again. Jackson Blackthorne had ended his pain forever.

Dora gently placed her hands on either side of her son's head and lifted his face so she could look at him. She moaned when she saw the damage Blackjack's men had wreaked. "My beautiful baby boy. What have they done to you?"

"Cut me down."

The words startled Dora, and she let go of Billy's head, which flopped forward on his chest. "You're alive!"

"Get me . . . down," he whispered.

Dora fumbled at the knots in the rope, which had drawn impossibly tight with the weight of Billy's sagging body. She wedged her shoulder against his chest to ease the tension on the knots and heard him groan.

"I need help," she cried. "Let me go get Emma."

"No." He gasped with the pain of breathing, but said, "Don't let her . . . see me . . . like this."

"I'll try not to hurt you," Dora whispered.

"Just get me . . . down."

Her fingernails were bitten to the quick, and she couldn't get a good hold on the rough hemp knots. "I can't do it!" she wailed. "They won't come free."

"Keep . . . trying."

Tears blurred her vision as she clawed at the knots. She cried out in joy when the top one came loose. Billy fell toward her, and she quickly braced both palms against his chest to catch him.

He screamed in pain, and she sobbed in desperation. "You have to hold yourself upright."

She thought her heart would break when she saw the excruciating effort he made to do as she asked. When the last knot came free, she circled her arms around him and eased his broken body as carefully as she could toward the ground.

But he was too heavy, and they fell the last foot or so. She knew from his harsh gasp and the hissing breath he took, that she'd hurt him again.

"I've got to go call 911. Will you be all right?"

He grabbed her wrist, and she saw that his knuckles were bruised and the skin broken. Why, oh, why had he tried to fight when the odds were so stacked against him? Johnny Ray would have run as fast and as far as he could.

But, she realized grimly, Billy wasn't Johnny Ray's son. He was a Blackthorne. With every bit of the pride and arrogance and defiance of that breed.

She tried to pull free, so she could call for help, but Billy held on.

"Wait," he gasped. "What are you . . . going to say?"

"I'm going to tell the truth. That Jackson Blackthorne had you brutally beaten."

His tongue came out and slowly traced his split lower lip. "No."

"You can't let him get away with this!" Dora cried.

"Tell them I got . . . stomped by . . . a bull."

"The biggest, baddest bull around," Dora said bitterly. "And his name is Jackson Blackthorne."

"Mom. Please. Do what . . . I ask."

"I don't understand! Why are you protecting him?"

"Not him. Her."

Dora felt her heart squeeze. He must be in love with the girl, if he was willing to protect her from learning about the terrible beating her father had given him. She could no longer keep the truth from her son. He had to be told who he was, so he would understand why he had to stay away from Summer Blackthorne.

She opened her mouth, but the words wouldn't come. She couldn't tell him the truth. He would never be able to forgive her. He would go away and never come back. The truth could wait. There was a little time yet. After he'd healed. Then she'd tell him.

But it couldn't be put off indefinitely. Because she was sure Billy would defy Blackjack and try to see Summer again. And next time Blackjack would kill him. Or he would kill Blackjack. Even outnumbered, he'd fought back this time. Next time Billy would be waiting to meet his father. And there would be patricide . . . or a slaughter of the innocents.

"I'm going to call 911," she said, standing and pulling free of Billy's grasp.

"What are you . . . going to . . . tell them?"

Dora used the elbow-length sleeve of her cotton housedress to wipe her eyes and her runny nose. "I'll tell them you got stomped by a bull."

The paramedics eyed Billy strangely when he persisted in the story his mother had told, but Dora realized they had no choice except to believe him, when they had no other information to go on.

As she watched her son being driven away in the ambulance, red lights flashing and siren blaring, Dora realized what she had to do. It would mean the end of everything. She would lose the ranch, because she couldn't manage without the monthly Blackthorne check. But it was time to do what she should have done twenty-five years ago.

She was going to tell Blackjack he had a son.

Dora stayed at the Bitter Creek General Hospital long enough to learn that Billy had two broken ribs and needed five stitches above his eye, two on the bridge of his nose, twelve along his chin, and nine inside his lip. Both eyes were swollen closed. Miraculously, no teeth had been broken, though several were loose.

The doctor had reset his nose, but it wasn't ever going to be straight again. He had multiple bruises and contusions on his face and body. He also had some internal bleeding, but it had been stopped without operating.

Dora was surprised how cold the air felt when she stepped outside. The heat of the day had fled and left her clutching her bare forearms to stay warm.

She had thought a great deal, while she waited for news about Billy, about when and where to tell Blackjack what she had to say. Eve would likely head her off, if she tried to reach him at the Castle. So it had to be somewhere in town.

Dora recalled reading in the Sunday paper that the Bitter

Creek First National Bank was having a special board meeting that evening. When it was over, Blackjack would go to the Lone Star Cafe. And she would be waiting for him.

BLACKJACK WAS TIRED. THE BANK BOARD MEETING HAD gone on forever and been as contentious as it always was. He headed for his regular booth at the back of the Lone Star Cafe, but to his surprise, someone was already sitting there.

It took him a second to recognize Dora Coburn. She was wearing a bloodstained, flowered cotton dress, and clumps of hair had escaped the bun at her nape and made her look frazzled. He hadn't expected her to confront him about what he'd done to her son. Not here. Not looking like that.

"Sit down, Jackson," she said.

His heart speeded up, and he wondered if this was going to be the time when the patches they'd done on his heart with the veins from his leg decided to give out. "What is it you want, Dora?"

"Sit down, Jackson," she repeated.

In deference to his struggling heart, he slid into the booth opposite her. He sought the waitress's eye, and she brought over a cup of coffee and set it down in front of him.

"You were right, Dora," the waitress said with a wink and a smile. "Here he is."

"There's something I need to discuss with Mr. Blackthorne," Dora said.

"Sure thing," the waitress said. "Just wave if you want more coffee."

Blackjack drank his coffee black and bitter. He took a

small sip, because he could see it was steaming, and he didn't want to burn his tongue. He'd faced down too many men with a grudge not to recognize the look on Dora Coburn's face. He had no remorse for what he'd done. He'd only been protecting his daughter from dangerous riffraff. To his surprise, he couldn't hold Dora's penetrating gaze without lowering his own.

"You shouldn't have done it," she said.

He lifted his gaze to her face and said, "Billy had his chance to do what I asked, but he refused. Then he got in a few punches, and the boys got mad and took it out on him."

"He's your son."

At first, Blackjack wasn't sure he'd heard her right. He looked for some sign that she was joking. But her dark, piercing eyes were staring soberly back at him through cheap plastic frames.

"What?" It was a stupid response to what she'd said, but he couldn't think of what else to say. What she'd suggested was preposterous. Absolutely impossible. "I don't know what you think you're going to accomplish by making up a lie as enormous—"

"I'm not lying," she said inexorably. "I was pregnant with your son when I married Johnny Ray Coburn."

"I don't believe you." He couldn't believe her. If he believed her, he'd just had his own son beaten up by three hard, angry men. If he believed her, his daughter had befriended—and maybe been more than friends with—his son. His body felt cold, and the flesh rose on his arms.

"It's absolutely true," Dora said. "When I went to the Castle to tell you I was pregnant, your wife came to the door, instead. Eve arranged everything. She provided the ranch and the husband and agreed to pay me a stipend—" Dora smiled oddly as she said the word. "For so long as I kept your son a secret from you. I deposited this month's check on Friday."

Blackjack felt the blood draining from his head. His heart was hammering. He reached for his coffee cup, realized his hand was shaking, and balled it into a fist, which he pounded on the table, rattling the spoon against the cheap ceramic cup. "How the hell did this happen?"

"You were there with me, Jackson, in the front seat of your pickup."

"Goddamn it! You should have told me."

"I'm telling you now."

"When it's too late!"

She shook her head. "It's not too late to do something to help your son. Billy's suffered enough. If someone leaves Bitter Creek, it should be your daughter. Send her away. Marry her off. Otherwise, I'm afraid of what might happen."

Blackjack blurted, "You let that bastard Johnny Ray Coburn beat my son."

"Johnny Ray didn't do anything worse than what you just did yourself," she shot back.

"But I didn't *know*!"

"Blame Eve if you don't like the way things turned out," Dora said angrily. "Johnny Ray hated raising your son as his own. He hated the checks, though he was quick enough to spend them on liquor. He thought it was funny—and fitting—that your bastard should end up mucking out stalls at Bitter Creek."

Blackjack groaned and covered his face with his hands. He rubbed at his throbbing temples. How could his wife have done something so cruel as to deny him his child? He wondered if she'd turned to Russell Handy to pay him back for his affair with Dora. But if so, why hadn't she ever flaunted her lover, or told him she knew about his bastard son?

"Didn't you ever notice how much Billy looks like you Blackthornes?" Dora said. "He's tall and lean and has your black hair and your square chin. Or he did, before your men rearranged his face. The only thing about him that's mine are his eyes. They're dark and sullen and angry. Because he's had to fight the world every step of the way, starting with his father."

"His stepfather," Blackjack corrected bitterly. *I have another son.* A son who was a known troublemaker. A son who'd earned the name "Bad" Billy Coburn.

"All you had to do was take one good hard look at Billy to see the truth," Dora was saying. "And he's so smart. He didn't get his brains from my side of the family. I barely got through high school. Billy loves to read, and he's always dreaming and planning how someday—"

"He can have his dreams," Blackjack interrupted. He owed his blood that. "I'll give him the money to do whatever he wants with his life. But he has to leave Bitter Creek."

Dora shook her head. "That's not fair. You can't send my son away."

"Summer's staying," Blackjack said. "And one of them has to go."

Dora made a disgusted sound in her throat. "He won't leave her. Haven't you figured that out yet?"

Blackjack frowned. "You haven't told him I'm his father? That any relationship with Summer is impossible?"

"Why should I be the one to hurt my child? Billy's been hurt enough. Why don't you tell your daughter the truth? Let her break it off."

"Summer is not to hear a word about this. Do you understand me? Nothing!" He didn't want his daughter knowing he'd been unfaithful to her mother. He didn't want her knowing she had a bastard brother, who'd become her best friend—and maybe, God forbid, more. He didn't want her burdened with his mistakes. She was the light of his life. He loved her more than anyone in this world, and he would give anything, sacrifice anything, to protect her.

"I tried to tell Billy the truth," Dora said. "I couldn't do it."

"Maybe that's for the best," Blackjack said. "He doesn't have to know. He can just leave town. I'll make him an offer he can't refuse."

"That sounds like a threat."

"He can't stay, Dora. He has to go. And I don't want Summer knowing why he's leaving."

"You always were a selfish bastard, Jackson."

"I never said I wasn't."

Blackjack left the Lone Star Cafe and went straight to the hospital. There was no sense postponing what had to be done.

He didn't expect the sudden ache in his gut when he pushed open Bad Billy Coburn's hospital door and stepped inside the dimly lit room.

His son—his bastard son—was covered with a white sheet to his waist and had a tube strapped to his arm and running to a bag of some clear liquid. A green-faced monitor beeped steadily, proving that the battered figure on the bed was still alive.

Blackjack walked to the edge of the bed and looked down on his son. Billy's rangy Blackthorne body filled the bed from top to bottom. The boy's black hair—

Blackthorne hair—was lank and needed a trim. His square Blackthorne chin was stitched across the center. His nose was swollen to twice its size, and the hospital had put some sort of cold compress over his eyes, apparently to reduce the swelling.

"Who's there?" the boy said.

Blackjack cleared his throat, which had swollen closed. He didn't understand the feelings roiling inside him. He'd planted the seed, that was all. But he couldn't help feeling connected to the weed that had sprouted. This was his son. His blood. Stolen from him and kept a secret for twenty-five years. Damn Dora and Eve both!

He wondered what he would have done if Dora had found him that day. Would he have urged her to give up the child for adoption? Would he have offered her money to raise it? Or would he have brought the child into his home and made him a part of his family?

Eve would never have stood for that. She must have realized—as he was realizing now—that he would never have given away what belonged to him. That he would have kept his bastard son and dared the world to point a finger at him. His indiscretion would have been exposed for all the world to see. Eve had avoided the problem by making sure he never knew about the child in the first place.

He felt a welling of sorrow for what he'd lost. A welling of regret for what his son had suffered. A welling of deep, coal-black anger for what his wife had taken from him.

"Who's there?" the boy repeated.

"Jackson Blackthorne," he managed to say.

The boy made an animal sound in his throat and reached up to yank the compress from his eyes. The boy's dark eyes, barely visible through his slitted eyelids, burned with hatred. "Get out," he rasped.

Blackjack saw more stitches above the boy's right eye and on the bridge of his nose. "I'll have a plastic surgeon fix up your face."

"Get out."

Blackjack saw how much effort it took the boy just to speak. He remembered the sound of his son's ribs breaking and felt his gut clench. "You've got some busted ribs. Makes it hard to breathe. Just lie there and listen to me."

The boy tried to rise, groaned, and lay back down.

Blackjack put a hand on his son's bare shoulder and felt his heart squeeze with emotion. "Stay down. You're only hurting yourself."

"Get your hands . . . off me."

Blackjack jerked his hand away when he heard the venom in Billy's voice.

"What are you . . . doing here?" the boy demanded.

"I want you gone from Bitter Creek."

"Go to hell."

"I'll give you enough money—"

"Put it where the . . . sun don't shine."

Blackjack's lips flattened. He saw the insolence, the obstinance, and the determination of a dozen generations of Blackthornes in his bastard son, and admired him for it. But nobody—not even this newfound son of his—told him no.

"You're leaving, Billy. Make up your mind to it. One way or another."

"My mother needs me."

Blackjack saw the concession of pride it took for the boy to make such a plea, humbling himself for the sake of his mother. And acknowledged two more Blackthorne traits in

Bad Billy Coburn—duty and responsibility. And damn
Dora again for letting that no-good Johnny Ray Coburn
beat the crap out of her son—and, by God, his son—until
Billy got big enough to stand up for himself.

"I'll pay whatever you think she'll need to make ends
meet," Blackjack said.

Billy was already shaking his head, and Blackjack
could see it physically hurt him to do it. "I won't be . . .
bought off."

Blackjack knew damn well what was keeping Bad
Billy Coburn in Bitter Creek, Texas. He knew what he
had to say to get the boy to leave.

"I'm your father."

He hadn't meant to blurt it out that way. He saw the
shock in Billy's eyes. The need for denial.

"Can't be—" the boy rasped.

"It's true," Blackjack interrupted. "I didn't find out
until today. Your mother came to me, wanting to know
how I could beat up my own son."

He recognized the moment when Bad Billy Coburn
realized the significance of being Jackson Blackthorne's
son. *He was related to Summer Blackthorne by blood.*

The guttural sound that issued from Billy's throat was
filled with such anguish, such incredible suffering, that
Blackjack hurt inside. When he stepped forward to offer
comfort, the boy lurched upright, grabbing at his ribs,
biting his already wounded lips to hold back his cry of
agony.

Blackjack was stopped in his tracks by the virulence
in his son's voice as he spat, "You've delivered . . . your
message. Now . . . get out."

It was clear Bad Billy Coburn didn't want a damned

thing from him. But he wanted something from his son. He wanted his silence. And he wanted him gone.

"You can see how it wouldn't be smart for you to see my daughter anymore," Blackjack said. "She doesn't know who you are. And I'd like to keep it that way."

"I'll bet you would," Billy muttered.

"I don't want her hurt," Blackjack said. "And I don't think you want that, either."

Billy looked at him with dull black eyes. The fight had gone out of him. "No," he said. "I don't."

"Like I said, I'll take care of your mother and sister. And I want to do something for you, if you'll let me. I—"

"There's nothing—"

Blackjack held up a hand. "I wasn't going to give you something for nothing."

"I don't—"

"Let me finish," Blackjack said irritably. "Then, if you don't want what I'm offering, you can turn me down."

Billy gave a jerky nod.

Blackjack took a deep breath and said, "I'm a past president of the Texas and Southwestern Cattle Raisers Association. I've got a lot of favors owed from friends. If you want, I can set you up as a field inspector for the Association."

"You need . . . a college degree to—"

Blackjack waved him into silence, but he was surprised that Billy knew the requirements for the job. "I can have that requirement waived," Blackjack said. "At least temporarily. You'd probably have to go back nights and get a degree, if you think you could handle that."

Billy said nothing. But he wasn't interrupting, so Blackjack kept talking. "A field inspector enforces the law—hunts down rustlers and horse thieves, carries a gun, and has the power to arrest wrongdoers. Think you can handle that?"

Instead of responding to the question, Billy said, "You said there's . . . a price . . . to be paid."

"I want you working as far from Bitter Creek, Texas, as it's possible to get. And you will make sure my daughter hates the sight of you before you leave."

"Done."

Blackjack wasn't sure he'd heard right, Billy's voice was so soft. When the boy stuck out his hand to seal the bargain, Blackjack knew he'd gotten what he wanted. He was surprised by the strength of Billy's grasp, and by the directness of his gaze. Until he remembered how Dora had faced him down. There was good blood there, too, he realized. As he shook his son's hand, Blackjack conceded that Bad Billy Coburn was a man to be reckoned with.

Which made him angry all over again. Not at Billy. At his wife, who'd robbed him of the chance of knowing his son. There was no way to turn back the clock. No way to recapture those lost years. And no way to go forward from here. "Good luck," Blackjack said.

"Don't need luck," Billy said. "Don't need anything . . . from anybody."

Blackjack left the hospital thinking how fast the twenty-five years since Billy's birth had passed. And how, if he wasn't careful, he could end up spending the next twenty-five years married to a woman he no longer loved, instead of sleeping at night beside a woman he'd loved for longer than the thirty-three years he'd been married.

It was time he did something to rectify the situation.

When he got home, he found Eve in the study, poring over his business papers, something she'd been doing a great deal lately. Maybe she'd known all along that he would one day make the choice he'd made in his son's hospital room. Maybe she'd known all along that when push came to shove, he'd choose Lauren Creed over a parcel of land, even if that land had been in his family for generations.

He stood in front of the desk, his hands balled into fists at his sides, and waited for her to look up and acknowledge him.

She lifted her head, removed her reading glasses, and said, "What is it, Jackson?"

"I want out."

"I don't."

"You can have it all. Take whatever you want. I'm through with you."

She laid her reading glasses carefully on the desk and looked up at him, her blue eyes wide with alarm. "What is this all about?"

"You heard me. I've had it. I'm done with you."

"What brought this on?" she asked, leaning back casually, resting her elbows on the arms of the swivel chair, and letting her hands fall into a soft knot in her lap.

"I went to the hospital and spoke with my son. The son you kept a secret from me."

She lifted a brow. "Why would you give a damn about a saddle tramp like Bad Billy Coburn?"

"Because he wouldn't have been a saddle tramp if I'd known about him twenty-five years ago!" Blackjack raged.

"I did what I had to do. It's over and done."

"The hell it is! You let me leave this house today knowing I would be shedding blood of my blood. May you rot in hell for it!"

"If we're comparing sins, what about Dora?" she demanded, rising abruptly to her feet.

"She was a one-night stand."

"How many other one-night stands were there?"

"This is getting us nowhere. I want you out of my life."

"If I leave you, Jackson, I'm taking everything."

"Take it all! I don't give a damn. Just get out of my sight."

"Very well. Summer and I will leave in the morning. My lawyer will be in touch with you."

"Summer stays here."

Eve sat back down, carefully crossed her legs, straightening her skirt exactly to her knees, then swiveled the chair slowly back and forth. She met his gaze and said, "Summer goes with me, Jackson."

"Summer is my daughter and—"

"No, she's not."

Blackjack felt his knees buckle and managed to fall into one of the horn-and-rawhide chairs in front of the desk. He couldn't catch his breath. His heart was pounding so hard he put a hand to his chest to hold it there, as he stared with stricken eyes at his gloating wife.

"Ah," she said. "Gotcha."

"When? Who?" Then he knew. The only person it could be. "Russell Handy." He saw her smile as he said the name of his *segundo,* his right-hand man, the man she'd had an affair with all those years ago.

"Why did you do it?" he asked. "Because of Dora?"

She shrugged. "That was part of it, I suppose. He paid attention to me. He loved me. Loves me still, I believe."

"Are you sure Summer's not mine? There's no chance you're mistaken?"

"If you'd paid the least attention, you'd have seen that she looks nothing like you. You're not Summer's father. Russell Handy is."

"The law—"

"The law has nothing to do with this. If you want to keep your daughter, you'll have to keep me, as well."

"Once I tell her—"

"Tell her what? That her mother had a tawdry affair, and that her real father is in prison for murder? Of course, if you reveal my sin, I'd have to reveal yours. When shall we tell your beloved daughter that she's fallen in love with a man who should have been her brother—your bastard son?"

Blackjack realized that she meant what she said. If he tried to leave his wife, she would ruin their daughter's life. He would have given Eve everything he had to escape his marriage. But he couldn't win his freedom at the price of his daughter's happiness. He made one last effort to convince his wife of the futility of continuing a marriage that was in ashes.

"Why won't you let me go? I loathe you. I despise you. I will never spend another night in your bed. For God's sake, I love another woman."

Eve smiled bitterly. "She has your love. I'll have you. I think that's a fair division of the spoils."

Chapter 15

BAY HAD FEARED THAT OWEN WOULD DEVELOP a worse infection, or that his fever would get dangerously high, and she wouldn't have the right herbal medicines to help him. None of that happened. In fact, the morning after his operation, her patient was more ornery than anything else.

"I don't understand how you can spring back so quickly," Bay said. "Yesterday I thought you were at death's door."

"It's my superior genes."

"Oh, please. If anything, it was my superior surgery."

"From the way you described those stitches in my back, I expect to be able to attend Halloween parties as Frankenstein without wearing a costume," Owen said.

Bay grimaced. "Not my best work. I thought having a few big stitches without anesthetic was better than having lots of neat little ones."

"For once we agree wholeheartedly on something."

"Are you really feeling as okay as you sound?" Bay asked, as she laid her palm on Owen's forehead to check his temperature.

He pushed her hand away. "Mothers do that. I'm a

grown man. There's a thermometer in the first-aid kit that'll give you an accurate reading."

"I don't need a thermometer. I'd say your temperature's 101 degrees. Above normal, but where I expected it to be."

"You want to make a bet on that?" Owen said.

She opened the first-aid kit, retrieved and shook the thermometer, and handed it to him. "Be my guest. What's at stake here?"

"Your professional reputation."

She lifted a brow. "Would you like to put your money where your mouth is?"

"What have you got in mind, Red?"

"We've stretched our rations, but now we're running low on water. If I'm right, I want to know what you think our chances are of getting out of here alive."

"Done. And if you're wrong—"

"Stick that thing under your tongue," she said. "And leave it there till I tell you to take it out."

Bay poured Owen another cup of mesquite tea and said, "Sit up."

Since he was lying on his stomach, Owen had to push himself upright with his arms. He hissed in a breath as the stitches in his back protested.

"Be careful," she said, as she handed him the cup.

"Believe me," he said around the thermometer. "I'm not making any fast moves."

She checked her watch, then said, "Okay. Take a look."

"I'll be damned. One hundred and one degrees on the nose. How'd you do that?"

"Practice. Now tell me. What are our chances?"

He sipped his tea and made a face. "You've got me over a barrel here, Red. I don't want to lie. But—"

"I want the unvarnished truth."

He met her worried gaze and said, "What is it you think is going to happen?"

She shrugged, unwilling to admit how scared she was. "I don't understand why no one's come looking for us."

"Lots of folks are probably looking for us. They can't find us here because of all that overhead camouflage."

"Why don't we tear it down?"

"That's a good idea. Have you figured out how we're going to get up that high?"

She grimaced as she looked up at the cliffs from which the netting was hung. "Nope."

"That's all right. I don't think we want to do that anyway until I've recovered enough physically that I can handle whoever comes through that opening in the cliffs."

"It isn't going to matter how healthy you are, if they show up with guns," Bay said. "We won't be able to defend ourselves."

Owen made a *tsking* sound. "Oh, ye of little faith. We can set booby traps to take care of them."

"What if they get past them?"

"They won't. Besides, I have some other tricks up my sleeve."

No matter how many suggestions Owen made for ways they could protect themselves, Bay wasn't convinced she was going to get out of the camp alive. Her fatalistic vision of the future caused her to see everything in a different perspective.

And made her reckless.

Over the next few days, as Owen recuperated, Bay let

herself enjoy looking at his masculine physique. At his sinewy arms. At his powerful hands. At his rugged jaw and sharp nose. At his washboard stomach and flat belly. At his muscular thighs and calves and feet.

She told herself that she only touched him to find out whether he was still feverish. But she managed to caress his face. And the small of his back. And the backs of his knees. She imagined his mouth doing all kinds of things to her.

Bay did all those things because they brought her pleasure, and because she figured she ought to enjoy the last few days of her life.

She hadn't really considered the effect all that touching might have on the man in question. Until he started returning the favor.

At first she thought she was imagining it. His fingers lingered on hers as she handed him another cup of mesquite tea. He tucked her hair behind her ear when she was bent over him, to help get it out of her way. His hand rested on her knee as she sat beside him checking the stitches on his back. And his eyes followed her everywhere.

As Bay warmed up the last of the *MREs* for supper, she realized that her idyll with Owen was over. Now that the military rations were gone, they had to do something to get themselves out of here, or they were going to starve to death. Actually, they would probably die of thirst before that happened, since they only had two days' worth of water left.

Bay set down her spoon and asked, "Why haven't you ever gotten married?"

Owen lifted a brow. "I could say the job keeps me too busy to have a wife. But that's not true. I'd like to be married. I've simply never found the right woman."

"What about kids?" Bay held her breath waiting for his answer. And then had to breathe, because he didn't answer right away. Although she'd had unprotected sex with Owen, she didn't have to worry that she was pregnant. Which should have been a comfort, but never was. It hurt to be reminded that she was a woman who could not bear children.

"It might be nice to have a couple of kids," he said at last. "I'm not sure what kind of father I'd make."

"You mean because you didn't have a good role model?"

Owen smiled. "I guess I'll always see my father with different eyes than you do. I think most parents do the best they know how. My father taught hard lessons, because he believed it's as true of men as it is in nature— only the strong survive."

Bay had been a vet long enough to know that Owen had made a valid point. The weak died during hard times—or were overpowered and devoured by those stronger than themselves. "Maybe those weren't such bad lessons to learn," she said. "My father taught me you never quit."

"Sounds more like plain old muleheaded stubbornness to me."

"If my father hadn't been so stubborn, your father would have owned Three Oaks a long time ago."

"Touché," Owen said. "I guess I would like to have kids someday. To pass on what I've learned about life. To share some of the good times. To leave a part of myself behind for posterity."

Bay felt her heart sink. It was one more confirmation of her belief that most men chose a wife not only for companionship and sex, but because she had qualities he wanted to see in his children. Which made a lot of sense when you'd grown up on a ranch and knew full well that you bred the best bull to the best cow to get the best calf.

Unfortunately, she'd let herself imagine what it might be like to have a relationship with Owen Blackthorne. Their lives might have fit together very well.

During the day, she'd be busy helping animals in trouble, while he'd be busy helping people in trouble.

In the evenings, they'd come home to their rustic cabin on the Pedernales River near Fredericksburg, sit on a big wooden swing hanging from the back porch rafters, and watch the sun set in golden majesty.

On weekends, they'd head for the smoke-filled bars off Congress Avenue in Austin, where famous country-and-western performers dropped in to play a set, and where they could waltz and do the Texas two-step and the cotton-eyed Joe.

In the spring, bluebonnets and Indian paintbrush would create a patchwork quilt of violet and orange around them, and they'd blow up tubes from giant tractor tires and float lazily down the river for hours and hours.

At Thanksgiving they'd head back to South Texas to celebrate with . . .

Bay's imaginary balloon burst.

To which family's ranch could she and Owen go and be sure they'd both be welcome? *Neither one.*

What would happen at Christmas? Her family always gathered for the holidays. Trace and a pregnant Callie had come all the way from Australia last year and brought Bay's niece and nephew. What would happen if she tried to put Owen and Sam in the same room together? Or Owen and Luke?

She shuddered at the thought of sitting down to

Christmas turkey at the Castle with the person—or per-
sons—who'd arranged her father's murder. Never. Not
ever could she do that. Bay understood now what might
have motivated Callie and Trace to go all the way to Australia to live. Maybe the solution for her and Owen would
be to stay in Fredericksburg and let whoever wanted to
visit come and see them.

Bay couldn't believe she was spending all this time
working out solutions to imaginary problems. No romantic relationship had ever existed between her and Owen
Blackthorne—other than a brief sexual liaison. And none
ever would.

Except maybe *another* brief sexual liaison.

"Hey, Red. Penny for your thoughts."

Bay flushed. Was the man a mind reader? Well, he'd
asked, hadn't he? "I was thinking of sex, if you must
know."

"Great minds think alike," he said with a grin.

"Your back isn't—"

"It'll have to be the missionary position, Red, since
my back's still a patchwork quilt. Wait. I have a better
idea. Why don't I sit right here, and you come get on my
lap."

Bay stared at him, not quite sure whether he was serious.

Owen got up and turned the short wooden bench away
from the table to make room for her, then patted his
thighs. "I'm ready."

Bay's skin felt hot all over. "Are we really going to do
this?"

"There's no TV show I want to watch. Monopoly's
out. Don't have a deck of cards. Couldn't handle another
one of your bedtime stories. I think this is probably the

best entertainment we're going to be able to come up with tonight."

Bay laughed. "You're crazy." But she was enticed.

He curled his index finger and gestured her toward him. "Come here, Red. Let me take off your clothes."

That prospect was even more beguiling. "All right. You asked for it."

"I just can't believe I'm going to get it," he said with a grin that made her body coil with pleasure.

Bay knew she'd have to be careful of Owen's stitches, but that should be simple, if all she did was sit facing him on his lap. She pulled off her boots and socks while she was still sitting across from him, then rose and walked barefoot on the sandy soil until she was standing in front of him.

"Let's see. Where to start," he said as he looked up at her. Their eyes met, and she saw his need. And the heat of desire.

"Maybe I ought to do a little touching through this cloth before I remove it," he said, as he splayed his hand across her belly. "Spread your legs for me, Red."

Bay did as he asked, feeling open and exposed and vulnerable, even though she was still fully clothed. She set her hands on his shoulders to steady herself, as he slid his hand down between her legs and nudged them even wider.

"You feel soft, Red," he said, his voice low and rough.

His touch was certain, adept and unerring. In no time at all, her knees were threatening to buckle. She settled onto his lap facing him, still clothed.

"Two can play this game," she said, as she slid her hand down between them and held him the way he was holding her.

She watched his eyes flare with heat as she measured the size of him with her hand. She loved hearing him groan, as her thumb traced the shape of him. She leaned forward, and their mouths met and meshed.

So much feeling. It hurt. Because it felt like the last time. It couldn't be much longer before something happened. They would be rescued and separated forever by the feud between their families. Or they would die here together.

The two hands that lay between them, his and hers, found one another and were suddenly woven tight.

Bay looked into Owen's eyes and said, "I wish . . ."

"What is it you want, Red? Tell me."

She shrugged. "I wish things were different. That's all."

"Trace and Callie made it work," he said softly. "Why couldn't we?"

"Trace and Callie escaped to Australia to make it work. You've already said you won't leave Texas, which means we'd have to deal with our families. I can tell you with some certainty that Sam will never forgive you. A camp for kids with disabilities won't give him back his legs."

She put a hand on Owen's lips to stop him from interrupting. "Even if Sam were willing to pardon you, I can never forgive your mother for what she did to my father."

"That sounds like a quitter talking."

Bay flushed. They already knew each other well enough to know which words would hurt. "I wouldn't give up if I felt there was any hope we could make this work. I don't like to quit. But I know when to walk away."

"So what was this supposed to be?" he asked as he grabbed her thighs and pulled her tight against his arousal.

"Good-bye," she whispered.

"Then we'd better get it right."

He shoved her off his lap and stood her upright so he could unsnap and unzip her trousers. He yanked them down, along with her underwear and said, "Get out of those and come here."

While she was freeing her feet from her trousers, he unsnapped and unzipped his own pants and peeled open the fly, freeing his erection. He grabbed her by the waist and yanked her toward him, lifting and spreading her legs as he pulled her downward, so she barely had time to latch onto his shoulders before he was buried inside her to the hilt.

His eyes burned into hers with anger. His hands gripped her hips as he held them bound together. She could feel him pulsing inside her.

"What are you waiting for?" she demanded. "Finish it."

"If this is going to be the last time, Red, I'm damn well going to take my time!"

And he did.

Bay was drenched with sweat long before he brought her to climax. And he wasn't satisfied with doing it once. He brought her joy again, before he filled her with his seed, unaware that there was no fertile ground in which it could grow and bear fruit.

She collapsed against him, her arms clutching his neck, her mouth pressed tightly against his flesh to prevent the wail of sorrow that sought voice. She swallowed back one sob before another broke free.

Owen held her tight against him, his hands smoothing her hair, his voice a comforting murmur. "It's okay, Red. We'll figure something out. This doesn't have to be the end of things between us."

"You don't understand," she wailed.

"Of course I do."

"No, you don't," she persisted. "I can't have babies. I can never give you children, Owen. I'm sterile."

"Oh, God. I'm so sorry, Red."

Bay lifted her head to look into his eyes. "I'm sorry, too," she whispered. "You see why it wouldn't be worth the effort of solving all those other problems to be together when there's this much bigger problem that can't be solved."

"How did you find out you're sterile?" he asked.

"I wasn't born that way. I got pregnant when I was raped," she said. "And . . . things went wrong."

He closed his eyes and bit his lip.

"Do you want to hear the rest?"

He nodded without opening his eyes.

"It was an ectopic pregnancy—where the egg starts growing in the fallopian tube instead of waiting until it gets to the womb. I ended up in the hospital, and when I got out of surgery, the doctor said I wouldn't be able to get pregnant again, because one of my fallopian tubes would be blocked by scar tissue."

Owen opened his eyes. "*One* would be blocked?"

"I latched on to that hope for a long time myself," she said. "Remember that professor I told you about? The one I fell in love with? I did my best to have his baby, but I never got pregnant. When he found out what I was doing, he admitted he had a wife and kids, and that was the end of that."

"Lots of people adopt kids. Or maybe a fertility clinic can harvest eggs and—"

Bay kissed him sweetly on the mouth. "You're a good man, Owen Blackthorne. I never thought I'd be saying that," she admitted with a smile. "Would you really be happy raising someone else's kids?"

"They wouldn't be someone else's kids, damn it! They'd be ours."

Bay stared at Owen. "You can't want to adopt."

"Why not?"

"It's—"

"Too easy?" Owen challenged.

Bay stared at him. Her entire adult life she'd felt unlovable, because she was unable to conceive a child. Here was a man telling her that it didn't matter one bit to him whether she could bear children or not.

Bay used her hands to lever herself out of Owen's lap, and as their bodies separated, she stepped away from him. She was suddenly cold, as the night air hit her un-protected flesh. She bent and picked up her underwear and put it on, then pulled on her trousers, as Owen re-dressed himself.

She was sitting across from him, pulling on her socks, when he leaned forward, his elbows on his knees, and said, "I've tried telling myself that what I feel when I look at you is merely the result of being isolated with a beautiful woman in a life-and-death situation."

Bay felt goose bumps rise on her arms. She was a *beautiful woman*? "That must be what it is," Bay said as she pulled on her boots. "I mean, here we are having sex when we hardly know each other."

"I wouldn't go that far," Owen said.

"Then what's my favorite color?" Bay asked.

"Blue."

She smiled smugly. "You're guessing, and you're wrong."

"What is it?"

"Green. What kind of movies do I like?"

"Romantic comedies."

Bay's eyes widened in surprise. "How did you know that?"

"You're a romantic from the top of your head to the tip of your boots."

"How do you figure that?" Bay asked.

"You could have settled for sex with that professor of yours. But you wanted love and family and happily ever after."

Bay met Owen's forthright gaze. "That's all the more reason for me to keep my distance from you. With us—because of our families—there can't be a happily ever after."

"Maybe not," Owen conceded with a sigh. "But we can—"

The distinctive *whup, whup, whup* of a helicopter could be heard in the distance. Bay looked at Owen, and they both jumped up from the table and ran toward the crevice in the cliffs that led to the open space where they expected the helicopter to land.

"You know what to do," Owen said.

"What if this doesn't work?"

"It'll work. Do exactly what we planned, exactly as we planned it."

He had already turned to leave when Bay called him back. "Owen, wait!"

She ran to him and gave him a hug. "Be careful."

He gave her a kiss and ruffled her hair. "Don't worry about me, Red. I'll be fine."

He turned and disappeared into the crevice in the limestone, leaving Bay behind in the valley to wait.

Chapter 16

OWEN'S PLAN WAS SIMPLE. HE WOULD WAIT until the helicopter landed and whoever was in it stepped out, then detonate a claymore mine that had been placed where it wouldn't hurt anyone, but would be sure to make a lot of noise and send whoever had flown in on the helicopter diving for cover. He would then take advantage of the confusion to grab whatever weapons he could and gain the upper hand.

Owen heaved a sigh of relief when he realized there were only two men in the helicopter. He recognized them as the two Dobermans. They were wearing suits, which suggested they'd come from either Alpine or Midland.

He was a little concerned when they both stepped out of the helicopter with Uzis. Especially if all they'd expected to find here was Luke Creed's dehydrated body. He waited until he was sure they were both clear of the helicopter before he detonated the claymore.

Owen was already moving when both agents lunged for the ground. As he'd expected, they both landed facedown, with their hands cupped over their heads to protect them. He grabbed one Uzi from the ground where it had landed and kicked the other as far away as he could. He had to wait for broken rocks to stop falling before he could say, "Stay down. Extend your arms in front of you, so I can see your hands."

When James Brophy reached toward his suit coat, Owen shot a burst from the Uzi near his feet. "Let me see your hands."

"All right. Give me a second."

"A second's all you've got," Owen said.

When both agents lay prone with their hands in front of them, he fired two shots to let Bay know it was safe for her to join him, instead of three, which was the universal distress signal, and would have meant she should detonate the booby traps they'd laid. To his chagrin, she stepped out of the crevice a moment later.

"I told you to wait at the camp!"

"I wanted to be able to help if anything went wrong."

Brophy lifted his head, and Owen said, "Stay down." He turned to Bay and said, "Bring me that other Uzi." When she returned, he hung it over his shoulder by the sling.

Brophy said, "I thought you were dead." He looked toward the crevice. "Where's the kid?"

Owen lifted a brow and exchanged a look with Bay. "You don't know?"

"I left him tied up in the tent with your brother Clay watching over him."

"You took your sweet time getting back," Bay said angrily. "They could have died of thirst by now."

Brophy shrugged. "It wasn't possible to get here because—"

The other agent said, "Keep your mouth shut."

"What kind of organization am I dealing with?" Owen

asked. "Foreign terrorists? White supremacists? Munitions dealers? Who are you working for?"

The two agents exchanged a look before Brophy said, "Shove it up your—"

"There's a lady present," Owen interrupted. "Watch your mouth."

Bay held out the looped rope they'd turned into makeshift handcuffs and said, "Shall I put them on now?"

"You gents put your hands behind your back—one hand at a time—and stay still for the lady."

Brophy glanced at the helicopter, which only had two seats and said, "What are you going to do with us?"

Owen's eyes narrowed. "We're going to leave you here, like you left that boy."

Owen watched carefully as Bay leaned over to place a rope around the first agent's wrist. Before she could tighten the knot, both agents leaped to their feet and charged, Brophy at Bay and the other man at Owen.

The agent coming toward Owen had already pulled the gun from his shoulder holster when the first spray of bullets from Owen's Uzi caught him in the chest and threw him backward. By the time Owen had angled the gun toward Brophy, he had Bay in his grasp, his hand around her neck in a half nelson, so all it would take was a little pressure to break her neck.

"Hey, Terry," Brophy called to his partner.

"He's dead," Owen said flatly.

"Damn you! I ought to break her neck."

"You'd be a dead man before she hit the ground."

"Drop the gun," Brophy said. "And back up."

Owen shook his head.

Brophy applied pressure to Bay's neck until she groaned.

"All right," Owen said, extending the Uzi in front of him as though he might drop it at any moment. "Maybe we can make a deal."

"No deals. Put down that Uzi and—"

Bay moved so fast, Brophy never knew what hit him. One moment he had Bay in a chokehold, the next she had broken free, and he was on the ground.

Brophy reached into his coat for a weapon, but he was a second too late. Owen's bullet had already found his heart.

Owen saw the stricken look on Bay's face as she stared at the carnage. "I had no choice," he said.

"I know," she whispered. "I just . . ."

Owen crossed to her and pulled her into his arms. "You did good, Red. You did great."

"I never thought I'd have to use those self-defense lessons," she said.

She was trembling, and Owen wished the two men alive again so he could punish them for frightening her so badly.

"We need to get out of here," he said.

"We can't just leave them here," Bay protested.

"We'll send the cavalry back for them," Owen promised, as he collected the ID from the unidentified agent. "Terry Watkins," he muttered. "Who the hell are you working for—besides the FBI?"

He turned to Bay and said, "Do you think you can fly that helicopter?"

Her gaze shot to the Bell helicopter. She nodded. "Yeah. I can fly it."

"Let's get the hell out of here."

Owen collected the two agents' SIG-Sauers and

barely had time to put on his seat belt, before Bay had the helicopter in the air. The instant he was wearing his headset, Bay said, "Who do you want me to contact first?"

"I don't want to call anyone just yet," he said. "Especially not on an open radio frequency."

"My mother and my brother Sam must be frantic with worry."

"A few hours more won't make any difference," Owen said. "Better not to let anyone know where we are for now."

"Why not? Who is it you're afraid of?"

Owen grimaced. "That's the problem. I don't know who I can trust."

"Where do you want to go?" she asked.

"Can we get back home?"

Bay tapped the fuel gauge and said, "Don't think so. What's your second choice?"

Owen thought a moment and said, "I guess the person I most want to see is Paul Ridgeway."

"If I had to guess, I'd say he's one of the bad guys," Bay said.

"He's not going to be able to do anything to us at the FBI office in Midland. I want to see his face when I tell him we left two dead FBI agents in the Big Bend with the VX mines."

"I'm confused," Bay said. "If they didn't know what happened to Luke—"

"It means my brother rescued him, like I said. We'll find out for sure when I confront Paul and—"

"I know Paul Ridgeway is a friend of yours," Bay interrupted.

"Not a friend," Owen corrected. "An almost-relation."

"What if Ridgeway denies that he's involved? What

are you going to do then? After all, he's in charge of the investigation. Who's going to investigate him?"

Owen frowned. "Paul's a man who's devoted his life to maintaining law and order. I can't imagine why he'd be involved with something like this."

"Maybe he needs the money," Bay said. "Or maybe he went a little crazy after his daughter was murdered."

"And what? Became a terrorist? I don't buy it."

"Well, the Dobermans obviously aren't at the top of the food chain," Bay said. "Someone they know is running the show."

"Maybe they needed the money. Maybe they hired themselves out to some Colombian drug lord who wants to wipe out the competition," Owen said.

Bay sighed. "I suppose anything is possible. But I can't believe they could be flying an FBI helicopter in and out of the Big Bend without Paul Ridgeway noticing—which suggests to me that he's involved."

"Not necessarily."

"I don't want to argue. I just want to call my mom at the first opportunity and let her know I'm all right and find out if Luke has shown up."

"Fine. I better check in with my boss, too, and let him know what's going on."

Navigating was simple with all the instruments available in the helicopter. It was early evening when they landed at the Midland-Odessa Airport. It looked deserted.

When the rotors stopped, Bay turned to him, her eyes brimming with tears, and smiled. "We made it."

Owen felt his throat thicken with emotion. "Yeah, Red. We did."

"Look at us," she said, pulling at her filthy T-shirt and shoving her lank auburn hair off her shoulders. She reached out and brushed at his ten-day-old beard. "We look like derelicts." She sniffed and said, "Whew! I smell wood smoke . . . and me . . . and you."

Owen laughed. "We may be a little rank, but we're alive."

"Yeah," she said with a smile. "We are."

It seemed like the most natural thing in the world to kiss her. He leaned halfway and she leaned halfway and they met in the middle of the cockpit.

It felt like coming home. It felt like a toasty fire on a bitter cold night. He broke the kiss and looked deeply into her eyes, to see if she felt it, too.

What he saw was fear. And denial.

"Everything I felt in the Big Bend is still there," he said. "And we're nowhere near the wilderness."

He saw her swallow before she said, "It won't work, Owen. I'll always have fond memories—"

"Damn it, Red. Don't you dare give up on us! Don't you quit!"

She made an angry sound in her throat, shoved open the helicopter door, and climbed down. He started to follow her and realized he was still belted in. He left the Uzis, but he checked the rounds on one of the SIGs, then stuck it in the back of his camouflage pants and covered it with his T-shirt. He finally caught up to Bay halfway across the tarmac.

"I don't see why it's necessary for me to stay with you any longer," she said. "I can just as easily make my calls and ask my questions about Luke on my own."

"Oh, no you don't. If Ridgeway is involved, he isn't going to want any witnesses left behind. Let me call my boss and see what he wants me to do."

"I'll stay long enough for you to make your call. Then I'm gone," she said.

They found an outbuilding with a pay telephone, so they wouldn't have to walk through the terminal looking like the terrorists they were hunting.

"Why don't we try calling your brother first?" Bay suggested as Owen picked up the receiver. "To see if he really did rescue Luke."

"That's not a half-bad idea, Red."

Owen made a collect call to his brother's office in Austin and was annoyed when no one would accept the charges. He made the call again, person-to-person to Clay Blackthorne, and was told that his party wasn't available to accept the call. He made a third call, person-to-person to Clay's secretary. She answered and said, "Where's Clay?"

"That's what I was going to ask you," Owen said.

"We haven't seen him for a week," his secretary replied. "Nobody knows what's happened to him. It isn't like him to disappear without a word. Do you know where he is?"

"No, I don't," Owen said, perplexed. "Thanks, Sylvia," he said, and hung up the phone.

"What did you find out?" Bay asked.

"Clay hasn't shown up for work in a week. His secretary has no idea where he is."

"Isn't that a little suspicious? Doesn't that sound like he's one of the bad guys?" Bay said.

"It's odd," Owen conceded. "But I'm not willing to believe Clay is acting on the wrong side of the law. Maybe he's keeping your brother safe somewhere. Maybe he needed to disappear so he wouldn't have to answer awkward questions."

"Yeah. Like where he put the stolen VX mines," Bay retorted. "I want to go home."

Owen caught Bay's arm before she'd taken two steps.

"Let me call my boss first and let him know we're all right, and see what he suggests."

Owen had no trouble getting hold of his Ranger captain on the phone.

"Where the hell are you?" Captain Mabry demanded. "I've had men looking high and low for you in the Big Bend. We thought you were dead. Are you both all right?"

"Bayleigh Creed and I are at the Midland-Odessa Airport," Owen replied. "We're fine. We found the VX mines and a whole lot more munitions besides."

"Good. You'd better report to Paul Ridgeway."

"Two of Ridgeway's FBI agents showed up with Uzis at the camp where the mines are kept. I had to kill them to escape."

There was a long silence on the other end of the line before Captain Mabry said, "What are you suggesting?"

"Nothing," Owen said. "I'm telling you what I know. By the way, have you heard anything about my brother Clay or Luke Creed?"

"The FBI is running this show. We've been pretty much cut out of the loop. You'd have to check with Ridgeway to see if there have been any developments on Luke Creed. What's going on with Clay?"

"Clay hasn't shown up for work in a week." Owen started to tell his boss that Clay had flown out of the hijackers' camp with Luke Creed the previous week, but held his tongue. He wondered which law enforcement agency had contacted Clay. Exactly who was he working for? Obviously, the Texas Rangers knew nothing.

"Is Clay involved in this VX business?" Mabry asked.

"I don't know," Owen answered, though it appeared Clay was in "this VX business" up to his neck. "Are you saying I should contact Ridgeway?" he asked his boss. "Even though the two FBI men I killed worked for him?"

"He's the man running the show," Mabry said. "Unless you have some reason to suspect him personally."

"Only guilt by association," Owen said.

There was another silence. "Do you think he's involved?" Mabry asked.

"I can't imagine why he would be," Owen said. "But I can't imagine why two FBI agents who work for Paul would be, either. Any suggestions?"

"I'll see who I can find who might be able to give us more information on the two men you killed. Give me their names."

Owen recited the information from their IDs.

"Can you tell me where those mines are, so we can put a guard on them?" Mabry asked.

"I'd have to take you there."

"Call me after you talk with Ridgeway," Captain Mabry said.

"Then you think I should see him?"

"There's not much he can do to you in downtown Midland," Mabry said.

"My thoughts exactly," Owen said.

"I'll call Ridgeway myself and have him send a car to pick you up. Tell him what you know. But watch your back."

"I will," Owen said.

"I'll call your folks and the girl's folks and let them know you're okay."

"I'd appreciate that," Owen said and then hung up.

"What happens now?" Bay said.

"Captain Mabry is going to call our parents to let them know we're all right. We're going to the FBI office to meet with Paul Ridgeway."

"I want to talk to my mother," Bay persisted.

"What can you tell her that Mabry can't? Do you know where Luke is?"

Bay made a face. "What if Ridgeway is one of the bad guys?"

"Even if he's involved, he's not going to be able to do a thing to us at the FBI office in Midland, especially when my boss knows that's where we are," Owen said. "He might very well know what's happened to our brothers."

"All right," Bay said. "I'll go along for the ride."

When the government car showed up at the airport to pick them up, the driver was Paul Ridgeway himself.

He got out of the car and said, "After I spoke with Captain Mabry I realized it would be dangerous for the two of you to show up at the FBI office in town. There might be other agents involved in this, and I don't want to risk something happening to you. My suggestion is for you to get right back in that helicopter and fly to Alpine. I have a cabin there where you can stay until we figure out who else might be involved."

Owen exchanged a look with Bay. "The government doesn't mind loaning us its helicopter?" he said dubiously.

Ridgeway smiled. "You've already borrowed it once. I could arrange for a pilot, but the fewer people who know you're alive and well, the better."

"Captain Mabry said—"

Ridgeway interrupted Owen. "Mabry told me about James Brophy and Terry Watkins. You can imagine what a flap it's going to cause when it becomes known that two FBI agents were responsible for the murder of a Texas Ranger and the theft of those VX mines. I need to make sure someone doesn't eliminate the only two witnesses who know where all those missing mines are located."

"I'd rather go home," Bay said.

"Soon," Ridgeway promised. "Give me a little time—twenty-four hours—to see who else in my office might be implicated."

Owen was watching Ridgeway, looking for some sign that he was lying, or that he knew more than he was saying. He didn't see or hear anything that sounded suspicious. Except for sending them off in the government's helicopter. But that could be explained using Ridgeway's own logic. The fewer people who knew he and Bay were alive, the better.

"Where is this cabin of yours? Can we land the helicopter there?" Owen asked.

"Actually, you can. I can give you directions that will get you there. There's a helipad next to the house."

"How rustic is this cabin?" Bay asked. "Is there a shower?"

Ridgeway smiled. "It comes with all the modern conveniences. Except a phone."

Owen felt his heart pick up a beat. "No phone? How are we supposed to stay in touch?"

"I'd offer you my cell phone, but it won't work in those mountains. It's only for twenty-four hours," Ridgeway said with an apologetic smile.

Owen wasn't comfortable being cut off, but he had a couple of Uzis as protection, and they could still fly back out in the helicopter if they didn't like the looks of things when they arrived. "All right," Owen said reluctantly. "Let me call my boss and let him know where we're going to be."

"Captain Mabry and I talked this over, and he agreed with my assessment of the situation," Ridgeway said. "But if you want to call him again—" He held out his cell phone.

When Owen hesitated, Bay took the cell phone and said, "I'd like to call my mother."

"By all means," Ridgeway said.

But when Bay tried to use the phone it read "Low Battery."

Could Ridgeway have planned to have a low battery? Owen met Bay's suspicious look with a shrug. "Guess you'll have to wait another twenty-four hours to talk with your mom."

"And your brother Luke," Ridgeway added.

Both Owen and Bay turned to stare at Ridgeway. "You know where Luke is? And Clay?"

Ridgeway smiled. "Clay has Luke hidden away somewhere safe. You can be sure of that."

"His office has no idea where he is," Owen said.

"Think about it," Ridgeway said. "Where would your brother go if he needed a place where no one would be likely to find him, and he wanted to keep Dr. Creed's brother safe?"

Suddenly, Owen knew. "You mean he's gone to the hunting cabin at Bitter Creek? That's perfect! But why not tell his office where he is?"

"We have no way of knowing who we can trust," Ridgeway said, "or how far-reaching this conspiracy is."

"And you're going to figure all this out in the next twenty-four hours?" Bay asked the FBI agent skeptically.

"The investigation is making great strides, Dr. Creed. Yes, I expect this whole matter to be concluded within the next twenty-four hours. By the way," he said, "both Clay and my daughter have stayed at the cabin. You should both be able to find clothes they've left there that will fit you."

Owen's suspicions about Ridgeway began to subside. Ridgeway was aware that Clay was hiding Luke at their father's hunting cabin at Bitter Creek—something nobody else seemed to know—and Clay would only tell that to someone he completely trusted.

Ridgeway escorted them to the helicopter. "How are you for fuel?" he asked.

"Based on the directions you gave me, we should be fine," Bay replied.

"What are you planning to do about those two dead agents and the VX mines?" Owen asked.

"They're not going anywhere," Ridgeway said. "We'll take care of them once we've rooted out the bad seed."

Owen stepped into the helicopter. "How will we get in touch with you?"

"I'll fly in and see you," Ridgeway said. "What time is it? Seven. I'll be there about seven tomorrow night."

"Good enough," Owen said.

They were in the air before Owen spoke again on the headset. "I don't know whether to trust him or not."

"If we're voting, I vote not to trust him," Bay said.

"What did he do that makes you doubt him?"

"Dogs run in a pack," Bay said. "Those two Dobermans followed Ridgeway around like he was the alpha male."

"He knew where Clay and Luke were staying," Owen argued.

Bay shook her head. "You told him where Clay and Luke were staying."

"I did not. I—" Owen frowned as he tried to remember his conversation with Ridgeway. "Are you sure?"

"He insinuated that he knew where they were. You confirmed the location. Will he be able to find the cabin?"

"He can figure out where it is. A couple of U.S. presidents have stayed there. The Secret Service did security checks before they spent the night."

Bay shot him an anxious glance. "I'm worried, Owen. What if Ridgeway's on his way right now to kill your brother and mine?"

Owen grimaced and shook his head. "That would mean he's coming after us next. If that were true, why would he give us the helicopter? I think you're seeing monsters where there aren't any."

Bay sighed. "They're out there. We just haven't identified them yet."

"Let's go to the cabin and sit tight for twenty-four hours. Clay can take care of himself." Owen put up a hand to stop Bay's protest. "If Clay went to the trouble to fly Luke out of that camp, he isn't going to let the bad guys get to him now. It's entirely likely there's some kind of guard on both of them."

Owen firmly believed what he was saying. But that crawly feeling along his spine was back. Something wasn't quite right. He wished he could figure out what it was.

"All I want is a long, hot bath," Bay said. "And a soft bed."

Owen brushed his hand over the beard on his cheeks and chin. "I could use a shave and a hot shower. And a soft bed—with you in it."

"Don't push me, Owen."

"You told me you never quit. Why are you quitting when it comes to us?"

"There is no us. There can't be an us."

"Too late for that argument, Red, when I've already been inside you."

"You're a Blackthorne," she said. "How am I supposed to trust you?"

He looked long and hard at her, then said, "My being a

Blackthorne isn't the problem. The problem is I'm a man. And every man you've ever trusted has betrayed you—from your father on down."

"My father—"

"Spent all his time with your crippled brother. Some boyfriend took advantage. A trusted professor did the same. I don't suppose you've let anyone else get close. Until I came along. But I'm not going away, Red. I'm here to stay."

"Until some other woman catches your eye," she muttered. "Like your friend's widow."

"Julia? We've always been good friends, but there's nothing else between us. Never has been. Never will be."

They arrived at the helipad, which Ridgeway had said would be lit up by a caretaker, who would also make sure the lights and hot water were on in the cabin. The helicopter was on the ground before Bay spoke again.

"Maybe you're right," she conceded. "Maybe my lack of trust has nothing to do with you being a Blackthorne. But it's there, Owen. I don't know how to make it go away."

"Give me a chance. Let me prove to you—"

"How?" Bay asked. "What can you possibly do that would make me believe I can count on you when the chips are down?"

"I don't know." Owen smiled ruefully. "I suppose you'll just have to trust me."

Bay met his gaze, her eyes bleak. "I'm sorry, Owen. I can't take that chance."

Chapter 17

 BAY SOAKED IN A TUB OF HOT WATER AT PAUL
Ridgeway's cabin for almost an hour. She'd
never had a bath that felt so good.

"Hey. Are you almost done in there?" Owen called
through the door.

"I don't want to get out," Bay called back.

"Fine," he said, opening the door and stepping into the
tiny room. "I'll be glad to join you."

Bay laughed. "As you can see, there isn't room in here
for two." She was covered in bubbles. "I've been trying
to figure out how to rinse my hair."

"Let me help," Owen said, dropping to his knees on
the soft shag rug beside the ancient, claw-footed tub.
"Let's see. Why don't you lean back over my arm."

Bay did as he asked and a moment later Owen was
cupping water from the tub with his other hand and pour-
ing it over her soapy hair.

"Close your eyes," he said, "so you don't get any soap
in them."

It was going to take forever to rinse all the soap out
of her hair if he did it a handful of water at a time, but Bay
didn't care. It felt wonderful to be supported by his arm and
to feel the warm water running over her scalp.

"There," he said at last. "No more soap. You can open your eyes now."

When she did, she realized the bubbles had finally melted away, and she was completely exposed to his gaze. "Owen?"

His gaze was tender rather than lustful, and therefore all the more threatening to her peace of mind. She could be wooed with tenderness . . .

He kissed her on the nose and said, "Out. I need a bath. We can continue this later."

Bay willingly stepped into the large, fluffy white towel Owen held out for her. She opened the bathroom door and felt a rush of cold air from the rest of the cabin.

"Brrr," she said, closing it again.

"There's a roaring fire in the fireplace in the living room where you can warm up and dry your hair. Do you suppose there's any hot water left?" Owen asked hopefully as the last of her bathwater drained out.

Bay caressed his smooth cheek. "You shaved. It feels soft."

He caught her hand and kissed her palm. "Go," he said, opening the bathroom door again. "Before I change my mind and you end up making love to a man who smells like a bear."

Bay realized what she'd done and pulled her hand back. That sort of intimacy had to stop. She inched past Owen and said, "Good luck with the hot water. I'll see what I can do about making us a midnight snack."

The six-room cabin was made of logs and had pegged wooden floors and a stone fireplace, where Owen had lit a crackling fire. Bay stood in front of the fire for a moment and let it warm her before she headed for the bedroom that had obviously been used by Paul Ridgeway's daughter Cindy. It was disturbing to find that the bedroom had been left exactly as it must have looked more than a year before, when Cindy Ridgeway had been murdered.

There were still tubes of lipstick on a dressing table, and a Tami Hoag novel beside the bed with a page marked where Cindy had stopped reading. The room was full of ribbons Cindy had won barrel racing in rodeo competitions as well as two college debate trophies. Apparently, Cindy had been both athletic and smart. Which only made sense, if she'd attracted a successful, intelligent man like Clay Blackthorne.

Bay felt like an intruder going through Cindy's drawers, but she found underwear, a pair of jeans that fit almost to a T, and a sweatshirt that negated the need for a bra. She pulled on a pair of boot socks but didn't bother putting on her boots. She'd seen a diary in the underwear drawer but resisted the urge to peek into the life of the woman whose room she occupied—though she was definitely curious.

Bay nosed around the room, picking up pieces of Cindy Ridgeway's life and putting them back down. A tiny figurine of a quarter horse, mane and tail flowing. A Dallas Cowboys Cheerleaders calendar with important dates marked leading up to her wedding. A framed picture of Cindy and Clay, both smiling, both looking extraordinarily happy. It shook Bay for a second, because Clay looked so much like Owen.

There were differences. In the eyes. Clay had seen a different world than Owen, she supposed. And in the smile. Clay's smile looked more open and friendly than Owen's. The couple looked happy together. She felt sorry the girl's life had been cut short.

Bay picked up a book that featured Western artists, sculptors, and photographers, wondering whether Owen's mother might be featured in it. According to the index, one of Eve Blackthorne's oil paintings was included in the book.

Bay was searching for page 42 when Owen showed up in the doorway. She didn't hear him coming; he was simply there. "Oh, you frightened me," she said, clutching the book to her chest.

He was wearing a pair of jeans with a crease pressed into them, a ratty maroon Texas A&M sweatshirt, and a pair of white boot socks. "What do you have there?" he asked.

She laid the oversized book down across her forearms so he could see. "It's a collection of Western artists. Your mother's in here. I was going to look at her painting."

"Later," he said, closing the book. "Let's eat first. I'm starving."

Bay carried the book with her to the kitchen and laid it on the tile counter. "What are you in the mood for?"

"What's in the fridge?" Owen asked, pulling open the door. "Uh. Not much in here. Guess Paul didn't have a chance to stock it."

Bay went through the cupboards. "There's tomato soup. And crackers."

"Guess that'll have to do," Owen said. "What I wouldn't give for a juicy hamburger."

"Tomorrow," Bay said. "We'll be out of here in twenty-four hours."

Neither of them had much interest in the soup. It was too similar to the military rations they'd been eating. A half hour later they headed for the overstuffed corduroy couch in front of the fireplace. Bay had brought the book of paintings with her.

Owen took it away from her again and set it on the brown-and-white-spotted cowhide that served as a rug. "Later," he said. "I want to sit here for a while and put my feet up."

A couple of dark brown corduroy ottomans stood in front of the couch, and Owen plopped down and put his feet up. He patted the couch beside him. "Have a seat, Red."

Bay plopped down beside him, putting her feet up on the same ottoman he was using. "This definitely beats those benches at the camp."

Owen leaned over and sniffed her hair.

"What are you doing?" she said, leaning away and staring at him.

"Smelling your hair. It smells like coconut."

"Compliments of Cindy Ridgeway. It must have been really sad for your brother to lose her like he did."

"Yeah," Owen said. "Clay took it pretty hard."

"And Ridgeway? It must have been awful losing his only daughter like that."

"He looked pretty stoic at the funeral," Owen said. "But Clay said he was a mess for a while."

Owen slid an arm around her shoulders, and she nestled her head against his chest as though it were the most natural thing in the world. As though they'd been a couple forever and always spent cold evenings cozied up together on the couch in front of a crackling fire. "Owen . . ."

"What is it, Red?"

"Nothing," she said. Then, "This is nice."

"Yeah. It is."

She looked up. He looked down. Their eyes met and held. He leaned slowly toward her, giving her plenty of time to object. But she wanted that kiss. Needed it.

His mouth was utterly soft, yearning. He touched her lips briefly, then looked into her eyes again. "I think I'm in love with you."

Bay leaned back abruptly. "What?" She felt the pressure of Owen's hand at her shoulder, keeping her from bolting.

"I'm in love with you," he repeated.

"You can't be," she said.

He laughed softly. "You wouldn't think so, would you? I mean, I've known you, what, two weeks maybe? You must admit, though, I've had a pretty good look at who you are. We've been through experiences together that most couples never encounter. I've liked what I've seen, Red. You were right about being reliable in a crunch. And you're smart and sexy and—"

"Whoa. Whoa," Bay said, putting a hand over his mouth. "Where is all this coming from? Have you forgotten who you are? Who I am?"

He gently took her hand away from his mouth and kissed her palm, causing shivers to run up her arm. "I know exactly who you are. The woman I love."

"How am I supposed to respond to that?" she said, feeling a spurt of panic.

He lifted a brow. "I know what I'd like you to say."

"That I love you, too?" Bay's heart was pounding. She was finding it hard to catch her breath.

"I'd prefer you made it a statement, rather than a question," he teased gently.

She didn't move when he leaned over to kiss her, but her heart squeezed at the tenderness of the gesture. She was used to men saying they loved her to get her into bed. It was a conventional male ploy. But Owen wasn't aroused. His eyes gleamed with some emotion she refused to admit might be love. She felt desire curl tightly inside her until she ached with wanting him. Needing him.

"Be practical," she said in a quiet voice. "You're feeling what you're feeling precisely because we've been isolated together under some pretty unusual circumstances, and I've been the only female around."

"I think I fell in love with you at your father's funeral," he said. "When you left Sam sitting there in his wheelchair and walked over and challenged me to find the man who murdered your father."

"That's ridiculous," Bay said. But she was remembering how it had felt to look into Owen's eyes that day, how she'd been so afraid of what she'd seen and felt.

He slid a finger under her chin and used it to tilt her mouth upward toward his. She stared into his eyes until it was uncomfortable to do so, then closed her eyes and let herself feel the gentleness of this powerful man, as his lips touched her own.

"Oh," she murmured.

"Is that *Owe* as in *Owen*?" he teased. "Or, *oh* as in—"

"*Oh* as in *ohmigod*," she whispered. She wanted this. She'd been waiting her whole life for this.

She simply didn't believe it would last. The betrayal of her college boyfriend had hardened her heart. The betrayal of her married lover had shattered it. She'd glued the pieces back together, but it was so very fragile now. If Owen broke her heart again, the resulting shards would be impossible to repair.

She couldn't take that risk. She wouldn't take that risk.

She leaned back and looked into his eyes. "I don't love you, Owe . . . n," she said. "I won't love you."

She saw the pain flicker in his eyes before it was

hidden behind a gaze that had turned to ice. She knew the risk he'd taken, revealing his feelings to her. She had the urge to offer solace. But it was too danger-ous to feel sympathy for him. She had to protect herself first.

She was expecting a scene. She was expecting protes-tations of undying affection. She was expecting him to fight for the right to love her.

Instead, she saw a muscle jerk in his cheek as he clenched his teeth, remaining silent.

She put a hand to his nape and brought his head down so she could kiss him good-bye.

He straightened, so her hand fell away, then removed his arm from around her shoulder as he reached down and picked up the book of Texas artists. He cleared his throat and said, "What page did you say my mother's painting was on?"

She stared at him, feeling an ache so painful inside that she wasn't sure she could bear it. So. That was it. He hadn't really loved her. He'd only been saying the words. She'd been right not to trust him with her heart.

As the tears welled in her eyes, she realized she'd al-ready offered him her heart without realizing it. And he'd broken the damned thing without even trying.

"Which page?" Owen asked brusquely, as he thumbed through the book of Texas artists.

"It's called *A Perfect Lady,*" Bay said. "Page forty-two."

Bay forced herself to stare at the painting when Owen set the book across their knees. She was surprised to see writing above a painting of a girl on a horse at a rodeo. " 'To my own Perfect Lady. All my love, Dad,' " Bay read aloud. "I can't believe this," she said as she turned to look at Owen. "Your mother painted Cindy Ridge-way!"

Owen wasn't looking back at her. He was staring at the painting. "Yeah. And made her even more beautiful than she was. That's what my mother does, you know. She takes the imperfect world and makes it perfect. *A Perfect Lady.*"

Bay looked at the reproduction of the oil painting and saw the things she hadn't noticed at first. In the photo of Cindy and Clay she'd found in the bedroom, Cindy's right eyebrow arched higher than the left. In the painting, they were symmetrical. In the bedroom photo, her chin was too sharp, but that had been softened. And her eyes were a little too far apart, but they'd been moved closer together, so Cindy possessed startling beauty in the painting.

"The painting is beautiful," Bay said. "But it's not real. Nobody's perfect. Nothing's perfect. The more I look at it, the less I like it," she said flatly. "If Paul Ridge-way really loved his daughter he would hate this paint-ing. Because it doesn't show her as she really is. But maybe that's how Paul saw his daughter. Perfect."

"Oh, shit," Owen said.

"What's the matter?"

He slammed the book closed and dropped it on the floor as he rose to his feet and headed down the hall. Bay followed after him.

She found him staring at the same painting, which was hanging on the wall. "This is the 'perfect lady' Hank was talking about," he said.

"What do you mean?"

"Remember that clue I told you Hank left me in his hat? He told me to find the perfect lady, and I'd find the thief. Here it is, *A Perfect Lady,* hanging in Paul Ridgeway's house. I'm not sure how those VX mines are connected to Cindy Ridgeway's death, but I'm willing to bet that somehow they are."

"How?" Bay asked.

"Only Paul Ridgeway knows the answer to that. But now I have the motive I was missing for why Paul might be involved with those VX mines. It isn't money. It has something to do with the death of his daughter. Maybe that vagrant who killed her was involved with those mines, or maybe Paul's using the mines to exact some sort of revenge.

"Hank must have found out something that implicated Paul. Then we came along and killed his two Dobermans. You can bet Paul isn't going to leave us alive to talk. We know too much that can incriminate him."

"Maybe we better get out of here," Bay said.

Owen swore under his breath.

"What's wrong?"

"I told Paul where to find Clay and Luke. He's had us sitting tight here while he goes after them."

"You don't know that they're at your father's hunting cabin," Bay said.

"Whatever government agency got Clay involved in this mess might have them hidden in a safe house somewhere," Owen conceded. "But we've got to find out for sure. It's time to get the hell out of Dodge."

WHEN THEY WERE AIRBORNE IN THE HELICOPTER, OWEN said, "Who can you reach with that radio?"

Bay tried the radio and said, "It's not working."

"It was working before!"

"Well, it's not working now," Bay said certainly. "It's broken."

"Paul wasn't taking any chances," Owen muttered. "Let's get back to the airport in Alpine. My jet's there. We can phone my boss and get him moving toward that hunting cabin."

They reached the airport in Alpine as the predawn light made shapes from shadows. As they approached the helipad, Bay said, "There's a car on the tarmac waiting for us. Two men in suits with guns are standing next to it."

"Yeah, but whose side are they on?" Owen wondered aloud.

"What do you want me to do?" Bay asked.

Owen took one look at the gas gauge and realized they didn't have many options. "Don't land here," Owen said. "Head for the hangar where I left my jet."

As Bay headed the helicopter in the direction Owen had ordered, the two men got into their car and followed.

"This is going to be close," Owen said.

"Can we get your jet off the ground before they catch up to us?"

Owen smiled. "Before we headed for Alpine, I made sure it was refueled and ready to go. I made a deal with one of the maintenance men to leave it outside the hangar. If we can get there with a little room to spare, we can beat them."

"Maybe they're the good guys," Bay suggested. "Maybe they aren't involved with Paul."

"Then why the show of force?" Owen asked. "What are they doing here watching the airport?"

Owen was out the door of the helicopter the instant Bay landed. "Come on," he urged. "Let's move!"

He ran toward the jet, hoping the mechanic had done the flight check he'd asked him to do, because there wasn't time for it now. He could see the faces of the two men he assumed were Paul's thugs through the car windshield. He got into the pilot's seat and waited for Bay to step into the jet and close the door behind her.

The thugs got out of their car and headed toward them on the run.

"They're not shooting," Bay said. "Maybe we should wait and see what they want."

"What if what they want is to take us someplace more private to shoot us?"

"All right. Go. Let's go!"

Owen taxied the jet onto the runway and had it in the air moments later. He picked up the radio to contact the tower and swore. "The radio doesn't work!"

Obviously, his own mechanic hadn't been the only one at work on the jet. Owen wondered what else might have been "fixed." He checked the fuel gauge and the hydraulic fluid levels and they seemed fine, but that didn't mean a leak hadn't been put in the lines somewhere.

"We're in trouble, aren't we?" Bay asked.

"As far as I know, all that's been sabotaged is the radio. Paul has a pretty good idea where I'm going, so he won't have any trouble following us. The only question is, will we get there in time?"

"You said Clay could take care of himself and Luke."

"He can," Owen said. "But I suppose it depends on how much firepower Paul shows up with. Or whether he decides to bring along one of those VX mines."

"He'd never do that. Would he?" Bay asked, her eyes wide with horror.

"Who knows what that crazy sonofabitch will do," Owen muttered.

"What are you going to use to fight him?" Bay asked. "I presume you have guns we can pick up at the Castle."

"There are plenty of guns at the hunting cabin," Owen said. "But there's no phone there, either—my father's idea of 'getting away.' It makes sense to stop at the Castle long enough to call in the cavalry. On the other hand, there's a landing strip right by the hunting cabin. We could go directly there. That would save us some flying time."

Bay bit her lip. "What do you suggest?"

"A few minutes could make all the difference," Owen said. "Or no difference at all, if Clay and Luke aren't at the cabin. Or if I'm way off base with what I'm supposing is the truth." Owen aimed the plane's nose up, gaining altitude as fast as he could.

"I don't think you're mistaken about Paul Ridgeway," Bay said. "If that means anything. But maybe we should stop at the Castle and tell someone what we know in case . . . in case something happens to us."

"I see what you mean, Red. We'll call Mabry as soon as we land."

One of the jet engines flamed out.

"It seems Ridgeway wanted to make sure we didn't tell anyone what we know," Owen said grimly.

"Are we going to crash?" Bay was so scared, her lungs had seized up, and she had a death grip on the edge of the seat.

"We've got plenty of altitude to work with. We can fly on one engine if nothing else goes wrong."

No sooner had Owen spoken than the hydraulic system failed. "Guess that stop at the Castle is out," Owen said. "We'll shoot for the landing strip at the cabin."

Bay had never panicked in an emergency, but she was having trouble catching her breath, and her heart was racing so fast it hurt. "If you think about it, this was the smart way for Ridgeway to be rid of us. We crash and there are no bullet holes to explain."

"Just a foolish pilot who left the airport in such a hurry he didn't do his flight check. No one will know we were forced into that hurried flight by two thugs with guns."

Bay let go of the seat with her left hand and clutched Owen's thigh. "I'm frightened, Owe."

He wished he could take his hand off the controls to comfort her, but with diminished hydraulics, he needed all his strength to keep the jet level and steady in the air.

"Think back on that paper you did on hydraulics. Any useful suggestions?" he asked with a grin.

She frowned and shook her head. "But I did another one on the most common causes of airplane crashes that—"

"That sounds ominous."

"How much do you know about soaring?" Bay asked.

"Why do you ask?"

"A Canadian pilot flew a jumbo jet to a safe landing after it ran out of fuel by applying soaring techniques to keep his plane in the air."

"I went soaring once over Vermont to get a good, quiet look at the fall foliage," Owen admitted.

"So all you have to do is keep the wings level and do a little sideslipping if the wind blows us off course—"

"Got it," Owen said. "Assuming we lose that second engine and need—"

The second engine flamed out.

Owen looked at Bay, who looked back, her eyes wide with terror. "Don't panic," he said. "I have plenty of experience. As I recall, that soaring trip lasted several hours."

"You're a laugh a minute," Bay said.

"Any last words you want to impart?" Owen said, his features turning grim. "If you're so certain we've come to the end of our rope?"

Owen wasn't sure what he wanted her to say. Maybe that she loved him, after all. Or that she regretted not taking the chance of loving him. She had to feel something. He couldn't feel what he did unless there was something coming back from her. Maybe he was trying to make something happen that was never destined to happen. Maybe he was knocking his head against a brick wall, and all he was going to get for it was a big, painful lump.

"Owe," she said. "I do have feelings for you."

"Feelings," he said. "Can you be more specific?"

"I think I might—"

"Hold that thought, Red," he said as the jet started to plummet. "I think I'm going to be busy for the next few minutes."

Chapter 18

BILLY HAD SPENT THREE DAYS IN THE HOSPITAL and another week in bed at home. There hadn't been much else to do but stare at the ceiling and think. The one thought he couldn't get out of his head was *I'm a Blackthorne*.

It explained so much he hadn't understood. Why he had never been able to please his "father," no matter how hard he'd tried. Why his mother had always looked so sad. Why he'd grown so much taller than his "father," and had crow-black hair instead of brown, like both his parents. Why he'd been so much smarter than his "father," who'd made so much fun of him for getting good grades that he'd stopped doing it. Why his "father" had always seemed so angry and had taken it out on his only "son."

Billy had always believed he didn't fit somehow. Now he knew why. And that knowledge had changed everything.

Summer Blackthorne is my half sister.

That information had been stunning. And devastating. No wonder they'd felt such an affinity for one another. No wonder they'd become friends. He shuddered to think what might have happened if . . . Maybe the same instinct that had drawn them together had kept him from letting their relationship get any more intimate than it had. No wonder his mother had gone crazy when she'd seen them kissing on the porch.

Knowing he was related to Summer didn't make the ache in his heart hurt any less. Of all the wounds he'd suffered, that one was the worst. Summer had been his ideal life partner, and now she was forbidden to him. He was glad he didn't have to tell her the truth before he left.

One good thing had come out of all of this. He was going to have the chance to make something of himself. Billy had watched a Texas and Southwestern Cattle Raisers Association field agent at work at the stockyard, when he'd been stuck doing more menial tasks, like drawing blood from cattle for brucellosis card tests.

He had yearned for the respect the agent commanded. Had admired the badge he wore, which mimicked the Texas Ranger badge, except for bearing the head of a longhorn in the center of the silver star. Had imagined himself toting a gun and hunting down cattle rustlers and horse thieves.

Billy knew the work of a TSCRA agent was ordinarily more mundane than exciting. But it was a job helping people and would give him a purpose in life, which was something he'd lacked until now. It sounded like he was going to end up with a college education, too. Though it might take him longer going to class at night while he worked. He would finally become the kind of man who might appeal to a woman like Summer Blackthorne.

Except, he could never, ever have her.

Billy wanted to hide his face in his pillow and cry. But his response to adversity had always been to fight back. Being a Blackthorne didn't change that attribute . . . or maybe was responsible for it. He was going to get well and get on with his life. He'd find someone else to love. Find someone else to love him.

First he had to meet with Summer. He dreaded the thought of lying to her about why he was leaving, of making her hate him.

He heard a knock on his bedroom door and then Summer's voice saying, "Billy? Are you in there?"

Before he could reply, she had shoved open the door, closed it behind her, and locked it. Splotches of mascara were smeared under her eyes, which were swollen red from crying. Her golden curls were shoved into a clip on top of her head, from which numerous strands had fallen. She was dressed in jeans and a Western shirt and boots which, although they might be her oldest clothes, were still nearly new.

He pushed himself into a sitting position in his iron-railed bed and pulled the sheet up to cover himself to the waist, since he was naked beneath it. "What are you doing here, Summer? My mom's going to be back any minute, and you know how she feels—"

"God, Billy. You still look so awful! That bull really stomped you bad."

She'd come to see him when he was in the hospital, suspicious that he'd ended up hurt so soon after her father's visit. He'd reassured her that Blackjack had nothing to do with his injuries, that he'd gotten cornered by his bull.

She was so trusting of her father—and so naïve—that she'd believed his lies.

He'd told her not to visit him when he got home, because he'd dreaded a showdown between Summer and his mother. Yet here she was.

He took a good look at her face and realized she'd been crying. "What's wrong?" he asked.

She wrung her hands as she paced back and forth at the foot of his bed. "I had to see you. I have something to tell you."

Billy's heart leaped to his throat and made it impossible to speak. She'd found out somehow. He could tell from the stricken look on her face. The tears welled in her eyes as she moved toward him. He inched backward, not wanting her to touch him, feeling unclean and guilty, though he had nothing to feel guilty for.

She sat gingerly on the foot of his iron-railed bed, as though she didn't want to touch him—or be touched—either. He could understand her feelings.

"I know what you're going to say," he said. "There's no reason for us to be talking about this. The past is the past, and we go on from here."

Furrows appeared on her brow. "How did you find out?"

"I think the better question is, how did you find out?"

"I overheard my parents talking the day of your accident. I've been wanting to talk to you about it ever since. At first you were in too bad shape for me to lay all this on you. Since then . . . I haven't had the courage."

"Summer . . . you don't have to say anything. I'm going to be leaving—"

She threw herself toward him, crawling the last foot to reach his arms, which to his surprise were open to receive her. He pulled her close, even though her energetic movements were wreaking havoc with his broken ribs. "Shh. Shhh," he whispered, as he brushed the hair away from her face and kissed her brow. "It's all right. Everything's going to be all right, Summer."

"Nothing's ever going to be right again," she sobbed.

"My daddy isn't my daddy. And my real father's a murderer!"

Billy felt his flesh get up and crawl. He put his hands on either side of Summer's head and forced her away far enough that he could look into her eyes. The misery there was palpable, and he felt his gut twist with the force of her pain. "Who told you that?"

"I heard my mother and father arguing in the study, and I went to see if I could stop them. I was outside the door when I heard Momma telling Daddy that he isn't my father. My real father is Russell Handy!" she choked out. "I ran away as soon as I heard. I've been crying in secret ever since. And not just for myself. Owen's boss called and told us he's safe, but now Clay's missing, and I think he might be dead!

"But then I remembered the twins aren't even my real brothers. I mean, they're my *half* brothers, 'cause we have the same mother, but . . . we don't have the same father."

Tears welled in her eyes as she sobbed, "I don't know what to do. I don't know who I am!"

Billy hissed out a breath of air. "Oh, God, Summer." His arms surrounded her, and he clutched her tightly against him, despite the ache in his ribs. "I'm so sorry."

He was sorry for her pain, for her disillusionment, for her confusion. His own relief was enormous. He was overwhelmed by emotion and blinded by tears of joy.

We're not related. We're not brother and sister.

He blinked his eyes to clear the blurry mist. When he opened them again, he released his hold on Summer and lifted her chin with a forefinger. He smiled tenderly at her, then gave her a soft kiss on the mouth.

It was the kiss of a friend. And a lover.

He was not related to her by blood. He was Blackthorne's son; but she was not Blackthorne's daughter. They could spend their lives together, and no one could stop them.

Summer looked at him with eyes that were far more wounded by her mother's betrayal than his body had been by her father's brutal attack. "What am I going to do, Billy? I feel like running away and never coming back. Come with me. We'll run away together and—"

He put his fingertips to her lips, his heart squeezing as he realized the trap in which he was caught. "I can't run away, Summer. I have to take care of my mom and Emma."

"They'll manage, Billy. They'll get by. What about us? We're entitled to a life, aren't we? I've got some money—"

"But I don't," he interrupted. "I've got nothing, Summer." If he ran away with her he would never have anything, never be anything, because he would be too busy working menial jobs to put food on the table and a roof over their heads. He would lose the opportunity Blackjack had offered him to become a TSCRA field inspector.

Summer was too young and spoiled to know what it would be like to live without all the money and conveniences she took for granted. When the defiance waned, when the first blush of excitement wore off, she would be left in surroundings more grim than she could imagine. She might love him enough to endure them. It was more likely she would first resent him, and then despise him.

The opportunity to be more than a mere cowhand or a lowly saddle tramp loomed large. He was afraid to lose it.

Billy thought there must be something wrong with

him not to grab for this chance at happiness with Summer. Maybe it would only last for a little while, but while it lasted . . . But that was precisely the point. He'd spent the past ten days imagining how he would go away and become a man worthy of Summer's love. If he could only convince her to wait a few years, there might be a chance they could spend the rest of their lives together.

Unfortunately, the only way he could grasp at the gold ring Blackjack was offering, was by spurning the brass ring Summer had thrust into his hand.

But to get what her father had offered, he had to make her hate him. That was the deal. His mother and sister taken care of and the position as a field inspector in exchange for leaving Bitter Creek . . . and making Summer hate him.

What should he do? Leaving Summer behind was risky. What if she ran off and married some other man? But that had always been a risk. He had no control over her behavior. Only over his own. Whether it was a flaw in his character or not, he wanted to be proud of himself and what he did. He wanted that job as a field inspector. He didn't think he would be a good spouse for Summer if he couldn't offer her a husband who was at least her equal.

Not socially. Not financially. But inside. Where it mattered.

Billy felt like he was being ripped apart. He wanted Summer. And he wanted that job. But he couldn't have both.

"I have some news, too," Billy said as he edged backward from Summer against the pillows stacked at the head of the bed.

She looked at him expectantly.

"I got a job offer. One that's going to take me away from here."

She frowned. "What about your mother and Emma? A minute ago you said you couldn't go away with me because—"

"They're being taken care of as part of the bargain."

"What bargain?" she asked suspiciously.

"Your father offered me a job as a TSCRA field inspector, if I'd go away and leave you alone."

"But you're not going to take it." Then, after a pause, "Are you?"

"It's an incredible opportunity for someone like me."

She was inching away from him on the bed, staring at him as though he'd morphed into some kind of monster. "An incredible opportunity? What would you call the offer I just made you?" she asked in a sharp voice.

He reached out a hand, and she scooted across the bed out of his reach. "Don't touch me. You're no better than any of the other 'undesirable' beaux my father has bought off!"

"Summer—"

She was off the bed and headed for the door. He'd hardly been on his feet the past ten days, but he struggled out of the bed, grabbing the sheet to keep him decent. He managed to catch her only because the lock on the door gave her trouble. He put one hand on her shoulder to turn her, but she whirled around and slapped him.

His face paled, then flushed where her hand had struck him.

She grabbed her mouth with the hand she'd used to strike him and gave a cry of anguish.

He reached for her again, to offer comfort, and she backed up against the door as though she wished she could magically disappear through it.

"Don't, Billy. I don't know you. I thought I did, but if you can do this thing—take money from my father to stay away from me—then I was wrong about you."

He wanted to say he loved her. But what purpose would that serve, except to hurt her even more? "What are you going to do?"

She smiled bitterly. "Are you asking if I'm still going to run away? Where would I run to? Especially when no one would be waiting for me when I got there."

"Are you going to tell them you know the truth?" he asked.

She closed her eyes and clamped her lower lip in her teeth. He saw she was trying not to cry. She kept her gaze lowered as she said, "I love my father. Blackjack, I mean. He was as surprised as I was to find out what my mother did with Russell Handy."

She lifted her gaze to look into his eyes and said, "I don't want . . . my daddy . . ." She swallowed hard. "To look at me differently. To act differently. He would if he knew that I knew he wasn't really my father. Can you understand what I'm saying?"

Billy understood far better than she could imagine what it was like to have a father who knew he wasn't really your father. "I understand." He swallowed over the lump in his own throat and whispered, "I'm sorry, Summer."

"Sorry isn't good enough, Billy. You of all people . . . choosing money over me. I *hate* you. Do you hear?" she sobbed. "I hate you! How could you? You were supposed to be my *friend*."

She yanked open the door and slid through the opening. He could hear her boots pounding on the hardwood floor as she ran away.

He closed the door until the latch clicked, then leaned his forehead against the cool painted surface.

He didn't fight the sobs, even though it hurt his injured ribs to cry. He knew he'd done the right thing. So he didn't understand why it was so hard to breathe, why he felt empty inside, like a gutted steer. Summer had never been his in the first place. So how could it hurt so much to know that he'd lost her forever?

"HOW COULD YOU DO IT, DADDY! HOW COULD YOU!" SUMmer raged as she marched into Blackjack's study.

Blackjack rose as his daughter confronted him from the other side of his desk. He took one look at the tears streaming down her face and felt his pulse begin to jackhammer. What the hell had that bastard son of his told his little girl? "What is it I've done, baby?" he asked in a soothing voice.

"You know damn well what you've done! Paid Billy to get out of town, that's what!"

Blackjack crossed around his desk and sat on the corner of it, with his arms folded over his chest. *So, the boy had kept his part of the bargain,* he thought. *Good for him.* "You know I couldn't make Billy Coburn do anything he didn't want to do."

"Why did you do it, Daddy?" she cried. "You knew how I felt about him. Why did you have to send him away? He was the only true friend I had."

"You can always come to me," he said, opening his arms.

Tears pooled in her eyes again. He saw the hesitation before she careered into his embrace. He closed his arms around her and held her tight. He could feel her hands clutching at his shirt, as she pressed her face against his chest and cried. He put a hand on her head and crooned, "Everything's going to be fine, baby. Don't you worry about anything. Someday the right man will come along."

"Billy is the right man for me," she sobbed.

"No, baby. No, he isn't. Otherwise, he wouldn't be running away like he is. He would have stayed and fought tooth and claw to have you."

If Bad Billy Coburn had known the truth, Blackjack thought, *I do believe that boy would have faced me down to have you.* He was glad the situation hadn't arisen. His daughter had suffered enough. He was going to do everything in his power to make sure her life was happy from now on.

"What can I do, baby? How can I help?" he asked.

"Nobody can help," she wailed. "I'm so miserable!"

"I've got a new computer program that figures grain versus grass growth ratios for our Santa Gertrudis stock. I thought you might be able to help me understand it."

Her crying stopped abruptly. She lifted her tear-streaked face and stared at him from reddened eyes. "You want me to help you?"

"If you think you can teach me how the damned thing works."

She took a step back and swiped at her eyes with the back of her hand, leaving a stripe of mascara across her left temple.

He gently wiped it away with his thumb, then smiled and said, "We Blackthornes have to stick together."

She winced and lowered her eyes.

He wondered what he'd said that had caused her to back off again. "You're a lot more computer literate than

I am," he said. "I could really use your help. What do you say?"

"All right," she said in a voice that was raspy from crying. She looked up at him and said, "I love you, Daddy. I love you so much."

He felt his throat swell with emotion. He hooked his arm around her neck, as he might have with one of his sons, and said, "I love you, too."

"What's all that wailing I heard going on in here?"

Blackjack let his daughter go and turned to face his wife. "Summer found out—"

"Daddy."

He glanced at his daughter, who shot him a look of pleading. "Summer found out I'm going to make her work for me all summer. No traveling to exotic ports of call."

"And that has you in tears?" Eve asked, eyeing Summer's tear-streaked face. "I thought you might have gotten some bad news about Clay."

"No. I—" Summer swiped at her face with her sleeve, removing all evidence of her tears and the rest of her makeup. "I had plans with a friend of mine," she said, her voice hoarse from crying. "I'm sorry I'm not going, that's all."

"Maybe you and I can take a trip this summer," Eve suggested.

Blackjack said firmly, "I need Summer here, right by my side, working with me."

"Very well," Eve conceded with a smile. "Can you excuse us, Summer? Your father and I have something to discuss."

"Sure, Mom. I'll be in my room when you need me, Daddy."

"I'll call up there for you," he said as she turned to leave.

"Close the door, will you, dear?" Eve said.

As soon as Summer closed the door behind her Blackjack said, "What do you want?"

"For a moment there, I thought you might have broken down and told her the truth," Eve said.

"I told you how I feel. I don't want her ever to know that she's not my blood and bone."

"But involving her in the business? That's new."

"She can handle it."

Eve shrugged. "I thought you had other plans for her. Marital plans. If I heard right, a friend of yours in Houston has an eligible son."

"That can wait for a while."

"Well, it's good to know I won't miss the wedding."

"How long were you planning on being gone?" Blackjack asked.

"I'll be traveling the rest of the summer. When I get back, I expect to hear that you've gotten that Creed woman out of your system."

Blackjack's lips pressed flat. He knew an ultimatum when he heard one. But he didn't have to like it. "When are you leaving?"

"As soon as I can get packed," Eve replied.

"Without waiting for news about Clay?"

"If the bad penny has shown up, I don't think the good one can be far behind."

Blackjack snorted in disgust.

She crossed to stand in front of him. "Would you like to kiss me good-bye?"

Blackjack thought of all the cutting remarks he could make. But he needed her help keeping their secrets. And it appeared they were going to be living in the same house together for some time to come. A gesture of conciliation would cost him nothing and might reduce the level of tension between them.

He leaned down and kissed her on the cheek.

"You can do better than that," she said, putting her arms around his shoulders and standing on tiptoe, leaning into his body so her breasts rested against his chest.

He waited for some feeling of arousal, but it didn't come. He reached up and took her hands from around his neck. "Don't do this, Eve."

She pressed her lips against his and darted her tongue into his mouth. He exhaled sharply as he felt a stab of desire and took a quick step back.

She smiled at him, her eyes gleaming with satisfaction. "You always did want me that way, Jackson. Even through the rough times you wanted my body, even if you never quite liked me. Maybe when I get back you'll need a woman. I can wait."

She left him standing alone in the library, vibrating with anger—and unexpected and unwelcome sexual arousal.

Blackjack knew he couldn't work anymore. He'd been keeping himself busy so he wouldn't miss Ren. He'd stayed away from her since his confrontation with Eve. But Eve was leaving soon, and she'd be gone all summer. Surely he could find ways of seeing Ren without getting seen by whatever detectives Eve had hired to keep an eye on him.

Presuming Ren would be willing to see him.

Blackjack was already on his way out of the house. He stepped into his pickup and gunned the engine. He knew where he was going. He needed to explain to Ren what had happened. How Eve was blackmailing him. How a divorce was impossible now. How he needed her too much to give her up forever. How life was too short to sweat the small stuff.

He found himself smiling wryly. Ren was hardly likely to call his marriage to Eve "small stuff." But love had to count for something. And the woman he loved was Ren.

He found her at the corral, training one of his cutting horses. She was poetry on a horse as she kept the animal focused on the cow it was cutting from the herd.

Ren had told him she'd won a bunch of ribbons as a competitor in her youth but hadn't ridden a cutter after her marriage until Jesse died. He watched her stop the quarter horse on a dime—and give back five cents change—before she ended the training session. She was as graceful and elegant as the horse she rode.

He realized Ren had been so focused on what she was doing that she hadn't even known he was there until she stepped down from the saddle and handed the reins to one of her cowhands.

It was hard to read the look on her face. He smiled, hoping to get a smile in return. It appeared briefly, but was gone again before she reached him.

"I'm surprised to see you," she said. "Did we have an appointment that I missed?"

"I'm not here on business," he said.

"Then you should leave."

"We have to talk," he said, following her as she headed toward the house.

She eyed him sideways. "You've made progress on your divorce?"

"That's what I wanted to talk to you about."

She stopped and turned to face him. "What is it you've come to say?"

"There isn't going to be any divorce."

He watched her eyes slide closed, saw the sad wobble of her chin before she gritted her teeth. When she looked at him again, her eyes glistened with unshed tears. "Well. I guess that settles that."

She started walking again, and he grabbed her arm to stop her. "That settles nothing!"

She stared at her arm where he was holding her, and he let her go. She started walking again, faster this time.

"You're going to give me a heart attack trying to keep up with you," he said.

She glared at him, but slowed her step. "Go away, Jackson."

She reached the back porch of the house and turned to face him. "I don't want you to come in. Sam's working on the books in the study and . . . Sam blames your son Clay for Luke's disappearance. I don't think it would be a good idea for you to come inside."

"We can talk here," he said, grasping her arms to keep her from running again.

"I think you've said everything."

"I offered Eve the ranch. I offered her everything, if she'd just give me a divorce."

He saw her eyes light up with hope and spoke quickly to lessen her disappointment. "She won't let me go."

"I don't understand," she said, her eyes troubled. "If she won't divorce you, why can't you divorce her?"

"Because if I do, she'll tell Summer that she isn't my child. That her father is Russell Handy."

Ren gasped. "Is that true?"

"Eve says it is. I checked, and it's true Summer has a blood type that can't be genetically linked to mine."

"Oh, Jackson. I'm so sorry."

"For obvious reasons, I don't want Summer to know the truth. So Eve is holding me hostage. I'm not proud of what else I have to tell you, but it's part of what Eve is keeping secret from Summer in exchange for my staying married to her."

Ren cocked her head and waited for him to speak.

"Billy Coburn is my son."

"How is that possible?"

Blackjack grimaced. "I had a brief affair with Dora Coburn twenty-five years ago. A one-night stand. I didn't know Billy was my son until about a week ago, when Dora told me. Eve had been paying her to keep Billy's existence a secret from me."

"Oh, that poor, poor boy. He's paid dearly for your mistake."

"I know that," Blackjack said irritably.

"What are you going to do now that you know?"

"About what?"

"To help Billy," Ren said.

Blackjack was glad Billy had accepted the offer to become a TSCRA field inspector. Glad he didn't have to confess that he'd had his son beaten so badly he'd ended up in the hospital. "Billy's going to be a TSCRA field inspector. A friend of mine is arranging to waive the college degree and any other requirements for the job that Billy doesn't meet."

She pressed a hand against his cheek and said, "That was a kind and generous thing to do, Jackson."

He opened his mouth to confess the truth and shut it again. He was on thin ice with Ren as it was. No sense jumping up and down on it. "I hoped that knowing the reason I can't get a divorce might make a difference to you. That you might reconsider your decision—"

"Mom? Who are you talking to?"

"You've got to go," Ren said, pushing him away. "I don't want Sam to see you here."

"We have to talk," Blackjack said, refusing to back off. "Meet me at my hunting cabin this afternoon, as soon as you can get free."

"I can't do that. I—"

"Mom?"

"I'm not leaving until you agree to meet me."

"All right," Ren said, looking desperate as she heard the mechanical whine of Sam's wheelchair approaching. "I'll meet you after Sam's gone home."

He squeezed her hands. "I'll be waiting for you."

As he headed for his truck, he heard the kitchen screen door slam behind Ren as she entered the house and Sam's query, "Who was that?"

REN ANSWERED HER SON WITH THE TRUTH. "I WAS TALKING to Jackson Blackthorne."

"What did he want?" Sam demanded.

"His visit was personal, if that's what you're asking," Ren replied.

"Did I hear right? Are you planning to meet him later this afternoon? With Luke still missing?"

Ren flushed but kept her head high. "My plans don't concern you, Sam."

Sam fisted his hands on his useless knees. "When my mother decides to lie down with the bastard who murdered my father, it's my business. I won't stand for it. I won't let it happen. Dad would roll over in his grave if he knew—"

"Precisely," Ren snapped. "Your father is dead. I'm no longer his wife. If I choose to love another man—"

"Love?" Sam interrupted in a scathing voice. "Are you telling me you *love* Jackson Blackthorne?"

Ren nodded. "Yes. I do. And whether I choose to see him or not is nobody's business but my own."

Sam shook his head like an angry bull. "I'm making it my business. Because I loved my father. And because the man you say you love is as much responsible for his death as if he'd pulled the trigger himself."

"You know that's not true!" Ren protested.

"I'm giving you fair warning not to see him again," Sam said.

"Warning? What is it you're going to do?" Ren asked.

"If he lays a hand on you, I'll do what Dad would have done. Kill him."

"That's crazy talk!"

"It won't look like murder," Sam said, his eyes narrowed in malice. "It'll be an accident. A hunting accident like the one that killed Dad. Or a car accident. Or he might accidentally swallow some poison. Or—"

"That's enough!" Ren was trembling, because she believed Sam would do what he'd promised. His hatred of the Blackthornes had festered for thirteen years, ever since he'd lost the use of his legs. To her shame, she'd allowed Jesse to feed that hatred without intervening. Now she would pay the price for standing back and letting this insane feud between the Blackthornes and the Creeds go on and on without trying to stop it.

"What can I say to change your mind?" she said to her son.

"Say you won't ever see him again," Sam replied.

Ren realized she had a choice. She could ask her son to leave, to take his hatred and go away and never come back. Because nothing was going to be resolved by her avoiding Jackson Blackthorne. The feud would still be there to haunt future generations of Creeds.

But right now, with Luke missing and Callie living in Australia, Sam and Bay were the only family she had left. And she didn't want to send him away.

In much the same way as Blackjack had chosen to remain in a miserable marriage rather than ruin his daughter's happiness, her first loyalty must be to her son. She was certain that, with time, she could make Sam see reason. Meanwhile, she and Blackjack would have to wait.

"I need to see him once more."

"Not on your—"

She held up her hand to silence Sam, so she could finish. "Once more. So he doesn't come here again. So he knows it's finished between us."

"When? Now?"

She nodded, her throat thick with emotion. "I promise after I tell him good-bye, I won't ever see him again."

Chapter 19

"DO YOU THINK WE'RE GOING TO MAKE IT?" Bay asked Owen, as she stared out the window at the clouds below them. Without the noise of the jet engines, it was eerily silent. And they were headed down. Fast.

"I wish I could say yes. But that would be a lie," Owen replied as he manhandled the controls with superhuman effort to level the plane.

Bay was gripping the seat so hard, her fingernails were putting crescents in the soft leather. "What are our chances?"

"Honestly? I wouldn't bet the ranch we're going to get onto the ground in one piece."

Bay felt her stomach turn over. "Thank you for telling me the truth."

"I figured you might want to say a prayer or something," he said as he fought to level the plane.

"I've already done that," she admitted. "I think it's leveling off," she added hopefully.

Owen grunted with effort as he pulled on the yoke. "Yeah. Maybe."

"How much longer till we're on the ground?"

He shot a quick grin at her. "Do you want the time if we make a soft landing? Or if we go in headfirst?"

She laughed, something she wouldn't have thought possible under the circumstances. "I think I'll opt for optimism. How much longer for a soft landing?"

"Maybe fifteen minutes."

"That's not very long."

"Especially if it turns out to be the rest of your life," Owen said under his breath.

Fifteen minutes was a great deal more time than Bay needed to have her life flash before her eyes. She hadn't married. She couldn't have children. There was even another vet to take up the slack in Bitter Creek, so she wouldn't be missed.

There wasn't much left of her family. The nine people who had sat down to dinner at Three Oaks each night when her father was alive—in the days when Callie was still married to her first husband and had given her a niece and nephew—had dwindled to herself, her mother, and Sam.

And Luke. Wherever he was.

She didn't regret making this journey to search for her brother. She only wished she'd been more successful in finding him. She was sorry she wasn't going to be there to help when Paul Ridgeway came hunting for him.

And she wished she'd told Owen she loved him.

She glanced at his profile, which looked so much like all the Blackthorne men. How strange that she should fall in love with him. How strange that of all the men she'd known, she'd learned to trust a Blackthorne. But she did. Which might have something to do with the fact her life had been in Owen's hands more times than she could count during their journey, and he'd always come through for her.

She felt the plane sideslipping, and they lost altitude. She put a hand to her stomach in an effort to keep it in place. She was scared to the bone, but trying not to lose her infamous cool. "I feel like a kid in the backseat of my parents' station wagon, but I can't help asking. Are we there yet?"

"Soon," Owen bit out.

For the first time, Bay noticed the sweat on Owen's forehead and above his lip. A day's growth of beard shadowed his face. There were dark circles under his eyes. He was barely recovered from the VX nerve gas and the infections he'd fought. Yet he'd never once complained. Or revealed his own fears.

"What's your greatest regret?" she asked.

He turned to look at her, then focused his eyes on the windshield in front of him. "You."

She felt an ache in her chest. "That you admitted you loved me? Or that you took me with you?"

"Both."

"Will it help if I say I'm in love with you?"

He shot another quick look in her direction, but a sudden gust of wind hit, and he had to focus on sideslipping the plane. When it was steady again, he focused piercing gray eyes on her and asked, "Are you in love with me?"

"I think so."

"Where does that leave us?" he asked. "I mean, considering all the barriers you mentioned the first time I brought up the subject."

"I guess we'd have to find a way to make Sam accept you."

Owen shook his head and swore.

"What's wrong?" Bay asked anxiously, looking out the window at the deceptively fluffy cushion of clouds, wondering if the plane was going down like a bullet any second.

"Why do our families always have to get involved in this?"

"You know the answer to that without me saying it," Bay replied.

"What happens if you can't convince your brother to accept me into the family?"

"I haven't gotten that far in my planning," Bay admitted.

"Neither of us is getting any younger," Owen said.

"I'd be grateful if we just get a little older," Bay quipped.

"I'd laugh, but right now, that isn't funny."

Bay sobered. "Is there anything I can do to help?"

"Tighten your seat belt," Owen said. "I think it's time we put this plane on the ground."

They came out of the clouds suddenly, and Bay could see the ground beneath them. It was flat all right, but covered with tightly bunched mesquite trees, whose roots traveled as much as a hundred feet underground to find water, and whose spiny branches scratched festering wounds in cattle where blowflies laid their eggs.

She turned to Owen and asked fearfully, "Where's the runway?"

"It seems to be a bit overgrown."

Bay searched for the runway again, looking for a break in the vegetation. "I don't see it. Oh, there it is."

Overgrown was an understatement. There was more green than brown in the strip of land. Bay hoped it was grass. "I see the cabin, too," she said. "Ohmigod! It's Luke. And Clay."

The two men were in an open jeep, racing for the runway. Obviously, they'd realized Bay and Owen were in trouble and wanted to be there when they landed—or crash-landed—to help.

"See," Owen said with a flashing smile. "I told you Clay had rescued your brother."

"It sure looks that way," Bay said, returning his smile. "I'm so glad they're both safe. Apparently, Ridgeway hasn't been here yet, either. So that's a bit more good luck."

"Save some of that luck for our landing," Owen murmured. "We're going to need it."

"Oh, God," Bay shrieked.

"What?" Owen snapped.

"There's a mesquite tree growing in the middle of the runway!"

"We'll be landing just beyond it," Owen said grimly. "I hope," he added under his breath.

Bay couldn't even reach for Owen's hand, because he needed both of them to control the yoke. She tightened her seat belt yet again, so she felt like she was wearing a strait jacket—appropriate dress for someone as crazy as she had to have been to come along on this trip.

But even if this was the end, she realized she couldn't regret the journey. Because she'd fallen in love.

She closed her eyes tight and started to pray. *Our Father, Who art in heaven . . .*

She heard the wheels chirp as they hit a bit of pavement, felt her stomach lurch as they bounced up again, heard Owen's vicious curse as he fought the jet back down.

Hallowed be Thy name. Thy kingdom come . . .

"Hot damn!" Owen crowed. "We're down."

Bay opened her eyes. And barely managed not to scream. They were careening down the overgrown runway, brakes screaming as Owen stood on them. She closed her eyes and kept on praying.

Thy will be done . . .

She was trembling all over when the plane finally rolled to a stop.

Owen gave a sigh of relief. "That was some ride."

Bay felt Owen's lips on hers and heard his laugh as he said, "You can open your eyes now, scaredy cat."

She opened her eyes and reached out a shaky hand to grip the one he'd extended to her. "Thank you, God," she croaked.

"I'm the one who landed the plane," Owen said as he disconnected her seat belt. "How about thanking me?"

She was in his lap before he could release his own belt, her hands gripping him tightly around the neck, her lips pressed against his.

Safe, she thought. *With this man I'm safe.*

A moment later the door opened, and Clay stepped inside.

"Jesus Christ, Owe," he said. "Why were you flying without engines?"

"Somebody sabotaged them," Owen said. "Correct that. Paul Ridgeway sabotaged them."

"He's the brains behind the whole thing," Luke said as he joined them. "He's the one who stole the VX mines—and a lot more besides."

Bay was still too shaky on her feet to stand on her own, and Owen lifted her into his arms and carried her out of the plane, with Clay and Luke on his heels.

"What's wrong with Bay," Luke demanded. "Bay, are you hurt?"

"Put me down, Owe," she said. "You're scaring my brother."

"He'll recover," Owen said, hanging on to her.

Bay reached out to clasp Luke's hand. "I'm so glad you're safe. Why didn't you ask for help? I was so scared for you!"

Luke looked sheepish. "Because I thought Clay was the one who'd stolen the mines. That is, until Paul Ridgeway showed up at that camp in the Big Bend."

"Let's get back to the cabin," Owen said. "We're too exposed out here. Have you got a cell phone?" he asked Clay. "Our radio was down, too. We need to call in the cavalry."

"Uh-oh," Clay said, as they all piled into the jeep, Clay and Luke in front, and Owen and Bay in back, Bay still in Owen's lap.

"No phone?" Owen asked.

"I didn't bring the plug to recharge mine, and the battery's dead," he admitted. "I never thought we'd be here this long. But the powers that be didn't want us moving until they found you."

"Surely someone's checking in with you periodically, to make sure you're okay."

"The Justice Department knows where we are," Clay said. "Hank contacted them before he went into the Big Bend for the last time, said he had a snitch who'd given him some information that might lead to whoever it was who stole those VX mines, and he was going to check it out. He wouldn't name the suspect, but he suggested it was someone in the FBI office in Midland.

"The Justice Department contacted me because of my relationship with Paul Ridgeway, and off I went."

"You could have told me," Owen said.

"Sorry about that. The Justice Department said I had to keep the whole business under my hat."

"How did you find Luke?" Bay asked.

"I convinced Paul that I should be a part of whatever it was he had going. He sent me off to inventory his cache, and I found Luke and all the evidence the Justice Department needed. But you were still missing, so they stashed us for a while."

"How often do you check in with the Justice Department?" Owen asked.

"Every four hours. I missed my last call a half hour ago, so they'll be sending someone to check on us."

"Let's hope they get here before Ridgeway does," Owen said. "If they don't, how are you fixed for weapons?"

Clay lifted a brow. "You're expecting an armed attack?"

"Ridgeway knows you're here," Owen said. "Or at least, that this is where I thought you might have taken Luke."

"The gun room is full of shotguns and hunting rifles," Clay said. "We can protect ourselves."

"At least you're alive," Owen said. "I figured we'd be too late, that we'd find the two of you dead."

"You never told me that," Bay said.

"I'm glad I was wrong," Owen said, as he slapped his brother on the back.

"Why don't we light out of here?" Bay said. "Why not keep on driving until we get somewhere safe?"

"We're better off at the cabin," Owen said. "The Secret Service put in all sorts of security to make it safe for presidential visits. There isn't any place safer that we could get to in the limited time I'd guess we have."

"So all we have to do is lock down tight and wait for the cavalry?" Bay asked.

"That's it," Owen confirmed.

Bay heard what he wasn't saying. *Unless Ridgeway gets here first.* The big question was, how many men would Ridgeway bring along with him?

"How many—" Bay began.

"How many—" Owen said.

Both of them stopped, and Bay gestured for Owen to continue.

"How many men were with Ridgeway at the camp?" he asked Luke.

"The most I saw at one time was five guys, including Ridgeway," Luke replied.

"I took care of two of them, so that leaves two men— probably the two who chased after us at the airport in Alpine—and Ridgeway for sure," Owen said.

Bay breathed an inward sigh of relief when they arrived at the Blackthornes' hunting cabin. It bore little resemblance to Paul Ridgeway's rustic hideaway. This hunting cabin was two stories high and looked more like some kind of Southern mansion made of logs. It was also shrouded by shrubbery where the bad guys could be hiding. Bay glanced at Owen and saw he had a SIG in hand, and that his eyes were surveying the land around the cabin.

"See anything?" she asked.

He shook his head. "But this place could definitely use a gardener."

She slipped off his lap and got out of the jeep. "I'm okay," she said when she saw the concern in his eyes.

She turned to Luke as he hopped out of the jeep and gave him a hard hug, which she was surprised to feel him return. Her teenage brother was notoriously unwilling to be seen embracing his older sister.

"Are you okay?" she asked, releasing him and looking him over, frowning at the yellowing bruises and healing cuts on his face.

"I'm fine." He reached down to touch her pinkened cheek. "What about you?"

"It's nothing." She slipped her arm around her brother's waist and hugged him again, to reassure herself that he was real, and that he was really well.

When Bay entered the main room she saw most of the furniture was still covered by sheets. Two wing chairs had been uncovered and pulled up to the fireplace, which was where Luke and Clay had apparently spent most of their time.

She brushed a lock of hair away from Luke's forehead, revealing a circle of pale yellow skin where a bruise was healing. "Are you sure you're all right?"

"I got a little beat up," he said. "But then Clay showed up—"

"And saved your butt," Bay finished for him. She realized the twin brothers were standing side by side watching them, and that it was making Luke uncomfortable to be hovered over by his big sister. She let go of him, crossed to Clay Blackthorne, and held out her hand. "I want to thank you for saving my brother's life."

"You're welcome," Clay said. "If it hadn't been for Luke, we wouldn't know nearly as much as we do about Paul's motives in this whole business." Clay pulled the sheet off a brass-studded leather sofa that was centered on the fireplace and said, "Make yourself comfortable. It's quite a story."

"Before anyone gets too comfortable, I think we better check out our arsenal," Owen said.

"Right," Clay agreed, as they all headed for the gun room.

Bay had never seen so many guns. They lined the walls in glass and wood cases. "There are enough weapons here for an army," she marveled.

"Unfortunately, there's only the four of us," Owen said, as he began opening gun cases and removing weapons. "How are you with a rifle, Red?"

Bay saw the speculative look Luke gave her at Owen's use of the nickname and flushed when she realized Clay was giving Owen an equally piercing look. "I can hold my own," she said, as Owen handed her a varmint rifle.

"We'll keep shotguns handy at the front and back doors," Owen said as he passed Clay two shotguns and two boxes of shotgun shells. "And rifles with us at all times," he said as he handed Luke a rifle.

They spent the next hour making sure the cabin was secure, before they returned to the main room.

"I guess now we wait," Luke said, as he slumped into one of the two chairs in front of the fireplace and settled one ankle across the opposite knee.

Clay took the chair across from him, a rifle across his knees, and exchanged a glance with Owen. "I hate waiting," he said.

Owen sat on the arm of the brass-studded leather sofa. "So do I. Maybe you can fill me in a little more on how you got involved in this mess."

"Sure," Clay said. "The Justice Department suspected someone in South Texas was stealing a lot of mines from around the country, but they couldn't figure out where he was holding them once they were stolen. Then Hank Richardson pointed a finger toward Paul's office.

"I didn't want to believe Paul was guilty, but when he came to see me during maneuvers to find out when the VX mines were being moved, and then the mines were stolen, I realized he was guilty, after all."

Bay found herself reluctant to leave Luke's side. She draped her arm across the back of the wing chair in which he was sitting and asked, "So why did Ridgeway steal all those mines?"

"He wants to mine the border between the U.S. and Mexico," Luke announced.

"What?" Bay and Owen exclaimed together.

"That was my reaction, too," Clay admitted.

Luke continued, "He wants to keep out illegal aliens like the vagrant who killed his daughter. He wants to make sure no other innocent will ever be killed by some desperate wetback coming across the border."

"He really has gone crazy," Owen murmured as he glanced out the window to make sure there was no movement.

"You have to admit," Clay said, "it would make anybody think twice about illegally crossing the border from Mexico."

They all froze as they heard someone at the door.

Bay saw the confused look Owen and Clay exchanged. It didn't make sense for Paul to come to the door. But who else could it be?

They were all on their feet facing the door, rifles and shotgun in hand, when the lock turned and Jackson Blackthorne stepped inside.

Blackjack surveyed the arsenal of weapons aimed at him and demanded, "What the hell is going on?"

"I THINK THE BETTER QUESTION IS, WHAT ARE YOU DOING here?" Owen said. "How did you find out we were here?"

"I had no idea you were here," his father blustered. "I came here to—"

"You're meeting my mother here!" Luke interrupted angrily.

Owen exchanged a grim look with Bay, who also seemed unsettled at her brother's pronouncement.

"I'm right, aren't I?" Luke insisted.

"Not right away, I'm not," Blackjack said. "But I did tell her to meet me here this afternoon. I can see maybe that wasn't such a good idea. What is going on here?" he asked again.

"We're waiting for Paul Ridgeway to come looking for us," Owen explained.

"I need to warn Ren to stay away," Blackjack said, heading back toward the door.

At that instant a barrage of bullets exploded through a window, shattering glass and thudding into the opposite wall.

"Get down," Owen shouted, grabbing Bay and covering her body with his own as they fell to the floor.

Everyone else hit the floor at the same time.

"That's supposed to be bulletproof glass," Clay pointed out from his prone position on the floor.

"Must have been made to keep out a different kind of bullet," Luke said. "It sure as hell isn't working on these!"

"I have a VX mine with me," Paul Ridgeway shouted. "All of you come out with your hands up, or I'm going to detonate it."

"Is this a good time to tell you again that I love you?" Bay said quietly, as she stared up at Owen.

"Anytime's a good time," Owen replied, as he gently kissed her on the lips. "I love you, too."

"Now that you two have that settled, how about figuring out how we can all have a long and happy life," Luke said.

"Right," Owen replied as he rolled off Bay and wormed his way over to Clay. "Do you think you can talk some sense into Paul?"

"I can give it a try." Clay worked his way over to the window, stood with his back to the wall, and yelled, "Paul, you've got to give yourself up. There'll be cops all over this place soon."

"Not soon enough to save you," Paul shouted back.

"Cindy wouldn't want this, Paul," Clay said.

"I'm doing it for her, Clay. She wouldn't want another young woman to suffer the same fate as she did. Sacrifices have to be made for the greater good. Your deaths will ultimately mean saving a great many innocent lives."

Clay made eye contact with Owen, shook his head, and whirled his finger in a circle to indicate Paul was crazy.

"Now what?" Luke asked.

"Maybe I can sneak out the back," Blackjack said, "and warn Ren away."

"He'll have someone out back with a gun aimed at the door, Dad," Owen said. "You'd never make it."

"We have to do something!" Blackjack said. "Otherwise, he'll detonate that mine, and we'll all be dead anyway."

"You should have stayed away from my mother in the first place," Luke snarled.

"Luke, that's enough," Bay said.

"Just because you're in love with one of them doesn't mean it's okay for Mom," Luke railed.

"Why not?" Bay shot back. "You were quick enough to turn to a Blackthorne for help when you were up to your neck in trouble! What's so wrong with the Blackthornes?"

"Hear! Hear!" Owen said, applauding her speech.

"You shut up!" Bay snapped at him. "I'm talking to my brother."

Owen smiled at her, loving her every bit as much for her fiery temper as for her defense of his family. He couldn't wait to make her his wife. Assuming they lived that long—and she agreed to marry him.

Luke wouldn't let the matter rest. "Dad would—"

"Daddy's dead," Bay said, interrupting him in a fierce voice. "We should let him—and his hatred of the Blackthornes—rest in peace."

"Easy for you to say," Luke muttered. "What about Sam?"

"What about Sam?" Bay said. "He's the victim of *an accident*."

Owen's brows rose nearly to his hairline. He'd never expected Bay to take his side where Sam was concerned. He was beginning to hope there might be a future for them.

His hopes were dashed in the next moment, when Paul Ridgeway shouted, "I've got Mrs. Creed. Come on out, or I'm going to kill her."

Blackjack immediately stood. "I'm going out there. Maybe he'll take me in exchange for Ren."

Owen saw the astonished look on Luke's face at Blackjack's offer and the satisfied look Bay exchanged with her brother that said, *See. He does love her.*

"Stay where you are, Dad," Owen said, as he rose to his feet.

"I should be the one to go," Clay said, also getting up. "Paul knows me. I might be able to talk to him."

"You've already tried that," Blackjack countered. "It didn't work."

"I think we should all go," Owen said.

Bay and Luke were on their feet now, as well.

"You want us all to get killed?" Luke said snidely.

"With any luck at all, Paul's only got two men with him," Owen reasoned. "He's certainly got one of them watching the back door—maybe both of them. There are five of us—too many for him, or even the two of them, to watch if we're all moving at once."

"That sounds like the kind of plan that can get somebody killed," Blackjack said.

"I know what I'm doing, Dad," Owen said. He pulled the SIG from where he had it tucked in his jeans at his back. "You're going to provide the diversion. I'm going to shoot Paul."

"He's not going to let you get anywhere near him with a gun," Clay said.

Owen saw the worry—and love—for him in Bay's eyes as she asked, "Can't we wait for the cavalry to arrive?"

"Paul isn't going to give us that much time," he said as he crossed to her. "I'll be fine."

"You can understand my concern," she said, straightening his collar as an excuse to touch him in front of their male audience. "I don't want to lose you now."

"I don't want to lose you, either," he said, kissing her in spite of their audience. He let himself enjoy the smell of her, the taste of her, the softness of her. He planned to love her until they were both old and gray. He hoped things worked out that way.

"If you two are done professing your undying love, let's see what we can do about not dying," Clay said with a grin.

"Be careful," Bay said as she smoothed Owen's shirt across his shoulders.

"You be careful, too," Owen replied, as he quickly kissed her one last time.

"Let's hear this plan of yours," Blackjack said.

"Here's what I think we should do," Owen began.

Once he was convinced that everyone knew their roles in the drama that was about to begin, Owen crossed to the front door and opened it wide. "We're coming out," he said.

"Come one at a time, your hands over your heads," Paul ordered.

Owen came out first, the SIG hanging down his back, held by a shoelace that went around his neck. At the right moment, he was going to reach for it and hope his aim was true.

Clay came next, then Luke and Blackjack. Owen's plan depended on Bay. She was going to provide the distraction. It had been her idea, one he'd protested. She'd convinced him she was the only one Paul was likely to believe might actually faint from nerves—even though anyone who knew Bay would laugh at the suggestion.

"I'm good in a crisis," she'd argued. "I can do this, Owe. Let me help."

He was afraid for her. Afraid that Paul or the men with him would fire at the first sign of movement from Bay. He had to be fast. He had to fire first.

Owen hadn't expected three men to be waiting for them. Was there a fourth man in back? There had to be. Maybe more than that. Damn.

The two thugs facing him held Uzis. Paul held no weapon at all . . . only what appeared to be a detonator. His other hand tightly gripped Lauren Creed's arm.

"I'm sorry, Ren," Blackjack said.

Owen watched her glance skip from Bay to Luke before she looked at Blackjack and said, "I love you, Jackson."

"That's enough of that," Paul said.

"Are you going to shoot all of us?" Owen asked. "That's going to leave quite a mess to explain, isn't it?"

"All that rancor between Blackthornes and Creeds is going to come in handy," Paul said with a smile. "It'll be easy enough to make it look like you've shot each other. Especially with Mother Creed and Father Blackthorne having a clandestine meeting here to provide a motive for all that murderous anger erupting from the rest of you."

Owen found himself exchanging glances with his father and brother, then with Luke, and finally with Bay. Paul's plan would work, all right. The authorities would believe it. Over the years, there had been bad blood aplenty between Blackthornes and Creeds.

They had one chance to save themselves. To save all those whose hate had turned to love. To live happily ever after.

Owen dipped his chin as a signal to Bay. *Now.*

She moaned loudly as she fell, to draw attention more quickly. Everyone scattered to the four winds.

Owen fell forward, his gun in his hand before the first bullets struck the outside of the house. He put a bullet between the eyes of the man who was firing, not taking a chance that he might be wearing a protective vest. The second thug ran for cover.

As planned, Clay had headed back into the house to retrieve the shotgun they'd left by the door. He blasted the second man through the broken window before he could reach safety.

Owen heard shots from the back of the house and yelled, "Luke, keep a watch out for anyone coming from the backyard. There's another agent back there!"

Blackjack had headed straight for Ren, catching a bullet in his arm before he managed to snatch her from Paul Ridgeway's grasp and roll away with her into the bushes where they were hidden from view.

Owen slammed into Ridgeway, but Paul held on to the detonator as they fell to the ground. When they landed, Owen lost the SIG.

"It's not a VX mine," Paul gasped. "It's a claymore. And your friend Dr. Creed is lying right on top of it."

Owen didn't know whether to believe him or not. "Bay, move away from there," he shouted.

"She isn't going anywhere," Ridgeway said. "She's been shot."

"What?" Owen had his hands around Ridgeway's throat but resisted the urge to squeeze the life out of him. "Bay," he shouted again.

He got a response from Luke, who'd crawled over to his sister. "She's been shot. She's bleeding bad!"

"Get her out of there," Owen yelled.

"Stay where you are, all of you," Ridgeway ordered. "Or I'll push this button, and you'll all die."

The claymore was an antipersonnel mine that sprayed tiny pellets that shredded flesh. There wouldn't be enough left of anyone in its path to bury.

"Do what he says," Owen shouted. "Don't—"

Owen hit Paul's wrist with a chopping motion that deadened the nerves and caused him to drop the detonator. He smashed his fist into Paul's face, knocking him cold. He found his SIG and stood over Paul Ridgeway, the barrel aimed right between his eyes. "This is for Hank, you sonofabitch!"

"Owen," Blackjack said as he rose from the bushes. "Don't do it."

Owen stared at the man who'd killed his best friend—and maybe the woman he loved.

"Don't," Blackjack repeated. "You've done your job."

Owen put pressure on the trigger, but realized he couldn't do it. He shoved the SIG into his father's open hand, picked up the detonator very carefully, and called, "Luke, come here."

Luke came running.

"Can you disarm this thing?"

"Yeah. Sure," Luke said, taking it from him.

"I have to check for that other man out back," he said. "See if Clay—"

Owen heard the whine of machinery, and Sam Creed's wheelchair came rolling into view from around the side of the cabin. He had a rifle across his lap. "I took care of the one out back."

"Holy shit!" Luke said. "Sam! What are you doing here?"

"I came to make sure Mom said good-bye to Blackjack," he admitted with a wry grin. "And stayed for the show."

Owen was already kneeling beside Bay, who was lying in a pool of blood. "Red, can you hear me?"

Blackjack approached him holding his wounded arm, Lauren Creed at his side. Clay came out of the house and joined them. Luke walked beside Sam until they reached the crowd at the porch.

"How bad is she hurt?" Sam asked.

Owen sat Bay upright and held her close to his chest. He could see the crease on her scalp where the bullet had plowed through flesh. "I don't know," he said in an anguished voice. "If she dies, you're all to blame," he said, turning accusing eyes on his family and hers. "This damned feud has to stop. Here. Now. For good."

He turned his gaze to Sam and said, "I'm sorry for what happened to you. It was an accident, plain and simple. I love your sister and I am, by God, going to make her my wife." He turned to the rest of them and said, "And we're going to be showing up for holidays, and you'd better damned well make us welcome."

Owen was crying, the tears streaming unashamedly down his face. "I love Bayleigh Creed. Do you hear me? I love her!"

"I think everyone can hear you just fine," Bay murmured.

"Oh, God, Red," he said, smiling down at her through the blur of tears. "I thought you were dying."

She lifted a shaky hand to her head, but he caught it before she could touch the wound. "My head hurts like hell. But I enjoyed the speech, Owe."

"I hope it worked," he said, sending his gaze from one to another of the family gathered around him, daring them to deny him his chance at a life with the woman he loved.

"I've got no problem with you and Bay getting together," Sam said at last. "I draw the line at my mother and your father having some sleazy affair."

Owen saw Bay's mother flinch and watched his father's jaw tighten at Sam's indictment.

"I told you I was coming here to say good-bye to Jackson," Bay's mother told her son. "And that's what I meant. We won't be the cause of anyone's unhappiness."

Except their own, Owen thought, as he looked from one miserable pair of eyes to the other.

"Can you drive us to the hospital?" Owen asked Sam.

He nodded. "I've got my van. There's plenty of room for anybody who wants to come."

"I'll stay here with Paul," Clay said. "Until the cavalry arrives to take charge of him."

"I can drive Luke to the hospital with me," Bay's mother said. "We'll meet you there."

That left his father alone. "How about you, Dad?"

"I'll drive myself to the hospital." He put a hand on Owen's shoulder and said, "You handled yourself well, son. I'm proud of you."

Owen felt his throat swell with emotion. It was the first time his father had ever said those words. "Thank you, Dad. I hope you're going to come to the wedding."

"Wouldn't miss it," his father said. He turned and walked away, his broad shoulders squared, his head high.

Owen shook his head as he realized that despite everything that had been said here today, the battle between the Blackthornes and the Creeds wasn't over by a long shot. His father wasn't going to give up that Creed woman any more than Owen was going to give up her daughter.

But maybe hostilities would cease for a while. Long enough for him to marry Bay. Long enough for them to start their life together.

He lifted Bay into his arms and headed for Sam's van. "We have a chance now, Red," he whispered.

Her eyes were closed, and he wasn't sure she'd heard him until she murmured, "Pretty good job of peacemaking for a lawman, Owe."

"Yeah," he said. "It was."

"I love you, Owe."

"I know, Red. I love you, too."

Epilogue

THE BRIDE WAS PREGNANT.

It wasn't apparent, unless you looked at the glow of joy on her face. The weather was cool for September, and Bay wore a long white dress with fitted sleeves that buttoned all the way to her wrists.

"I can't believe this is really happening," Bay said as her mother rearranged her veil one last time.

"I'm so happy for you, darling," her mother said.

Bay saw the sadness in her mother's eyes that belied the smile on her face. She kissed her mother's cheek and said, "Someday."

Her mother laughed. "What does that mean?"

"You know what it means. I'll keep my fingers crossed for you."

The church was full of friends and neighbors, Blackthornes on one side of the aisle, Creeds on the other. Callie and Trace had come all the way from Australia with their three children and sat on the bride's side, since there were so many fewer people there.

As the eldest Creed male, Sam was leading Bay down the aisle. He showed up in the vestibule and said, "Are you ready?"

Bay smiled once more at her mother. "Ready."

"Luke's waiting for you," Sam said to their mother. "He'll walk you to your seat."

"Be happy," her mother said as she squeezed her hands.

"I will," Bay promised.

Bay leaned down and kissed Sam on the cheek. "Thank you, Sam."

"Just be happy," he said gruffly.

"I will," she promised for the second time.

Bay put her hand on her brother's shoulder as he turned his wheelchair and headed for the aisle of the church. The wedding march began, and the guests stood and turned expectantly to watch.

Bay couldn't take her eyes off Owen, who stood in a morning coat at the altar of the First Baptist Church waiting for her to join him. He looked so tall and strong and handsome. And in love. Oh, he looked at her with such love.

When she reached the front of the church, Bay noticed her mother appeared pale. She realized why when she saw that Eve Blackthorne was sitting beside her husband. Next to them sat Summer Blackthorne, with her arm looped through the arm of a handsome young man Owen had told her was visiting the family from Houston.

"Who gives this woman . . ." the preacher intoned.

Sam looked somber as he handed her over to Owen's care and then turned and wheeled himself to the first pew alongside the rest of her family.

Bay laid her hand trustingly in Owen's and met his gaze as he began to recite the vows that would join them forever. Bay's throat had swollen closed, so her voice was whispery soft as she said, "I, Bayleigh, take you, Owen, to be my lawfully wedded husband."

To love and to cherish, in sickness and health. Until death do us part.

They were powerful words, made more potent by Bay's knowledge that it wasn't going to be just the two of them, that they would be sharing their joy with a child. Bay hadn't told Owen yet. She'd been holding this special gift close to her heart, waiting for just the right moment to tell him.

"I now pronounce you husband and wife," the preacher said with a beaming smile. "You may kiss the bride."

"And the mother of your child," Bay murmured as their lips met.

Owen jerked upright. "What did you say?"

Bay grinned. "I'm pregnant!"

There was both laughter and applause from the guests.

"I'd say this is a timely ceremony," the preacher said. "God bless you and your blessed event."

Owen was clasping her hands and staring at her. "Are you sure? When did this happen?"

Bay laughed at the look of astonishment in his eyes. "Twelve weeks ago. And we're going to have—"

He put his fingertips across her lips and grinned broadly. "I don't want to know if it's a boy or a girl. Not until he—or she—arrives."

Bay grinned back. "All right, Owe. Whatever you say. If you don't want to know now, I can keep a secret."

She was sure that whenever *the twins* arrived, he would be delightfully, deliriously happy to welcome his new family.

Author's Note

Everything I know about VX nerve agent, I found on the Internet—including the formula for how to make it. Seven cities in the United States have storage and disposal facilities for the vast stockpiles of chemical warfare agents—including mustard gas left from WWI, and Sarin, Tabun and VX nerve agents—contained in bombs, mines, mortar rounds, rockets, spray tanks, and artillery projectiles. These weapons are stored in earth-covered igloos, with and without their explosive components. All chemical weapons in the United States are scheduled to be destroyed by 2007.

Letter to Readers

Dear Readers,

I hope you enjoyed *The Texan!* Summer Blackthorne and Bad Billy Coburn will be back soon—and the feud between the Blackthornes and the Creeds will be resumed—in *The Loner,* the next book in the Bitter Creek series.

If you missed Trace and Callie's story, *The Cowboy,* you should be able to order it on the Internet or find it in your local bookstore.

If you'd like to read more about the Blackthorne family, look for my Captive Hearts series set in Regency England, including *Captive, After the Kiss, The Bodyguard,* and *The Bridegroom.* For those of you intrigued by the Creeds and the Coburns, my publisher will soon be reprinting the Sisters of the Lone Star trilogy, *Frontier Woman, Comanche Woman,* and *Texas Woman. Frontier Woman* will be in bookstores August 7.

I love hearing your comments and suggestions. You can e-mail me through my Web site at www.joanjohnston.com. I answer e-mail as soon as I receive it. Snail mail is . . . a little slower (and I thank you for your patience). You can write to me at P.O. Box 8531, Pembroke Pines, FL 33084. If you'd like a reply, please enclose a self-addressed stamped envelope.

Happy trails,
Joan Johnston